‘*I...am...not...yours!* Do you hear me, barbarian?

‘I won’t belong to any man. Ever again!’

Rorik’s eyes gleamed down at her. ‘You belong to me, little wildcat. But don’t worry. I’ll give you time to get used to the idea.’

‘Give me time—’ The sheer arrogance of his statement made her gasp. ‘Why, you overbearing, boorish...*kidnapper*. I’ll show you what time—’

She didn’t get a chance to finish. Rorik leaned forward, lifted her wrists over her head and slowly lowered himself over her. Yvaine’s eyes widened as his body covered hers. Heat enveloped her instantly.

She tried a tentative wriggle, then went utterly still, her breath seizing, as the movement brought her harder against him. Their eyes met, his blazing, intent; hers wide and wary.

‘Aye,’ he growled. ‘Now you know. I could take you right here, if I was the barbarian you think me.’

Julia Byrne lives in Australia with her husband, daughter and a cat who thinks he's a person. She started her working career as a secretary, taught ballroom dancing after several successful years as a competitor, and, while working in the History Department of a Melbourne university, decided to try her hand at writing historical romance. She enjoys a game of cards or Mah Jong, usually has several cross-stitch projects on the go, and is a keen preserver of family history.

Recent titles by the same author:

AN INDEPENDENT LADY
(part of *The Regency Rakes* collection)

THE VIKING'S CAPTIVE

Julia Byrne

MILLS & BOON®

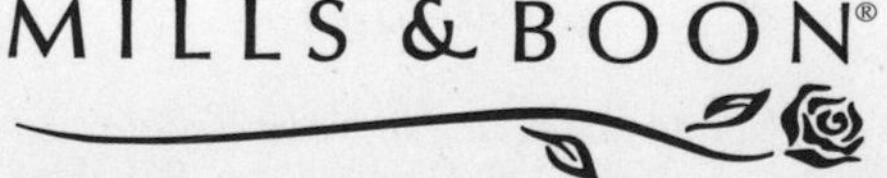

All the characters in this book have no existence outside the imagination of the author, and have no relation whatsoever to anyone bearing the same name or names. They are not even distantly inspired by any individual known or unknown to the author, and all the incidents are pure invention.

First published in Great Britain 2003
Large Print edition 2003
Harlequin Mills & Boon Limited,
Eton House, 18-24 Paradise Road, Richmond, Surrey TW9 1SR

ISBN 0 263 18003 4

Set in Times Roman 14 on 14½ pt.
42-0903-85785

Printed and bound in Great Britain
by Antony Rowe Ltd, Chippenham, Wiltshire

For my mother,
in loving memory.
Thank you for always being there,
and for always believing in me.

AUTHOR NOTE

At the beginning of the tenth century Englishmen and Danes had been occupying their own territories in England in comparative peace for several years, thanks to a treaty between Alfred the Great (he of the burnt cakes) and Guthrum, King of the Danes. Individual rebel bands of Danish or Norse raiders occasionally attacked the English coastal towns for plunder, but they didn't cause the widespread devastation of the brutal Viking armies prior to the treaty.

After King Alfred's death in 899, however, the increasing number of raids, plus the fact that dissatisfied English nobles recruited Norsemen whenever it suited them, prompted Alfred's son, Edward, to begin reclaiming the Danelaw. He eventually succeeded in 918. The Danes remained in England, but were Christianised and acknowledged Edward as King.

GLOSSARY

Bur	Farm building
Faering	Small rowboat
Fylgja	Animal spirit believed to accompany all Norsemen
Hnefatafl	Board game, possibly similar to the present day Fox & Geese
Jarl	Wealthy landowner (equivalent of English earl)
Pell	Velvet
Ragnarök	Doom of the gods
Shieling	Mountain farm dwelling, used in summer
Skyr	Dairy food made from creamy curds
Styri	Steering oar on ship
Thing	Norse parliament and law court (also Allthing, Gulathing)
Thrall	Slave

Christian and place names are usually pronounced phonetically, excepting those spelt with a 'j' which is silent, e.g. Katyja (pronounced Katya).

Chapter One

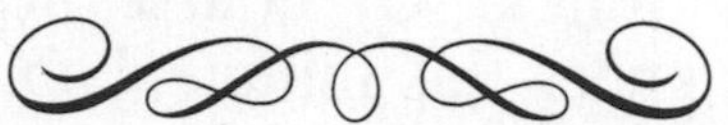

England in the Year of Our Lord 904

Smoke blanketed the sky, a thick black pall, hanging over the town beyond the manor walls and filling the air with the suffocating odour of burning thatch. She could almost hear the hungry flames, even above the terrifying clamour of axe against shield, sword against sword, and the screams of the townswomen.

And louder still, borne on the wind that whipped at her hair as she ran from the stable, there rose a steady roar, a sound inhuman, like the howling of a thousand wolves.

The chilling roar brought her to a dead stop halfway across the manor compound. One hand clutched a hooked tunic to her breast; with the other she pulled a kirtle into place over the chausses she'd snatched from the stableboy's loft, her gaze on the empty road outside the palisade. The big wooden gates stood open, no defence at all.

Had everyone fled to the woods? she wondered. Even her husband?

No. The answer to that came immediately. Considering the sins on Ceawlin's conscience, he'd more likely taken refuge in the church.

Fool! Did he think those murderous savages would respect the sanctuary of the church? Hadn't he listened to the tales of slaughtered monks, plundered treasures, desecrated holy relics? Of course not. Ceawlin was probably on his knees this minute, babbling prayers for deliverance from the wrath of the Norsemen.

Her mouth curled in a scornful smile. It suited her purpose if the Lord of Selsey thought only of his own safety, leaving his wife to the mercies of their attackers, but still she felt contempt for such a man.

She hesitated a moment longer, wondering if she should close and bar the gates, then shook her head, turning away. Gates wouldn't hold against the heathen horde outside. But they would sack the church first in their quest for loot. She still had a little time.

Clutching her tunic tighter, she raced across the compound towards the hall, glad of the freedom of her borrowed raiment. If she managed to escape she'd be able to travel quickly and more safely disguised as a boy. And if not, if by some evil chance she was caught, at least death would be quick.

But she refused to think of failure. She *would* escape. She must.

With a final glance over her shoulder at the lowering black cloud, she ran into the hall.

The terrifying sounds were instantly muted as the silence of the empty building surrounded her. The hush gave an illusion of safety. Her racing pulse slowed, her breathing steadied. All she had to do was find a dagger and some coins and leave. Once outside the gates, it would take only a minute to gain the safety of the forest—and her freedom.

What she sought lay under the big carved chair at the high table. She knew it was there. Jankin had innocently told her of the hidden chest months ago, not realising…

Dear God. *Jankin.* He'd been sent to the town that morning. Had he managed to hide, or was he even now lying dead, his life cut brutally short—?

No, don't think it.

Resolutely suppressing the hideous pictures in her mind, she hurried down the hall to the dais at the end of the long room. Kneeling behind the table, she felt under her husband's chair.

The chest was there in its niche; small, but heavy. She put her tunic aside to use both hands, dragging the chest from its hiding place and around to the end of the table where she could open it more easily. Its wooden base shrieked protestingly as it scraped over the floor, momentarily drowning out the noise outside.

But not quite cloaking the thud of approaching footsteps.

She whirled as the intruder spoke, a terrified gasp breaking free.

'So, Anfride was right. The Lady Yvaine of Selsey is no better than those heathen fiends outside. You seek to rob me also.'

'Holy Saints! Ceawlin.' She came to her feet, waiting for her heartbeat to slow before speaking again. She ignored Ceawlin's mention of her unmarried sister-in-law. Anfride was as malicious as her brother and had always disliked her. She'd long ago given up trying to make a friend of the woman.

Just as she'd long ago vanquished fear of Ceawlin. It hadn't been easy. Though he hadn't mistreated her physically, being in awe of her connection to the powerful royal house of Wessex, he was spiteful with the meanness of the weak and cowardly, cruel to those below him and self-indulgent in his pleasures. But she'd been married to him for five years and was no longer the uncertain child who'd arrived at Selsey.

Now she despised him.

He glared at her through close-set eyes before pointedly lowering his gaze to the chest at her feet.

Yvaine lifted her chin. 'I do not rob you, Ceawlin, but only retrieve what was mine.'

'What was yours, wife? What was *yours*? You own nothing here. Or were you hoping I'd be killed by yonder savages, leaving you free of me and mistress of my wealth?' Ceawlin flicked her clothing with a contemptuous gesture. 'Do you think to hide behind your boy's clothes while you await my death? Stupid woman. Your face betrays you and 'tis too late to seek the church.'

'Too late for you also, Ceawlin, if you linger here.'

He threw back his head and laughed at that, a shrill cackle that echoed shockingly in the empty hall.

And Yvaine felt the first icy trickle of dread slide down her spine. So might demons laugh, she thought. Mad. Evil. She had to get away from this place. But how was she to get past Ceawlin? The table stood at her left; he in front. If she made any sudden move towards the open space to her right, he'd be after her like a hound after a hare.

'Hah!' he barked as if aware of her frantically racing thoughts. He leaned forward and thrust his face close to hers. 'You think I've no wit for planning, Yvaine, but mark this. I intend to use you as surety for my life.'

For a moment Yvaine could only stare at him. 'You think I'll stay here to be used as a *bargaining* counter?' she finally got out. 'Let me clear your foggy wits, Ceawlin. I came in here to retrieve the dowry I brought you, but if I have to leave without it—'

'Leave? That was your scheme?' He snorted. 'A foolish one. I'm your lawful husband. I say what you'll—'

'Lawful *husband*?' The words burst from her, incredulous. The smug satisfaction on Ceawlin's sharp, rat-like features was intolerable. She thought of the past five years; the insolence of serfs too afraid of their master to serve her, the spite, the threats, the deliberate destruction of her treasured manuscripts, the disappearance of any animal she petted.

The memories flicked at her like tiny whips. For one reckless instant danger was swept aside as a torrent of emotion surged and swelled inside her until it broke over her in a wave of molten fury.

'*Husband!* You don't know the meaning of the word. And this my family will know. No longer will I stay here to be scorned, half-starved, used to hide your true nature. I have been silent all these years, but no more. You wallow in vice! You have no honour, no decency. Hear me now, my Lord of Selsey. *I would walk to Rome barefoot to have our marriage annulled!*'

The silence that followed her outburst seemed to throb with the echo of her words.

Then Ceawlin's face turned a mottled red as rage contorted his features. 'You speak so to *me*?' he almost screamed. 'You forget yourself, wife.'

'I forget nothing,' she spat back. 'But you do, Ceawlin. Do you hold your life so cheap that you stand here berating me?' She pointed to the chest between them. 'There lies your treasure. Take it and hide.'

She started forward as she spoke, intending to push past him, but as quick as an adder striking, his hand flashed out and fastened around her wrist. Yvaine bit back a startled gasp, her eyes flying wide as Ceawlin's fingers tightened with deliberate cruelty.

'So you wish to leave, my lady? You wish to be free of me?'

The snarled anticipation in his voice sliced through her anger like steel cleaving mist. Yvaine went very still, waiting.

'Then so you shall be,' Ceawlin hissed. 'When *I* say, in the manner *I* devise. But first—' with a vicious jerk he began to pull her across the hall towards the thick centre post, at the same time loosening his belt with his free hand '—you need a lesson in wifely respect. 'Tis long overdue and your noble connections won't help you now.'

'Are you mad?' she cried, throwing herself back against the numbing grip on her arm. Fear surged as she realised Ceawlin was stronger than his flabby, over-indulged body appeared. Desperate, she lashed out, her nails raking across fat knuckles.

Almost casually he turned and backhanded her across the face, then yanked her forward so roughly she stumbled and fell to her knees.

Dazed, she flung out her other hand, trying to recover her balance, only to have both wrists captured and bound with Ceawlin's belt. He jerked her arms above her head, looped the ends of the belt around the solid post and fastened them, then stood back to examine his handiwork.

Yvaine shook her head, trying to clear her vision. How had it happened so quickly? Her ears were still ringing from Ceawlin's blow when she realised she was trapped. The sheer horror of it had her clawing aside fear as frantically as she'd fought Ceawlin's grip. 'You *are* mad,' she whispered. 'When the king hears of this—'

'When Edward hears of this,' Ceawlin retorted, ''twill be through a letter from me telling of my beloved wife's capture by Norse pirates.' He chuckled at the notion and gave a cruel jerk on the belt. 'Aye, I've waited a long time for this, wife. A long time. Anfride's potions didn't work, but this will. And the role of bereaved husband will suit me well.'

Potions? No. She shook her head. There wasn't time. 'Ceawlin, listen to me. Those fiends won't spare you because you have me tied and trussed for them.'

But Ceawlin only laughed again as he retraced his steps and bent to open the chest. This time the effect of that high-pitched giggle was terrifying. She forced herself to shut out the sound, forced herself to think. What was she to do? Ceawlin was beyond listening to warnings or reason. And she would not beg. She would not plead.

She strained at her bonds, ignoring pain as the leather bit deeper. A warm trickle of blood ran down her arm. She ignored that, too, twisting her hands in an attempt to get at the buckle.

Ceawlin's footsteps sounded behind her again. He was coming back, eyes glassy with excitement, a thick rope, knotted at one end, dangling from his hand. A prayer for strength flashed through her mind and was gone. Yet 'twas not the threat of a beating that had terror pushing her heart into her throat, but the greater danger. Coming closer, stalking her on silent feet. To be left here, helpless, for those barbarians to find…

A beating was nothing to what they would do to her.

'You'll lose your life for this indulgence,' she choked. Her throat felt so tight she could scarcely speak, but she clenched her teeth and summoned the only possession Ceawlin hadn't been able to take from her: her pride. She would not cringe before this depraved beast.

But as Ceawlin bent down, one damp hand scrabbling at the back fastening of her kirtle, Yvaine couldn't suppress the shudder that coursed through her at his cold, clammy touch. He ripped the kirtle away, leaving the sleeves dangling from her bound wrists and baring her body to the waist.

'If you live through this raid, I'll kill you myself,' she vowed, her voice shaking with rage and fear. 'I don't care how long it takes. I'll kill you.'

But Ceawlin only smiled, his face flushed with an eagerness that sickened her. 'We'll see how much your threats are worth when I've finished with you,' he gloated, and raised his arm.

The sight of a girl huddled by the centre post in the hall stopped Rorik cold in his tracks. She was so still, he thought for a moment she was dead. If so, it was not by the hand of a Viking. His men were still busy looting the church or fighting any merchant foolish enough to oppose them.

A distant knell of discomfort sounded at the back of his mind with the thought. He shrugged it off. Christians and their churches meant nothing to him. Except as a means to an end.

He cast a quick glance about the hall, his gaze sweeping past the tapestries covering the rough thatch walls to rest on the cooking pot hanging above the circular fireplace to his left. Preparations for a meal lay on a table nearby, showing signs of hasty abandonment: a knife flung to the floor, scattered spices, an overturned jug of wine. The stream of liquid had reached the edge of the table and now dripped, slowly, to the rushes below.

A wealthy manor, he mused. And empty except for the girl. Despite the royal standard flying from the roof, no guards had appeared when he'd strode unchallenged through the gateway and across the compound.

But if all had fled, who was this, half-lying, half-crouching in the shadows of the big room. Why had she been abandoned here?

His sword ready to strike, Rorik moved forward with the soundless tread of the hunter.

He was still several paces away when a ray of noon sunlight flashed through the smoke-hole in the roof, bathing the figure on the floor in a brilliant circle of light. The girl stirred, as though the warmth of the sun had brought her to life. Slowly, so slowly she seemed scarcely to move, she lifted her head and stared straight at him.

The impact stopped him as if he'd run into a wall; he was barely aware of halting again, of lowering his sword.

She was a creature of golden light. Magical. Her hair lay in tumbled disarray about her shoulders, the colour of deep, rich honey. The flesh of her arms glowed a paler gold. And her eyes! Wide and slightly tilted at the outer corners, set in a face of such delicate beauty she seemed more the stuff of long-ago dreams than reality, her eyes made him think of a wildcat he had once cornered. It had gazed at him with that same golden fire, and he'd been unable to bring himself to kill it. Unable to destroy the fierce pride of something so wild and free.

Then the sun slid past its midday zenith. The ray of light vanished, and the magical golden creature with it. And as his eyes narrowed against the disappearing light, he saw that her raised arms were tied to the post, that a boy's kirtle hung from her wrists, and her extraordinary eyes, if they had ever held fierceness, were now dull and lifeless.

The girl stared back at him, unmoved and unmoving.

Uttering a soft curse, he came forward quickly, going down on one knee beside her and lifting a hand to brush her hair from her cheek. Someone had struck her face. But it wasn't the bruise already staining the fragile line of her cheekbone that made him go still. He looked down as the veil of her hair shifted, revealing what had been hidden, and felt his body harden in a rush so powerful, his breath left his lungs on a sharp expulsion of sound.

She was bare to the waist, her breasts rising and falling with her uneven breathing, her entire body trembling. Her fear was a palpable thing, quivering in the air between them, and yet he was lowering his hand without thought; as if he had no will beyond the sudden need to touch, to take.

She was exquisite. Small, delicate, with an untouched fragility about her that caught at his heart. And when her soft rose-tipped breast filled his hand, he felt something deep inside himself tear loose, as if part of him had become hers, never to be reclaimed.

He looked back at her face, fighting the fierce urge to close his fingers more firmly around the sweet flesh moulded to his palm. She neither spoke nor flinched away from his touch, but beneath his hand her heart fluttered like the frantically beating wings of a panicked bird, and her eyes, those golden cat's eyes, were anguished.

Shaken, Rorik drew his hand away. It was like tearing away his own flesh, inch by agonizing inch. Was she a witch to move him like this? He'd known lust before, but *this*…

Suddenly furious, he jerked upright. What in the name of the Gods was he doing? He was here for a purpose, damn it. And she was English. *English.*

He reached down to yank the kirtle's sleeves roughly over the girl's arms, intending to cover her again before he cut her hands free.

Another shock jolted through him before he'd touched the first laces. Desire leached out of him as if it had never been, and he, who had looked upon the most gruesome of battle wounds without flinching, was sickened by what he saw.

She'd been cruelly beaten. Not with a whip, he saw at once. Her skin was unbroken, but angry red weals crisscrossed her back from shoulders to waist, surrounded by ugly bruises that were already darkening to purple.

Rorik's mouth hardened into a grim line. He knew the marks of a knout when he saw them. By Thor, he gave his men plenty of leeway, but if one of them had done this—

Bending, he cupped the girl's face in one hand. Her blank gaze told him she was probably beyond speech, but he tried anyway.

'Who did this to you, maiden?'

There was no response, but her lashes flickered as she looked away from him to the shadows at the end of the hall. Rorik heard it at the same time. Rapid footsteps approaching a leather door-curtain in the corner behind the high table. There was no time to warn her. Hoping her shock-induced silence would continue, he straightened and stepped behind the post, his sword held aloft and ready.

Ceawlin brushed aside the curtain and hurried into the hall, tucking a laden sackcloth bag into his tunic.

Yvaine watched him approach through the mist that dimmed her vision. She wondered if she ought to tell him there was a Norseman nearby, but the thought was strangely distant. And faded completely when he spoke.

'Still undiscovered, my lady? Perhaps 'tis as well. I'd enjoy watching your pride stripped by those barbarians, but 'twould be unwise to linger. Tell them I hope they won't torch the hall, considering the gift I've left them. A building is so much more costly to replace than an insolent, disdainful wife.'

'Tell me yourself, Englishman,' suggested the Viking, stepping into the open. He studied the short, bloated figure in front of him and lowered his sword in a slow arc, until it pointed straight at Ceawlin's heart, inches away. His eyes slitted.

The chill of that ice-cold glare sank into Yvaine to her very bones. She didn't wonder that stark terror wiped the look of pleasure from Ceawlin's face. She could only marvel that she didn't feel the same fear. The Norse giant standing over her was a formidable enough vision, and he'd done something—

What had he done? She couldn't think clearly. But then, minutes ago she hadn't thought at all. Not until his deep voice, softly questioning, had brought her back from a mindless abyss of pain. She couldn't recall his words, but her surprise that he spoke English, and the rough velvet of his voice…those she remembered.

Yvaine lifted her gaze to his face. She had to look up a long way. He stood several inches over six feet, and every inch of the journey passed over solid muscle, from his long legs encased in woollen chausses and thonged leather boots, to his broad shoulders covered by a sleeveless chainmail tunic. Heavy bands of twisted gold encircled his powerful arms, and more gold adorned his belt.

She couldn't see his face clearly, couldn't tell if he was dark or fair. An iron helm covered most of his features, the nose guard, sharp curving sides and frowning onyx inlays above the brows creating a visage meant to terrify. From this fearsome mask glittered eyes the colour of a mid-winter sky, a cold, light grey. And below the nose guard his mouth looked brutally hard.

Her eyelids flickered when he jerked his head at her, but that arctic gaze never left Ceawlin's face. 'You did this.' It wasn't a question.

The realisation that he hadn't instantly been killed had restored some of the colour to Ceawlin's ashen face. He attempted a fawning smile. 'How else does one treat a wife who dares to scorn her husband?' he whined propitiatingly. 'Perhaps you'll have more success in teaching her respect for her masters.'

The Viking's head tilted slightly. 'You'd give up your wife to me?'

'Aye…aye…if you want her.' Ceawlin's words tripped over themselves in his eagerness. 'Do as you please with her. She may be a defiant wench, but she's not uncomely. Look—' He reached down a hand to her face.

'Touch her and you lose that hand!'

The snarled threat had Ceawlin's eyes bulging. His mouth fell open as the Norseman's sword flashed with deadly swiftness to hover over his outstretched arm. 'Is she not enough?' he babbled. 'Here—' Not daring to withdraw the arm extended towards her, he extracted the pouch from his tunic with his free hand and held it out with shaking fingers. 'Take my treasure as well.'

The Viking made no move to accept the proffered bag. Contempt sliced through the rage in his voice. 'For what do we bargain, Englishman? Your life? Your costly hall? Only your arm, mayhap?' He lowered his blade until it rested on Ceawlin's forearm. 'What do you demand for a paltry bag of coin or jewels and a beaten wife?'

'No…no…you don't understand.' Ceawlin's arm trembled so violently beneath the Viking's blade that a thin line of red appeared. He squealed like a suckling pig at the sight and snatched his arm back.

The sword point followed to aim at his heart again.

'I only beat her today…never before…and the wench is untouched…I swear…' The disjointed phrases tumbled from Ceawlin's slack mouth in a panicked rush, only to cease abruptly when surprise flashed in the Norseman's eyes. Yvaine saw calculation overlay the raw terror of her husband's face. He licked his lips.

'You've already sacked the town, looted the shops, plundered the church. Surely this wealth and the girl are worth my life. A virgin will fetch a high price as a slave if you don't want her for yourself. Or give her to your men. There's much pleasure to be had in watching such sport.'

The air in the room seemed to still and ice over. Yvaine shivered as the chill brushed her flesh. She heard the Viking speak again, his voice as biting as the winds howling across the frozen wastelands at the edge of the world, and knew that everyone in the vicinity of a rage so terrible was going to die.

'By Thor, I knew you English were lying, faithless traitors, but what manner of man throws his wife to an army already drunk with blood-lust?'

'But isn't that what you want?' Ceawlin shouted, waving his arms in his agitation. 'You rape, you loot, so take her. Take her now. You'll see I speak the tr—'

The last word shattered into a strangled scream that tore aside the mists threatening Yvaine's mind. Murderous intent flashed in the Norseman's eyes; stark horror filled Ceawlin's. The blade, which had been held with such controlled stillness, suddenly whirled above his head, then slashed downwards with a vicious rush of air.

When Ceawlin's body hit the floor only inches from her face, Yvaine didn't even flinch. She watched her husband's killer sheath his sword and draw a wicked-looking dagger from his belt; saw the lingering traces of ferocity in those chilling eyes as he bent towards her.

He was going to kill her, too. She felt nothing.

His dagger made quick work of the leather binding the girl's wrists. Abruptly released, her arms would have fallen, but Rorik held her hands with one of his, kneeling again. The killing rage was leaving him, but he still had to force the gentler note into his voice when he saw the bloody streaks encircling her wrists.

'Easy, little one. Let your arms down slowly.'

She didn't utter a word, her face remaining blank, but he saw her whiten as the blood returned to her limbs.

Rorik pulled the kirtle more securely over her arms, covering her nakedness but leaving the back open. Then, without a second's hesitation, he lifted her bodily over his shoulder and rose to his feet.

He had no fixed purpose in mind as he carried the girl from her home. He only knew he couldn't leave her behind. Not like this. Not hurt and helpless. No echo of discomfort sounded. He ignored the fact that she was English. Let the Norns weave trouble for him if they would because of it. He had killed for her.

She was his.

Chapter Two

Noise surrounded her, ebbing and flowing as if in a dream. Voices shouting, the roar of flames, a shrill cry abruptly cut short.

A woman ran past, screaming, pursued by two men. She wondered vaguely who it was, then her gaze fell on a body lying by the riverbank and grief, layered upon shock, layered upon pain, became too much to bear.

Her mind simply shut down; shutters slammed against the battering of a violent storm. She heard her captor speak sharply to the two men, saw them break off their pursuit of the fleeing woman, but none of it made sense.

She had no idea where she was being taken, and cared less.

'Rorik! Since when have you carted off boys when there's richer plunder to be had? You want the church, my friend, not the cow byre.'

Rorik eyed the tall, bearded warrior who barred his path. His helm was dented, one muscular arm sported a gash, but his blue eyes twinkled, and a sack, overflowing with gold and silver, was slung over one shoulder.

'I see you've collected your share of spoils, Thorolf.'

'Nobody ever called me backward,' Thorolf retorted, turning and falling into step beside him. 'But this is the first time I've seen you take anything. Don't tell you're collecting new thralls for your stepmother. She'll only wear them out within a sen'night.' His voice altered to a shrill falsetto. *'Go here, go there. Do this, do that.'*

Rorik's mouth twitched at his masterly imitation of his stepmother's discordant tones.

'I wouldn't hand a dog over to Gunhild,' Thorolf continued, casting a cursory glance at the limp form draped over his friend's shoulder. 'Let alone a puny boy like that. You're not really taking him home, are you? He won't last the voyage.'

'We must've been at sea too long,' Rorik said dryly. 'Take a good look, you lackwit.'

Thorolf sent him an indignant glare but obliged. He goggled at the sight of golden-brown hair hanging down to Rorik's knees.

'Thor's hammer! 'Tis a woman.'

'Oh, well said, Thorolf. How encouraging to know my men are so observant.'

Sarcasm rolled off Thorolf as easily as insults. 'But I've never seen you carry off a female in all the years we've been a-viking together,' he protested. 'What's more, you've always stopped the men from doing so.'

Rorik shrugged, the girl's slight weight hardly impeding the gesture.

'What's Othar going to say?' Thorolf persisted, beginning to look dubious.

'Why should he say anything?'

'Because he thinks he ought to have what you have. Better yet, he wants more. You have a woman. He'll fill the ship with 'em. Damn thing will probably founder.'

'Where *is* Othar?' was the only response to this grumble.

Thorolf shifted his booty to a more comfortable position and sidestepped around a burning chunk of thatch. 'Probably chasing some unfortunate wench. Odin's ravens know why. There're plenty of willing girls in the Danelaw if he can't wait until we get home.'

He caught the quizzical glance Rorik sent him and grinned sheepishly. 'So I agree with you on that point. It doesn't mean I think you were right to bring Othar with us.'

'He's my brother. Where else should he be, but with me?'

'Well, I can think of—'

A sharp movement of Rorik's hand cut him off. They had reached the point where they'd landed and the four guards left on board the longship were already alert to their leader's approach.

Ignoring their curious stares, Rorik stepped on board. The girl shifted in his hold, but she made no sound and he thought she'd probably swooned. Just as well. He didn't want her hurting herself in an attempt to escape. Once they were underway it wouldn't matter. There was nowhere to run to on a ship. Except the tent.

His gaze swept the seventy-foot length of the vessel and rested frowningly on the leather shelter in the prow. It shouldn't have been there.

'Why is the tent up, Orn Hooknose?'

A warrior, grizzled of beard and lined of face, stepped forward. 'Your brother and his friends brought women back, my lord. To use as they please until they sell them.' The man scratched the hawk-like feature that had given him his nickname and aimed a thoughtful look at his leader's burden. 'Knowing your views on captives, we thought it best to keep the wenches out of sight until you returned.'

Rorik's eyes narrowed. Trust old Hooknose to remind him of his own rules. Orn wouldn't indulge in speculation with the other men, though. He'd sailed with Rorik's father and was loyal to the death.

Dismissing the man with a nod, he turned to Thorolf. 'We've been here over an hour. Call the men back, my friend.'

Thorolf grunted agreement and reached for the elk horn hanging from the mast in the centre of the ship. But as Rorik went to move past him he put out a restraining hand.

'I know you couldn't leave Othar at Einervik after what happened,' he said, lowering his voice so the others wouldn't hear. 'But be careful, Rorik. He's jealous of you. Always has been.'

'He'll get over it as he grows older.' Rorik cast an amused glance at Thorolf's sober countenance. 'But my thanks for your counsel.'

'Aye, I can see you're taking due notice,' Thorolf muttered, and vented his feelings on the elk horn.

The blast set the seabirds shrieking as they wheeled and dipped above the mast. The incoming tide was beginning to turn. Rorik eyed the swiftly flowing current, calculating speed and distance. With luck they'd reach the Thames estuary and the North Sea before they were discovered by one of the warships of the late King Alfred's fledgling navy.

Normally he'd welcome such an encounter. Hel, a sea battle might finally release him from a certain vow. But he hadn't taken the girl from one battlefield only to dump her in another.

He paused outside the tent to watch the crew as they answered the call of the horn. They were in rowdy humour, drunk with triumph, yelling battle cries and thumping each other's shoulders as they leapt on board. He could expect a scuffle or two over the division of loot but, for the most part, they were good, seasoned men who'd sailed with him before. Any trouble with the women would come from Othar and his cronies.

Eyes narrowed in thought, he pushed aside the leather curtain of the shelter and entered.

Three women and a girl child were huddled together against the far side. They stared at him with varying degrees of hatred and fear.

Ignoring them, he seized one of the skin bags used for storage by day and sleeping by night. He flipped it open and spread it over the rough planks, then lowered the girl on to her front. Her eyes were closed, but when he turned her head to the side and laid his fingers against her throat, her pulse beat steadily. She stirred slightly as though trying to find a more comfortable position, and a small whimper escaped her lips.

He frowned as he studied the makeshift bed. It would have to do for now; he'd find something softer along the coast. At least she had the other women to tend her. That she needed them was the only reason he was keeping them on board. Although the terms of their captivity were going to be changed and—

'Savage! Accursed barbarian!'

Rorik jerked his head up, as surprised as if one of the iron rivets in the hull had suddenly addressed him. His gaze clashed with the accusing glare of one of the captives, a dark-haired, sturdy wench in a blue woollen gown that matched her eyes.

'Is that the measure of Norse manhood?' she demanded, shifting her glare to his captive's bruised flesh. 'To beat a woman until she's senseless.'

'I didn't do this,' he growled before he could stop himself. And then wondered why in the three worlds he was defending himself to a bunch of captive women.

He stood up so abruptly his head only narrowly missed the overhead awning.

Cursing silently, he turned on his heel and strode outside. He grabbed a skin waterbag and tossed it into the tent. Then he rummaged through another sack.

At best, the treatment of wounds tended to be crude and spartan on board ship, but Rorik prided himself on never having lost a wounded man on a voyage. He produced a pot of sheep fat and, pulling aside the curtain, threw it to the sullen girl.

'Do what you can for her,' he instructed curtly, and let the curtain fall again, stamping down on an utterly senseless urge to care for his captive himself.

By Odin's missing eye, he must have gone soft in the head. He'd spent enough time fussing over a woman. He had a ship to run.

Dreams slid through her mind. Nightmare visions of Ceawlin's jeering face, red flashes of pain, crazed laughter. And then, as though to mock her with the hope of rescue, Ceawlin's face disappeared, and there, through a dazzling haze of dust motes, stepped a warrior from an ancient legend. Tall and powerful, surrounded by light, gold flashing off his helm and shimmering along the naked blade of his sword.

She tried to cry out, to call to him. He would save her if she could only make him hear, but he was gone in a wave of agony, leaving blackness wrapping around her like a shroud. And voices. Norse voices, speaking of men and ravens. Jankin's body lying by the river. Grief like a torrent of tears rushing through her head.

'Am I weeping?' she whispered, and couldn't tell if the whisper was hers because other voices immediately struck her senses, rapping like sharp little blows against her head.

'My lady?'

'What is it? Does she live?'

'Hush! She spoke. Lady, do you hear me?'

She could hear the rushing noise. And there was movement beneath her; a strange kind of rocking—

They were taking her away.

Yvaine jerked upright, a thin cry bursting from her lips. The sound was abruptly cut short as fiery pain lanced across her back. Whirling black clouds threatened her senses.

'No, lady. You must be still.'

The voice sounded somewhere above her. Gritting her teeth, she looked around. She was in a tent. A girl hovered nearby, her face anxious. Further away a woman sat, holding a child in her arms. Another woman crouched next to them, head bent over a rosary as she muttered prayers beneath her breath.

The girl nearest her knelt and spoke again. 'You should rest, lady. You've been hurt. Do you remember what happened? Did those barbarians do this?'

Yvaine blinked at her, trying to think. 'You know me? Who are you?'

'I'm Anna, lady. The silversmith's daughter. I saw you in the manor once when I delivered a buckle to your lord.'

'My lord?' A sound that wasn't quite a laugh escaped her. 'He's dead.'

Anna nodded. 'And they took you. Well, we shan't suffer a like fate, I think.'

Yvaine barely heard her. 'They killed Jankin, too. A slave. A mere slave. Too simple to fear Ceawlin's spite against anyone who was kind to me. He was my only friend.'

'Well, now we're all slaves and friendless,' remarked the woman holding the child. Her voice was brusque but not unkind. 'I'm Britta,' she added. 'And the child here is Eldith.'

The little girl gave a timid smile.

'They took a child?' Yvaine whispered. 'Blessed Jesu...I suppose we should be grateful she's alive.'

'Aye, but for how long?' Britta shivered 'Vikings kill for the pleasure of it. 'Tis what befell Eldith's father, my master. He tried to run and was slain.'

Yvaine glanced at the woman mumbling over her beads. She neither looked up nor spoke. Only her fingers moved, ceaselessly counting the rosary. The other two waited, as though instinctively looking to the lady of the manor for answers.

A fine source of help, she thought, on a silent, despairing laugh. She could scarcely think when every breath she took was laced with agony. But still they waited.

'I think Anna is right,' she murmured at last. 'They won't kill us. Sell us, mayhap.'

'Then we might as well make the best of the situation.' Anna settled herself more comfortably against the bulkhead, shrugging when Yvaine gaped at her.

'I was little more than a slave in my father's house, lady. Worked day and night with not a groat to show for it, nor hardly a decent meal. I'm no stranger to slavery.'

'Nor I,' Britta added. 'But at least in your father's house, Anna, you weren't forced to share the master's bed. That could well change before this day is out.'

'No!' Shaking visibly, staggering with the effort, Yvaine managed to gain her feet. 'I won't! I won't submit to rape. Better to escape…take our chances in the river.'

'Escape? Your wits are still wandering, lady.'

'Britta's right.' Anna sprang up and caught Yvaine's arm. 'There's a ship full of Vikings out there. We can't escape. And you're hurt.' She tried to urge Yvaine down to the crude skin bedding. 'Come, lady. Lie down and save your strength. God knows, you'll need it.'

Yvaine threw her off. The movement sent whips of fire across her back, but she managed to stay upright.

'Listen to me,' she gasped. 'There are no waves. That means we're still on the river. Can you swim?'

Anna goggled at her. 'No, but… What are you saying, lady?'

'I will *not* be captive to another man. Never! I don't care if I risk my life. Better to try and fail than…' She stopped, willed steadiness to her voice, strength to her trembling limbs. 'Once we're at sea, there'll be no chance of escape. Do you come with me or not?'

Anna stared at her, mouth agape. Britta shrugged and bent to speak to the silent child. The muttering droned on in the corner.

'Then pray for me,' Yvaine whispered, and whirled towards the curtain. She was through it before Anna's quickly outflung hand could stop her.

Light exploded before her eyes, flashing off sparkling water, blinding her. Dazed, she flung up a hand, stumbled. Her foot struck something hard, sending it clattering across the deck. She faltered, trying to blink her vision clear.

And those few seconds' hesitation were her undoing. Every eye on the ship turned to her. Before she could move, a yell came from the stern.

'Othar! Stop her!'

Mindless with terror, still half-blinded, Yvaine sprang for the side. Her hands reached, groping desperately for the topmost plank. Before she could take hold, footsteps thundered behind her. Heavy breathing rasped through the air, she could almost feel it, hot on her neck.

Sheer instinct had her swerving like a hunted deer, darting for the opposite side, only to have another Viking leap into her path. He spread his arms, laughing, his mouth a gaping maw in an unkempt reddish beard. Behind her, her first pursuer let out the blood-curdling yell of a hunter.

Gasping for breath, she dodged again. The bulkhead flashed before her eyes, feet away. Her chest was on fire. She lunged. Her fingers touched, clung…

And an arm came from nowhere. She was flung to the hard oak planking, unable to prevent an agonised scream rising in her throat when her back hit the Viking's abandoned oar.

The scream sliced through Rorik with the ice-cold kiss of a naked blade. Already halfway up the ship, he leapt the remaining distance in seconds, roaring as if charging into battle, and knocked his brother's hand away as Othar reached for the neck of the girl's kirtle.

'I said *stop* her, not kill her!'

Othar looked up, surprised anger turning his face petulant. 'What's got into you, Rorik? She's only a thrall. Let's have some fun.'

Rorik went down on one knee beside his captive. She glared at him, but pain was clouding the golden fire in her eyes. Holding her arms, he carefully pulled her upright.

'She's mine, Othar,' he said, knowing full well his brother was going to challenge that statement.

Othar wasn't the only one. A low growl rumbled through the crew, the warning before a storm.

Every muscle in his body tensed. Odin curse it, why couldn't she have stayed senseless until he'd warned the men off her? Didn't she know they would've fallen on her like slavering wolves if he hadn't reached her in time?

'Little fool!' he snarled in English. 'You think drowning is such a desirable fate that you'd risk arousing my men to achieve it?'

''Tis more desirable than slavery to you fiends of Satan,' Yvaine spat.

She tried to wrench out of his hold and staggered as the relentless throbbing of her bruised back sent a wave of sickness through her. The dazzling water beyond the ship dipped and swayed. She felt herself swaying with it and squeezed her eyes shut.

The Norseman's grip tightened until she could feel the throb of her blood beneath his fingers. Holy Mother, he was strong. Those powerful hands could snap her in two in a heartbeat. But…he wasn't hurting her. His hands felt protective…and utterly steady. As if he knew she couldn't stand alone, that she was summoning every ounce of willpower to stay conscious.

She lifted her lashes and gazed up into eyes the colour of ice crystals.

'So you can speak now,' he said in a calmer tone. 'What are you called?'

The dazzling swaying water came back, reflected in his brilliant grey eyes. Yvaine gritted her teeth. If she was going to drown in those icy depths, she would drown with pride intact.

'I am Yvaine of Selsey, second cousin to King Edward,' she enunciated clearly. And crumpled between his hands.

Rorik caught her up in his arms before her knees had done more than buckle. He cradled her against his chest, gazing down at the sweep of her lashes against her cheeks, the gentle curve of her mouth, and again felt that odd wrenching deep inside. And knowledge. A sure, irrevocable knowledge.

His! This hurt, proud, recklessly courageous girl belonged to him.

He didn't think past that. Shoved the other sensations to the back of his mind. They went too deep, to a place he hadn't looked into for a very long time. Right now, he had a more immediate problem on his hands.

Slowly, deliberately, he turned to face his men. Several were on their feet, wolves closing in on a prey they knew was weak and helpless.

He glared at them across her limp body.

They shuffled, stepped back. Discomfort and wary acknowledgement replaced the avid purpose in their eyes. Some even looked sheepish, the expression sitting incongruously on rugged, weatherbeaten faces. Without a word, Rorik met each pair of eyes in turn.

They sat again, and started rowing.

Except Othar—and one other.

'Not so fast, Rorik. What do you mean, she's yours? We all share the loot.'

'We don't share women, Othar. As of this moment, every female on the ship is under my protection. They won't be forced. They won't be sold unless I approve the arrangement.'

Othar's light blue eyes, almost level with his own, went cold. The boy rocked on the balls of his feet, but he made no further move, seeming undecided about what to do next. The red-bearded Viking took a step nearer.

From the corner of his eye, Rorik saw Thorolf moving towards them. 'Why don't you take a turn at the styri?' he suggested to Othar. 'And get us out to sea.'

His brother slowly relaxed his belligerent pose. 'You're going to let me steer?'

'If you like. Keep the speed up and hoist the sail as soon as we reach open water.'

Othar cast a long, considering look at Yvaine, then turned a scowl on Thorolf who now stood a pace away.

'You don't have to play the watchdog,' he sneered. 'If Rorik wants to keep the wench, let him. We have others. Right, Ketil?'

'Aye, and plenty of time.' The red-bearded ruffian stared into Rorik's eyes for a second before moving away to his place at the oars. 'We won't be on the ship forever. Eh, Gunnar?' He cuffed the man seated in front of him and took up his oar.

His friend turned with a grin that displayed several missing teeth. 'Time is useful, Ketil Skull-splitter. Very useful.'

Othar laughed and started back towards the stern. 'Come on, you men,' he yelled as he passed them. 'Put your backs into it.'

'Swaggering young cub,' muttered Thorolf. 'He'll probably run us aground.'

'Othar can steer in this calm water.' Rorik jerked his head towards the sea, where white caps could be seen dancing over the surface. 'But keep an eye on him, will you.'

'Aye, but this won't be the end of it, Rorik. I didn't like the look in Ketil's eye. Or Gunnar's. And a ship's a damned inconvenient place for men to be fighting over women. You've said it yourself often enough. Get rid of the wench. Get rid of all of them.'

'What do you suggest I do? Toss them overboard?'

'Of course not. Put them ashore somewhere. They're only going to cause trouble. I can see it.'

Rorik's jaw tightened. 'Before you start prattling like a soothsayer,' he bit out, 'you'd better see something else. Come with me.'

He strode towards the tent, brushing through the curtain just as the dark-haired girl went to peep out. She withdrew at once.

Her swift retreat didn't improve his mood. 'You won't be harmed if you behave yourselves,' he snapped. 'We're not all monsters.'

She glared at him. 'So *you* say.'

Behind him, he heard Thorolf sigh. 'Trouble.'

'Stop bleating like a damned sheep and look at this.' He laid Yvaine down, flicked back the edges of her kirtle and glared up at his friend. 'Well?'

Thorolf leaned closer. 'By the runes! Who did that?'

'Her husband. I killed him.' He didn't wait for a comment on this terse explanation. 'How can I put her ashore like this? She'd never survive.' His voice lowered as he touched a hand to her hair. 'Even as brave as she is.'

Thorolf's jaw dropped. He gaped at Rorik for a full ten seconds before he managed to clamp it shut again. 'Uh...right. Wouldn't survive. As brave as she is. So...what did she say her name was?'

'Yvaine of Selsey.' Rorik frowned. 'She's some kind of cousin to Alfred's son.'

'Alf—' Shocked comprehension had Thorolf jerking upright. 'But...she's a woman.'

'Aye. So you said before.'

'And you think that's just what the Gods ordered? Because she's cousin to the King of the English? For Thor's sake, Rorik, what do you have in mind for her? Ransom? Another beating? Shall we throw her overboard in truth?'

Rorik shot to his feet, his face hard. 'That's my decision to make. All you need do is make sure Othar is steering us in the right direction.'

Thorolf studied his leader for another tense moment and decided not to say 'trouble' again. Rorik was clearly not in the mood to listen to ominous forebodings or grim warnings. Indeed, his friend looked ready to knock the teeth down the throat of anyone who tried issuing such omens.

But as he backed out of the tent, he took with him an uneasy memory of a vow of revenge against the English king that had been sworn on the blood of betrayal eight years ago. A vow that went to the very heart of Norse honour.

Since then, he'd never seen Rorik strike anyone other than warriors who were his equal in battle, but it took no great leap of logic to see the Lady of Selsey as a means by which he could achieve his final act of vengeance against the king himself. Even if it meant going against his own nature.

And if that happened, Thorolf decided grimly, they wouldn't need a soothsayer to see dangerous shoals ahead.

And he didn't mean the sandbar Rorik's spoiled brat of a brother was probably heading for.

* * *

Yvaine drifted in a timeless haze of semi-darkness and pain. Sometimes she felt someone spreading an evil-smelling salve on her back. Another time a hand held a cup to her lips, but it was too much effort to drink. She turned her face away and the hand disappeared.

A few minutes later it was replaced by a large hand that pressed the cup hard against her mouth, forced her lips apart, and ruthlessly tipped the contents down her throat.

After that, she drank whenever the cup returned. Usually it held water. Sometimes the contents were hot and tasty. Broth, she decided, before she slipped back into the merciful darkness.

Once she woke to feel herself lifted and gently lowered again on to a thick bearskin. She sighed and snuggled her cheek against the unexpected luxury. A hand stroked her hair from her face. It wasn't Anna. Anna's hand was small, her touch light and quick. This was the large hand that had forced her to drink. She stiffened in vague alarm, but a soothing murmur stilled her and she drifted.

And then, aeons later, she opened her eyes and was herself again. The cruel throbbing across her back had lessened to a dull ache that was bearable; movement would no longer rob her of her senses. She could think.

But with the return of awareness came terror, a crushing weight of it, constricting her chest so she could scarcely breathe. Her heart seized; her limbs turned leaden. For a moment, just for the moment it took for her heart to start beating again, she wished she'd stayed senseless forever.

Then she clenched her teeth, swallowed to ease the icy fingers of fear gripping her throat, and pushed herself to a sitting position. There'd be time enough for terror when she knew what the future held. And she wasn't alone.

'The saints be praised. You're with us again, my lady.' Beaming with relief, Anna came to sit beside her. She held out a cup and Yvaine took it.

'Where are we?' she croaked when she'd taken a few sips of water. Her voice sounded like rusty mail being hauled from storage.

'Somewhere off the coast of the Danelaw, heading north,' Anna told her. 'The Norsemen beach the ship every evening so they can prepare hot food. Broth or gruel mostly. Some of the men stay ashore all night, but we're not allowed to leave the ship. Well—' she gestured slightly '—only for a few minutes morning and night.'

'Aye,' said Britta shortly. She stroked Eldith's hair and drew the child closer. 'We're forced to live like animals in this cramped shelter.'

'Prisoners in truth,' Yvaine murmured. But even as panic threatened again, something else nagged at the edge of her mind. A sound that had been constant and now was gone. She turned swiftly towards the dimmest corner under the prow when she realised what the silence meant.

'The other woman. Where is she?'

Her companions glanced at each other.

'Poor thing,' Anna murmured. 'We never knew anything about her, lady. She refused to speak, except to mutter over her beads. Then last night she got up and threw herself into the sea. The men on board were asleep. I suppose they thought if we tried to escape, 'twould be towards land, and that way was guarded.' She shook her head, sighed. 'Her body was found early this morning, washed up on the beach. They buried her at least.'

'May God have mercy on her soul,' Yvaine whispered, crossing herself.

'Aye. 'Tis a terrible sin to take your own life. Still, she was escaping from pagans. A martyr's death, you could say.'

'But she hadn't been molested,' Britta added hastily. 'None of us have.' She thought about that for a minute. 'That's not to say some of them wouldn't treat us like common harlots,' she amended. 'Especially that cold-eyed lout Othar and his friends. Blessed Mary, what a pair *they* are. Skull-splitter and Ale-swiller. Names well earned, I warrant. But they go in awe of Rorik.'

'Rorik?'

'Their leader. The one who captured you.' Britta eyed her curiously. 'Do you remember him, lady?

A young warrior. Big. Powerful. Glittering eyes, watching. A large hand…

No! She wouldn't remember. That time in Ceawlin's hall was part of her nightmare.

'No,' she murmured, aware that Anna's gaze, too, had turned curious with her long silence.

She glanced away, towards the leather curtain. One corner had been drawn back to admit some light into the shelter. Warm summer sunshine beckoned, a welcome distraction.

'Are we allowed to breathe some fresh air?' she asked, suddenly desperate to escape the confines of the tent. She had to be outside, had to *think*. Because out of the array of facts she'd just learned, one stood out clearly. If the Norsemen beached the ship at night, they might still escape.

'Thorolf usually fetches us,' Anna said doubtfully. Then she shrugged and helped Yvaine to rise. 'But I see no harm if we stay near the tent, behind the rowers. I'll come with you in case you feel weak.'

Yvaine gave her a smile, and was about to assure Anna that she felt much better, when they stepped into the open.

The instant barrage of curious, assessing eyes tore the smile from her face as if she'd been struck. Frozen, she stared back, unable to do more in that first moment than wonder, stupidly, why the men weren't rowing.

The answer came as she staggered and almost fell. The ship was under sail, ploughing through the waves with a speed that caused her to grab for the side in startled surprise. A quick glance showed her that, far from making any threatening move towards her, most of the crew were seated on wooden chests along the sides, tending to equipment or keeping watch on the shrouds attached to the sail. To her everlasting relief, the men in the immediate vicinity seemed to have looked their fill.

And, after that first furtive glance, she had no intention of finding out if the rest had done likewise.

'Dear God,' she whispered. 'There seem to be hundreds of them.'

Anna gave her a wry smile. 'Aye, so I thought at first. But there's only forty, and they ignore us for the most part.'

If that was so, Yvaine thought, perhaps she should jump over the side now, when they'd least expect it.

Taking a shaky breath, she forced her gaze past the men to the water beyond—and felt her heart plummet straight to her feet.

Jumping overboard would avail her nought. Fore and aft and to one side of the longship, the open sea stretched to the horizon; dark, fathomless, surging constantly as though spurred by the force of some vast invisible power.

And on the landward side…a lonely, windswept beach, its sandy hillocks covered in swathes of long grass that, stirred by the wind, looked eerily like the hair of long-departed souls. There was no sign of human habitation. No sound except the haunting cry of a kestrel as it swooped above the dunes in search of prey.

The empty landscape had her gripping the side in an agony of helpless frustration, but at the same time she felt the sun, warm on her face. The air was fresh, tangy with the scents of the sea. The cry of the kestrel called to something deep within her. She was alive. *Alive.* And if the other girls were to be believed, they hadn't been harmed. Indeed, she'd been cared for.

She turned to Anna on the thought, grasping at the small, everyday task of thanking someone, as though that alone might restore some normality.

'What have you been putting on my back, Anna? Now that I have air in my lungs, I have to own that even the threat of being watched by every lout on this ship pales before the stench inside that tent. I thought 'twas because we'd been confined, but—' She craned her head to look over her shoulder, sniffed cautiously. 'I seem to have brought it with me.'

Anna laughed. ''Tis sheep's fat. The stuff smells vile, but 'tis wondrously healing. Your bruises are fading already.'

'Indeed.' She reached out to give the girl's hand a quick squeeze. 'My thanks for all you've done. 'Twould have gone ill with me, I fear, if you hadn't been here. I only wish I could repay you, but...'

'I need no payment, lady. Besides, I alone didn't care for you. Rorik, himself, watched over you often. Indeed—' her voice lowered '—he watches you now.'

And with those four words, the fragile shield of normality she'd been trying to build shattered like the spray flying from the prow above them. Yvaine fixed her gaze on the sea, her fingers pressing into the wood beneath them. 'Where?' she whispered.

'The stern,' Anna said in the same low tone. 'Do you wish to retire, lady?'

'Retire?' She gave a short, rather desperate laugh. 'Of what use is that? I'd sooner jump over the side and swim for shore.'

'You already tried that,' Anna said drily. 'Besides, Rorik would be after you before you'd so much as wet a toe. What he takes he holds, mark me well.' She glanced warily over her shoulder. 'I may have spoken with him only briefly, but I've come to know his friend, Thorolf, somewhat better, and if half the tales he tells are true—'

'Tales?' Yvaine turned. 'What tales?'

Anna looked back at her, solemn-eyed. ''Tis said Rorik has never been defeated in battle, not even when he wrestled a great ice-bear with only his hands and a knife. Can you imagine it, lady? 'Tis why the men call him the Bearslayer. He wears the beast's tooth on a cord around his neck and—'

'Wait…wait!' Yvaine waved her hands to stop the flow. 'An ice-bear?' She frowned. 'This Thorolf weaves a fine story, Anna, but I wonder you paid him heed. A bear made of ice? We should all see such a creature.'

'But—'

'No, no. Trust me on this. 'Tis only a tale. A Norse saga. I know all about them.' And not for the world would she admit that icy little fingers had tiptoed up her spine during the telling.

'Then what of Thorolf's accounts of battle, lady? With his own eyes, he's seen—'

'Aye, feats of great daring, I have no doubt. Have you ever heard a tale of battle that didn't include such things?'

'They must have some truth in them,' Anna retorted with heavy meaning. 'Or we wouldn't be standing here unharmed when there are forty Vikings not ten feet away. What do you think would happen, lady, if Rorik didn't have the men under control?'

The question effectively robbed Yvaine of the urge to discredit Anna's tales; there could be only one answer. The ruffians, whose very presence made her want to shrink into the smallest possible space, were kept under control because the man who led them was more brutal, more ruthless, more savage than his crew.

And she would have to face him, she realised, shaking inside. Before she could plan any escape, she would have to face him, assess the danger, try to outwit him.

It might not be so hard, she thought, trying to bolster her courage. He was heathen, a barbarian. He probably didn't look beyond the next bloodthirsty battle. But if they engaged in a battle of wits, the outcome might be different. Perhaps she could lull him into thinking them so cowed it would be safe to let them spend the night ashore. Then if she could lay her hands on a weapon—

She turned, her gaze darting over the ship, from oars to pails to bundles of goods. There was nothing here to aid her. Nothing. Only ropes, a thick block of wood, a dragon—

Dragon?

She looked back at the stern, to the flash of gold that had caught her eye. Not a dragon; the steering oar, shaped like a long sea-serpent, the gilded eyes catching the sun in a way that seemed to breathe life into the carved beast.

For a moment she was caught by the fanciful creature, captivated by the artistry. Then she saw the hand, large, long-fingered and strong, wrapped about the solid wood as though holding the dragon in check.

A cool whisper of air brushed her skin, lifted the hair at her nape. Her gaze shifted, as though drawn by a force beyond her control; skimmed over a muscled forearm, past gold armrings, across a broad shoulder, upward.

And there, watching her with the glittering intensity of a hawk sighting prey, were the light, piercing eyes of her memory.

Chapter Three

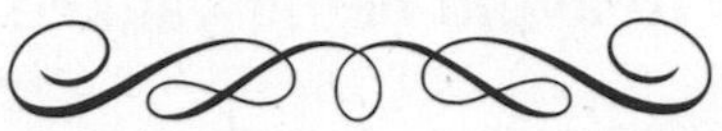

Everything stopped. Time, thought, movement. The entire length of the ship separated them and yet she felt as powerless beneath her captor's gaze as if he'd shackled her to the deck. When he finally glanced aside to address the man standing next to him, her breath shuddered out on a ragged sound that echoed her heartbeat.

'Thorolf comes to speak to us,' Anna warned softly. 'No need to fear him, lady. He's more civilized than some of the others.'

'They're savages,' Yvaine muttered. And didn't ask herself why she needed to make a point of it. 'Every last one.'

'Hmm. Was your husband any better?'

Before she could answer that pointed question, she was confronted by a blond, bearded Viking. He glanced at Anna, then held out an imperative hand. 'Come, lady.'

Not knowing what he intended, she stepped back. 'Not at your bidding, barbarian.'

Thorolf sighed, seized her wrist and, without wasting any more words, began towing her towards the stern.

Shock had Yvaine nearly tripping over her own feet. She'd expected force—and it was—but not quite as she'd anticipated. She finally got her voice back when she realised where they were going. 'Loose me at once, you misbegotten savage. I'm not a sack of loot to be dumped at your leader's f—'

She broke off to avoid being yanked willy-nilly over a cross-rib.

'Hush your noise, lady.' Thorolf threw her an impatient glance over his shoulder. 'Would you make an outcry in front of the men? Rorik merely wishes to speak with you.'

'And this is the manner of his fetching? Who taught him courtesy? Your swineherd?'

He muttered something in Norse, then stopped, swinging about to face her. 'Do you think Rorik can leave *Sea Dragon* to steer herself while he runs after you? Women! Nothing but trouble, first and last.' Turning, he stomped onward. 'Watch out for that bailing pail.'

Yvaine blinked at his back. The incongruity of an annoyed Viking making sure she didn't stumble over the unfamiliar hazards in her path was beyond comprehension. Of course, he was just as likely to kill her if she followed her instincts and gave in to the urge to break free and run.

Aye, and where is there to hide? she asked herself grimly. Behind the three men lounging at the base of the mast, idly casting dice?

As if the trio had heard the thought, they looked up. Their attention fastened on her instantly, like leeches to human flesh. Yvaine shuddered and turned her face away. To her strained senses, the laughter that followed her held a hideous anticipation that reminded her of Ceawlin.

'Ignore them,' Thorolf said and, when her gaze darted up to his, he startled her again with a wry smile. 'Perhaps Rorik should've come for you, lady, although Thor knows even he can't stop the men from looking. But these seas are treacherous and he's waiting for a tricky wind change. Best helmsman in all Norway, you know.'

No, she didn't know. She didn't know anything. The entire world had gone mad, leaving her floundering in confusion and disbelief.

For there, standing before her, up close, without his helm, was the warrior of her dreams. Not the coarse brutish ruffian she'd anticipated, not the mindless barbarian she'd feared, but a man who could have stepped straight out of the Norse legends that had enthralled her as a young girl.

How could that be? she wondered, frantically trying to recover her image of a witless savage. He was tall and strong, aye, but he didn't possess the finely moulded features she'd always attributed to those legendary heroes, nor even the ordinary male good looks she'd grown accustomed to at her cousin's court. He was too tough-looking. Too hard. This was the stern, savage beauty of slashing cheekbones, straight high-bridged nose, firmly chiselled jaw. And in the direct scrutiny of those piercing grey eyes, she saw an ice-cold intelligence that was more daunting than any brute force.

Without speaking, without movement, he took her breath away.

'You recover quickly, lady. Freyja must have watched over you.'

Yvaine jolted at the sound of his voice. Deep, with a husky timbre that made her think of darkest night, it stroked over her taut nerves as if he'd touched her.

'Credit your heathen Gods if you will,' she retorted, flushing with the belated realisation of the way she'd been staring at him. She hadn't even noticed that Thorolf had left them. 'No doubt they approve of men carrying off helpless women and selling them into slavery.'

The Viking's brows rose. Glancing up at the mast, he made a slight adjustment to the tiller, then returned his gaze to her face. 'Your husband would have abandoned you to slavery. I won't.'

Tilting her chin in disbelief, she affected an absorbed interest in the sea beyond him. But she was aware of him still. Saints preserve her, she was aware of every little detail.

The way the wind ruffled shoulder-length hair that was lighter than her own and streaked by the sun. The way he stood, long legs braced against the movement of the ship; the powerful ripple of muscle in his arm as he held the vessel on course; the tiny lines at the corners of his eyes when he narrowed them against the light.

So sure of himself, so utterly male. Standing there challenging the unpredictable forces of nature and harnessing them to his will. How could she ever escape such a man?

Did she want to?

The question had her gasping before she could stifle the sound. Her knees buckled.

'Here,' he said gruffly, shoving a wooden sea-chest closer with his booted foot. 'Sit down before you keel over. You're probably weak from hunger.' He reached to a sack at his feet.

Yvaine dropped to the chest without a murmur. It wasn't obedience; her legs simply gave way. Where had *that* thought come from? Had she forgotten she was dealing with a Viking? He wasn't going to take her for a sail along the coast, then return her with a polite word of thanks for her company.

An object that resembled a strip of leather landed on her lap. She stared at it as one eyeing a serpent poised to strike.

''Tis dried fish, not henbane,' her captor murmured. And at the note of wry humour in his voice, she looked up—into eyes that were no longer cold. He smiled at her. A slow, heart-stopping smile that completely transformed his stern features, melting the ice in his eyes and replacing it with something warm and wicked. Something that invited her to forget about forced abduction and slavery and follow where he led.

Dear God, why would the man even need force? she thought dazedly. That smile would make a willing thrall of any woman. It caressed, it embraced, it enticed. It threatened to destroy the walls of stone she'd built around her emotions.

Heaven save her, hunger really had addled her wits. She had to get her strength back. Fast!

Tearing her gaze from Rorik's, she snatched up the fish, put it between her teeth and bit. Then nearly choked when he leaned over and swiftly unfastened her kirtle.

Screams tangled in her throat, sounds without voice. She tried to leap up, only to feel strong fingers clamp around the nape of her neck, anchoring her to the chest. Her heart slammed against her ribs in a terrified rhythm she was sure he could hear. Was he going to tear her clothes off in front of his men?

'Be still,' he murmured. 'The sun will be good for your back, and the men can't see anything.'

His fingers relaxed, cupping the nape of her neck rather than gripping it. She felt his hand move to her back, a fleeting touch. Then he straightened away from her.

Relief had her slumping on the chest as every muscle went limp. He wasn't going to tear her clothes off. At least, not yet. Indeed, his attention was no longer on her at all, but on his ship. He pulled hard on the steering oar, bellowing out orders.

Men swarmed up the mast, sure-footed on the ropes as they brought the sail around. She fixed her gaze on the huge expanse, realising, after the space of several heartbeats, that it wasn't particularly war-like. It was criss-crossed in diagonal lines of red and white, but there was no fierce black raven such as she'd heard described.

Surprised, she followed the line of the mast upward. A triangular, gilded wind-vane was swinging around to landward. Pennants attached to holes along its lower edge flew proudly in the breeze and, higher still, the small figure of a dragon gazed out over the horizon with remote, far-seeing eyes.

The light was dazzling. She lowered her eyes, vaguely aware of the heat bathing her back. The sun did feel good; warm and healing. She absently took another bite of fish.

'Tell me, lady. Why did your husband take the time to beat you in the middle of a Viking raid?'

The question, coming without warning, jerked her upright again as if Rorik had taken a whip to her.

'Well?' he prompted when she sent him a quick, startled look. 'Had you goaded him beyond reason? Lain with another man? What had you done to be so grievously punished at such a time?'

'Oh, that's right, assume I was to blame.' Outrage restored her voice in a hurry. 'Goaded Ceawlin beyond reason? Aye. The very fact that I breathed goaded him for the entire five years we were wed.'

'Five years?' His brows snapped together. 'You must have been a child.'

'I was fourteen,' she said curtly. 'What of it? As for a beating, you Norse probably do the same when your wives defy you. Or worse.'

'In my land, lady, a woman may divorce her husband for the treatment you were subjected to, unless he can prove she was a faithless wife. In my land, a woman may divorce a man for being a poor provider, or lazy. Or for baring his chest in public.'

'Baring his *chest*?' She glared at him. 'You must think me a lackwit, if you think I'd believe that tale.'

Amusement edged his mouth. 'Far from it. But I speak the truth. My own uncle employed the ruse to rid himself of a wife whose tongue was honed to a sharper edge than any battle-axe on this ship. If a man bares his chest publicly 'tis considered bad taste and provocative. By the same token—' He reached out, touched the honey-gold tresses tumbled about her shoulders; a gentle caress that was over before she thought to evade it. 'A married woman must cover her hair.'

'Oh.' Hot colour rushed to her cheeks. Until that moment she hadn't given a thought to her appearance. Now, for some strange reason, she was acutely aware that several amenities had been missing from her life for a couple of days. Such as soap, and a comb. She wondered if Rorik was aware of the pervasive odour of sheep fat that hovered about her, and then wondered why the thought had even occurred.

'Well, 'tis a pity I couldn't divorce Ceawlin,' she muttered, annoyed with herself. 'But our marriage was supposed to benefit my cousin. And why are we even discussing the matter?'

'Because I would know you, lady. I would especially know about this cousin.'

'The king?' She frowned. 'You want to know about Edward?'

'Edward,' he repeated thoughtfully. 'Aye.'

'But what—?'

She stopped dead, the answer striking her like a thunderbolt. *Ransom.*

Of course! Oh, why hadn't she thought of it before? The means to her freedom was right here to hand. Vikings wanted loot; she could offer it.

Relief made her head spin. She had to struggle to keep her voice steady, to hide her eagerness.

'What do you want to know?' she asked as amounts of coin and jewels danced through her mind.

'Why your cousin married you to a brute and a coward at such a tender age, for a start.'

'I—*what*?'

'The question was simple enough, lady. You said you were married five years ago. 'Twould have been about the time Alfred died, by my reckoning.'

'Aye, but...' She narrowed her eyes at him. 'How did you know that?'

''Tis not important.'

'But—'

'I will have your answer, lady!'

'Oh, aye. Right away. At your command, O Leader of Pirates.'

'Sarcasm won't change the fact that I do command here. Speak!'

Yvaine dug her nails into her palms, reaching for patience. Sarcasm would also not win her release.

'Five years ago,' she began with great care, 'Edward was crowned King of Wessex. However, our cousin Athelwold challenged Edward's right to the throne. When he failed to win enough support, he fled to the Danelaw and tried to gain followers there. 'Tis not unknown for Saxons to hire Norse warriors when it suits them, so Edward thought to ally himself through marriage to some of Athelwold's English thegns. Ceawlin was one of them.'

'That's why the king's standard flew over your hall?'

'Aye.' She shrugged. 'Ceawlin would have it so, even though the king never set foot in the place. Mayhap he thought proclaiming his royal connection was support enough for Edward's cause. Heaven knows, he was too cowardly to fight for either side, but Athelwold was killed in battle last year, so it no longer mattered.'

'Except you would have been bound to a man who mistreated you for the rest of your life.'

She gaped at him. '*You* have the effrontery to make that statement?'

'I haven't mistreated you,' he pointed out mildly.

'Holy Saints! How do you describe murder and kidnapping? As doing me a favour?'

'You tell me, lady.' He studied her for an uncomfortably long moment. 'You were beaten almost unto death. If your husband still lived, and resented your presence as you say, how long would you have survived? There are many ways to kill a woman while she lies senseless.'

Yvaine moved restlessly under that cool, steady gaze. Uneasy memory stirred. Something about Anfride's potions.

'Ceawlin could hardly kill me before witnesses,' she muttered.

'What witnesses? The place was deserted and might have remained so. I've heard of people not returning to their homes for days after a raid.'

'Aye, because there's nothing for them to return to after you finish burning and looting.'

'Not all of us burn and loot, little one.'

His voice had dropped to a dark tone she thought she'd heard once before. She shivered. No. Impossible.

'Do you think me blind?' she scoffed. 'I saw the smoke from your fires. I saw your friend, Thorolf, with plate and silver, I—'

His brows went up. 'You recall a lot, little cat, for one so grievously hurt.'

'I recall you killing,' she retorted. 'I recall seeing others lying dead. Even now one of your captives has thrown herself into the sea, and…

'Ah. You blame me for that?'

'You caused her to be—'

'No!' His voice was suddenly stern, those light eyes piercingly intent. 'Do you accuse me of her death, lady?'

Yvaine glared at him. 'No,' she said at last. 'I cannot. Precisely.'

The hard line of his mouth eased. 'You would seem to have a fine sense of justice, lady. It should surprise me, but somehow...' He shook his head. 'You also have courage. Too much, I think, to follow that unfortunate woman's example.'

'Sometimes it takes more courage to die than to let oneself by used.'

'You know damn well I'm not going to hand you over to my men,' he chided. 'Despite your husband's charming suggestion that I do so.'

'Well, then, you do have a problem, don't you. I'm not destined for slavery, I'm not destined for your men. The only thing left is to rape me yourself.'

And, Holy Mother, if you have any mercy, you'll let me sink through these planks beneath my feet and disappear into the sea.

Nothing happened. Except that Rorik raised a sardonic brow.

'Not the most enticing offer I've ever received,' he drawled. 'But an interesting challenge, none the less. 'Tis plain to see you need taming, lady.'

The blood drained from her face in a heartbeat. 'The way Ceawlin tried?'

He was down beside her before the last whispered word vanished on the wind. Without meaning to, Yvaine flinched.

'Thor's hammer,' he said very softly, 'have I given you reason to fear me so greatly? Do you truly believe I'd strike you after seeing what that bastard did to you?'

'How do I know?' She shook her head, desperately trying to rally enough wit to defy him. The task was well nigh impossible. He was too close, too big, too overwhelmingly male. And this close, somehow different. Still tough, still hard, but the sun slanted over his cheekbones, touching his mouth so that his lower lip looked fuller, softer. And though his eyes were narrowed, she saw concern, and something that looked... almost questioning.

She wrenched her gaze away, inexplicably shaken. 'How can I tell you what you'd do? You took me from my home. I saw you kill Ceawlin. Even if you thought he... But he'd never touched me until then. In any way. So—'

'What!' Rorik reached out, captured her face with one large hand and jerked it around to his. Yvaine's heart thudded at the flare of heat in his eyes. In the clear light they shone almost silver.

'What are you saying?' he demanded. 'That he had you in his bed for five years and never touched you? Was the man dead even then?'

'Well, he didn't...I mean, he wasn't...that is, he had other interests.' Yvaine winced at the babbled explanation. Coherent speech was beyond her, but Rorik seemed to know precisely what Ceawlin's other interests had entailed. His fingers tightened painfully for an instant, before he tore his hand away and shot to his feet.

* * *

If the mast had suddenly fallen on him he couldn't have been more stunned.

Rorik stood rigid, only his seaman's instincts keeping his hand on the steering oar as the truth hit him with the force of a battering ram. The Englishman *hadn't* lied. Yvaine was innocent. She was his.

By the Thunderer, *she was his*. No other man had seen her naked, touched her sweet flesh, held her—

The violent rush of blood to his loins warned him to stop that line of thought, but what stunned him was the wild conflict of emotions raging within him. Protectiveness. Tenderness. Where had they come from? He'd felt liking for the women he'd bedded, affection for one or two, but never this. Never to the point where he was torn in two; rent savagely between aching desire and an equally fierce need to protect the object of his desire. Even from himself.

Gods! He couldn't think about this now. Couldn't think about the grinding need to plunder, to hold; to ravish, to shield. He was all that stood between Yvaine and forty men. If he once broke the rule he'd laid down while the women were on board, none of them would be safe.

Clamping his hand harder around the steering oar, he forced his gaze from Yvaine's startled face to her kirtle. The loosened garment had slipped sideways, giving him a tantalising glimpse of the slender column of her throat and one delicately curved shoulder. It wasn't the distraction he needed, but the unpleasant suspicion that struck him at that moment, wrenched his thoughts from the storm howling within him.

'Is that why you're wearing those clothes?' he snarled. 'To cater to your lord's *other interests*?'

Shocked bewilderment sprang into her eyes, but he couldn't soften the rage in his voice. The thought that her husband might have forced Yvaine to dress as a boy, in order to bed her to get a son, sent reason hurtling overboard. He could have killed the viperous bastard all over again. Slowly.

'To cater—' Bewilderment changed to comprehension, then to a fury that almost matched his own. 'How *dare* you!'

'I didn't mean willingly,' he growled, calming down somewhat in the face of this reaction.

But Yvaine sprang to her feet, the reason for her boy's attire sweeping through her on a tide of rage. 'I was going to leave him,' she cried. 'I was going to return to Edward. And I would've succeeded had it not been for you! Thief! Plunderer! You even took the money I needed and—'

'What money?'

'That bag Ceawlin was so anxious to give you. It had my dowry in it.'

His eyes narrowed. 'I don't need the paltry wealth of such a nithing.'

'Well, *I* did! Now I have noth—'

She stopped, her gaze suddenly riveted to the hand she was waving about. A heavy gold ring, set with precious garnets and sapphires, adorned one finger. She tugged it off.

'Except this,' she said breathlessly, holding it out. ''Tis valuable and rare. Will you take it in payment for sending a messenger to Edward? He'll ransom me and the others, I swear it. You'll not lose by setting us free.'

Something dangerous flashed in his eyes. 'How do you know what I'll lose, little cat?'

'Nothing of honour, surely. All men understand the rules of ransom. Even Vikings. Take the jewel. I have no need of it now Ceawlin is dead, and never wanted it in the first place.'

'Your husband put that ring on your finger?'

'Aye, but—'

Rorik whipped the ring out of her grasp before she could blink. Without even glancing at it, he drew back his arm and flung the jewel as far as he could. 'Then let Aegir's daughters have it,' he muttered with savage satisfaction.

Yvaine stood as though tied to the deck and watched in appalled disbelief as her property soared in a shining arc and disappeared beneath a rolling wave.

'I can't believe you did that.' She turned on him, fury curling her hands into tiny fists. 'To think that a moment ago I wondered if you might be different. But you're nothing but a savage...an ignorant barbarian...a—'

He stepped forward and clamped his free hand over her mouth, silencing her by the mere threat of those powerful fingers closing hard around her jaw. 'Enough,' he said with ominous quiet. 'You can spit at me as much as you like in private, lady, but I'll be damned if I'll let you do so in front of my men.'

'In private!' She spluttered behind his hand. And immediately froze, staring up at him, as the movement of her mouth against his calloused palm sent heat streaking through her.

He tensed as if she'd struck him. His eyes narrowed, turned fierce. Then with a gentleness in shattering contrast to the blazing intensity in his eyes, he lowered his hand to her throat, touched his fingers to the pulse leaping there.

'Aye, in private,' he growled, and she trembled uncontrollably at the dark promise in his voice. 'When you can release the fire frozen inside you by that travesty of a marriage.'

Dear God, she was going to faint. His blatantly stated intent, allied to the gentle touch of his fingers, had her senses reeling. She couldn't let it happen. *Couldn't.*

'Aye,' he murmured as though privy to her thoughts. 'You'll fight me, little cat. Until you know me better, I wouldn't expect otherwise. But while you fight me, think on this.' His gaze, utterly focused, held hers. 'Had I left you where you lay, I doubt you'd have lived. If you'd escaped your husband unhindered, you'd never—'

'I don't *care*.' Horrified that the first man to wring a response from her was a marauder to whom she was nothing but an object to be used, she wrenched herself out of his hold and backed away. 'I *might* have lived. I *might* have reached Edward. You had no right to stop me.'

'Damn it, *I* didn't—'

'But you're right about one thing,' she swept on. 'I *will* fight you. I'll make you wish you'd never set eyes on me. I'll—'

'Do you think that hasn't already crossed my mind?' he snarled suddenly, shocking her into silence. 'I don't carry off women as a matter of course, lady, but damn you to the far reaches of Hel, I saw you lying in that hall and forgot why I was there. I looked at you, captured and helpless, and forgot your kind is usually at war with mine.' His voice lowered to a guttural growl she barely recognised as human. 'By the Gods, I touched your naked flesh and almost took you where you lay.'

She remembered! Heaven help her, she *remembered*. Being tied, being trapped, being touched.

She stood there, fighting for air, for the strength to defy him, while memory swept through her with a force that left her shaking; while her mind reeled beneath a vision more terrifying than any memory. A vision of herself engulfed by the Viking leader, their limbs entwined, his head bent over hers, the hard mouth taking…

A shuddering wave of sensation tore through her. She almost staggered under the force of it.

With an almost soundless cry, she turned to flee.

Chapter Four

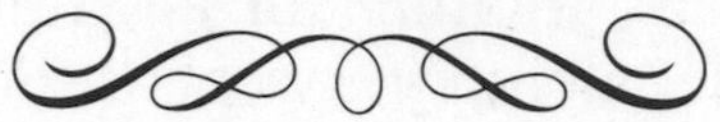

He whipped an arm about her waist before she'd taken a single step.

'Fight me here in the open,' he warned, 'and you'll have every man on this ship licking his lips while he awaits the outcome.'

The words were like a slap in the face. Yvaine dragged in a shuddering breath and almost choked on it when the movement brought her closer against him. His mail tunic had been replaced by a loosely belted kirtle, but it made no difference. The arm about her was like iron; the rest of his body as hard. Heat surrounded her, turning her limbs to water. His scent, a tantalizing mixture of male, salt air and sun-warmed skin, had her senses swimming.

Desperate to escape the devastating assault, she made a small frantic sound and strained away from him. 'Let…me…go!'

'So you can fall on your face? Damn it, stop trembling like that. I'm not going to hurt you.'

'You expect me to believe that? When you say you want me and damn me to hell in the same breath?'

'Ah.' He was silent a moment. 'You know little of men, sweet virgin. I hadn't realised how complete is your innocence.' He lowered his head to hers. 'Here's your first lesson. A man is not at his most patient when he holds the woman he wants in his arms and can't take her.'

'Then let me suggest a cure for such a grievous malady. Release me at once.'

She felt some of the tension leave his body; felt his mouth curve against her hair. 'But you tremble still. 'Tis difficult enough to keep one's footing in these seas.'

Holy saints! After frightening her out of her wits, was he *teasing* her?

Out of the maelstrom of emotions battering her senses, she managed to wrest some pride. 'I won't fight you in front of these savages,' she muttered. 'But nor will I give you the satisfaction of seeing me fall. Especially at your feet.'

'That wouldn't give me satisfaction, little cat. If you look like falling at my feet, I'll catch you and we'll reach the ground together.'

'And angels will change their halos for forked tails.'

He laughed. And kissed her swiftly on the cheek. 'This time I'm only going to fasten your kirtle. There's nought to fear in that.'

'No,' she whispered through the pulse pounding wildly in her throat. 'Nought to fear.'

He released her, slowly, as though he wasn't sure she believed him. It wouldn't have mattered. She couldn't run until her legs stopped trembling.

Nought to fear? He had no conception of a woman's fears. Until now, neither had she.

The thought made her shiver.

'Don't make it easy for me,' he growled.

She barely heard him. Barely realised he'd felt that small betraying tremor. She had to get away. Had to think about this new threat that had sprung at her from nowhere. He'd fastened the first laces and moved to the next. There were three ties; two would keep her decently covered.

The instant the second knot was drawn tight she sprang free and ran, stumbling over the uneven planking until she was forced to slow down or fall.

Her heart pounded, her stomach churned. Reaction had her shaking so badly only sheer momentum kept her upright. That, and the promise of shelter. The tent beckoned, a safe haven.

A safe haven? That flimsy tent? A strip of leather won't keep him from you.

No! Don't think about it. Keep moving.

The base of the mast loomed in front of her. She swerved, remembering the three dice-throwers. This time they were easy to ignore.

Until one man rose to his feet and moved in front of her, bringing her to an abrupt standstill.

He looked vaguely familiar. She frowned, wondering why it should be so, then, cursing herself for her hesitation, went to step around him.

He stretched out an arm and propped his hand against the mast, blocking her path. He made no move to touch her, but his cold blue eyes raked her up and down with calculated insolence.

After all she'd been through it was too much. Her teeth clenched on a snarl of pure rage. 'Get out of my way, you accursed heathen!'

The Viking threw back his head and laughed. 'A spitting wildcat,' he announced to nobody in particular.

But his amusement was mirthless, malicious. He opened his mouth to speak again.

'Let her pass, Othar.'

'Did you hear the way she—?'

'Stand aside!'

Rorik's voice cracked behind her with the force of a whip. Yvaine jumped. He must have handed over the steering oar and moved like lightning. She flinched as he closed his hand over her arm, but didn't try to avoid his touch.

Othar scowled and moved aside, his face reddening when some of the nearer men sniggered.

Yvaine didn't wait to see anyone else's reaction to the unpleasant little scene. She hurried towards the tent, painfully aware of Rorik keeping pace by her side, of his hard fingers gripping her arm. And still she didn't shake him off. How could she? She needed him. Without his protection she'd have no choice but to throw herself overboard before the crew fell on her like dogs snarling over a bone.

But his protection came at a price.

Fixing her eyes on the shelter, she quickened her pace; a hunted creature seeking the safety of its den.

'Another lesson,' he murmured when they reached it. 'When the quarry flees, the hunter is all the more determined to catch it.'

'I'm sure you consider me already captured,' she retorted, refusing to look at him. 'That being so, you could at least allow me the privacy of my prisoner's quarters.'

'You're a long way from captured, sweet prisoner. The trick, in this instance, is the bait.'

'Wallow in delusion if you must. You have nothing I want. Except the means to my freedom.'

'Stubborn little cat.' He laughed softly, and sliding his hand down to hers, he spread her fingers wide, lacing his between them with a slow insistent pressure that, for some odd reason, made her legs go weak, as if… Dear God, as if he'd laid her down and was spreading…

No! She shook her head; struggled to keep her footing against the wave of terrifying vulnerability that threatened to drag her under.

'Such big eyes,' he murmured. 'Such a tiny hand. You fear me now, little maiden, because you're innocent. It won't always be so.'

'Because you intend to rob me of my innocence!' She flung the words at him, looking up at last.

'No,' he corrected. 'Because you'll learn not to fear me.'

'I'm not afraid of you,' she denied. 'And you'll take nothing from me that I don't want to give.'

Rorik's eyes narrowed briefly. *Aye, you will be mine, little cat. Already you know it, without knowing. 'Tis why you fight so hard.*

But he couldn't tell her that. Not when the confusion in her eyes belied the gallant angle of her chin. Not when she stood there, so small and soft, in the midst of male violence.

Something exquisitely painful pierced his chest even while his free hand clenched against the need to pull her against him, to press his body to hers and find some ease from the ache that had tormented him from the moment he'd touched her. He wanted to see fire in her eyes, not fear. He wanted her willing.

Aye, and how willing was she likely to be when he'd taken her from her home and dumped her in conditions that could test the hardiest of men?

The question came out of nowhere, blind-siding him. Rorik shook his head. Gods! Was he now doubting his actions? He'd taken her. 'Twas done.

But he looked down at her, at the sweet, tremulous curve of her mouth, at the way she kept her gaze on his, glaring, without yielding an inch, and was shaken by an overpowering urge to give her something, anything, to ease the shock of that transition.

'Would you like a bath?' he murmured.

Her eyes blinked wide. 'A *what*?'

Despite the ache of frustration, he smiled. 'Tonight we'll beach near a river. After that we won't sight land until we reach thc Jutland peninsula, two days' sailing away. I thought you might like a bath.' Bracing himself for the tearing sensation he knew would follow, he separated their hands.

Yvaine stared at her fingers. They were still there, still hers, but they pulsed gently from the pressure of his, a faint throbbing that was echoed somewhere deep inside her. A sudden longing swept over her. For something familiar. Something safe. Something utterly mundane. Like a bath.

'Without you,' she blurted out. Then blushed wildly when his brows shot up. 'I meant as a guard,' she muttered, scowling.

He laughed wryly. 'At this moment, sweet lady, you'll be safer with Orn Hooknose. He has granddaughters older than you.'

'More shame to him, then, that he's on this ship.'

'Hmm. I'm beginning to see what my uncle meant about his wife's tongue. Don't worry, little cat, Orn won't touch you. He'll be there for your protection.'

'You mean he'll be there to make sure we don't escape.'

Every trace of amusement vanished from his face. 'Don't even think about it,' he bit out with icy precision. ''Twould be as foolish as your attempt to jump overboard the other day.'

Yvaine lifted her chin. 'I knew what I was doing. I can swim.'

'Indeed?' His expression turned sardonic. 'A useful accomplishment. But if you run off into the Danelaw you'll be in well over your head. The English aren't very popular there at present, thanks to your enterprising cousin. A girl alone, and as beautiful as you are, would be forced into a whorehouse so fast you'd think slavery a blessing in comparison.'

When she didn't answer, his eyes narrowed. 'Perhaps a bath wasn't such a good idea, after all.'

But Yvaine wasn't about to let the opportunity slip out of her grasp. The possibility of escape beckoned. The promise of ridding herself of the pervasive odour of sheep fat almost outweighed it.

'Even a bath in the sea would be welcome,' she murmured wistfully. And Rorik felt his heart melt.

'Tell the other women,' he instructed curtly, and turned away, now regretting his offer but utterly incapable of disappointing her. 'You'd best all bathe together.'

Yvaine stood in the opening of the tent and watched him stride away. He never faltered, never swerved from his path, never doubted his purpose.

Oh, for a tithe of that sureness, that strength. She felt as if she'd just been pummelled by the heavy stones used by the laundresses to press water from the wash. Her legs shook, her arms hung limply at her sides…

'My lady? Are you all right? You've been gone so long I was worried.'

Yvaine turned. And suddenly not only her legs, but her entire body was trembling. 'Anna.' She almost collapsed against the girl. 'I just realised. I've been bandying words with a Viking, and—'

She stopped, shook her head. 'Bandying. What a useless description. I argued with him, defied him, *angered* him…but he didn't…'

'Hurt you?' Anna ventured, steering her into the tent.

'No, he didn't hurt me.' Yvaine gazed blankly at her surroundings. 'I think…in some way…'twould have been easier if he had.'

When Anna stared at her, uncomprehending, she made a small, dismissive gesture. 'Pay no heed to me, Anna. I spoke without thought. No woman wishes to be hurt.'

'No, lady.' The girl continued to eye her doubtfully. 'Perhaps you should sit down. 'Twill be an hour or two before the ship is beached.'

'Aye.' She sank to the bearskin, grateful for the reprieve. The battle had exhausted her. A mere battle of words, of wits—that she'd actually thought she might win.

Oh, foolish arrogance. Reckless pride. What had made her think such a thing when for five long years she'd surrendered every battlefield, refused every fight, schooled herself never to show anger, never to betray fear, never to give in to wrenching loneliness. At first because she wouldn't give Ceawlin the satisfaction, and then—

And then, when fear had finally worn thin that first winter at Selsey, the young girl, who'd married to please the only family she had left, was gone, and she'd turned cold. Cold all the way through. So cold she'd thought her heart had been buried forever beneath the frozen snowdrifts surrounding the manor.

Now spring had come with a vengeance; feeling overwhelmed her. Wave after wave of anger and fear and something...*urgent*. She felt it with every part of her being, as if all her nerves were thrumming like lute strings too violently plucked. She wanted to pace, needed desperately to move to escape the sensation, and had to force herself to stillness, while her heart beat like the wings of a hundred birds fleeing the turbulence of a summer storm.

And through it all, carried on the winds of confusion that swirled through the tempest, the vision that had sent her fleeing from the Viking leader played over and over in her mind, like an ancient bard who remembers only one verse.

With a tiny sound of despair, she wrapped her arms around her upraised knees, laid her head down and closed her eyes.

What had he done to her?

They bathed in a small pool, formed by a collapsed section of the riverbank where the low-lying leafy branches of an ancient oak created an illusion of privacy. The westering sun, filtering through the leaves, sent light and shadow rippling across the shimmering surface. Further out, a path of liquid gold flowed lazily towards the shore. Later, when the tide turned, the flow would drift inland, towards the forest—and freedom.

Yvaine gazed into the trees, and counted the hours until nightfall.

She'd finally found a measure of peace, had told herself that Rorik had done nothing more than kidnap her. She wasn't the first woman to be so used, nor would she be the last. Indeed, in these uneasy times it happened frequently; sometimes for revenge, but more often because the woman was an heiress and a man was looking for a wealthy bride. At least she didn't have to worry about those two possibilities.

And though she'd never admit as much to Rorik, she suspected he *had* saved her life by kidnapping her. She hadn't known about Anfride's potions at the time, but three times in the past few months she'd been overcome by stomach pains and illness for no apparent reason. The feeling of impending danger that had been growing on her since the last episode had spurred her to seize the chaos of the Viking raid as cover for her escape.

Her plan had failed, but that didn't mean she'd willingly stay with the man who'd carried her off because he'd rescued her from another violent male.

'You are very quiet, lady. Does your back pain you still?'

Yvaine glanced over her shoulder. They'd bathed and Anna was braiding her hair. Though soap had still been lacking, one of their guards had produced a bone comb and brusquely shoved it into Britta's hand. She and little Eldith sat watching as Anna's nimble fingers moved through the thick strands of hair.

'No. At least, only a little. If I'm quiet, 'tis just that this is our last night in England, and—'

'You're not thinking of running, lady,' Britta glanced from Yvaine's face to the forest. 'Those warriors Rorik sent to guard us might have their backs turned, but I warrant their ears are alert to every sound.'

'Besides, where would you go?' Anna asked. ''Tis a long way to Selsey and you'd have to cross the Danelaw.' She tied Yvaine's hair with a scrap of cloth torn from her kirtle and leveled the comb at her. 'We may be captives here, but at least we have some protection.'

'I know, but...'

She let her protest fade. Anna was right. So was Rorik, come to that. This part of England was firmly held by the Danes, despite Edward's efforts to reclaim it so he could fulfill his father's ambition of a united England. There would be little safety here and, if the other girls were truly reconciled to their fate, she would be completely alone.

The knowledge sent chills through her, but how could she persuade the others to escape against their will, especially with a child? Danger, hunger and fear would be their constant companions, and who was she to say their lives would be no better in Norway? Anna claimed to have been little more than a slave; Britta looked as though grinding labour had been her lot since she could remember; and poor little Eldith would have suffered the fate of orphaned children, and become a slave anyway in exchange for food and shelter.

She alone had somewhere to turn, but how was she to get there?

Nothing helpful occurred as they were herded back to the beach. They cleared the forest and the ship came into view, still some distance away. Indecision racked her. She glanced back towards the river, her footsteps slowed. Sheer madness to run now; they were surrounded. But the forced waiting raked at her nerves like tiny claws.

'Better you not fall behind lady,' said a gruff voice beside her. 'Night draws close, and the Bearslayer's patience isn't boundless.'

Yvaine turned her head. A pair of light blue eyes in a crinkled nut-brown face stared back at her, not unkindly. Above the man's grizzled beard was a hawk-like nose of truly impressive proportions. Hooknose without a doubt.

'Bearslayer,' she echoed sceptically, answering him in Norse, although he'd used enough English to make himself understood. She ignored the flicker of surprise in his eyes. 'I suppose you, too, are going to tell me he killed an ice-bear.'

'He did, lady. Not that I saw the deed myself, but—'

'No, nor anyone else, I warrant.'

'You speak with haste and without thought, mistress. That puts you at a disadvantage when dealing with my lord, gentle though he's been with you.'

'Gentle!' Yvaine sniffed. 'I've seen little evidence of it.'

'Now you speak without knowledge. An hour in Ketil's company would change your mind.' Orn jerked his head, indicating a group of men walking towards them. With dismay, Yvaine recognised the three dice-throwers.

'Othar,' muttered Anna, moving to her other side as she halted. 'He makes my flesh creep. You wouldn't think he and Rorik are brothers, would you?'

'Brothers?' Startled, Yvaine looked at the boy, using the small crowd as a shield. The vague sense of familiarity she'd experienced earlier was now explained, but she had to agree with Anna. Othar was tall and fair, but he seemed a mere shadow of his brother, his sullen face a blurred image of Rorik's stern, cleanly etched features, his build already that of a man who spent more time in an ale-house than on the jousting-field.

But the main difference was in the eyes. Rorik's grey eyes held the chill of winter in their glittering depths, but she'd also seen them warm with amusement, or blaze with sudden, fierce desire. Othar's blue eyes held the flat, inward stare of a man who sees only himself. And their expression turned ugly when he heard Anna's remark.

'You won't be on the ship forever, wench, so watch your tongue or I'll cut it out the minute we reach Kaupang.'

His gap-toothed friend apparently found the prospect appealing. He grinned, before turning a curious stare on Yvaine. The third man was already watching her, his eyes as cold and unblinking as a snake's.

'Try not to spoil a peaceful summer evening, Othar.' Hooknose spoke with an impatient authority she could only hope was effective. 'We have to get these thralls on board before Rorik returns.'

'Don't give *me* orders, old man. If you let them linger overlong at their bath the consequences rest on your head.'

'Aye. Enjoy the watch, did you, Orn?' Gap-tooth roared with laughter at his own wit.

His friend's expression never altered. 'Orn fears the Bearslayer's wrath too greatly for that.'

She felt Orn stiffen beside her. 'And you, Ketil? Do you fear it no less that you address me against his orders?'

Ketil flicked a glance at Orn, but remained silent.

'Ketil spoke to me, Orn.' A ripple of unease crossed Gap-tooth's face. 'We don't want any trouble. You know what Rorik said about private feuds while we sail with him.'

Othar snorted. 'You mew like a new-born kitten, Gunnar.' Barrelling forward, he thrust his arm against Orn's chest. 'Out of my way, greybeard. I'll show you how to hurry these thralls along.'

'I doubt it,' Orn scoffed, standing his ground. 'If I were you, Othar, I'd not rely too heavily on your brother's protection. As I told the lady—'

'Lady? I see no lady here.' Othar shoved Orn aside and seized Yvaine's braid in a grip that forced her face up to his. 'She's nought but a thrall who'll learn who's master. Isn't that so, wench?'

She gave him her coldest stare. 'You are not my master. And I am not a slave.'

Othar clicked his tongue in mock disapproval. 'When Rorik's finished with you, you'll be a slave and nothing more. Then I'll take my turn. You think it won't happen?' He grinned. 'I'll show you.'

Tightening his grip, he bent his head, but Yvaine was already struggling. She whipped her arm up and had just aimed a blow at his ear when she was abruptly released.

Othar was spun away from her so fast she almost fell. She had one brief glimpse of the rage on Rorik's face, before he slammed his fist into Othar's stomach.

The boy doubled over, falling to his knees and retching. Before he'd hit the sand, Rorik had turned on the others. 'Get everyone back to the ship,' he snarled at Orn. 'And you two, go with him. One word out of either of you, and you'll be left here for the Danes to find.'

Neither Ketil nor Gunnar argued.

Shaking, Yvaine reached for Anna's hand.

She was jerked away from the girl before she could blink. Rorik pulled her to his side but spared her neither word nor look. 'Get up,' he ordered his brother.

Othar staggered to his feet. 'You'll be sorry for that, Rorik. When our father hears of this—'

'And keep your mouth shut.'

Othar shut his mouth, scowling.

'Perhaps I didn't make myself absolutely clear two days ago,' Rorik began. His voice could have frozen hellfire. 'The Lady Yvaine is not a thrall. You will not treat her as one. Ever. Now apologise.'

'Apolo—'

Othar saw his brother's free hand clench and bit off the rest. His bottom lip stuck out. 'Your pardon, *lady*.'

She nodded, scarcely listening. Othar was the least of her worries. When he swung about and strode back to the ship, she forgot him instantly. Danger stood beside her, not with a sulky youth. Danger cloaked in a form of protection she dare not trust.

Wrenching her arm free, she stepped back. 'Well, your brother has tendered an apology, albeit reluctantly. I'm still waiting for yours.'

He sent her a look that could have shrivelled lightning. 'You have a reckless notion of humour, lady.'

She gave him back look for look. 'Then you should laugh yourself silly at my next words. I demand that you ransom me immediately.'

'You expect me to conjure your cousin out of air?'

'Of course not. Send a message to him.'

'And sit around here waiting for his reply I suppose.' He grabbed her wrist, turned on his heel and started towards the ship. 'You're right. If I didn't have my hands full with the trouble you've caused, I would laugh myself silly.'

'*I've* caused?' The injustice sent her voice soaring. ''Tis not my fault if your stupid brother—'

He stopped so abruptly she cannoned into him. He cursed, steadied her, and stepped back. 'What the Hel else do you expect him or any other man to think when you're running around dressed like that? Look at you! Kirtle falling off. Chausses clinging like a second skin. Gods! In Norway you'd be outlawed for dressing like a man.'

'I didn't ask to be kidnapped,' she yelled, trying to fling off his hand. 'If you don't like the way I dress then set me free. I'll be only too happy to see the back of you.'

Rorik's teeth snapped shut on a curse that blistered her ears. Jerking his hand from her arm, he wheeled about and raked his fingers through his hair. Then stood, fists clenched tight on his hips, staring out to sea.

Yvaine studied the back she'd expressed a desire to see. She wished she'd kept her mouth shut. He stood so tall and straight, broad shoulders tapering to narrow hips and long legs; a dark lance spearing through the golden disk sinking into the sea beyond him. His very stance was a blunt statement of invincible strength.

'I went inland to find a gown for you,' he said, so abruptly she jumped. 'But no one was there. The whole damned village had gone.'

She eyed him for a moment, weighing caution and defiance. 'The Danes had fled? Well, who could wonder at it?'

'No, not Danes. English.' He turned. 'There are some in the Danelaw. We trade with them.'

'You astonish me.'

A shadow of a smile came and went. He looked away again, towards his ship, and a strange kind of silence fell. Almost peaceful, she thought. The sea lapped at the shore in little wavelets that chased each other back into deeper water. A gull marched along the water's edge, leaving a trail of prints in the sand. Further up the beach, a cooking fire had been lit, the flames just visible against the golden sky.

She lifted her head and took a deep breath of the balmy air, letting the serenity of the beach, bathed in the lambent glow of sunset, settle about her. Just for a moment she could almost imagine she was on a journey. That her captor was her escort, her protector, her champion.

Then she turned her head, their eyes met, and a sharp little arrow of awareness pierced her insides that had nothing to do with safety or protection.

'Did my brother hurt you?' he asked softly.

She shook off the strange sensation and sniffed. 'Saints, no. What is a strand of hair or two?'

'Clearly nought, for you seem to be none the worse for losing them.' He reached out and ran his hand down the braid hanging over her shoulder.

She smacked his hand away before he felt the tremor she couldn't suppress. ''Tis not your brother I fear. He's nought but a boy, and a sulky one at that.'

'In Norway, lady, a boy is considered a man at twelve. Othar's sixteen. He no longer thinks like a child. Unfortunately, he's been indulged by his mother from birth, and thinks all women should do the same.'

'Hmph. The fault seems to run in the family.'

'My mother died when I was born,' he murmured. 'By the time my father took Gunhild to wife I was ten and, I assure you, she did not feel inclined to indulge me.'

'Ah, well…' She ruthlessly banished a picture of a motherless little boy. 'It must have been your father who instilled in you this odd notion that murder and kidnapping are nought but summer pastimes.'

'Egil raided a-plenty in his youth,' he acknowledged, amusement glinting briefly. Then he sobered. 'But he's very ill now. He won't see out the summer.'

'Then I wonder that you left him.' She'd meant the words to sound snippy, critical. They came out softly, faintly questioning. She could have kicked herself.

He sent her a quick, searching glance, frowned and took her arm. 'I had a vow to fulfil. Come. You need food and rest. 'Tis time you were back on the ship.'

And with that the brief moment was gone. Yvaine went without protest, but later that night, when she lay on the bearskin with the others, her mind was a seething mass of confusion; plans for escape tangling hopelessly with questions that had no answers. For some reason she kept thinking about the sense of peace, almost of companionship, that had fallen over her and Rorik on the beach. She knew he'd felt it, knew his anger had dissipated as abruptly as her own.

And that was another thing. She'd never shouted at anyone in her entire life. Indeed, when she'd finally recovered from their first encounter, she'd vowed to treat her captor with the same cool composure she'd used towards Ceawlin. And what had she done instead? Argued with him, yelled at him, continued to throw verbal darts at him—secure in the knowledge that he wouldn't hurt her. At least, not in a rage.

Was she mad as well as reckless to put that much belief in the man's honour? To treat him as if they'd met under different circumstances and—

Different circumstances. Now there was a question. How *would* she have felt about Rorik if she'd met him at Edward's court? Would she have seen the toughness, the hard edge of danger? She thought so. They were too close to the surface to be completely hidden. But how would she have responded to the fleeting moments of humour? To the hints of gentleness?

Yvaine shivered and hugged herself against a sudden chill. Why was she asking such questions? They hadn't met at Edward's court. Rorik had kidnapped her. He'd murdered her husband before her very eyes—never mind that she wasn't broken-hearted over the deed. He was pagan, a Viking. He'd stolen the freedom she'd risked her very life to gain.

And he'd done something else, she realised in that moment. Something that made her heart stand still, something more terrifying than all the rest. Something she hadn't thought possible.

He'd brought her alive again.

Suddenly, escape was more imperative than ever.

Chapter Five

Thin, translucent clouds drifted, wraith-like, across the face of the moon.

Yvaine glanced skyward as she slipped out of the tent. The misty light seemed as bright as a beacon to her anxious eyes, but if she waited for deeper darkness, dawn would be upon her before she'd gone more than a mile or two into the forest.

She hovered in the shadows cast by the shelter, searching out deeper patches of night in which to hide—and trying not to picture her fate if one of the men sleeping in two rows down the centre of the ship heard her and woke.

And yet, she had to pass them. She had no choice. The ship had been beached prow first. If she clambered over the high, curved side at this point and jumped down to the gritty sand at the water's edge, the guards on the beach would see or hear her for certain.

The first few steps wouldn't be so bad; several yards separated her from the sleeping men. After that, she could only pray that the cacophony of snores and grunts might muffle her footsteps.

Holding her breath, expecting with every passing second to feel hard fingers reach out of the darkness and seize her ankle, she tiptoed forward, moving as silently as the drifting clouds. Her goal was the centre of the ship, the shallowest part, where she could slip easily over the side and let herself down into deeper water. Then she could swim parallel to the shore until she was a safe distance away.

She hadn't thought past that point. Couldn't afford to. Slipping soundlessly through the night was taking all her attention.

Except for one tiny part of her mind that was conscious of a faint whisper of regret.

She closed it off and counted paces instead. A few more and—

Without a sound a shadow loomed out of the night. A hand was clamped over her mouth, she was locked to a hard male body. Moonlight glinted, cold and merciless, on the dagger an inch from her breast.

'Not one word,' growled a soft voice in her ear. 'Or I'll slit your throat.'

She couldn't utter a word. She had no breath, no voice. It wasn't Rorik. That was the only thought in her head.

She felt herself being dragged over the side, felt the gentle tug of ripples against her chausses. The sea was warm compared to the ice sliding through her veins.

Why didn't anyone stir? If she'd made a tithe of the noise her attacker was making, the entire crew would have been on her in seconds. But now they chose to keep snoring.

Oh, God, she had to think. Where was he taking her? He was moving swiftly, up the beach, away from the guards where they'd be out of sight, out of hearing. He didn't speak again; only his breathing broke the silence. Light and rapid, the excitement in the sound finally had comprehension exploding in her brain.

He wasn't only preventing her escape. His purpose was far more sinister.

Panic jolted her into action before she remembered the dagger at her waist. One arm was pinned by the Viking's grip, but the other was free. Flinging it out, she brought her elbow back into the man's ribs with all the strength she could muster, at the same time kicking out with her legs.

The suddenness of her attack took him by surprise. His hand slipped from her mouth and she drew breath to scream.

To her horror the only sound that emerged was a thin gasping cry that wouldn't have carried more than a few feet. Before she could drag in enough air for another attempt, he cut off her breath with a stranglehold around her neck.

Roaring filled her ears; blackness threatened. She felt the Viking pull her down to the sand, felt his weight pinning her there while he tugged at the neck of her kirtle. An image of Skull-splitter flashed through her mind; revulsion had her choking. She went limp. He must have thought she'd swooned, because the arm across her throat lifted.

And this time her scream was piercing, cutting through the night.

The man above her cursed once, viciously. Then as a shout came from the ship, he sprang to his feet and vanished into the darkness as quickly and silently as he'd appeared.

Yvaine rolled, hugging herself into a tight little ball. She had to clench her teeth to stop them chattering.

She couldn't stand, couldn't run. There was something she had to do, but she couldn't think what it was. And when she remembered, darkness no longer shielded her. It was too late. She looked up, straight into Rorik's face. The flaring light of the torch he held illuminated his expression with brutal clarity. A phalanx of warriors stood at his back.

He reached down, grasped her arm and lifted her to her feet. 'Were you taken from the tent?' he demanded. His voice was low, but held the promise of death to anyone who crossed him.

Yvaine could only shake her head. She didn't even consider lying. It would have been useless. Those glittering eyes probed to her very soul, and at her silent answer they turned violent.

'You went *willingly*?'

'No...*no!*' She winced at the snarling fury in his voice. 'I was trying to escape. I don't know who—'

He cut her off with a slashing movement of his hand, then turned, thrust his torch into the hands of the warrior nearest him and ordered his men back to the ship with a few terse words.

The night closed around them again, broken only by the fitful moonlight, but the darkness did nothing to hide Rorik's mood. Yvaine felt menace coming from him so strongly it was almost visible.

'By Thor, I ought to take the flat of my sword to your sweet backside,' he grated. 'Where in Hel did you think you were going?'

'Swimming,' she offered weakly.

He seized her arms in a grip that raised her to her toes. 'Don't be so damned flippant,' he snarled. 'Little fool! I warned you. Do you know how close you came to being raped?' His eyes flashed silver as the moon appeared from behind a cloud and his fingers tightened. Yvaine got the distinct impression he wanted to shake her. Hard.

'Take your hands off me,' she snapped, reckless anger coming to her rescue. She wrenched out of his hold and backed away. 'Do you think I cared for your warnings? You said yourself there were English in the Danelaw. I might have found shelter with good people who would help me return to Edward. And even if I didn't, I'm dressed as a boy, so—'

'*By the Gods, woman!* Only a blind man would be fooled by that ridiculous disguise, and even he'd know the truth the minute you opened your mouth.'

'I would've tried to escape if I'd been naked!' she yelled back. 'Did you think me so tame I'd stand still for your ravishing? You'll know better, my lord.'

'No,' he said, taking a step closer. 'You'll know that you belong to me. That you're mine. That—'

Yvaine whirled and ran. It was useless and she knew it. Even taking Rorik by surprise she couldn't hope to outrun him, but his fierce claim of possession caused her to panic instinctively. She flew down the beach as though pursued by demons, only to be brought down by a neat tackle before she'd covered more than a few yards.

He twisted as they fell, protecting her from the impact, then rolled. For the second time that night Yvaine lay flat on the sand, her chest heaving as she struggled to breathe, overwhelmingly conscious of a man's weight over her.

Then the suffocating pressure lifted, she was flipped over and imprisoned between Rorik's thighs as he knelt above her. He reached out and captured her wrists when she lashed out at him.

'Stop that,' he ordered, his calm tone at odds with his anger of a moment ago. 'You can't fight me. You'll only hurt yourself trying.'

'What do you care?' Panting, trying with every futile twist of her body to throw him off, she fought back with the only weapon left to her. 'You intend to hurt me anyway. Coward! Pirate! No real man would use a woman so.'

His eyes narrowed. 'Be grateful I know 'tis panic speaking, otherwise you'd regret those words.' He smiled faintly. 'Also be grateful I don't abuse what is mine.'

'*I…am…not…yours!* Do you hear me, barbarian? I won't belong to any man. Ever again!'

Rorik's eyes gleamed down at her. 'You'll belong to me, little wildcat. But don't worry. I'll give you time to get used to the idea.'

'Give me time—' The sheer arrogance of his statement made her gasp. 'Why, you arrogant, overbearing, boorish…*kidnapper*. I'll show you what time—'

She didn't get a chance to finish. Rorik leaned forward, lifted her wrists over her head and slowly lowered himself over her. Yvaine's eyes widened as his body covered hers. Heat enveloped her instantly. He didn't crush her, but the awareness that she was thoroughly helpless beneath his much greater weight was absolute.

She tried a tentative wriggle, then went utterly still, her breath seizing, as the movement brought her harder against him. Their eyes met, his blazing, intent; hers wide and wary.

'Aye,' he growled. 'Now you know. I could take you right here, if I was the barbarian you think me.'

He certainly could, she thought, swallowing the sudden constriction in her throat. He was primed and ready. Hard, huge, nudging the place where her thighs were clamped together with just enough pressure to be threatening.

She swallowed again and hoped she could speak. 'No honourable man would even be capable—'

He laughed. A low growl of amusement that sent a ripple of heat from her throat to her toes. Her fingers clenched in his hold as she fought the sensation.

'Sweet innocent. A man couldn't hold you beneath him and not be capable.' His gaze held hers as he lowered his head. 'A man couldn't hold you beneath him and not do this.'

'No…'

'Hush.' His breath bathed her lips. 'Just a kiss, little cat. Nothing more.'

'I don't care what it is. If you try to kiss me, I'll…I'll sink my teeth into you.'

He was so close she felt him smile. 'Go ahead,' he challenged softly. 'Bite me.' His mouth brushed her lips, leaving fire in its wake. Then closed with devastating gentleness over hers.

Time stopped; thought blurred. Yvaine tried frantically to remember what she'd threatened to do. Instead, a whirlwind of confusion buffeted her mind. His mouth was warm and gentle on hers, in stark contrast to the hard male flesh pressed firmly to the most vulnerable part of her body.

She didn't know which was more dangerous; tried to gather her wits to fight him, and couldn't hold on to any one thought. Her senses swung dizzily between the threat of violent possession and the unexpected sweetness of his kiss. And when she finally forced her lips apart, forced the command to retaliate into her mind, she discovered to her dismay that she couldn't bring herself to hurt him.

And then she couldn't think at all, because he slipped his tongue between her lips and...oh, so gently...stroked it over hers.

A tingle of heat streaked her, making her cry out. But even as she softened, Rorik wrenched his mouth from hers. He pushed himself to his feet, pulled her upright and gave her a none too gentle shove towards the ship.

'Move!' he growled.

Dazed, her head spinning from the abrupt shift, Yvaine stumbled forward. Confusion, anger, shock that she'd all but responded to him, jostled about in her head until she wanted to scream. She hadn't even managed to escape. And now see what came of it, there were tears on her cheeks.

She swiped a hand angrily across her face. She never cried. She wasn't going to start now.

A choked hiccup escaped her. Before she could muffle it, she was spun around and pulled into Rorik's arms.

'Oh, God, little cat, I didn't mean to hurt you.'

She froze; for several seconds incapable even of thought. Had she heard aright? Had a Viking just invoked her Christian God? Expressed regret? Offered comfort?

The questions hammered at her brain until her head threatened to ache. Who *was* he, this man who had taken her from her home, but watched over her while she'd lain senseless? Who had cursed his desire for her, but refused to release her? Who had held her beneath him, but hadn't forced her?

An urgent need to know welled up inside her, so strong it almost drowned out the warnings of danger clamouring at the back of her mind. The same danger that had sent her fleeing from him; that tempted her to stay.

'You didn't hurt me,' she said curtly, and pushed away from him. Somewhat to her surprise he let her go.

'What of the man who attacked you?' he asked, his voice as terse. 'Did he hurt you?'

'No. He had a dagger, but he didn't use it, even when I screamed.'

'Of course not, you little fool. He wants you alive, in case you hand him another opportunity.' Suddenly he was looming over her. 'But you won't, will you, my lady?'

Yvaine glared up at him, refusing to be intimidated. 'Since we're leaving England tomorrow, there would be little point.'

'True, but the more I learn of you, lady, the less faith I place in your sense of prudence.'

'Well, that will teach you to make enquiries the next time you consider kidnapping someone, won't it.'

His mouth curved; even in the fitful moonlight she saw it and, for some strange reason, felt fresh tears sting her eyes.

'I'll remember that,' he said. Then, frowning. 'Do you know who it was?'

'No. And what does it matter? You'll probably be grateful to him when you stop to think about it. He prevented my escape.'

He moved abruptly. No, not movement, she thought, with a belated sense of caution. It was the air that stirred, as if every muscle in his body had tensed, sending icy currents flowing outwards.

'Indeed,' he said in a harder tone. 'But console yourself with the knowledge that you wouldn't have made it to Winchester, even if your escape wasn't discovered 'til morning. I would've come after you. Now, back to the ship. We both need some sleep.'

Easy for him to say, Yvaine thought resentfully, when she finally crept into the tent and lay down next to her sleeping companions.

She sent up a brief prayer of thankfulness that she didn't have to offer any explanations. The task would have been beyond her; she had too much else on her mind. With her attempt at escape in ruins, she would now have to concentrate all her energies on convincing Rorik to ransom her. And if that didn't work…

She shied away from the prospect. It was far too nerve-racking to contemplate. Better to plan another escape—which wouldn't be easy, because once they left England, she'd have to recruit someone to help her.

Hope stirred faintly, only to sink without trace. Thorolf and Orn were the only men she'd consider trusting with her safety, and they were completely loyal to Rorik. The only alternative—and she'd have to be desperate—was Othar. She didn't trust him, but he was three years younger than her and she suspected his posturing was mainly for the benefit of his friends. Away from them, she might be able to bribe him with offers of a large ransom, especially given his present animosity towards his brother.

Of course, before she attempted any such risky strategy, it would be wise to know more about him. And—if she was cautious about it—to know more about Rorik. After all, it was only sensible to learn all one could about one's adversary.

Slightly comforted by this conclusion, Yvaine turned over and settled down to sleep. She'd start tomorrow, she promised herself, with a few polite questions. She would behave with dignity. She would refuse to be drawn into argument. She would be civil, but distant.

And she would steadfastly ignore the annoying little voice at the back of her mind, that was wondering why common sense and strategy just happened to coincide with her own curiosity.

'My lady, you are not going to walk all the way to the stern alone when the man who attacked you is watching and waiting.' Anna frowned in disapproval.

Britta nodded in dire warning. Both girls had been horrified when Yvaine had related the tale of the previous night's activities over their breakfast of gruel and fruit. They'd emerged from the tent a short time later to find the ship underway. The shores of England were but a memory.

Yvaine shifted her gaze from the misty line dividing sea and sky and studied her two companions. 'He's not going to attack me in front of the entire crew, Anna.'

'We shouldn't even be outside,' Britta muttered. 'Already I hear whispered comments and furtive jests. And you may be sure the brute who attacked you is whispering and jesting with the rest so as to appear as innocent as a babe.'

'Aye.' Anna glanced nervously over her shoulder. 'Since we don't know who it was, 'tis best to avoid the lot of them.'

'He was tall,' Yvaine said slowly. 'And wore a skin tunic. But that's no help. Only Rorik and Thorolf wear chainmail, and that only on the day they sacked Selsey. 'Twas probably filched from some murdered soldier,' she tacked on grimly.

'Thorolf told me Rorik had them specially made, long before they went a-viking,' Anna said. 'I wonder what they did back then?'

'I don't care to know.' Yvaine stuck her nose in the air. Then, remembering her plan, ruined the effect of this lofty attitude by adding, 'What else did Thorolf tell you?'

'Well, yesterday I asked him about the slaves on Rorik's estate, lady, thinking to discover what sort of life you might expect. Most of the men purchase their freedom within three years by working longer hours. Imagine that. A lord who frees his slaves.'

'Hmm. What of the women?'

Anna grimaced. 'Well, a man may buy a woman's freedom if he wishes to marry her, but—'

'An expensive way of acquiring a wife,' put in Britta tartly. 'I can't see that happening to one of us. Marriage to another slave, mayhap.'

''Tis more than I hoped for in England,' Anna pointed out. 'My father would never have allowed me to marry. I was too useful to him.'

Yvaine eyed her thoughtfully. 'I suppose the freedmen are replaced by more slaves captured in England.'

'No. Thorolf told me that Rorik uses the money paid by freed slaves to purchase more. He also lends money to freemen so they may buy a small farm, or set up in trade. He's the son of a jarl and very wealthy.'

'Then why does he need to plunder? I remember now, he scorned Ceawlin's treasure as though 'twas nought. And heaven knows, he hardly needs to employ force to take a woman to his bed, so—'

She suddenly realised her companions were staring at her as if she'd expressed a desire to join the ranks of those willing females, and felt hot colour burn her cheeks.

'Well, if I'm to outwit the man, I need to know these things,' she informed them, turning aside before her face got any redder.

Fortunately for her dignity, her gaze fell on a Viking who was coiling rope nearby. Inspiration struck when she recognised him. She crooked an imperious finger.

'You there. Orn. I would ask a favour of you.' Ignoring the strangled sounds of protest coming from behind her, she took a step forward.

Hooknose straightened, looking wary.

Yvaine pinned her best lady-of-the-manor smile to her face. 'Would you kindly escort me to your commander?'

Orn frowned. 'I'm ordered to stay here, lady. To keep you out of trouble.'

Her smile froze. 'Indeed? Consider, then, how much more trouble there'll be if I go alone. Or if you try to stop me.' From the corner of her eye, she saw Anna and Britta clutch each other.

'Hmph. 'Tis clear Rorik didn't administer harsh enough punishment when you tarried on the beach last night,' muttered Orn. Then, as Yvaine glared at him, a wry smile crossed his face. 'But 'twould be strange indeed if the Bearslayer raised his hand against a woman. Come, then, mistress.'

With a glance at her companions, who were obviously torn between awe at her foolhardiness and the expectation of her immediate demise, Yvaine hurried after him.

'Why do you say that?' she asked. 'When he's taken us against our will.'

'I don't fathom his reasons for taking you, lady, but the others were taken by Ketil and Gunnar. Be grateful Rorik has forbidden them privileges denied the other men.'

'Dear God,' she whispered involuntarily, her gaze sweeping over the men until she located Othar's friends. Ketil was watching her, but, as their eyes met briefly, she realised there was no special awareness in his unblinking stare. She knew, without any doubt, that he hadn't attacked her last night.

Then he shifted his attention to Orn, and as if the older man sensed the cold scrutiny, his pace slackened. He looked around, located Ketil and smiled in unmistakable anticipation. His hand went to his dagger.

Yvaine felt the hair at her nape rise. She doubted anyone with the name Skull-splitter would balk at much, but Orn seemed like a reasonable man and was at least thirty years older than Ketil. What had happened to cause the hatred she felt emanating from him?

She shook off the question as they walked on. She already had enough to worry about. Particularly the wild leap her heart gave when she saw Rorik standing by the steering oar, not six feet away. This time the impact of his presence was devastating. A vivid memory of how it felt to lie beneath all that heat and power and muscle threatened to rob her legs of strength.

She clutched the side and hoped he put her unsteadiness down to the motion of the ship.

'Good morning.' He raised an interrogatory brow at Orn.

'Don't blame me,' Hooknose grumbled. 'She threatened to saunter past the men on her own.'

Yvaine's mouth fell open. 'I did *not* threaten to saunter.'

'Never mind.' Rorik waved Orn away and turned a narrow-eyed look on her. 'Well, lady, you achieved your purpose. What couldn't wait until I came to you?'

Yvaine clamped her lips shut on the urge to inform him she could have waited until doomsday. She was supposed to be trying good manners and diplomacy.

'Thank you for sharing the fruit with us this morning,' she began ''Twas a welcome change.'

His brows lifted. A second later, a wicked gleam lit his eyes. 'Ah, well, we like to fatten our slaves before we sell them.'

Politeness threatened to fly over the side. 'Indeed? I suppose you plundered somebody's orchard for the purpose.'

'Aye.' He grinned. 'But 'twas a Danish orchard.'

'A fine thing,' she muttered, fighting an insane urge to smile back. 'You even steal from each other.'

'Ah. You English see Vikings as one people, don't you, but Norse and Danes are often at war. Usually over trading rights and land. We're on the brink now.'

'One would think you'd both taken enough English land without having to squabble over it,' she retorted, but without real heat. She'd grown up with the fact. 'The Danes rule England from the Thames to the Humber and you Norwegians further north. Everyone knows the town of York as Jorvik these days, and I wager there are many places where the old names are forgotten.'

Rorik shrugged. 'Are we doing any differently from you Saxons? Your ancestors drove the Britons as far west as Wales and Brittany. Not to mention annexing Mercia more recently.'

'That was through marriage,' Yvaine answered indignantly. 'The Lady of Mercia is Edward's sister.'

'Aye,' he agreed, and, without warning, the grim expression she'd seen yesterday descended on his face. 'Alfred's whelps. And together they'll rule all England one day.'

'What do you mean?'

He gestured impatiently. 'The Danes in England are becoming weak, lady. They still hold the Danelaw, but they're farmers and merchants now, not warriors. One day your cousin will triumph and Alfred's dream will become reality.'

'Aye…well…' She pushed aside the intriguing question of Rorik's sudden bitterness in the interests of grasping the opportunity he'd just handed her. 'Speaking of Edward, when do you intend to send a request for my ransom?'

'Ah,' he murmured. 'We arrive at the real reason for this sudden desire for my company.'

With a monumental effort she kept the expression of polite enquiry on her face.

His eyes narrowed. 'I don't recall expressing any such intention, lady.'

'But...' She gripped the planking tighter. 'Kindly do not jest with me, my lord. I understand your pressing need to return home because of your father's health, but I see no humour in the prospect of an unnecessary voyage for myself. You will oblige me by sending a messenger to the king at once.'

A brow went up. 'From the middle of the North Sea?'

'Very well, when we get to Jutland you can put me ashore and—'

'You don't want to be put ashore there, little one.' The wicked smile glinted again. 'There's nought but dark cliffs and caverns along that coast. Only the Gods know what lives there.'

'Don't bother to scare me with your tales of trolls and giants,' she snapped, losing the last tattered threads of her patience. 'Or ice-bears for that matter. I'm not so easily—'

She broke off as he cast a quick glance downwards. A leather thong hung around his neck, threaded through the top of a silver amulet she knew represented Thor's hammer. Hanging beside it was a long, curved tooth. It looked ominously large and deadly.

Yvaine swallowed and decided a change of tactics was called for.

'Very well,' she said, as though frustration and apprehension weren't chasing each other around in her stomach. 'I'll go to Norway with you, and when we get there you can tell everyone I've come for a visit, while you make arrangements to return me to England.'

He stared at her as though she'd turned into a very small ice-bear right before his eyes. 'Why would you come for a visit, lady?'

'I shall study your Norse legends, my lord.'

'Study our Norse legends,' he repeated evenly.

'Aye. I presume you have a *skald* in your household. I shall replace the manuscripts I was compiling—until Ceawlin fed my collection to the cooking fire. Unfortunately, he didn't consider such learning to be useful.'

'You understand Norse?' His gaze sharpened. 'Aye, Orn told me yesterday you spoke to him in the language. How is that?'

She shrugged. 'The same way you learned English, I expect. Through travellers. In times of peace there were plenty of Norse visitors at court. One was a bard who stayed a while. I learned your sagas from him.'

'In that case, lady,' he said, his voice suddenly, unnervingly gentle, 'you know more of us than that we kill and plunder.'

'You forgot abduction,' she said tartly. 'And the fact that you have bards and *skalds* and highly skilled craftsmen doesn't excuse kill—'

She stopped short, her heart contracting on a sudden stab of pain as a picture of Jankin flashed through her mind. Oh, how could she have forgotten? He'd been so innocent, so utterly without guile. He wouldn't have resisted, wouldn't even have understood. Guilt overwhelmed her as she realised that, despite all that had happened, she'd barely taken a moment to mourn that senseless loss of life.

'What is it, little one?'

She turned on him, anger igniting at his careless question, the meaningless endearment. 'Did you kill anyone near the riverbank that day at Selsey?'

He frowned. 'The only person I killed was your husband, but…'

'You've killed on other raids,' she finished for him, and felt her eyes fill. 'Innocent people who…'

Rorik saw her blink rapidly as she turned her face away, and cursed silently. What could he say? He couldn't tell Yvaine the truth. Her cousin was involved. She'd immediately assume he'd taken her to use as bait.

Maybe he had, he thought. For a few hours after he'd learned who she was, maybe that purpose had tangled with the rest. Maybe it did still. All he knew was that he was driven by a need so fierce, a desire so urgent, it was almost…a *yearning*. As if there was an empty place inside him only she could fill, a hunger only she could appease.

Gods. He was thinking like a *skald*, composing a maudlin saga where the hero spends his time languishing over some unattainable female. He knew what was driving him. The memory of her soft flesh against his palm, the way she'd felt as she'd lain in his arms last night. The sweet innocence that had enveloped him when he'd kissed her. He'd wanted to take that innocence into himself, to absorb her, to be himself absorbed. Only the thought of her injured back, striking him when she'd cried out, had forced him to his feet. And his blood went cold at the thought of the other damage that could have been done to her.

He frowned suddenly, wondering how he was going to leave Yvaine at Einervik while he went off raiding.

The answer was immediate...simple, unsettling, but immediate.

'Set your mind at rest on one score,' he said curtly. 'This is the last raid I'll be leading.'

She turned her head at that, clearly startled. 'What?'

'You heard me. 'Tis done.'

'But...why?'

Again he hesitated. Why not tell her the reason for his raids? Why not let her assume she was bait? The tale might gentle her, make her feel less physically threatened. Yet, even through the tangled skein of needs, of desires, of reasons, he couldn't lie. Not to her, not even by implication. 'To please you?' he finally suggested. And, if there was more than one question in the words, he pushed it aside. 'If 'twould do so, little maiden.'

She studied him for a moment before turning away again. 'I suppose it would,' she said coolly. 'Since I've no wish to see even an enemy's soul burn in Hell for his sins.'

He laughed, torn between wry acknowledgement that he had a battle on his hands, and reluctant admiration for her stubbornness. 'You don't yield ground easily, do you, little cat. But your studies should have taught you that we Vikings take a different view of death. And we have many Gods to keep us from such a fate as you describe.'

'Best pray to them,' suggested Thorolf, overhearing this remark as he approached. 'I smell rain.'

Yvaine all but collapsed against the side as Rorik's attention shifted to Thorolf. She wasn't sure what had happened just then. On the surface, they'd been arguing, but for one fleeting instant she'd felt poised on the brink of discovery, only to have the moment snatched away.

'More than rain,' Rorik said. 'We're running straight before a storm.'

'What!' She jerked upright again. 'You've been standing there, amusing yourself by thwarting me at every turn, when there's a storm coming? Do something!'

'Take the *styri*,' he ordered Thorolf, and in a sudden change of mood that took her completely by surprise, he swooped, caught her up in his arms and, ignoring her startled squeak of protest, lifted her to his shoulder. 'Look to the south,' he advised, grinning up at her. 'And tell me what you think I should do.'

Yvaine looked, mainly because it was less dangerous than gazing down into those wickedly smiling eyes. She promptly changed her mind when she saw what awaited her gaze.

Black clouds were rolling over the horizon like giants erupting from some violent netherworld. Seething, growling, they advanced with ominous purpose. Every few seconds lightning flickered eerily within the dark roiling bulk, as though the god of thunder was stirring, preparing to wreak havoc on the puny humans below him. In that moment she could well believe that such a being existed. And that, *Sea Dragon*, once seeming so big and solid, would look like nothing more than a tasty snack.

'Blessed Saint Mary save us,' she uttered as Rorik lowered her to the deck. 'What are we going to do?'

'You,' he said, holding her steady against the motion of the ship, 'are going back to the tent. We'll do what we always do in these conditions.'

'Aye.' Thorolf gave her a wry grin. 'We have all of two choices, one of which is to leave the sail up and try to outrun it.'

'Dear God. What's the other?'

'Turn and face it,' Rorik said, glancing southward. 'If we leave the sail up, it'll be ripped to shreds while we think that storm is still a mile off. We'll ride it out. It won't be the first time.'

She turned her head sharply. 'For you, maybe, but—'

The rest slid back down her throat as he lowered his head to hers. 'Don't worry, sweeting,' he said, his warm breath caressing her cheek. 'I'll never surrender you. Not even to the sea.'

Thorolf coughed politely, and Rorik released her to take the steering oar from his friend. Faint colour was staining his cheekbones, but Yvaine was in no state to take much notice. The promise in his words had been disturbing enough; the deep note of tenderness in his voice shook her to the core.

'Thorolf will take you back to the tent,' he said rather curtly. 'You'll be safe there for a while.'

'For a while?' she echoed, alarmed. But Thorolf seized her arm and urged her back to the prow before she could question further.

'Don't give me any trouble,' he ordered. 'I've got enough to do so I can get back to Rorik. The ship has to be kept steady into the waves and when that storm hits, he'll see nothing but water flying in all directions. Two pairs of eyes at the steering-oar are better than one.'

Yvaine swallowed her protest and obeyed. Clearly the men knew what they were doing, and would do it better without hindrance. But her patience was sorely tried during an hour in which the wind began to strengthen and the ship to toss.

She and the other women braced themselves against the oak planks, shielding little Eldith as best they could, and endured the worsening conditions in a frightened silence that was broken only once.

'Thank the saints we're too scared to be seasick,' observed Anna with grim humour.

'Aye,' muttered Britta. 'A plague on all ships, I say.'

Yvaine could only nod agreement. She grabbed hold of a crossrib as the ship plunged into another deep trough. Her head banged against the narrowed side of the prow when they hit the next wave.

If the sea got any rougher they would be thrown all over the place. How did the men fare in such storms, exposed in an open ship that cleared the water by a mere three feet? Were they even still alive? She could hear nothing but the keening wind and the growl of approaching thunder.

Visions of an empty ship, its crew swept overboard, danced before her eyes, but before she managed to frighten herself enough to disobey Thorolf and investigate, two men brushed through the curtain, carrying a couple of skin bags. They didn't waste words. One burly fellow tucked Eldith under his arm. The other wrapped a bag apiece around Anna and Britta and began to hustle the women outside.

'Wait!' Yvaine stumbled to her feet. 'Where are you taking them?'

No one answered her. She took a step forward, only to come up hard against Rorik when he strode into the shelter. He was drenched from head to foot, but he looked reassuringly strong and safe.

'Oh, thank God,' she breathed, her hands coming up to grip his tunic. 'What in heaven's name is happening?'

Rorik covered her hands with his, bracing his legs to keep his balance.

'We have to take the tent down before it blows away,' he said. 'I'm going to tie you to the mast with the other women. You'll be safer there.'

'Tie me...no!' Terrified memory swept over her. 'Don't—'

'Hush, little one. No one's going to hurt you this time.'

'But—'

Rorik's grip tightened. 'Yvaine, listen to me. These little hands aren't strong enough to hold on to something for hours. One good wave would take you over the side.'

His firm tone halted her frightened rush towards panic. He was right. She knew he was right, but the memory of her helplessness when Ceawlin had tied her to the roof pole made her tremble.

'Trust me, sweeting.' Rorik wrapped one of the skin bags around her and urged her towards the curtain. 'I'll leave your hands free. It won't be the same as before.'

Yvaine went with him; she had no choice. This was his world, his battlefield. She could do nothing but place her life in his hands.

She braced herself as he reached out to draw back the curtain, only to jerk back in surprise when he halted and swung around to face her. She looked up, her heart starting to race at the intensity in his eyes. He was gazing at her as if fixing her face on his memory for all time.

Then, as her lips parted in startled enquiry, he pulled her against him with sudden fierce urgency and his mouth came down on hers.

Chapter Six

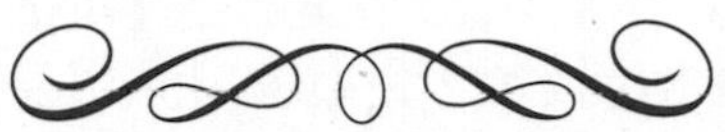

He kissed her as if she was his and they'd been parted forever. Raw hunger overwhelmed her. No gentle tasting, this. He ravished, he plundered.

And she yielded. She could do nothing but cling, while the fierce demand of his mouth sent a sweet, melting weakness flowing through every limb. When the ship slewed sideways, forcing him to break the kiss, she would have fallen if he hadn't been holding her so tightly.

For one heart-stopping moment his gaze, burning, intense, held hers. Then, without a word, he clamped her to his side and swept her through the curtain into the teeth of the storm.

The tempest engulfed her instantly. Shrieking, howling, the storm raced across the sky like condemned souls fleeing the fires of hell. Already dazed, she would have been helpless without Rorik's support. The wind and the rough rise and fall of the ship made it almost impossible to stay upright, and she was constantly blinded by the spray that hissed over the side every time *Sea Dragon* ploughed into the enormous waves.

Bent almost double, they reached the centre of the ship and she saw that the mast had been lowered. Dim figures crouched beneath it. Rorik tucked her close to the other women and secured her by lashing a rope about her waist and tying it to the solid wood.

'Stay beneath the mast as much as possible,' he yelled. 'And here, take this.'

He closed her fingers around a metal object. Yvaine peered at it through the gloom. Thor's hammer. But when she held it upright the two-headed amulet became a cross.

'Hold it so if you wish,' he said. 'Perhaps you'd better pray to that Christian God of yours. We're going to need all the help we can get.'

She looked up, seized by a sudden wrenching sense of urgency. Lightning exploded around them as the wind whipped his hair across his face. The very air seemed to crackle with the force and power of the storm. In the brilliant light his eyes blazed, silver fires burning. His mouth was set hard, the planes of his face as fiercely primitive as the elements themselves.

This was how she would remember him always, she thought. Fighting the raging forces of sea and sky to keep them alive.

He touched her cheek gently, and was gone.

Yvaine crouched in the darkness, feeling as if she'd taken a direct hit from that lightning bolt. As if in that split second she'd been rendered open, accepting, bared to her very soul—and filled with a calm, clear knowledge.

Then the fury of the storm swept over her, wrenching her back. She tried to make herself as small as possible, pressing against the solid wood at her back as though she could become part of it. The mast and the oiled skin bag kept most of the water off her, but the hissing of the sea below the hull sounded vicious and terrifyingly close. Planks shifted and groaned beneath her. She vaguely recalled hearing that the flexibility of Norse ships kept them from breaking up in rough weather, but the memory slipped through her mind and was gone.

The bone-jarring thud as they landed in a trough and the whoosh as the ship lifted into the next wave had her senses reeling. The noise was ear-splitting. Wind howled. Lightning cracked. And one explosion of thunder scarcely faded to a rumble before another tore the sky asunder.

She tried to pray but her brain wouldn't co-operate. She began to wonder if God would feel inclined to help forty heathens battle the storm for the sake of keeping four Christians from a watery grave. She hoped so, because she wasn't ready to die just yet. She wanted the adventure to continue. She wanted—

Her mind blanked. Lightning wasn't responsible this time; when thought finally returned, the storm raged in a realm so far distant she scarcely noticed it.

What did she want? To know what it was like to lie with Rorik? Did she want more than kisses, more than his arms holding her as if he'd never let her go—when he'd taken her for no other reason than desire?

And yet…somewhere deep inside, that knowledge thrilled her. Like his smile, it tantalised, lured, seduced. And as if it had been waiting only for this moment, when with danger all around, her defences lay shattered, an insidious little question crept into her mind.

Would it be so wrong? To yield. Just once. To know what it was like to be desired for herself? It wasn't as if she'd be surrendering to a mindless brute. There were depths to Rorik that drew her. And why should she cling to her virtue? She'd done her duty; she was a widow. And since she'd rather be swept over the side than have another husband foisted upon her, who would know or care?

A torrent of water cascading over the mast jolted her brutally back to the present. They could all be swept over the side. Before she worried about any future, both she and Rorik had to survive the storm. And his danger was far greater than hers.

The knowledge wrenched an involuntary cry from her. She raised her head, trying to see through the darkness and the driving spray. It was impossible. She could only picture Rorik in her mind, standing by the steering oar, without shelter or protection, pitting his strength against the wild sea.

Hunkering down against the elements, Yvaine began to pray in earnest.

There hadn't been a breath of wind all morning. After the violence of the storm the utter stillness was shocking. The sail hung limply. The bright pennants drooped from the motionless wind-vane.

Despite bailing water half the night, the crew had been rowing in rotating shifts since a grey dawn had broken over the becalmed sea. They said little. There was none of the usual jesting or tales of other voyages. What comments there were came from Othar and his friends, and had an edge to them.

Rorik scowled at the overcast sky. He was going to have to speak to his brother. He knew tempers were short. Lack of sleep and the eerie stillness had everyone edgy, but Othar's grumbling only added to the air of tension that hung over the ship.

He glanced at Yvaine as she sat on his sea-chest talking to Thorolf—who was supposed to be navigating. The other women sat against the bulkhead, the child between them. The fact that they were there in the stern, in full view, while the tent was drying, probably wasn't helping matters, but after the storm, he'd wanted Yvaine close.

Not that it had done him much good. She'd scarcely spoken to him all morning, although she seemed to be showing an inordinate amount of interest in navigation. And Thorolf wasn't discouraging her.

Rorik grimaced. Gods! Unsatisfied desire must be playing tricks with his mind. He'd trust Thorolf with his life.

'How's our course?' he asked as his friend picked up a yellowish stone. Aye, concentrate on steering. It was more productive than fantasies of the golden-eyed sorceress beside him clinging to him as she'd done last night when he'd plundered that soft, sweet mouth.

'Steady to the north-east.'

'How do you know without the sun?' Yvaine asked, peering curiously at the stone.

Thorolf handed it to her. 'See how the crystal changes to blue when held to the east. 'Tis the light from the sun. Even though we can't see it on a cloudy morning like this, the sunstone tells us we're going in the right direction.'

'Aye, but I'd like to go there a lot faster,' Rorik muttered.

His low growl sent a shiver of awareness through Yvaine. She hoped he hadn't noticed. For some reason, she'd expected the shocking thoughts she'd entertained during the storm to dissipate with the coming of dawn. After all, she'd been terrified for her life last night; rational thought could hardly be expected under the circumstances.

But the cold light of day was proving disturbingly ineffectual. The tantalising notion of surrender still whispered, siren-like, in her head. And when she told herself that danger and dependency had overturned her wits, images started tumbling through her mind. Images of Rorik's broad shoulders blocking out the moonlight when he'd knelt above her on the beach. The leashed power in the hard body pinning her to the sand. A mouth that could gently coax, or take with a fierceness that shattered every notion of resistance until she wanted nothing more than to surrender.

Madness. It had to be. Her mind was playing tricks with her, tempting her to submit because she had no choice. And yet there were always choices. She could fight; retreat into frozen martyrdom; even seize the ultimate escape offered by death itself.

As if that was going to happen, she thought with ironic self-mockery. If someone like Ketil had captured her, she wouldn't hesitate, but…

She looked up at Rorik and felt something soften deep inside her. No, death wasn't an option. Right now she doubted she'd even fight him. He was strong and hard, aye, but he was also human. He looked dead tired.

'Have you had any sleep?' she asked softly, and immediately felt heat flood her cheeks. She was indeed mad. Sweetness and understanding were *not* part of any plan to win her freedom.

The grim lines about his mouth eased. 'I will as soon as the wind comes up and I can set a course for sailing,' he said. 'Then it shouldn't be too long before we sight Jutland.'

'You always were an optimist,' Thorolf observed, peering at the sunstone.

Yvaine glanced at him. 'Are we far from land?'

'You may well ask,' he replied gloomily. 'Odin's ravens might know. I don't.'

'You said something like that once before,' she cried, remembering. 'I thought I was dreaming, or out of my mind, but you meant Hugin and Mugin, didn't you.'

'Thought and Memory,' murmured Rorik. 'I see you've heard of them, lady. They fly over the world every day and return at night to tell Odin all that has happened. Thus, he knows everything.'

'So does our Christian God,' she pointed out before she could stop herself. 'Without the help of any ravens.'

Rorik's eyes narrowed.

'Speaking of gods, I pray to Thor myself,' Thorolf said hastily. 'He's the most popular. Then there's Freyr, who looks after the crops; Loki, the troublemaker; Aegir, God of the Sea, whose daughters are the waves—temperamental like all women. But you should invoke Freyja, lady.' He leaned over and indicated Rorik's amulet which Yvaine had looped around her neck so she wouldn't lose it. 'Thor doesn't suit you.'

She quickly removed the silver hammer and thrust it at Rorik. He took it, capturing her hand in the process.

Thorolf picked up the crystal again and turned aside to show it to the other women. Somehow his action gave Yvaine the impression he was giving them some privacy.

'Thorolf's right,' Rorik murmured, stroking his thumb across the backs of her fingers 'Freyja is the goddess for you.'

'Oh?' She swallowed. The feel of his calloused thumb was doing strange things to her heartbeat. She tried to pull her hand free, without success. 'Why is that?'

'Well, for one thing, she's always attended by cats, and your *fylgja* is definitely a cat.'

'F...fylgja?' His thumb moved to the inside of her wrist; she felt her pulse jump along with her voice. 'Oh, aye...an animal spirit.'

'The animal spirit that accompanies you everywhere,' he elaborated. 'But Freyja is also the Goddess of Love.'

She made a sound that could have meant anything. Under his thumb, Rorik felt her pulse trip, then start to race, and had to steel herself against the urge to tighten his grip. He wished he could see her eyes, but Yvaine kept her lashes lowered, her face slightly averted. She didn't seem afraid of him; more torn, as though she hovered on the brink of some unseen precipice.

Awakening desire and wary innocence, he thought. Was there a more potent combination with which to torture a man? Holding her captive like this with just the touch of his fingers was sweet torment. He wanted to reassure her, to hold, to gentle, and at the same time ached to have her beneath him again, to peel back her kirtle so the slender fragility of her body was laid before him, awaiting the heat of his gaze. He'd be gentle at first, stroking, arousing, until the soft curves of her breasts warmed and swelled in his hands, and her rosy nipples peaked with the need for his mouth on them. And then—

The loud clatter of abandoned oars jerked him violently out of his fantasy.

Several men were on their feet, shouting and closing in on a pair frozen in a parody of an embrace. It was Ketil and Orn, standing less than an inch apart and glaring into each other's eyes.

Rorik cursed savagely as he released Yvaine's hand and sprang forward. But even as he moved, Ketil's muscles bunched and he shoved Orn away. A dagger was clenched in his fist, its blade wet.

Orn collapsed at Ketil's feet, frothy pink bubbles appearing at the corners of his mouth. One hand clutched at his chest.

Already dead, Rorik thought as rage and grief erupted within him. He fought back the deadly mix, closing the distance between himself and Ketil with lethal speed.

The man whirled to face him, but Rorik was already balanced and lashing out. His booted foot smashed into Ketil's wrist, snapping the bones like a collection of dried twigs. Ketil howled and dropped his dagger. Before it landed, Rorik had slammed Ketil against the side and had his own blade pressed to the man's throat.

'You've got ten seconds to tell me what happened,' he snarled.

'Rorik.'

The hoarse sound came from the man lying at his feet. Rorik glared at Ketil for a moment. The bastard's teeth were clenched in pain, but he was far from cowed.

'Seize him,' he ordered, and several men sprang to obey.

Othar and Gunnar weren't among them. Rorik registered the thought only briefly as he went down on one knee beside Orn. He'd get to them later. After he'd finished damning himself.

'My…fault,' Orn gasped as Rorik lifted him slightly and propped him against his knee. The position seemed to ease the old man's breathing, although Rorik knew he had only seconds. 'Challenged…'

'No. Don't talk, Orn.'

Hooknose gripped his sleeve. 'Ruined…my granddaughter. Floki dead…you knew…' He broke off, coughed.

'I know what happened after your son died,' Rorik said quietly. 'You felt you had to challenge Ketil, to seek reparation.'

'Challenged him…before we sailed. Kept…reminding him. Didn't break your rule, but wrong. Coward…tried to kill me…before he met me in combat.' He made a rasping sound that might have been a laugh. 'Looks like…he succeeded.'

'There'll be a price, Orn. I swear it. For you and for your granddaughter.'

A shadow of a smile flitted across Orn's features. 'Put my sword in my hand,' he whispered. ''Twas battle…of a sort.'

Rorik turned his head, but Thorolf was already there, handing him Orn's sword. He took it and wrapped the old man's fingers around the hilt, his jaw clenching when he had to hold the limp hand in place.

'Take your seat in Valhalla, Orn Hooknose,' he murmured. But Orn had already slipped away on a sigh to join those warriors who had died in battle, and the words went unheard.

Rorik lowered Orn's body to the deck and got to his feet. His eyes met Thorolf's for a brief instant. His friend nodded, his face grim. Justice was harsh on board ship—it had to be—but Rorik felt no compunction about this particular sentence.

He turned to the men holding Ketil. 'Rope him to the body.'

Ketil started shouting. 'Othar, you're supposed to be my friend! Tell your brother what happened. 'Twas self-defence. Orn struck first. I can prove it.' He jerked his head to the side, revealing a graze on one temple.

Rorik glanced at it, his eyes hardening. 'You heal quickly, Ketil,' he said with soft menace. 'That graze has already scabbed over. I suggest 'twas done during the storm.'

'Aye,' another man muttered. ''Tis clear what happened here. Ketil seized the chance to escape trial by combat.' He snorted. 'And he calls himself Skull-splitter.'

Rorik glanced at the speaker. 'Did you see what happened, Grim?'

Another man stepped forward as Grim shook his head. 'I can speak, Bearslayer. Ketil thrust something at Orn as he bent to take his place at the oars. I didn't know what until Orn fell, but Grim's right. Ketil thought to use that wound on his head to claim self-defence, but 'twas no fair fight. Your brother saw it, also.'

'Othar?'

The boy stepped out from behind the mast, his eyes darting from side to side. 'What are you going to do, Rorik? The provocation was Orn's. He said so, himself.'

'No man kills another in such a way on my ship and lives. No matter what the provocation.'

A low growl of agreement rumbled through the crew. Only Gunnar stayed silent. Like Othar, he'd hung back behind the mast; now he eyed Rorik as though fearing a similar fate was going to fall upon his own head.

'Then challenge Ketil, yourself, when we get to Norway,' Othar suggested.

Thorolf snorted before Rorik could answer. 'You know the laws as well as the rest of us, Othar. Orn's murderer goes overboard with his body.'

A gasp came from behind them.

Rorik wheeled. Yvaine stood a few paces away, her hands over her mouth as if she'd tried to stifle the sound. Her eyes were huge in her pale face.

'Rorik…'

Rage deafened him to the rest. The first time she'd said his name and it had to be under these circumstances. He strode forward and clamped his hands around her shoulders.

'Don't say another word,' he ordered. 'Not one word. This has nothing to do with you.'

She stared up at him, mute, but her eyes were eloquent with horrified comprehension. He turned her and gave her a gentle push towards the stern. 'Go back to the other women. Don't look if Norse justice makes you squeamish.'

Yvaine stumbled when he released her, but she didn't look back. There was a lot of shouting behind her—probably Ketil again—but she barely heard the commotion. Nor did she obey Rorik's order to return to the others, although she saw Britta tuck Eldith's face into her shoulder so the child wouldn't witness such swift and brutal reprisal.

She suddenly remembered that the pair would have been Ketil's property once they were off the ship.

Then a terrible silence fell, followed only by the soft hush of disturbed water against the hull. And still she didn't move; was barely conscious of breathing. He was a barbarian, after all. A man who belonged to a savage race of heathens. A race whose way of life was so opposed to any softer emotion, they saw nothing wrong in sentencing a man to so terrible a death, even for murder.

And *still* she wasn't horrified at the thought of surrender.

Heaven save her, she had indeed been struck by madness. A madness brought on by dependence. Hadn't she thought so only minutes ago? Rorik had saved her from Ceawlin, and now stood between her and his men. It was the only reason for this utterly senseless—

'This is *her* fault,' Othar shouted right behind her.

She jumped and whirled.

Rorik stood between her and his brother, so close she could have reached out and touched him. Unwilling to cower at his back, she stepped to the side so she could see both men.

The rest of the crew were being ordered back to the oars by Thorolf. Behind her, she sensed Anna and Britta move closer.

'I heard her claim that a God fit only for puling priests knows more than Odin,' accused Othar. 'And you listened. This evil calm is his revenge. And see what has come of it.'

Rorik's jaw tightened. 'I'm sorry you lost a friend, Othar. But Ketil brought about his own death.'

'He was worried that Orn would appoint a stronger fighter because of his age. Ketil had no surety of winning, of proving his innocence.'

'That's hardly the—'

'And how many more deaths will there be before you come to your senses and throw this bitch into the sea?'

'No one else is going to die.' Rorik bit off each word with savage inflection. 'At worst, we'll have to ration the water if this calm continues.'

'Share it with *Christians*?' Othar's voice rose. 'They're not that valuable as thralls, and you've forbidden us to use them as we like. I vote we kill them.'

'I haven't asked for votes,' Rorik said, turning away.

'No, you never want my opinion, do you?' yelled Othar. 'I suggested we spend the summer in Ireland, so we could raid Britain whenever we chose, but—'

'Land!'

The shout came from the top of the mast, cutting short Othar's tirade.

Thank God, Rorik thought. And immediately felt the hair at his nape rise. What had made him think that? He was done with Christianity. Finished with it eight years ago when—

He shook his head; fixed his gaze on the horizon where a thin line of grey showed. 'Get the sail up,' he shouted to Thorolf. 'If there's any wind coming off-shore, we'll ride it up the coast.'

'What!' Othar gaped at him. 'Are you mad? This is the west coast of Jutland. Do you want us to join the other wrecks lying at the bottom of the sea?'

Rorik's eyes narrowed. The waters off the Jutland peninsula were notorious for shipwrecks; most sailors rolled their vessels the few miles overland to the trading port of Hedeby on the Baltic Sea, which was the safer route. It also added a couple of days to the trip.

'We're not landing.'

'But—'

'There'll be little danger, Othar. Trust me. In weather this calm—'

Thorolf strode up to them. 'Even so, Rorik—'

'That's right,' roared Othar. 'Ignore me again. Put all our lives at risk! And I know why,' he added, lowering his voice abruptly. 'We have to take the shortest route home so you can have your English whore!'

Yvaine gasped as if Othar had struck her. Rorik felt her flinch even though several inches separated them. Fists clenched, he took a step towards his brother.

'No.' She reached out, touched his arm; the lightest, most fleeting of touches, but it stopped him cold. His gaze flashed to her face.

She was still pale, but her eyes met his unflinchingly. 'Let there be no more violence here today. Especially as your brother speaks the truth.' She lifted her chin. 'That *is* what you intend, is it not?'

Her eyes, dark with some hidden emotion, looked into his for a moment longer, then she turned, gestured to the other girls, and walked back to the prow.

She might as well have stabbed him.

Rorik watched her go and felt as though tiny shards of glass were piercing his heart. The wrenching sensation twisted inside him again—unrelenting need colliding with racking tenderness. The conflict was tearing him apart, and yet he couldn't release her, couldn't stop wanting her.

For the first time in years he was eager to reach Norway, because then he could take Yvaine to his bed and free himself of this constant ache she aroused in him. Surely once he possessed her this inner struggle would cease. She'd become just another woman, beautiful, desirable, but no longer inciting this strange need to protect, to cherish.

And then what? he thought, suddenly aware that Othar watched Yvaine's retreat with a curiously intent expression. He'd refused to think beyond getting home as quickly as possible, but now a savage wave of possessiveness washed over him, momentarily blinding him to everything else.

The thought of another man touching her aroused a killing rage in his blood that would qualify him for the berserkers if he ever wanted to join that elite body of fighters. Already he'd struck his brother. A brother who was younger and physically less powerful. A week ago he wouldn't have thought himself capable of such an action.

Given enough reason, he wasn't sure he wouldn't repeat it.

Stifling a roar of sheer frustration, Rorik turned on his heel and came face to face with Thorolf.

'We're going up the coast,' he snarled before his friend could argue. 'Put more men on the oars. I want this ship moving faster if you have to get behind the sail and puff!'

'Get behind the sail and puff,' he heard Thorolf mutter behind him as he stalked towards the stern. 'Right.'

The dark, looming bulk of Jutland had looked as inhospitable as Rorik had described it, but either the danger had been exaggerated, or the winds had been kind, for the rest of the voyage passed uneventfully. The coast of Norway rose out of a deep blue sea early the following morning.

Yvaine stood in the prow with the other women, watching the land open up before her. A few yards away, Thorolf leaned over the rail to dangle a wooden rod, marked at regular intervals, into the water.

'Sciringesheal,' he announced, pointing to a distant settlement at the head of a small inlet. 'Some call it Kaupang. Our summer trading port here in Norway.' He pulled the sounding rod clear, examined it, and yelled a signal to Rorik.

Yvaine glanced sternwards as Rorik pulled on the steering oar, bringing the ship into the wind. The sail began to flap, and men swarmed up the mast to furl the vast canvas. The big vessel rode gently on the slightly choppy waters of the bay, waiting to negotiate her way through a maze of small islands that protected the entrance.

At Rorik's command the oarholes were opened. Wood rattled as the oars were engaged. The ship began to move forward again under the smooth, practised action of the rowers.

Closing her mind to everything but the immediate present, Yvaine turned back to the port.

Wattle-and-daub buildings ringed the head of the bay. Rich fields rose behind them, sloping gently towards craggy hills that seemed to lean over the town, providing shelter against storms or attack. Trees dotted the lower slopes; several homesteads nestled among them. The whole place appeared snug and prosperous.

'It could be any port in England,' Anna remarked. 'Except for the mountains.'

'They look very big and cold,' ventured little Eldith in a hushed whisper.

Britta put her arm around the child's shoulders. 'There are mountains in England also, sweeting. I dare say one grows used to them.'

'In a month or two you won't even notice them,' predicted Thorolf. He turned to Yvaine, scanning her boy's attire, now somewhat the worse for wear. 'You're to stay in the tent, lady. Rorik will get you some decent clothes to wear as soon as possible.'

'How thoughtful,' she muttered as he crossed the ship to test the depth on the other side.

'Be grateful to him,' Britta said drily. 'I am.'

Yvaine frowned. 'What do you mean?'

Britta jerked her head in Rorik's direction. 'You may not have heard, lady. Yesterday, after Ketil's death, Othar claimed me, but Rorik ordered him to accept an offer for Eldith and me from the man who loaned us the comb the day we bathed. Apparently he lost his wife and daughter to sickness a few years back and is lonely.' She shrugged, and an unexpected grin crossed her face. 'He stammered and stuttered about his needs, God knows, but I understood him well enough.'

'And you can *smile* about it? Britta...'

''Tis better than staying with that lout, Othar, or being parted from Eldith and both of us sold to strangers. At least Grim was honest with me, and he seems kind enough. He even promised to wait a while, until I'm more at ease with him.'

'Aye. Rorik promised that I'd know him better, too,' Yvaine said grimly. 'As if that will make a difference.'

Anna gave her a quizzical smile. 'You think it won't?'

Yvaine stared at her, unable to answer. That same question had reverberated over and over in her mind until she felt like a mouse in a cage, scurrying in circles, getting nowhere.

Oh, why hadn't she forced another confrontation yesterday, instead of staying in the prow with the other women? Why hadn't she nagged, ordered, begged even, to be released? Now her fate was rushing towards her like a siege-engine out of control and she didn't know what to do about it.

'I don't know,' she murmured. 'I vowed never to be captive to another man. And now...I just don't know.'

Britta and Anna exchanged startled glances.

'What are you saying, lady? That you want him?'

'No, no! Of course not! 'Tis just...don't you think it wrong to surrender so tamely, Britta? You say Grim seems kind, but you're to be given no choice. Indeed, are grateful for a little time. 'Tis not...*right*.'

'Lady, what else can we women do but comply when men arrange our lives? Look at yourself: cousin to the king, a lady born and bred, but were you allowed to choose your own husband? Or even if you would wed at all?'

'But this isn't the same. At least marriage is respectable.'

'Well, as to that…' Britta flushed and darted a quick glance down the ship to her Viking. 'Grim dodged around the word, and mumbled something about children, but it crossed my mind that he meant for us to wed some day.' She eyed Yvaine thoughtfully. 'Would you feel better if Rorik intended the same?'

'No! I wasn't speaking for myself.' Then why, she wondered, were her arms crossed defensively over her body? Why was she backing away? And why hadn't she noticed what was happening with Britta and Grim?

Because she'd been too busy being shattered by the knowledge that the savage display of barbarity she'd witnessed yesterday hadn't turned her against Rorik.

Something shuddered inside her once, violently, before subsiding to a faint tremor. She held herself tighter. 'I'd rather choose the cloister. In fact, that will likely be my only choice if I ever get back to England. But we're here in Norway, and how can I submit…how can I even *contemplate* submission when he doesn't…when I don't…?'

'Mayhap in England 'twould be wrong to surrender,' mused Britta, completely misunderstanding her. 'But here our lives will be different. Who's to say what is right or wrong? Not I.'

'Nor I,' agreed Anna. 'Besides—' she indicated Britta '—some good has come of Rorik wanting you, lady.'

'But I said nothing to him about either of you. Except when I asked him to free us and he threw my ring into the sea.'

'Then perhaps there's hope for the man. Who knows, in another month or so he might even give up his heathen ways.'

Yvaine had to smile at this unlikely prospect, although the expression wobbled a bit at the edges. 'Somehow Christianity seems very far away,' she murmured. Then seeing the looks of concern on the other girls' faces, she straightened and held out her hands. 'But not far enough away that I can't pray for you both.'

'And we for you, lady.'

The ship bumped gently against the pier as they clasped each other's hands. No longer thegn's lady, tradesman's daughter and serf, but three women facing an uncertain future with courage and the will to survive.

Chapter Seven

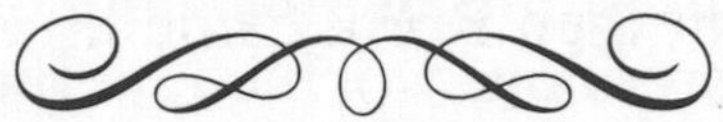

An hour later, uneasily aware of the silence in the tent, Yvaine contemplated a tub of water, a bowl of soap and a chest full of clothes and ornaments. They'd been delivered to the ship by a stout, elderly merchant who had treated her with the utmost respect.

She supposed she should be grateful.

Instead, she felt very small…and very lost…and utterly alone. Despite the guard on the pier outside, the prospect of climbing, naked, into the tub while the other girls were not by was distinctly disquieting.

She glanced at the curtain, telling herself not to be foolish. After yesterday, she doubted any of Rorik's men would dare venture near the tent, let alone enter it. She was perfectly safe.

For the moment.

Quelling a shiver, she stabbed a finger into the water as though expecting a leering Viking to leap out at her. Then whirled, snatching her hand back when light footsteps sounded outside.

The curtain was swept aside and a small, sturdy figure hurried through the aperture.

'Anna!' With a squeak of surprise, Yvaine sprang forward, flinging her arms around the girl. 'What…?'

'Rorik bought me,' explained Anna breathlessly, returning Yvaine's embrace. 'To be your maid.'

Yvaine drew back and gaped at her. 'My maid?'

'Well, I think that's what he said. He and Gunnar were speaking in Norse. Gunnar had taken me into a tavern just beyond the pier. He was boasting about carrying me off, but then Rorik came in, ordered me back to the ship and gave Gunnar some money, so it must be true.'

'But why?'

Anna pursed her lips. 'Mayhap after what Othar called you yesterday, Rorik thought to provide you with some respectability, lady. After all, you're no tavern wench who's used to dispensing her favours. To put it no lower.'

Yvaine could only stare at her while hope and puzzlement danced a dizzying reel in her head.

Anna was probably right. Rorik could be doing nothing more than throwing a sop to the conventions—if such conventions existed in Norway—but surely it was an act of kindness to see that Anna stayed with her. He could have given her a maid from his own slaves, rendering her completely alone among strangers and thus more dependent on him, if his only motive was to supply her with a façade of respectability.

Or, she thought, suddenly shaken, after Othar's blunt description of her yesterday, he could be supplying her with a maid who could testify that she hadn't been molested, because he intended to return her to England, unharmed.

A ripple of something that felt very like dismay brushed her mind. A wave of apprehension immediately followed. What was she thinking? Did she want to be kept here against her will? Taken before she was ready to give?

No, no. She didn't mean that! Ready to give what, for heaven's sake? Submission wasn't giving. Besides, Rorik would never force her. If she believed nothing else, she did believe that.

But if he still wanted her, how long could she stand against seduction? If he treated her with kindness, how long could she hold him off when her own emotions were in turmoil? What was she waiting for, anyway? What did she want?'

'My lady?'

Yvaine blinked, abruptly aware that she'd been staring at Anna for several long seconds.

'This is what comes of not asking these questions yesterday,' she stormed as worry and doubt got the better of her. 'Well, he'll soon learn that I won't be making any decisions until I have some answers.' Ignoring Anna's goggle-eyed expression, she stalked towards the curtain.

'But, my lady, your new clothes. Wait—'

Anna spoke to the empty air.

She saw him immediately, leaning against the side where it began the upward curve into the prow. There was nothing relaxed about his stance. His arms were braced, his big hands gripping the side rather than holding it. The tension in his body was palpable, but it wasn't caution that had Yvaine jolting to an abrupt halt. Sheer surprise held her spellbound.

Gone was the rough tunic, the iron helm, the barbaric gold armrings. Rorik still wore his sword, but the terrifying Viking warrior had, by some mysterious transformation, become a Norse nobleman. Tan woollen trousers, tucked into thonged boots, closely hugged the length of his legs. His red tunic, also of wool, was heavy with braid and rich gold thread. A long blue cloak of rare pell hung over his left shoulder, drawing her gaze to the broad sweep of his back, and upward.

Sunlight gilded his newly trimmed hair, and the backdrop of dark green hills threw into prominence his strong, sharply etched profile. He looked powerful, heart-breakingly handsome, and utterly daunting.

And she was suddenly aware that her own appearance more closely resembled something he'd fished out of the sea.

She took a step back, and bumped into an oar left lying on the deck.

He straightened, whipping around in the same fluid movement. Then went still.

The questions pounding in her head vanished beneath the look in his eyes. Desire, fierce and barely restrained, leaped out at her, bathing her in incandescent heat. Thought, breath, will, tottered and threatened to crumble. She tried to move, realising in a blinding flash of insight, that, after their first encounter, Rorik had kept the full extent of his desire from her while they'd been at sea. He'd held her, kissed her, true, but this was different. This was terrifying. This was ravenous hunger about to be unleashed by a man who knew a banquet was within reach.

'I…uh…just wanted to thank you for Anna, but…'

The fire in his eyes was instantly banked. It didn't help. The smouldering embers that remained mirrored the leashed power in him as he closed the distance between them in two long strides. He caught her arm before she could retreat further.

'And 'twas kind of you to see that Eldith stayed with Britta,' she babbled.

'I'm sorry you had to witness two violent deaths yesterday.'

She blinked at him. Yesterday? She scarcely remembered yesterday. She was too busy making a mind-numbing discovery about the present. That it was far easier to heed fear and run, when it wasn't mixed with a shivery kind of excitement.

'You're sorry?'

He gave a short humourless laugh. 'I'm not sorry Ketil's dead, given the circumstances, but none of it should have happened. I knew there was bad blood between him and Orn, but…I allowed myself to be distracted.'

Yvaine frowned. At the back of her mind she was aware of danger still, but there was something more here. Something imperative. She sensed it dimly and struggled to comprehend 'You couldn't have stopped it. I heard what was said. No one knew what Ketil intended until the knife—'

She shuddered and let that pass. 'I also heard that you'd forbidden them to speak to each other.'

'Only Ketil,' he said. ''Twas a condition of his service. And my misjudgement. Othar asked if his friends could join us and I thought he'd settle easier, so I agreed. But neither Orn nor I took account of what cowardice can drive a man to do.' He paused and glanced down at his hand still wrapped about her arm. 'What anything can drive a man to do,' he added beneath his breath.

His brows drew together and he released her, stroking the backs of his fingers against her arm. 'But 'tis done. Of what use to question?'

Because I need answers.

But her response was silent. She watched the movement of Rorik's hand against her arm with a kind of dazed fascination. It was a caress he might have used to gentle a frightened hawk, she thought wonderingly. His hand was so big, so powerful. She fought against the sharp awareness of his touch, the heat emanating from his big body. This was important. Whether Rorik knew it or not, he was showing her something of himself. She needed the knowledge, desperately.

'I understand justice,' she said haltingly. ''Twas the manner of his death…to be roped to the body, unable to free himself…'

'Ah.' Understanding softened the hard line of his mouth. 'You're remembering how it felt to be tied and helpless. But consider. It might have taken Ketil longer to die if I'd thrown him overboard, unfettered, and sailed away.'

'We weren't sailing.'

'True. But would you rather have witnessed him trying to climb on board and being beaten off until he was exhausted?'

When she didn't answer, he smiled. 'This is why I didn't want you witnessing such a death, little cat. You have a soft heart.'

The moment was over. Frustration muttered at the back of her mind with the thought. 'My heart might be soft, but my head isn't,' she retorted, jerking her arm out of his hold.

'No.' He lifted a hand and stroked the tip of one finger across her brow. 'But I'm in here just the same. Or if not yet, I will be.'

Yvaine's mouth fell open. 'You've made it clear 'tis not my head you're interested in,' she finally got out. 'As for the rest—'

'You misunderstand me, sweeting. Once I'm in here—' he raised his other hand to cradle her head between his palms '—the rest will follow.'

'Rest?' She gulped in air and tried to remember she was furious. 'And what then? Have you given any thought to afterwards, you...you *pirate*?'

His mouth crooked. 'You think there'll be an afterwards, sweet witch? Only if you free me from your spell.'

Yvaine gaped at him. *Her* spell? What was the man talking about?

'Why would I weave a spell that results in me becoming a prisoner, a discarded mistress, then a slave?' she demanded. 'If there's a difference between those things, which I doubt.'

She tried to wrench out of his hold, only to find that his grip, though gentle, was inescapable.

'Oh, there's a difference,' he assured her. 'But never fear, little cat, you won't see it. I intend to show you something else entirely.'

'But—'

'Hush,' he murmured, and lowered his mouth to hers. 'There's no need to be afraid. I want you, but I'll never hurt you. Yvaine.'

Dear God, had she ever heard him speak her name before? Surely not, for the sound of it whispered in that deep, dark voice, threatened to cloud judgement, stroked over nerves that were already quivering, shivered over flesh that was suddenly yearning. She *wanted* the warmth of his arms about her, the thrilling heat of his mouth on hers. She'd been cold for so long. So cold…

His mouth brushed hers, retreated, returned. Then took with a power that emptied her mind.

Questions, demands, even pleas, vanished beneath a cascade of thrilling sensation. Heat streaked through her, warming, weakening. She had to grasp his wrists or fall. She felt him shudder in response, felt power ripple through him even though an inch or two still separated them. A peculiar sensation of drowning began to wash over her, her lips parted…

The loud thud as someone jumped into the ship wrenched them apart almost violently. Rorik jerked his head up, his hands falling to her shoulders.

'Sorry, did I interrupt something?' asked Othar in a voice totally devoid of apology.

Yvaine barely heard him. She felt Rorik's gaze on her, unnervingly intent, before he released her and turned, shielding her from his brother.

'I'm glad you're back, Othar,' he said, ignoring the youth's rudeness. 'You can summon the men. I want to reach Einervik this afternoon.'

'This afternoon? But I've got a girl waiting and—'

'Then you'll just have to control yourself for once!'

The lash of his voice jolted Yvaine out of her daze. She stepped back, intending to retreat into the tent, then saw Othar's face and froze.

'For once?' he shouted. 'We've been at sea for more than a week!'

'Then the sooner we're home, the better. Now, *do it*!'

Fuming, but powerless, Othar obeyed. 'Witch!' he hissed at Yvaine as he passed her.

There was such malevolence in his voice, such rage in his eyes, she shrank back. 'I'm not a witch.'

'I'm not so sure about that,' muttered Rorik. Then as she turned horrified eyes on him, added impatiently, 'Don't take any notice of Othar. Witches are usually respected in Norway. They even travel around the country, visiting farms to foretell the future, or make spells for good crops. One comes every year to Einervik. My stepmother dotes on the woman.'

Yvaine shivered, not comforted in the least by this careless dismissal of heathen practices. A vast distance might be opening up between her and Christianity, but she wasn't ready to embrace paganism just yet.

She crossed herself. 'The priests say witchcraft is evil. The Devil's work. In England such—'

'This isn't England,' Rorik snarled, turning on her. 'You'd do well to remember that from now on. And to start with you can get rid of those English clothes. You look like a damned street urchin.'

Yvaine blinked in surprise before glancing down at herself. She knew she looked like a street urchin. A particularly scruffy one. That wasn't what startled her. An irresistible urge to laugh was welling up inside her. It had been so long since she'd felt such a thing she'd forgotten what it was like.

'Aye,' she said softly. And suddenly, irresistibly, she felt her mouth curve in a smile. She looked up. 'Perhaps 'tis as well it was only Othar who saw you kissing me.'

His stunned expression was quite wonderfully satisfying. There was no better time to stage a strategic retreat. Feeling ridiculously pleased with herself, she turned and walked into the tent.

'I swear, Anna, 'twas worth agreeing with him just to see his face. Never have I seen a man so confounded. But he'd better not see it as a sign of encouragement,' she added, narrowing her eyes at this heretofore unanticipated possibility.

'I wouldn't count on that,' mused Anna, drawing a beautifully carved comb of walrus ivory, discovered in the chest, through Yvaine's hair. 'He's too direct a man to see agreement as anything but encouragement, and yet…'

'What?'

'I'm not sure, lady. Sometimes he seems like two different men—and 'tis not the change of clothes that makes him appear so. You'll think me foolish, but I can't explain. Thorolf, now, he's the same all the time.'

'I know what you mean.' Yvaine frowned as she bent to lift a long-sleeved shift from the chest. It was made of the softest linen, dyed green, and was very finely pleated. She laid it aside and gazed thoughtfully at the exquisitely made under-shift she was wearing.

'Sometimes I wonder if I'm drawn to a ruffian because he can be gentle and honourable, or if I'm trying to convince myself he can be gentle and honourable because I'm drawn to a ruffian.'

'Hmm. It sounds complicated. I think I'll stick with Thorolf.'

'Why, Anna.' Yvaine turned to look over her shoulder. 'You've never said...do you care for him? Does he like you?'

Anna blushed. 'You go too fast, lady. He hardly knows I exist. But he's rather appealing—in a ruffianly kind of way.'

Anna gazed at her mistress, startled by what she'd confessed. Then both women burst out laughing.

The shared humour momentarily lightened Yvaine's mood. Succumbing to the lure of new clothes, she delved into the chest for another pleated shift; yellow this time, with short fluted sleeves. Beneath it, resting on a folded length of cream-coloured wool, lay several articles of jewellery.

'These brooches are beautifully crafted, my lady.' Anna leaned forward to lift out a gilded oval clasp, examining it with the eye of an expert. 'See how the animals are all intertwined. And look at this necklace of silver, set with crystals.'

'The Norse have some of the finest craftsmen in the world,' Yvaine agreed, picking up a necklace of sparkling glass beads. 'I shall wear this,' she decided, entranced by the flashing colours. 'With the yellow shift and the cream tunic.'

'But it has no sides.' Anna frowned as she shook out the length of wool.

'No. It hangs from the shoulders and covers the outer-shift at front and back. See, you fasten it in front with these oval brooches just below the shoulders, and this—' she held up a fine gold chain '—hangs from the right-hand brooch. Ladies attach all sorts of things to the ends of the chains. The household keys in most cases, but we have this comb and here is a little silk purse.'

'How do you know all this, lady?'

'The Norse legends,' Yvaine explained, checking to see that everything was fastened as it should be. 'I listened to them over and over as a child, but— Oh, Anna...' She swung about, hands clasped, her pleasure in the clothes fading. 'Never did I think I'd be one of those ladies who are kidnapped in the sagas. Of what use is all this finery when underneath I'm still English? Will it stop Rorik using me? Of course not. Oh, why didn't I plead with him to ransom me from the first, instead of arguing, instead of demanding? Why—?'

'Don't blame yourself, lady,' Anna interrupted drily. 'I doubt Rorik would have ransomed you then, and he certainly won't now. I've never seen a man more determined to possess a woman.'

Yvaine gazed at her in dismay. 'Are you saying he'll force me if I resist? That I *have* been deluding myself that he's honourable?'

'No. On Rorik's honour we agree. The real question is, can you resist him? Is it Rorik you fear, or yourself?'

Yvaine shook her head. 'You said something like that on the ship. I couldn't answer you then, and I can't now.'

'But you're drawn to him. I've sensed it, and now you say 'tis so.'

'Aye, drawn. Who would not be? He's handsome, he's protected us. God knows what would have happened if he wasn't the man he is, but...' She glanced away, towards the curtain. Beyond it lay her future—or her destruction. She didn't know why that thought had come into her head; it was just there, terrifying in its clarity. But so was something else—a vague awareness that struggled to surface.

'You know, Anna, I've just realised…' She looked back at the girl, slowly working it out. 'I've been relying on Rorik's sense of honour, but what of my own?'

'Your own?' Anna frowned. 'But a lady's honour is bound to a man's. You have no father or brother or husband here.'

'Exactly. And Rorik is both protector and predator, so I can't look to him. Indeed, why should I? My honour should be my responsibility. Don't you see? I've been waiting to see what he's going to do, worrying about surrender, as if I don't have a choice.'

'But—'

Yvaine swept on before Anna could point out the glaring flaw in this brilliant reasoning. 'I know he said he'd give me time to get used to the idea of belonging to him, but he can afford to say that because he thinks I'll succumb. Edward's too far away to rescue me, and by the time he learns what's happened 'twill be too late. There's no other man whose honour will be impugned. Why wouldn't Rorik expect me to give in?'

'But—'

'What I should be doing is demanding his respect for *my* notion of honour.'

'But you did. I mean, you demanded to be returned to your cousin.'

'That's just it. I asked to be ransomed as if I was a piece of property to be bartered between one man and another. I played by the rules of men, making the demands they would make. All of which Rorik ignored or refused because I'm a woman. Would he have flung my ring into the sea if a man had offered it? Of course not. And I accepted his decrees like a meek little prisoner. No wonder he thinks he'll succeed.'

Anna frowned. 'But you just said you don't know what you're feeling, so—'

'I don't,' Yvaine agreed grimly. 'But until I do, he'll refrain from trying to seduce me. There'll be no more kisses—'

'Kisses?'

'No more looking at me as if he wants to gobble me up in one bite. I may be a woman, but I'm a person, too. If I decide to have a...a...*liaison* with him, it will be because *I* want to.' She glared at Anna. 'Not because he's seduced me into it.'

'Hmm.' Anna folded her arms and contemplated her mistress's determined face. 'And how long do you think 'twill take him to seduce you into a liaison, lady?'

'Probably not long,' Yvaine muttered. 'But he doesn't have to know that.'

'Well then—' Concealing a grin, Anna turned to sweep back the curtain. 'Let us show these Norsemen that two Saxon women are not to be reckoned with lightly. Onward, lady.'

Yvaine took a deep breath and marched outside.

She cannoned straight into Rorik.

He grasped her arms, stepped back a pace and looked her up and down.

'Well?' she demanded, while her heart leaped into her throat and threatened to stay there. 'Does the lady meet with your approval more than the street urchin?'

His brows went up at her belligerent tone, 'I think you were safer as a street urchin, beautiful lady,' he murmured, and a smile flashed into his eyes that was very male, wickedly inviting, and utterly irresistible.

Yvaine sternly ordered her mouth not to curve in response. Bad enough that she'd smiled at him before; if she continued the practice, heaven only knew what might happen.

'Holy Saints!' exclaimed Anna, coming unwittingly to her rescue. 'We're not the only ones who look different.'

Rorik sent her an amused glance 'Come with us,' he instructed. 'Your place is with your mistress. And yours—' he gently tugged Yvaine closer '—is with me.' Releasing her, he took her hand and led her towards the stern.

Yvaine clutched thankfully at the distraction Anna had given her. It wasn't difficult. She had to look twice to recognise some of the men. Several of the crew had been left behind in Kaupang, including Gunnar she was thankful to see, but the rest now looked more like respectable tradesmen or farmers than Viking raiders—in startling contrast to the ship which was decked out in all her pagan glory.

The big sail was furled, but flying from the mast were two standards. The topmost pennant was red, embroidered with a large black raven, its huge wings outspread. Below this fluttered a smaller yellow flag decorated with a fierce red dragon. Painted wooden shields hung over both sides of the vessel, overlapping each other in alternate colours of red and black. They were too small to be useful in battle, and in any event larger shields would have covered the oarholes, so Yvaine assumed their use was purely ceremonial.

The triumphant return of the warrior indeed.

They reached the stern and Rorik took the steering oar from Thorolf with a word of thanks. Yvaine sank on to a nearby sea-chest, her troubles momentarily forgotten. Even Othar, who was staring at her as if he'd never seen her before, impinged only vaguely on her awareness as she gazed in awe at the scene before her.

They were making their way up a narrow fjord. The water arrowed before them, of a blue so clear it seemed to pulse with light and colour. Lush green fields clung to the shoreline, gradually giving way to dense pine forests that marched up the craggy slopes on either side of the fjord. And higher still rose the distant, snow-capped mountains, their peaks soaring towards a pale, cloudless sky.

The only sounds were the light splash of the oars and the occasional call of a bird. Then, rising gradually on the clear, still air, the call of a horn echoed through the hills. Just two notes, long and haunting.

Yvaine tilted her head, her lips parting in delight as she listened.

'Word has gone ahead of us,' Rorik said. 'Come here, sweeting. We're almost there.'

His remark brought her back to earth with a thud. She looked at him, nerves and anticipation warring within her, and knew the real battle was about to begin.

'How are you going to explain me?' she demanded. 'As the spoils of war?'

Rorik reached over, grasped her arm and drew her up to stand in front of him. 'Sheathe your claws, little cat. There'll be no need to explain you. One look at us standing together, and everyone will know you're mine.'

'Will they?' She tried to pull out of his hold, only to discover there was nowhere to go; that even if there were, her own senses were conspiring against her. She wanted to stay in his arms, to feel the strong beat of his heart against her back, the male heat and power surrounding her. The longing to go where he led, to let him protect her, was wrenching—and she had to fight it.

'How convenient,' she muttered, forcing the words out. 'Install me in the same house as your stepmother and go on your way. After all, we're only women. Possessions.' She turned sharply within the circle of his arm. 'And possessions don't think, do they? They don't *feel*. They don't—'

She had to stop; anything else and her voice would break. She was angry, aye, but her own words beat at her like savage blows. If Rorik installed her, as his mistress, or even potential mistress, in the household run by his stepmother, he would have no awareness of her as a person. No awareness of her sense of pride, of worth.

Pain clutched at her heart, almost making her cry out. She couldn't surrender under those conditions. No matter how gently he treated her. No matter how much—

She dug her nails into her palms and fought the tears stinging her eyes.

And didn't hear Rorik inhale sharply as her meaning hit him with the force of a battering ram. He opened his mouth to assure Yvaine that concubines were a commonplace part of Norse family life, that the position held almost as much status as a wife—and the words wouldn't come.

He stared down into tear-drenched eyes and saw exactly what he'd done. He, who had never taken a woman by force in his life, had carried an innocent girl from her home because he wanted her with a desire that, by now, was barely under control. Because of a gut-deep conviction that she belonged to him; a conviction so absolute he hadn't once considered her feelings.

Oh, aye, some deep instinct had urged him to remove her from a place where she'd been grievously hurt. The sight of the royal standard might have had something to do with it. He could even argue that he hadn't believed she was innocent. The fact remained that he'd placed her in a position that might destroy both her pride and any chance he had of—

He frowned and shook his head sharply. Any chance he had of…what? Why this sudden feeling that he could lose something incredibly fragile, something indefinably precious? There was nothing he wanted that Yvaine could withhold. He wouldn't force her, but every time he touched her he found an innocent, seeking response that threatened to shred his control into tiny little pieces and send him hurtling back to the savagery of his ancestors. He would have her.

But his arm tightened as though he would shield her even from himself, and he knew he was about to condemn his aching body to further torture without a second's hesitation.

'Don't,' he said, not even sure what he was protesting. She hadn't let the tears fall; hadn't used them to plead her cause. That, alone, was enough to rend him.

'I know everything's strange...different. I won't rush you.'

She didn't speak, only gazed up at him, so utterly vulnerable, he felt something tighten about his chest. As though a giant hand had seized his heart. He started to speak, to reassure her further, only to hear the clear notes of the horn again.

The meadows of his home were opening out before them, and there, on the grassy bank, an excited crowd had gathered, waving and calling out.

There was no time, then, for long explanations, but in that instant, savage desire and aching tenderness came together for the first time without conflict, and he knew, with utter certainty, what he was going to do.

Abandoning the steering oar for one brief moment, he captured Yvaine's face between his hands, pinned her gaze with his, and put every ounce of conviction he possessed into his voice.

'Trust me,' he said. 'For this moment, at least, put your honour in my hands and trust me.'

Chapter Eight

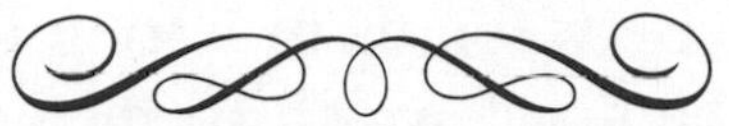

Trust him? What choice did she have? From the moment they stepped off the ship, Rorik's grip on her hand was her only anchor in the sea of noise and confusion that surrounded her.

Cries of delight rang in her ears as husbands and fathers were welcomed home. Men thumped friends and brothers on the back; children darted, laughing, through the throng. There was even a greeting or two thrown in her direction. She would have responded, but she couldn't translate fast enough to keep up. Her mind was still caught in the moment when Rorik had specified *her* honour.

Then, as the crew began to mingle with the crowd, expressions changed, became cool assessment. Speculation hummed on the air like a swarm of bees. When Rorik finally won free of the crush and led her across a narrow meadow towards several turf-thatched wooden buildings clustered at the foot of a pine-covered slope, the crowd followed, sweeping them through the doorway of the largest building on a tide of curiosity and anticipation.

The sudden cessation of daylight blinded her. She had a vague sense of walking along a short corridor, then they passed through another doorway, into a hall, and she could see again.

Her first impression was of size. The room was huge, longer than the King's thirty-foot hall at Winchester and far more luxuriously appointed. Two rows of posts, carved in intricate designs of plants and animals, supported the roof. Between them a long open hearth was set lower than the floor, which formed a wide platform around the perimeter of the room. Benches, broad enough for sleeping and made comfortable with furs, were set against the two long walls, on either side of a pair of carved, high-backed chairs that could have comfortably accommodated a giant or two.

A doorway in the far end wall led to an inner chamber. The jarl's private solar, Yvaine guessed. Another bench was set to one side of it, and on the other, an enormous loom held the beginnings of a colourful wall hanging.

Smoke rose in lazy spirals from the firepit, but the air was surprisingly fresh thanks to several square holes cut into the walls. Though their wooden shutters hung open, they were too small to allow much light into the hall; what illumination there was came from bowl-shaped lamps set on long spikes hammered into the floor. Wicks made of moss floated in pools of oil—fish oil, she decided, sniffing cautiously.

The flickering lights glinted on an enormous wooden shield that hung above one of the central chairs. Gold plaques and precious stones rimmed its edge, while the brightly painted centre depicted men and animals engaged in various improbable battles.

Below the shield, propped in the chair and wrapped in furs, an old man watched the invasion of the hall through half-shuttered eyes.

Yvaine knew him instantly; knew that, though wasted with illness, he'd once been as tall and powerful as his son, that, despite a face drawn and gaunt, he'd once possessed the same sternly chiselled features and glittering eyes.

When Rorik led her across the hall and clasped his father's outstretched arm, she was startled by the wave of fierce emotion she felt emanating from the old man. Then a woman spoke behind them, and a chill brushed her flesh.

'So, Rorik, this is the reason you've returned early.'

Yvaine turned to meet pale blue eyes. Othar's eyes.

'Gunhild,' said Rorik coolly.

Othar's mother looked her up and down, her sharp features pinched in an expression of distaste. 'Who is this stranger you bring amongst us, Rorik? One would say a Norsewoman by her clothes, but my son tells me otherwise.'

'In this case, he's right.' Ignoring the tightening of her lips, Rorik turned to his father and raised his voice so everyone in the hall heard him. 'Egil Eiriksson, my father, I present to you Yvaine of Selsey. My betrothed.'

Stunned silence greeted his announcement. It was immediately followed by an explosion of sound as shock and excitement sent voices soaring to the rafters. Gunhild's outrage overrode them all.

'What!' she shrieked.

Yvaine couldn't say anything. She could only stand there, eyes open to their widest extent, while she wondered what Rorik thought he was doing. If they were truly betrothed she *would* visit his family, but every member of his crew knew a romance worthy of the sagas hadn't taken place on board ship.

'By the Gods!' Another furious voice rang out, and as swiftly as they'd cried out, the crowd fell silent.

'We don't marry English captives!' Othar elbowed his way out of the throng and ranged himself beside his mother.

'Aye,' Gunhild added. 'If you want the girl then take her as your concubine. There's no need to marry her. A captive will bring you no dowry, and how do we know she's virtuous?' She cast a scornful glance at Yvaine before appealing to her husband. 'A necessary quality in a wife, Egil.'

Egil had been so still and silent, an oddly frozen expression on his face, that Yvaine suddenly wondered if he *could* speak. As if in answer, he gave a short bark of laughter and glanced up at Rorik.

'Gunhild has a point there, Rorik. You've had the wench on your ship for nigh on two weeks and even my failing eyes can see she's a beauty.'

'She's a virgin,' Rorik said shortly.

Egil's brows shot up. Before he could answer, Gunhild grabbed Yvaine's arm and jerked her around towards the nearest light. 'How do you know?' she demanded shrilly. 'The English always lie. Look at her well, husband. Look at those cat's eyes and tell me the creature hasn't cast a spell on your son.'

'Don't be ridiculous, Gunhild.' Rorik stepped forward and pushed the woman's hand away from Yvaine 'You may rule here when I'm away, but don't overstep yourself.'

'I will not be silenced. This touches your father's honour. Have you forgotten your purpose in England? Do you turn so lightly aside from avenging your cousin?'

Yvaine blinked, but there was no time to grapple with this unexpected reason for Rorik's viking raids.

'That purpose is done,' he said curtly. 'Enough English soldiers have died to avenge Sitric's death and the deaths of his men.'

'I didn't see you kill anyone on this trip, Rorik.' Othar's eyes gleamed with malice. 'And that's not all, Father. Rorik struck me in front of the men, and wait until you hear about—'

'Enough!' ordered Egil, struggling to sit upright. A shaking finger was pointed at Othar. 'I'll hear no tales from you, boy, unless you can tell me what you've done to help your brother avenge Sitric.'

Othar smirked. 'Well, some of those English vermin had to watch their wives and daughters pay for their sins.'

'Pah!' Egil's hand fell back on his chair. 'You call raping women a fitting revenge for the way Sitric died? Strutting young cub. You'd do well to remember why you had to leave Norway.'

'I have killed,' Othar claimed, turning sullen. 'Some fellow who refused to get out of my way. The drooling fool kept gaping at the ship as if he'd never seen one before and didn't even try to defend himself.' He shrugged. 'I think he was wanting in wits.'

'*You* killed Jankin?' Shocked comprehension wrenched Yvaine from the stupor induced by Rorik's announcement. She took a step towards Othar, knowing the answer as surely as if she'd seen it happen.

'How do I know?' he said, casting her a look of scorn. 'I didn't stop to ask his name, you stupid woman.'

'He was my friend,' Yvaine said quietly. 'My only friend.' And without warning her hand flashed upwards, striking Othar across the face so hard the impact whipped his head to the side.

Every female serf in the hall screamed and fled from Othar's vicinity. With a screech of rage, Gunhild went for Yvaine's face, her fingers curled into vicious claws.

Anna, whom, until then, Yvaine had thought lost in the crowd, tried to fling herself in front of her mistress. She was roughly shoved aside by Othar, who recovered from his stupefaction at having been hit by a woman, and leapt forward.

He met Rorik's shoulder, bounced off, and was sent sprawling on the floor.

Rorik stepped in front of Yvaine just as Gunhild lashed out. He grabbed his stepmother's wrist. 'You were just extolling vengeance, Gunhild,' he purred with silky menace. 'Would you deny my lady that same right?'

Gunhild's eyes were wild with rage, but when she cast a glance at her husband, Yvaine saw sudden caution flash through the anger. With an effort that turned her pale, she pulled a rigid mask over her temper.

'As you say, Rorik.' Jerking her arm free, she turned on her heel and retreated to the smaller bench against the far wall.

'As you say,' mimicked Egil with a harsh laugh. 'A rare show of meekness, wife. You may sit there on the women's bench and contemplate your likely lot if you insult any woman of Rorik's.'

Leaning heavily on the arm of his chair, he turned on Othar, his eyes flashing. 'And you, boy! Have you learned nothing yet? Get back on your feet when a man knocks you down, even when it's justified. By the Gods, if you can't behave like the son of a jarl—'

He broke off, his face going deathly pale. Sweat sprang out across his brow. Gasping, he bent forward, pressing a clenched fist to his chest.

To Yvaine's horror no one went to Egil's aid. Even Gunhild seemed more concerned with gesturing to Othar to leave the hall than anxious about her husband. Looking nervous, she remained on the women's bench, her hands folded in her lap in a pose of meek obedience. But before her eyes lowered, Yvaine caught the look of hatred directed at her and knew the woman wouldn't forgive her for striking the son she obviously adored.

Everyone else seemed torn between watching Egil and nudging each other as they exchanged low-voiced comments. She noticed Thorolf standing with his arm around Anna, and realised that he must have moved to break the girl's fall when Othar had pushed her aside.

She was suddenly aware that her palm was stinging painfully. She cast a quick glance at Rorik. His face was impassive as he watched his father, but as if aware of her gaze, he glanced down and she saw concern in his eyes. He really cared about the old man, she thought, and, in an impulsive gesture, reached out to take his hand.

His mouth curved briefly. He lifted her hand and pressed his lips to the palm that had struck Othar.

'Well, Rorik,' Egil slumped back in his chair. His voice was hoarse, and his eyes had sunk far back in his skull, but whatever pain he'd suffered seemed to have passed. 'Is this an example of what we can expect if you marry your little wildcat?'

Rorik grinned. Still holding Yvaine's hand, he kicked a bench around at an angle to his father's chair and sat, drawing her down beside him. 'Very likely,' he said.

Egil snorted, but half-amused respect flickered over his face as he peered at Yvaine. 'You'll have your work cut out taming her,' he muttered to his son. 'I don't blame you for wanting the task, but you don't have to marry the wench to do it.' A look of urgency came into his eyes. 'If you want a wife, there's Harald Snorrisson's elder girl, grown into a fine strapping woman who'll bear sturdy sons, and he'll probably give her that piece of land adjoining ours as her dowry.'

Rorik shrugged. 'I know what I'm doing.'

Egil watched him for a moment, then sighed. Now seeming very weary, he lapsed into a long, brooding silence.

The crowd continued to wait. Like an audience at a mummers' play, Yvaine thought uneasily. Watching for the slightest movement, listening for the faintest murmur. She wondered what they'd say if she told Egil he didn't have to worry about his son marrying an English captive, that—

'Your mother's blood calls you,' the old man murmured, jerking her attention back to him.

From the women's bench, Gunhild gave a derisive sniff. The sound seemed to rouse Egil further from his reverie. He sat up straighter and nodded at Rorik.

'So be it. A man can't escape the fate woven for him by the Norns, and since they stand ready to cut my thread you'd best marry today.' He paused, nodding again as though hearing some unspoken question. 'Aye, let it be now, in my presence, and whilst Thorolf's here as witness.'

'An excellent notion,' Rorik agreed. 'I was going to suggest it, myself.'

'What!' Yvaine came to life as abruptly as Egil. Letting a mythical betrothal float past her was one thing; when reality was snapping at her heels it was time to act.

'I thought…' When Rorik turned to her, she realised she didn't know *what* she'd thought. There hadn't been time to think. But now—

Oh, now it was clear, she decided furiously as he raised an enquiring brow. He was going to uphold her honour in a way that allowed him to take what he wanted.

Well, it wasn't going to happen. She wouldn't *let* it happen.

'I won't be forced into marriage,' she hissed in a furious undertone. 'I don't care what everyone thinks. We can go on being betrothed if you like while you send—'

'Mention Edward one more time,' he interrupted softly, 'and I won't be answerable for the consequences.'

'But—'

'My father's wish is clear.'

'Your *father*'s wish!' Sheer frustration threatened to propel her straight off the bench. 'Do you think me deaf and blind? Your father doesn't want you to marry me any more than the rest of your family do.'

'They'll get used to it. So will you, little cat.'

The careless endearment was too much. Yvaine promptly forgot their interested audience. 'Will I?' she said through her teeth. 'Well, here's something you can get used to, you arrogant, thick-headed male. You can force me to marry you, but I'm still English. I'll still consider myself free. I'll still make you wish you'd never—'

The rest of her tirade strangled in her throat when Rorik wrapped one big hand around the nape of her neck and hauled her against him. The fierce purpose in his eyes had her blinking in sudden feminine alarm.

'You may consider yourself still English, lady,' he began in a soft voice that nevertheless managed to reach every corner of the hall. 'That is your choice. But let me assure you that, by morning, this arrogant, thick-headed male will have made you feel very married indeed.'

Before she could argue, his mouth came down on hers. It was a kiss of sheer male annoyance. She could only endure, fuming.

When he finally raised his head, everyone except Egil and Gunhild broke into cheers and delighted laughter.

The air of merriment still prevailed several hours later. At least, it prevailed among the slaves and house karls, Yvaine amended silently as she watched them clear away the remains of the wedding feast. Egil had retired immediately after the ceremony, Thorolf had left to visit his mother, and Gunhild's expression was more sour than ever.

From her seat beside Rorik, she cast a glance at the woman who occupied the central position on the side-bench. Gunhild had taken great pleasure in pointing out that, after today, she, too, would sit there, since Norsewomen ate apart from the men.

The thought of sharing a household with such a spiteful creature, let alone the women's bench, had tears of frustration and anger stinging her eyes. She forced them back with a swallow of ale, then thumped her drinking horn down on the table, causing it to sway precariously.

Rorik instantly covered her hand with his, steadying the vessel. 'There's no need to be nervous, sweetheart,' he murmured, misunderstanding the cause for her clumsiness. 'I have no intention of hurting you.'

Yvaine closed her mind to the dark velvet of his voice and glared at him. From the moment Egil, Thorolf, and another jarl, hurriedly fetched from a neighbouring farm, had declared them wed, he'd been treating her with gentle patience. Probably because he thought he'd achieved his purpose, she decided grimly.

''Twould not matter if you did,' she retorted. 'I have no intention of letting you do anything to me.'

'Aren't you forgetting something?' he growled. 'We're married.'

'A few heathen words over a cup of ale doesn't make me your wife.'

'Hmm.' He released her hand and rose. 'I think we'll continue this conversation elsewhere.'

Yvaine immediately sprang to her feet—and was abruptly thankful she hadn't eaten much; her stomach seemed to turn over with the movement.

'I don't know what your custom is,' she said, trying to keep any hint of pleading out of her voice. 'But I would like some time alone.'

He inclined his head in a gesture that was oddly formal. 'That is our custom, lady. Some of the women will escort you to the marriage bed and make you ready.' He signalled to the women, then seemed to hesitate before touching her hand lightly. 'I regret that one of them has to be Gunhild, little one, but to exclude my father's wife would be a grievous insult.'

'I understand,' she said, equally formal. And refused to meet his gaze.

Bad enough that Rorik watched her like a hawk as Gunhild and two other women led her from the hall. Reason and logic would fail her entirely if she saw the masculine assurance in his eyes. The assurance of a predator who knows his prey has been captured.

She shivered as the big room disappeared from view and she was ushered into a small chamber off the entrance passage. The first thing she noticed was that there was no way out except through the doorway. The single window, similar to those in the hall, was too small to allow any escape.

She glanced at the wide bed, illuminated by an oil-lamp standing in one corner beside a wooden chest. The bed was so huge, only a narrow L-shaped space was left at its foot and on one side. She remembered the vision that had sent her fleeing from Rorik on the ship, and tiny claws skittered up her spine.

'No doubt you expected to take my bedchamber, and the household keys as well,' Gunhild said spitefully as soon as the door closed behind them. She gestured to the wrinkled old crone who'd accompanied them into the room to start removing Yvaine's clothes. The other woman was apparently waiting outside in the passage. 'But you and Rorik will have to wait.'

'I've no wish to take anything from you,' Yvaine said with perfect truth. She drew back as a gnarled, claw-like hand reached for one of her brooches. 'And I'd prefer to undress myself, or for Anna to do it, if we must have all this ceremony.'

'Such ignorance,' Gunhild sniffed. ''Twould not be proper for an Englishwoman to escort Rorik's bride to the marriage bed. The witnesses must be trustworthy, isn't that so, Ingerd? It must be proven that you're a virgin, that no man but Rorik enters this room tonight. And let us hope he won't regret doing so in the morning.'

The ancient crone cackled shrilly at this patently insincere hope. She was obviously Gunhild's creature, but she cringed as Yvaine turned a haughty look on her.

'Guard me then, if you must, but I will undress myself.'

'As you wish.' Gunhild shrugged. 'I've no wish to play servant to your ladyship.' She made a scornful sound as Yvaine began to divest herself of her clothing. 'Well, see what we have here, Ingerd. 'Tis as I've always said. Englishwomen are skinny and over-delicate. This one doesn't look capable of bearing sons, even if Rorik stays around long enough to get her with child.'

'You expect him to leave?' Yvaine asked. Smarting under the indignity of being naked in front of hostile eyes, but determined not to show it, she climbed beneath the bearskin Ingerd was holding back for her, head held high. The bed felt surprisingly soft, but, at that moment, she didn't have attention to spare for unexpected luxuries.

'Of course.' Gunhild cast her a mocking glance before opening the door. 'Do you think 'twould take Rorik eight years to avenge twenty, even thirty, men? I expect that task has long been done. He's developed a taste for raiding, and he'll need more incentive than your paltry charms to keep him at Einervik. Then we'll see who rules here.'

The door shut quietly behind the two women.

The instant Yvaine heard the key turn in the lock, she leapt from the bed and grabbed her under-shift from the pile of clothes Ingerd had left on top of the chest. Gunhild's spite was forgotten as she pulled the garment over her head. She had too many other things to worry about.

Not least of which was the possibility of angering Rorik beyond patience by putting all her clothes back on in defiance of custom.

She glanced down at herself and hesitated. Perhaps the shift was a reasonable compromise. The garment fell only to her knees and wasn't the sturdiest of coverings, but at least she felt less vulnerable. If nothing else, it might slow him down for a second.

Her stomach clenched on a wave of nervousness. Something that felt very like fear gathered in the dim corners of the room; helplessness hovered in the shadows. The combination threatened to fog her mind. And she *had* to think. She had to find an answer to the dilemma she now faced.

What was she to do? Try to resist him? Lie passive? Give in to the urge to respond that grew more powerful every time he touched her? Continuing to deny she was married was useless. Rorik considered himself her husband no matter what she said. But what had happened to the time he'd promised her? How was she to know him better when she was faced with a wedding night scant hours after setting foot in Norway?

Why should it even matter, she wondered, sitting down on the bed. Why was she fighting herself? She was realistic enough to know that women were given little choice in such matters. Five years ago, she'd even been willing to do her duty by Ceawlin, terrified though she'd been at the time. What was it that sent tremors coursing through her every time she thought of Rorik claiming his husbandly rights?

'Oh, fool!' she exclaimed, springing to her feet and wrapping her arms about herself. She was being ridiculous. Wasn't she already tempted to surrender, to give in to her curiosity and his desire?

But what else would she be surrendering?

The question had her starting to pace in the small rectangle at the foot of the bed. 'That isn't the point,' she muttered ''Tis the way he sees me that's important. I'm more than a captive who should be grateful he's married me. I'm more than a possession who can run a man's household and bear his children. I'm a person. I'm *me*!'

She turned at the wall and paced faster. 'He's already trapped me in another household where I'm despised and resented. He's not going to turn my whole life upside down and expect me to submit without a murmur. He's not going to take my body and leave my heart shattered. He's not—'

Oh, God.

She jolted to a stop, staring blindly in front of her. Her lungs were burning; she couldn't get enough air. She stood there, barely breathing, unable to move, while the truth pounded in her head until she could have screamed aloud in a desperate bid to drown it out.

How had she not known? Blessed Mother save her. How had she not known that her heart was involved?

Groping blindly, she lowered herself to the bed, slowly, as if any sudden movement would have her shattering inside. She put her hands over her face, dragged them down, pressed her fingers to her lips.

Of course she'd known. She'd known since the night of the storm, in that swift, clear moment of acceptance when she'd crouched beneath the mast with the image of Rorik, defying wind and rain and lightning, etched in her mind for all time.

She'd known, and had hidden from the truth, denied it, told herself it was gratitude, dependence, *anything*. Until he'd whipped away the shield of her honour by marrying her, forcing her to confront her real fear: that to love him and surrender to nothing more than desire would ultimately destroy her.

Even marriage wasn't enough, she realised in that moment. Because without love, desire would surely burn itself out; without love, obligation and honour would become shackles he might one day resent. Unless…

Could she win his heart in return?

She straightened, letting her hands fall to her lap. The task seemed overwhelming. She thought Rorik would always protect her, but given the total lack of any softening influence in his life, he might not be capable of love.

And yet… She'd seen him hold a dying man's hand around a sword hilt, his own fingers clenched so hard his knuckles had shown white. He'd cared enough about her fellow captives to see they had a chance at a reasonable future. Indeed, had only kept them on the ship for her sake.

He was relentless in his determination to have her, but when he'd touched her, held her, hadn't she sensed something more? Not merely gentleness. Tenderness, deeply hidden, but waiting.

And she already loved him. Given that, there really was no choice. If she was to surrender her freedom, her heart, then she had to fight for the chance to win his love in return. Even if it meant fighting him and her own instinct to yield.

And as that realisation struck, the key rattled in the lock.

Yvaine sprang to her feet as the door opened. She heard Rorik speak to someone in the passage, then he stepped into the tiny chamber and pushed the door closed. The room immediately shrank to the size of a closet.

Without thought, she leapt on to the bed, landed on her knees and scuttled to the centre of the bear-skin covered expanse.

Rorik's brows rose. He locked the door and turned to eye her consideringly. 'Don't you think this is taking maidenly nervousness a little too far?' he asked.

She lifted her chin. 'I suppose you expected to find me waiting dutifully in bed, but I have no intention of lying here like a sacrifice on some pagan altar.'

He smiled faintly. 'I've never been particular interested in sacrifices,' he said. And began to unfasten his belt.

Yvaine's gaze flashed to his hands. For some reason her legs went weak. She sank back on her heels, watching with a sort of alarmed fascination as he removed the belt and his dagger and tossed them on to the bed. He whipped his tunic and undershirt over his head and sent them into a corner.

'However,' he continued, 'you might be warmer under the covers.'

'No, thank you,' she squeaked, her gaze now on his chest. Holy saints, he was big. Despite her nervousness, her fingers flexed, as though they wanted to curl around those broad shoulders, to probe the muscles rippling under warmly tanned skin. A pelt of gold-tipped hair spread over his chest and arrowed downwards. She followed its direction, and blushed wildly. He still wore his trousers, but unlike the loose-fitting chausses of her countrymen, these left little to the imagination. He was decidedly large all over. And already aroused.

Swallowing, she jerked her gaze upward and tried to remember her plan. She didn't have a plan. He hadn't given her time to think of one.

'If you're this nervous with me,' he said, a rueful smile curving his lips, 'what were you like with Selsey before you knew the truth about him?'

'Who?'

He laughed. Taking a step closer, he propped an arm on one of the carved bedposts, and leaned against it.

She wondered if he thought the casual pose made him look less threatening.

'You surprise me, little cat. Is this the woman who tried to escape when she could scarcely stand? Who risked capture and rape by the Danes rather than remain under my protection?'

'Fine protection,' she managed. 'You kidnapped me in the first place.'

'True.' He was silent a moment, lashes half-lowered as though in thought. Then his gaze lifted to hers. 'But 'tis over and done. Can't we put that behind us, Yvaine, and go on from here? 'Tis not as if I took you from a gentle home, a doting husband.'

'That's no excuse.'

'No, it isn't. But tell me, if I hadn't killed Selsey, if I'd left you there, what would you have done? You said he hadn't mistreated you until that day. Why were you trying to leave him?'

She eyed him warily, wondering why he'd asked the question. It was difficult to concentrate. His very presence, overwhelmingly male, had every nerve braced and quivering; the gentle tone of his voice was in such stark contrast to the physical threat, she felt dizzy, as if her senses were being tugged in several directions at once.

For the first time, defiance was having to be forced. The oddly serious note in his voice confused her further, and yet wasn't this what she wanted? To talk, to gain some time, so she could decide what to do.

'Ceawlin didn't beat me,' she said at last. 'But 'twas a miracle I survived the winters. He gave me nought but the thinnest cloth for my gowns. He never allowed a fire in the solar—and I had privacy there only because he didn't want me. The food I was served was more suited to swine. Indeed, I was ill several times this past year, until I learned to eat nothing that hadn't been cooked in the communal pot.' She gestured slightly. 'Is that reason enough?'

He nodded. 'You were unfortunate in your marriage, I grant you, but not all men are the same.'

'Are they not?' she retorted. 'When men see women as nothing more than objects, to be moved this way and that at the whim of their desires and ambitions? Me, my cousins—' her voice hitched as a memory of childhood grief stabbed through her '—my mother.'

Rorik's eyes narrowed. 'Your mother? What of her?'

'She was killed by one of our neighbours, for no other reason than that he was feuding with my father and seized the opportunity to strike when he came across her in the woods one day. To him she was nothing more than a...*thing* he could steal from his enemy. Not that my father grieved overmuch,' she added bitterly. 'He didn't even bother to avenge her. In his ambition to get a son, he was too busy picking out another bride.'

'But you grieved.' His gaze sharpened. 'You have a father? When you mentioned ransom, you spoke only of Edward.'

'My father died of a fever before he could wed again. I was taken into the King's household.'

'To be married, in turn, for political gain.' When silence was her only answer, he nodded. 'And had you stayed in England as a widow, Yvaine? Indeed, if you'd escaped and been granted an annulment, which I presume was your goal, what would your cousin have done with you?'

'Probably married me off ag—'

She stopped short, finally realising his purpose. 'He might,' she amended pointedly, 'have given me some choice in my own future.' And if she believed that, she believed every monk in the land would abandon his vows and turn to a life of debauchery. Of course Edward would have married her off again. Given his present single-minded determination to unite England, he probably would have married her off to a Dane.

And judging by the look in Rorik's eyes, he knew exactly what she was thinking.

'What Edward would do no longer matters,' she pointed out. ''Tis your actions we're discussing. You saw, you wanted, you took. And now—'

'Now I've protected you, given you your proper position at Eincrvik. Isn't that what you were talking about on the ship?'

'No! I thought you'd take me to live somewhere else. I didn't think you'd *marry* me.'

His brows shot up. 'You'd prefer to be my mistress?'

'Aye—no!' Oh, how could she explain without leaving herself vulnerable? 'Don't you see? 'Tis being given no choice in the matter that strikes at me so. How would you feel,' she demanded suddenly, 'if you had no control over your own life?'

He frowned. 'As furious and frustrated as you are, I expect. But, sweetheart, we're back where we started. 'Tis done. I understand how you must feel, but—'

'Then give me time,' she interrupted, coming up on her knees as hope surged within her. 'Time to know you better. Time to settle.' *Time for you to fall in love with me.*

'Yvaine...'

'You promised.'

'I didn't swear a vow on it,' he murmured. 'And 'tis just as well, because whatever time I intended to give you ran out the instant we were wed.'

'Ran out!' She glared at him. 'Ran *out*?'

Rage slammed through her; fury like nothing she'd known. So he knew what she was feeling, did he? He knew she was furious. He knew she was frustrated. How observant of him. How very clever. How kind of him to mention it. Furious? He hadn't seen the half of it.

'As far as I'm concerned the sands haven't even started,' she yelled. 'What's more—'

Before she could enlighten him, he straightened, planted his hands on the crossed boards at the foot of the bed and leaned forward. His expression was stern, and utterly determined.

'Yvaine, we're married. Accept it. And while you're doing so, think on this. If there's no proof of your virginity in this bed come morning, your position in this household will be intolerable whenever my back's turned. I can't be here every minute so—'

'Women's spite? Why should that worry me? I've had five years of practice at ignoring it.'

His hands flexed around the boards. 'I know you're angry and upset. But if your response to me the last time I kissed you is any indication, you know damn well that sharing this bed with me isn't the worst fate in the world.' He paused, the implacable expression in his eyes replaced by a wicked gleam. 'In fact, 'twill be my pleasure to make sure you enjoy our wedding night as much I intend to.'

She didn't think; she didn't plan it. Rage had her hand whipping out as if it had a mind of its own. She snatched up the dagger lying a few inches away and sprang to her feet, staggering slightly as the plump mattress gave unexpectedly beneath her weight.

'You might wish to change your mind about that,' she said, whipping the leather sheath away and sweeping the blade in a reckless arc.

Every trace of devilment vanished from Rorik's eyes. He straightened, his narrowed gaze never leaving her face. 'What in Hel do you think you're going to do with that dagger?' he demanded with soft menace.

Yvaine didn't answer; she was too intent on keeping her balance. No wonder the bed had felt soft. What fool had thought to stuff a mattress with feathers? In England it would have been straw; a sturdier base from which to wave a dagger about.

'Put the knife down, Yvaine.' Rorik still spoke softly, but he took a step to the side which brought him to the corner of the bed.

Yvaine took a corresponding step back, aware that if he moved again the bedpost would no longer hinder him. 'When you promise me some time,' she countered.

'And if I don't?' He took the step that brought him to the side of the bed. 'Are you going to take a slice out of me with that dagger?'

'No.' She hesitated as the glimmer of an idea came to her. 'I'm going to— Stay back!' She waved the knife wildly and almost overbalanced when she saw the muscles in his shoulders flex.

'Jesu!' he exploded. 'Put the bloody thing down before you hurt yourself.'

'What?' She blinked at him. '*What* did you say?'

And in that moment he moved.

Too late, Yvaine jerked back to avoid his lightning swift grab for her hand. Her heel caught the turned back edge of the bearskin. She stumbled, the blade in her fist swooping downwards as her feet went out from under her. Ice sliced across her knee. With a startled squeak, she tumbled into the depths of the mattress.

Chapter Nine

'You little idiot!'

Rorik ground out the words between his teeth as he grabbed Yvaine's wrist, braced a knee on the bed and wrenched the dagger from her grasp. He sent the blade into the floor with a savage flick of his wrist. It stayed there, quivering.

He pulled Yvaine upright. 'Who were you trying to kill? Me or yourself?'

'Neither,' she said. 'And if you'll stop breaking my arm, I'll tell you what I intended to do. To my finger, that is, not my knee.'

She wasn't even contrite. Rorik ground his teeth again as another wave of fury roared through him. The little wretch had taken ten years off his life and she didn't even realise it. If it wasn't for the blood he could see—

He jerked his gaze down. 'Odin curse it.'

'That wasn't what you said a minute ago.'

'Never mind what I said a minute ago.' He hauled her closer, glaring straight into her eyes. ''Tis what I'm going to do that should worry you.'

'Well, I meant to cut my finger.' Her lashes flickered; whether in wariness or defiance he wasn't sure. 'But this will do as well.'

Defiance, then. What had he expected? Gods, he didn't know whether to yell at her or pull her into his arms. Both impulses hammered at his brain; both would probably drive him mad with frustration. And in the meantime, she was bleeding all over the bed.

Biting off another curse, Rorik released Yvaine's wrist, took the hem of her shift between his hands and ripped.

The force of his action almost sent her toppling backwards again.

'What do you think you're doing?' she began, shoving at his hands as he tore a strip of fabric away. Then yelped indignantly when he clamped the wadded-up strip down on her knee. 'Ouch.'

'Be still,' he growled. 'We have to stop this bleeding, unless you want everyone to think I took to you with the finesse of a rutting bull.'

She studied the thin trickle of blood that had run down the side of her knee onto the sheet. ''Tis only a few drops. I should think you'd be content. There's your family's proof that I'm virtuous.'

He reached out, captured her chin in his hand and forced her face up to his. It was a mistake. The softness of her skin, the faint trembling he could feel, pierced frustration and anger as if she'd taken the point of the dagger to his own flesh.

What chance did rage have, he asked himself, fuming, against soft vulnerability combined with fierce pride? Her courage, her sheer determination to fight him when they both knew he could have vanquished her easily by force, or even by seduction, had struck more truly than any sword or spear. And totally disarmed him.

But, by the Runes, he ached. Her softness, her sweetness, were here for the taking. His entire body was throbbing with the need to cover her, to take, to push himself into her again and again, until she could no longer deny she was his. Until she cried out in surrender, and yielded, everything.

It would happen, he swore silently. By Thor, it would happen if he had to wait for the Doom of the Gods to achieve it.

But it wasn't going to happen tonight.

Wrenching his hand away, he stamped down on needs that were edging past violent, and wondered if he'd lost his mind when he'd first touched Yvaine.

'Don't move,' he snarled. 'Don't speak. Don't even blink if you want the time you risked my temper to obtain.'

Yvaine swallowed and decided Rorik's temper had little to do with the terrifying restraint in his voice. A man on the knife-edge of control glared back at her. If he granted her five minutes 'twould be a wonder.

She barely refrained from flinching when he moved back, lifted the cloth from her knee and started bandaging the small wound. He didn't hurt her, but his movements were abrupt and jerky, completely unlike the powerful masculine fluidity he commanded at will.

He tied a knot at the side of her leg and got to his feet. 'You'd better not bend that knee for a day or two,' he said curtly, and turned his back on her. 'Get under the covers.'

Yvaine obeyed, eyeing him as if he might change his mind at any moment. Every muscle in his back was rigid, his shoulders braced, his fists clenched. She was torn between diving under the bearskin until she was out of sight and reaching out to touch him, to ease the brutal tension pulling his entire body taut.

'What now?' she ventured, sitting up in the far corner of the bed and pulling the bearskin to her shoulders.

He turned, swept her with one coruscating glance and bent to pull his dagger from the floor. 'You tell me, lady. Perhaps another conversation will enliven the rest of the night. Who knows, by morning, you might know me well enough to refrain from holding me off with my own dagger as if I'd intended to tear you apart.'

'From what I saw,' she muttered, 'that was a distinct possibility.'

He said something under his breath, turned to thump the weapon down on the chest, then wheeled back so suddenly, she jumped. He planted both fists on the bed and leaned forward. 'Don't worry,' he purred. 'When I take you, lady, we'll fit together like that dagger to its sheath.'

Yvaine didn't answer. Something else had just occurred to her: the problem of where this first fitting of daggers and sheaths was to take place now that she'd removed the bed as a possibility. She decided not to ask; glanced around the small chamber instead in a frantic search for a change of subject. The light from the oil-lamp flickered on the pelt bunched between her fingers, turning the tips of the creamy fur to silver, and inspiration struck.

'I've…uh…never seen a pelt this colour before. What manner of creature was it?'

Rorik's eyes narrowed. He continued to watch her for a moment with unblinking intensity, then he straightened. ''Tis the fur of the great ice-bear,' he said shortly. 'They live far to the north.'

'Then you really killed such a creature?'

'He didn't give me much choice.' A sardonic smile twisted his mouth. 'In that instance, lady, I had more success with the dagger than you did.'

'I had no intention of attacking you,' she retorted. Her gaze went to the curved tooth still hanging around his neck. It nestled in a whorl of hair. She felt a sudden longing to twirl her finger in the small curl, and clenched her hand around the bearskin. She wished Rorik would put his shirt back on. The longer he was half-naked, the stronger her need to touch him, to run her hands over the powerful contours of his chest and shoulders, to press her cheek to his warm flesh.

Doubt welled. Confusion and a strange, yearning ache warred with caution. Was she doing the right thing?

'Tell me something,' he said, and raised his brows when she jumped at the sound of his voice. 'How long will it take you to know me better, Yvaine?'

'I…hadn't thought that far.'

'You expect me to wait indefinitely?'

'No. Of course not. I just need to know…to know that you see *me*, not—'

'You think I don't see you?' he demanded, leaning forward again to plant his fists on the bed. 'You think I haven't seen *only* you these past few days?'

'That isn't what I meant.'

'I don't think you know what you mean. Unless you're seeking revenge for being given no choice.'

'No!' Dismay washed over her that he'd attribute such a motive to her. 'I just want some time. A few weeks, even a—'

'Very well. You have it.' The words were clipped. He straightened, turned, and snuffed out the oil lamp with a savage swipe of his hand.

Yvaine blinked in the sudden darkness. She couldn't believe she'd won.

Or had she?

Two thumps told her Rorik had taken his boots off and tossed them on to the floor. She slid down in the bed and lay still, barely breathing, as he climbed in next to her.

A minute passed in absolute silence. She racked her brain for something to say that might melt the chill all but forming icicles in the air between them. Remarking on the fact that Rorik still wore his trousers probably wouldn't be wise. Nor was she inclined to ask how long a reprieve he intended to give her.

On the other hand, she'd asked for time, not this ominous silence. Apart from finding out if Rorik could fall in love with her, it *wasn't* unreasonable to want to know her husband better. Especially when she was dealing with a Viking who used a Christian oath whenever it suited him? 'Jesu', he'd said. And tonight wasn't the only occasion.

She frowned as she remembered the night she'd tried to escape. Not only would she swear that Rorik had said 'Oh, God,' not 'Gods', when he'd pulled her into his arms, he'd also told her she wouldn't have made it to Winchester before being recaptured. She hadn't thought to question him at the time, but how had he known that Winchester, a full day's march from any coast, was the usual location of Edward's court? How, for that matter, had he recognised the royal standard flying over the hall at Selsey?

She turned her head. With the small window unshuttered, and her eyes now adjusted to the dark, she could just make out Rorik's long form stretched out on the other side of the bed. She thought he'd folded his hands behind his head, but there was no sense of relaxation about him.

'Rorik?'

His voice sliced at her through the darkness. 'Yvaine, I expect to spend a damned uncomfortable night. I suggest you not add to my problems by testing my control.'

Silence fell again, with an almost audible thud. Yvaine lay utterly still. Dismay threatened to overwhelm her. The uneasy suspicion that she hadn't thought through all the consequences of denying Rorik his rights in the marriage bed began to stir. And yet, how else could she protect herself? Loving him, how could she surrender her body while withholding her heart?

The answer to that was still beyond her reach when she fell into an exhausted slumber.

She awoke as she'd woken for the past five years. Tense, wary, instantly alert.

It was just as well. The first thing she saw was Rorik, watching her from less than a foot away. They lay facing each other. The early morning light streamed through the window making his eyes glitter like diamonds encrusted in ice. It also illuminated with nerve-tingling clarity, the intent, searching expression with which he studied her.

She stared back at him, hoping he wouldn't notice the pulse leaping in her throat.

He did, of course. A faint frown drew his brows together. He reached out and brushed a strand of hair from her cheek. 'Am I such an ogre, Yvaine, that you should wake like that? Braced as though awaiting a blow.'

After the stony silence in which she'd fallen asleep, the regret in his voice shook her immeasurably. 'No,' she whispered. 'It isn't you. I fell into the habit at Selsey.'

'Then you don't fear me?'

'No. At least... No.'

'Good.' A smile dawned. Coming up on one elbow, he captured the strand of hair he'd brushed aside and began to wind it around his fingers.

Yvaine immediately shifted to keep some distance between them, and found herself on her back with Rorik leaning over her. She blinked up at him, wondering how she'd managed to put herself in such a precarious position. She was glad Rorik's anger had passed, but for someone whose wedding night hadn't gone according to plan, he was looking far too pleased with himself.

She levelled her brows at him. 'What do you mean, "good"?'

'Well, in order to know me better, you'll have to permit a certain amount of intimacy. That would be difficult if you feared me.'

'Intimacy?' she squeaked. 'But...' She couldn't continue; her mouth had gone dry. When had that happened? For that matter, when had she lost the small advantage she'd gained last night? She had the distinct impression Rorik was about to turn the tables on her, but she wasn't sure how.

'Stop!' she ordered as he leaned closer as if to kiss her. She thumped a small hand against his chest and gasped as the heat of his skin struck her. Warmth enveloped her instantly. She wanted to curl closer, to nestle into that seductive heat.

'You're not going to seduce me into changing my mind,' she stated, and wondered who she was trying to convince.

'I wouldn't dream of it,' he murmured, a wicked twinkle in his eyes. 'But even if I did, you can always say no whenever you like.'

She eyed him cautiously. 'And you'll stop?'

'I'll stop.' Still holding her captive with nothing more than the fragile shackle of her hair, he bent and closed his mouth over hers.

Oh, the sweetness. The thrilling ripple of pleasure. His kiss was a seduction in itself, a siren call to surrender. Something softened, opened, trembled deep inside her. She wanted to sink deeper into the mattress, to feel the weight of his body over hers, to have him part her lips with his tongue. Not with the fierce pressure he'd used before the storm, but as he'd done that night on the beach, gently tasting, gently taking.

Tentative, uncertain of what she might unleash, she returned the pressure of his mouth. He shifted the angle of his head, shaping her lips to his, tracing their outline, enticing her to the same seeking movements. Her fingers pressed into the muscles of his chest. She lost all sense of time; knew only the slowly spiralling pleasure of his mouth moving on hers. And, again, that strange yearning ache.

He raised his head and looked down at her, eyes narrowed and glittering.

Yvaine swallowed and tried to speak. It took several attempts before she realised she didn't know what to say anyway. The hard beat of his heart against her palm seemed to have robbed her of thought.

But it was that powerful rhythm that restored a sense of caution. It was too heavy, too fast. Tension hummed in the small space between them. The muscles against her hand were like tempered steel.

''Tis morning,' she managed, in a voice that sounded as if she was calling a timid creature to her side, not trying to hold off a considerably more dangerous one. 'This isn't...I mean, we'd best be up and about—'

'I doubt anyone will expect us to be up with the thralls.'

'No, but...' She drew her hand away, clenching her fingers against the sudden loss of heat. 'That...reminds me. What am I supposed to do here?'

He watched her, as if weighing the strength of her resistance, then shifted his gaze to the curl he'd captured. Slowly he began to unwind it.

'While Gunhild is mistress here, why not rest, recover from the past few days. When she's gone you may do as you please. Within reason.'

She ignored that last bit. She wished she could ignore the hand that almost...oh, *almost*...brushed the tip of her breast as he straightened the curl wrapped around his hand. 'You intend to send her away?'

'I'll see she's well provided for, but I won't have her in the same household as you.'

'Oh.' She thought about that. 'What about Othar? Will you send him away, also?'

'Mayhap,' he said absently, watching the curl spring back when he released it. He immediately recaptured it and began to unwind it again. 'He needs to be kept busy.'

'Is that wh—?'

She broke off with a gasp as his knuckles brushed her breast in passing. Her nipple tightened on a thrilling little tingle of pleasure, but the sensation was so fleeting she wasn't sure if he'd meant to do it. 'Is that why he had to leave Norway? Idleness?'

His hand stilled. His gaze flashed to her face. 'You seem very interested in Othar all of a sudden.'

Yvaine swallowed. She'd barely been aware of what she was saying, had been talking only to retain some hold on her senses. Now it appeared she'd stumbled into another pit. 'He is part of the household,' she said. 'And your brother.'

He frowned. Then with an abrupt movement that left her feeling horribly bereft, he untangled his hand from her hair, turned and rose from the bed. Keeping his back to her, he flung up the lid of the chest, ignoring the clothes on top that promptly slithered to the floor, grabbed an undershirt and yanked it on.

Yvaine watched as he continued to dress, torn between relief and a sharp sense of loss. Then he turned to face her and the feeling of abandonment wasn't quite as keen-edged. The muscles in his jaw were locked tight, but his eyes weren't cool as she'd expected.

'Perhaps 'tis best you know,' he said. 'Othar was challenged to a fight and disgraced himself.'

She sat up, drawing the bearskin to her shoulders and wrapping her arms around her upraised knees. 'A duel? Do you mean a joust?'

'No.' He sat down on the edge of the bed and began to pull on his boots. 'He'd wronged a man. Forced the fellow's wife, or so she claimed. In our duels, the one challenged strikes first, and when Othar failed to draw blood with his first blow he ran from the ground. I had to pay compensation to prevent him becoming a target for revenge from his opponent's family.'

'Rather like our Saxon wergild,' she murmured. 'Where the victim's family receives payment from the culprit.'

'Aye, but in this case I had to take Othar away until the talk died down. Not only had he attacked, or tried to seduce, a virtuous woman, he'd branded himself a coward.'

'Hmm. No wonder he and Ketil were friends.'

A fleeting smile came and went. He stood, picked up his dagger, sheathed it, and fastened it to his belt. 'That was a little different, sweeting. Ketil offered marriage. Probably because Orn's family run a prosperous ale-house and Ketil saw an easy life ahead, with as much drink as he could hold. When Orn refused him, Ketil took the girl, intending to force her into marriage.'

Yvaine raised her brows, but not a flicker of awareness crossed Rorik's face. She narrowed her eyes at him. 'What happened?'

'She got him drunk and managed to escape unharmed. Unfortunately she didn't find her way home until the next day, so Ketil put it about that she'd spent the night with him. Orn, being the only suitable male in the family after his son died last year, challenged Ketil in order to prove him a liar.'

Yvaine fell silent, considering the different codes of behaviour implied in Rorik's explanation. Apparently he saw nothing odd in the fact that it was permissible for him, or any other man, to carry off a woman when a-viking, so long as they adhered to a strict code of honour at home. Was it because the victims of viking raids were English? But if that was so, why had he married her?

'That's where I'll be this morning,' he said abruptly. 'With Orn's family. I have to tell them what happened.'

She looked up, quick sympathy overriding all else. 'I'm sorry, Rorik. That sort of thing is never easy. But it wasn't your fault. Unless you can see the future.'

He halted, half-turned away from her, before reaching for the door. 'It shouldn't have been difficult in this case.'

'No, but— Wait!' she cried as he twisted the key in the lock. When he glanced back, frowning, she searched for something to say, to keep him with her a moment longer. His abrupt leave-taking, without a touch, or even a word of farewell, was dismaying. He was so changeable this morning; indulgent one moment, curt the next. For someone bent on seduction, he couldn't seem to leave fast enough. And she was as contrary.

'Rorik, what ails your father? I might be able to help him, ease his pain.'

His frown cleared, but the sombre look stayed in his eyes. 'The healers say his heart is tired. There's nothing to be done, nor will he accept help. And speaking of help,' he added before she could argue, 'you'll have to manage without Anna this morning. Though no accusation was made, Gunhild will be the first person to enter this room once we've both left it.'

'Oh.' She glanced down, not sure if guilt or embarrassment was heating her cheeks. 'I can manage to dress myself,' she muttered.

He nodded, hesitated as though he might say more, then opened the door and left.

The moment Yvaine stepped into the hall all activity stopped. The slaves tending the cookpots simmering over the fire looked up and stared. Ingerd paused in her task of shaking out the bench furs and fixed her with beady eyes. From a corner of the room Anna stepped forward, only to halt when the girl beside her caught her arm.

Gunhild rose from her seat at the loom and moved towards her, a gleam of anticipation in her eyes.

Yvaine braced herself as the woman approached. She would be polite if it choked her. 'Good morning to you, Gunhild.'

'That is yet to be seen,' Gunhild retorted, sweeping past her into the bedchamber. 'And 'tis nigh on noon.'

Yvaine grimaced at the woman's retreating back. Then, spying Egil hunched in his chair, watching the encounter, decided boldness might win her respect from that quarter. She crossed the room, walking with considerable care so she wouldn't favour her bandaged knee.

Instantly the air of tension in the room was dispelled. The slaves exchanged knowing smiles and turned back to their pots. Ingerd pursed her lips thoughtfully. The girl with Anna nudged her and said something that banished the look of concern on Anna's face.

And Egil's gaunt features relaxed into a faint smile. 'Here, girl,' he said, indicating the place beside him. 'You're moving as if you spent the night riding hard. Or being ridden,' he added with a rusty chuckle. 'You'd best sit down.'

Yvaine gave him a prim look and obeyed.

He chuckled again, and slumped back in his chair.

'Should you not be resting, my lord?' She eyed the bluish tinge about his lips. It had occurred to her that Egil could answer several questions that had nagged at her after Rorik had left, but she didn't want the information at the expense of the old man's precarious health.

'Plenty of time to rest in the grave, my girl. And call me Egil. We Norse don't hold with high-sounding titles. The name we're called on our name-giving day and a nickname earned later are good enough. Except for those with an ambition to be king,' he added grimly.

Yvaine tilted her head. 'That would be King Harald, I expect.'

'Hmph.' He peered at her. 'You're well informed. No tavern wrench, then. Aye, *King* Harald.' He gave a snort. 'Harald Fairhair he was once called, before he put a crown on his head and announced at the Gulathing he was King of all Norway. Nothing but a land-grabbing tyrant, if you ask me. And when he didn't grab a man's land, he demanded money.'

Yvaine raised her brows.

'You think those of us who go raiding aren't any better? You'll understand when you look about you, girl. We cling to the edges of the fjords here. During summer our sheep graze on the lower slopes, but the winters are long and hard, and further north there's nothing but ice and snow. Only the Lapps make a living there from fur trading and whaling, and Odin knows they're always on the move just to survive.'

'So you fight to win more land.' She nodded. ''Tis not so different in England.'

'Aye, but there you have land for the taking. When the men who defied Harald lost their farms, they had nothing. Not all turned towards England, you know. Nor even Normandy.'

'What became of them?' she asked, genuinely interested.

'Packed up and went to Iceland.' Egil shrugged. 'Sounds like a nice inhospitable sort of place, doesn't it? But the colony prospered. The people formed their own Thing with its law-speaker and justice for all.'

'But you stayed.'

'No one drives me off the land that's been in my family for generations,' Egil growled. Then added with a cynical snort, 'At least, not so long as we pay tribute.'

Yvaine watched him, wondering if the tribute exacted by the king was another reason for Rorik's viking raids.

'Aye, we kept the land,' the old man murmured. He sank deeper into the furs wrapped about his shoulders, staring into the fire as though the past could be seen in the flames. 'And yet, despite that, I was worried that

Sitric would go off to Iceland. He was always a rebel, and Rorik would've followed him into Hel itself.'

Yvaine went still, hardly daring to breathe. 'But he didn't?' she asked very softly when nothing more seemed forthcoming.

'No.' Egil stirred. 'Settlement was too tame for Sitric. The young hothead joined up with Guthrum, King of the Danes.' He sighed, shook his head. ''Twas the year I took Gunhild to wife. You'd have thought Sitric had battles enough here to fight. He and Gunhild hated each other on sight, and he resented the way she treated Rorik, especially after Othar came along. But that didn't stop him leaving one night without a word to anyone.'

'Not even to Rorik?' She frowned, remembering Rorik telling her he'd been ten that year. A rebellious older cousin, standing between him and an unpleasant stepmother, would have seemed like a hero to a young boy.

'Just as well,' Egil said drily. 'Sitric knew what I would've done if he'd taken Rorik with him. Thor's hammer! The boy wasn't yet full grown, although strong and as brave as any warrior twice his age.'

Yvaine smiled and he grinned faintly in response. 'Aye, I'm proud of my son. Why not? And Rorik was more than capable of fighting his own battles, so don't go thinking Sitric abandoned his cousin. He was a man to be proud of, also. I'd raised him from a lad, my dead brother's son, and he was like a son to *me*.'

'What became of him?'

'Hah! You have all a woman's curiosity, girl, but 'tis no gentle tale. Suffice to say that Sitric didn't see much excitement with Guthrum either. That same year

Guthrum and Alfred of Wessex signed a treaty and the Danes settled in the east of England. The Danelaw, you English call it. Sitric stayed in Guthrum's service, but he was restless. Every time he came home I wondered when he'd leave Guthrum for another leader, or to fit out his own ship. Then, after that last visit, four years after Sitric joined the Danes, Rorik went with him.'

'To England?'

'Aye, to England. And six years later Sitric died. That's all you need to know, girl. If Rorik wants to tell you more, he will. But know this. Family honour is the most important thing in a Norseman's life. If a kinsman is slain, then vengeance will be taken. There's no choice, no argument. Sometimes the head of a family, or the finest, may be killed, though he disapprove or not know of the initial crime. And it doesn't only apply to sons and brothers, but to cousins of the remotest degree, to foster children who've lost their own father, like young Thorolf, and to any who marry into the family. Honour, girl. Remember that.'

'Yvaine has a greater awareness of honour, father, than many a man,' Rorik said from the doorway.

She turned her head, her heart giving a little leap at the sound of his voice. He filled the doorway, tall and powerful, but, just for an instant, as he crossed the room towards her, she saw not the fierce warrior of her girlhood dreams, but a child who had never known a mother's gentle touch, a boy growing up among men whose code was harsh and unforgiving.

Doubt shook her, almost crushing her resolve. When he reached her, tipped her face up to his with one long finger, and brushed his mouth across hers, she drew back, wondering if the brief caress was nothing more than a step in her seduction.

A faint frown came into his eyes. 'Don't you, my sweet?'

'What?'

Egil chuckled. 'What did you do to the girl last night? First she can't walk properly. Now, a mere kiss of greeting and you've addled her wits.'

Yvaine blushed and straightened her spine. 'My wits are perfectly all right, thank you, my lord. I believe we were speaking of honour. I seem to be discussing the matter rather frequently of late. However—' she rose; the lady of the manor taking leave of impudent peasantry '—I'm sure you have other matters to discuss with your son and I, uh, need to speak to Anna, so if you don't mind...'

Anything else and she would find herself in a verbal morass. Ignoring Egil's broad grin and the narrow-eyed speculation on Rorik's face, she turned on her heel and stalked with as much dignity as she could muster to the other end of the hall.

'Good morrow, my lady,' Anna greeted her when she arrived, somewhat flushed, at the girl's side. 'As you see, they have me busy already.'

Yvaine peered at the table as though examining priceless relics. Anna seemed to be using a heavy glass smoothing stone to press the fine pleats of a linen shift. 'Mmm-hmm.'

Her maid frowned. 'Are you all right, my lady? They wouldn't let me near you last night or this morning, and you seem somewhat—'

'I'm perfectly well, Anna. Perfectly well. As for last night—' she took a deep breath '—apparently 'tis custom, when the bride's virtue is called into question for the bridegroom's family to, er, see to things.'

'Hmph. I could have told them you were still a maid, if only from the rumours flying around Selsey. But Rorik warned Thorolf and me not to mention you'd been married before. He said, 'twould only cause trouble, and no one else knows. Except Britta, of course, but she's not here.'

'Aye, well, what of yourself, Anna? You haven't been mistreated, I trust.'

'Indeed not. I have a cosy corner in the loft above the entrance, and food a'plenty. One of girls showed me how to make that curd mixture we ate last night. Skyr, they call it. 'Tis quite tasty. And this task is simple enough, once one gets the knack of it.' She cast a quick glance around the room and lowered her voice. 'But I'd watch Gunhild, if I were you, lady. While you were talking to Rorik's father, she came out of your bedchamber looking as sour as old milk. And earlier I saw her with Othar out near the dairy. They had their heads together like a pair of thieves, but when they saw me they broke off and went their separate ways.'

'Mayhap Gunhild was disappointed to find proof of my innocence,' Yvaine murmured, all too conscious of her bandaged knee. 'As for her talking to Othar—why wouldn't she? He's her son.'

'Aye, and as like as two peas, if you ask me. But still I say be wary. It wasn't natural, the way they stared at me, then parted so quickly. 'Twas somehow…furtive.'

'Hmm.' Yvaine left it at that. She had enough on her mind without looking for spectres where there were none. 'Egil just told me that Thorolf is his foster son,' she said to divert her maid.

'Aye. Thorolf's father used to go a-viking with Egil in their young days and was lost overboard in a storm. Egil has treated Thorolf as one of the family ever since. As he seems like to do with you, lady, judging by the way you were chatting there, so friendly.' Anna shook her head in wonder.

'Maybe Egil isn't as fierce as he tries to appear.'

'If that's so, you may put it down to age and illness. I warrant he would have been fierce enough in his prime from the tales Thorolf has been telling me. He's even kept his old ship. 'Tis moored down at the fjord with Rorik's vessel.'

'Is it? Perhaps I'll walk down that way.' Yvaine glanced about the hall, careful to kecp her gaze away from Rorik and his father. A walk sounded good. Some fresh air might even clear her mind. 'It seems I have time before we eat, and I've scarcely seen what my new home looks like. Do you come with me, Anna?'

'I have to finish pressing these shifts, lady. But if you intend to walk to the fjord, take care.' She levelled the smoothing stone at Yvaine in warning. 'I wouldn't put it past that Othar to push you into the water.'

Yvaine had to smile. 'He wouldn't dare,' she said. 'Besides, I can swim.'

Rorik kicked back on the bench and watched Yvaine walk out of the hall. She took the long way around, circling the firepit to avoid having to pass him on her way to the door.

He stayed where he was, resisting the urge to go after her, to tear down the wall of resistance she'd been busily erecting when she'd escaped him just now. He'd practically seen the stones go up, one by one, when he'd bent to kiss her.

So much for the plans he'd made earlier that morn, as he'd watched the dawn light move across her face. Even in sleep she'd touched something deep within him. With the golden fire in her eyes shuttered, there'd been a look of sweet, untouched innocence about her that aroused a need so urgent, so all-encompassing, even the memory made him ache. Gods, he'd wanted her; wanted to be inside her, part of her, to—

'Rorik? The light dims. Is it evening, my son?'

Rorik shoved frustration aside, and looked at his father. They'd begun speaking of Orn, of his last voyage, but Egil had fallen into a light doze, leaving him to his thoughts. Now there was a greyish tinge to the old man's face that looked ominous, and his breathing seemed laboured.

'Not yet, Father, but I'll carry you to your chamber. You should rest.'

''Twas Harald, you know.'

'Harald?' Rorik got to his feet. 'Snorrisson?'

'No, no.' Egil's hands moved fretfully on the furs. 'Harald Fairhair. I was telling Yvaine. He wanted land, and money.'

'A common ambition.'

'Aye. You know that, Rorik.' Egil looked up, almost pleading. ''Tis why I married Gunhild. She brought wealth into the family. Enough to buy more land from the King. I'd promised your mother, you see.'

Rorik frowned. A vague memory stirred, of himself as a very small child asking Egil about his mother, and having the subject brushed aside. Since then his life had been too full to admit more than fleeting thoughts of a woman he'd never known. He'd forgotten the occasion, and Egil had never mentioned the wife who had died in childbirth. Until yesterday.

He sat down again. 'My mother?'

'I...cared about her,' Egil murmured. 'So I promised not to go a-viking again.'

Rorik gave a short laugh. 'That I can understand.'

'Hah. Promised Yvaine, have you?' Egil eyed him with sudden disconcerting awareness. 'Aye, how a man's past returns to haunt him. But Yvaine isn't like your mother, Rorik. She's strong. A fighter. I lived to regret that promise, and yet... Even after your mother died I kept it. 'Twas the only reparation I could make,' he added in such a low tone Rorik barely caught the words.

''Twas not your fault she died, father.'

'Wasn't it? A man pays for his sins in this world, Rorik. But when I stopped raiding there was no wealth coming in to see us through the bad winters, or to acquire more land.'

'So you married Gunhild.' Rorik shrugged. 'She's efficient, I'll grant her that.'

'Aye, efficient. I thought her safe enough, too. She wasn't young, past childbearing age, or so I was told. But never underestimate a determined woman.' He struggled upright, reaching for Rorik's arm with sudden urgency. 'I never meant to get her with child, Rorik, but the woman tricked me. Or maybe Loki had a hand in the business, and now you'll have to deal with Othar.'

'I can handle Othar.'

'No! You don't understand.' Egil's fingers gripped like claws, the muscles in his throat worked. 'Listen to me. Don't give Othar any authority. I've ordered my ship to be refitted. Let the boy take it and—'

He broke off, his face going white. Sweat beaded his upper lip as he gasped for air. His grip tightened with ferocious pressure, but before Rorik could do more than seize his father's arm, Egil made an odd little sound in his throat and slumped forward, losing consciousness.

Chapter Ten

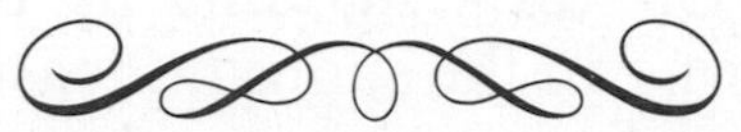

At Selsey she'd never been allowed beyond the manor walls, and when she'd walked within the compound there'd been nothing to soften the bare earth, no flowers to tend.

Here, the grass was a lush green carpet beneath her feet. Wildflowers bloomed in profusion, their scent rising on the clean mountain air as her skirts brushed their petals in passing. Bees hummed; the sun shone. Here she could walk unhindered.

The irony of it, given her present situation, made Yvaine smile wryly as she crossed the narrow meadow between house and fjord. She halted when she reached the shore and looked back at the cluster of buildings. The hall, a dairy, a huge barn that no doubt held lofts for the slaves, and beyond it an open structure of racks for the drying of fish. A blacksmith's hut was set a safe distance from the house, its occupant wielding a hammer with practised ease while a shaggy pony waited, its tail swishing in lazy counterpoint.

Behind the small settlement rose the forest, a dark thicket of pines that would provide shelter when winter's storms blew ice and snow down the valley. No doubt the place would be cold and bleak then, she thought, but the hall was snug. She could be happy here. If Rorik loved her.

Sighing a little, she started walking along the shore. A short distance away, men worked on a longship she assumed was Egil's. Beside them, *Sea Dragon* rocked gently at her mooring, bringing back memories of the past few days. Of Rorik standing by the steering oar, grey eyes glittering in the sunlight, teasing her, arguing with her, wanting her.

Even then she'd known he was her fate, her future. Perhaps if she'd listened to her heart from the beginning, she might be more certain now of what she was doing. Then again, what did she know of love? All she'd had were the dreams of her young girlhood, and they had been snatched from her by the reality of her empty marriage. She'd become a shadow, empty, unfeeling—until a pagan marauder had strode into her life and turned it upside-down. And in doing so had given her more than had any man. Gentleness, humour, the promise of passion.

While she, who professed to love him, held everything back.

Yvaine frowned; her footsteps slowed. Shouldn't love be a giving thing? Not something that counted the cost?

A sudden rattle broke through her thoughts. Startled, she looked up, to see a small boat being moored to the pier. The apparition that climbed out of it was enough to drive the puzzle of who was giving what to whom momentarily out of her head. Covered from head to toe in a hooded blue cloak embroidered with strange symbols, the figure was like no one she'd ever seen. Hairy calfskin shoes, tied with long laces, emerged from beneath the cloak's hem. The laces had large tin knobs on the ends that clanked as the visitor approached.

Yvaine gaped at this unmelodious footwear for a full five seconds before she managed to wrench her gaze upward. The next thing she saw was a pair of hands clad in furry gloves that looked for all the world like animal paws. One paw held a skin pouch; the other carried a long, wooden staff topped by a brass knob. Above the knob, set in a face that held the lines of countless years, a pair of gentian blue eyes regarded her with equal interest, and no little amusement.

'Ah! The golden child I saw in the flames. Good. I am in time.'

The stranger's voice was low, feminine, and unexpectedly sweet. She tucked the skin pouch away beneath her cloak and extended her hand towards Yvaine, touching her shoulder gently.

Yvaine decided there was no doubt as to the visitor's identity. Eyeing the furry hand warily, she took a step back.

'You fear me, little one? No need.' The woman smiled. 'I'm Katyja, who tells only of good things. Although for you—' her smile dimmed as she studied Yvaine. 'For you I must tell the truth if 'tis shown me. You must be warned.'

'Are you the witch Rorik spoke of?' Yvaine asked bluntly. 'Let me tell you, far from being in time, you're a little late. Not that your warnings would have done me much good from here.'

Katyja laughed. 'I see the future, child, not the past. We'll talk of that later. In the meantime, I've travelled far. This house has always welcomed me with good food and sweet wine. I hope nothing's changed.'

'Far from it, I imagine,' Yvaine muttered. Then, feeling guilty for her unmannerly outburst, summoned a smile. 'My regrets if I seemed tardy in my welcome. I'm afraid we English are unused to...uh...witches dropping by.'

Katyja laughed again as they began walking across the meadow. 'English! That explains the journey I saw, and yet, there was more. But no matter. Such things show themselves in their own time.'

'Hmm.' Yvaine decided such cryptic utterances were not comforting. She was about to search for another topic of conversation when Anna emerged from the house, hesitated, saw them, and began to run.

'Something's happened,' she said, alarm sprinting up her spine.

'The jarl,' Katyja said calmly. 'The Norns will cut his thread this night.'

Yvaine sent her a sharp glance, but before she could speak, Anna reached them.

'My lady, thank the Saints you didn't go far. 'Tis Rorik's father. He was talking to Rorik, then with no warning at all it seemed, he fell into a stupor. Rorik managed to rouse him, but he only mutters and tosses on his bed. Gunhild is at her wit's end and—'

Anna finally caught sight of Katyja and stopped, gaping.

'Your slave is also English?' Katyja asked. 'What is she saying?'

Yvaine repeated the news as they hurried towards the house. The instant they were through the inner doorway, Gunhild rushed forward.

'Katyja! Thank the runes you're early this year.'

'May the Gods look kindly on your house, Gunhild. I've come to see this child—' Her voice held a faint question and Yvaine realised she hadn't introduced herself. 'But I'll be glad to use my skill to make Egil's last hours more peaceful.'

Gunhild sent Yvaine a dismissive glance. 'My stepson's wife. Come. I'll take you to Egil.'

Katyja nodded. 'We'll speak later, child,' she murmured before following Gunhild.

'What an odd person,' Anna whispered, as they watched Katyja's tall figure disappear into the solar. 'And what in the name of all the saints are those things on her feet?'

'Shoes,' Yvaine said very firmly. 'Don't worry, Anna. She's a witch, but I think she means no harm. Indeed, I've heard such people have healing powers, but we've always been afraid of them in England because the Church has forbidden—'

She realised Anna was staring at her as if she'd expressed a desire to tie clanking tin knobs to her own shoes, and hastily decided this wasn't the time for a discussion on the merits of witchcraft.

Giving Anna a distracted smile, she hurried towards the solar, only to be met in the doorway by her husband and his stepmother.

'You have no place in there,' Gunhild snapped. 'Leave my husband to his own people.'

Yvaine ignored her. Looking up at Rorik, she touched a hand to his arm. 'Rorik, I'm sorry. Is there anything I can do?'

'No.' His tone was curt, but he covered her hand with his. 'My father wouldn't know you, and Ingerd is tending him. She was his nurse and knows his ways.

Perhaps under the circumstances you could supervise the slaves today, so Gunhild is free to sit with my father. I'll leave the two of you to work it out.' He gave her hand a quick squeeze and returned to the solar.

'How typical of a man's reasoning,' muttered Gunhild, but, this time, without rancour. 'Set two women to run the same household.'

''Tis only for a day or so,' Yvaine said, feeling more in charity with the woman. After all, she might be a widow before the day was out. 'You must be worried, Gunhild. I'll say a prayer for Egil's recovery.'

Gunhild considered her, eyes hooded. 'Do as you will,' she said at last. 'For what it's worth.' And with that enigmatic statement hanging between them, she turned and walked quickly out of the house.

'Your father rests quietly, Rorik. The end will not be long, I think.'

Katyja came into the hall and sat down in the visitor's chair opposite Rorik. She glanced at Yvaine, seated next to him on the jarl's chair, then at Gunhild, on the bench beside them. Her brows rose but she said nothing. The evening meal had been a family affair, eaten quickly and in a preoccupied silence that Yvaine, for one, hadn't felt like breaking. The karls and slaves chatted among themselves, but their voices were subdued, a low murmur in the background.

'You should rest, Gunhild.' Katyja lifted her drinking horn and took a sip of wine. 'Ingerd is with him.'

'Later, perhaps.' Gunhild indicated Katyja's empty trencher. 'Have you eaten your fill, Katyja? Is there something more we can offer you?'

Katyja shook her head and set aside her drinking horn. 'As usual, your house has looked after me well. Now 'tis my turn.'

'Forsooth, we need some good news,' muttered Gunhild.

'I'll look into the flames for you, Gunhild. But first—' Katyja beckoned to Yvaine. 'Come to me, child.'

Yvaine felt Rorik shift beside her. 'Refuse, if you wish,' he said. 'No one will think anything of it.'

But Yvaine caught sight of Gunhild's expression of scornful anticipation, and knew the woman was waiting for just such a refusal.

'Am I not a Norsewoman now?' she asked with a fleeting glance at him. Something she couldn't read flickered in his eyes. Then he shrugged and indicated Katyja.

Suppressing a slightly queasy feeling in the pit of her stomach, Yvaine rose and walked around the fire-pit. Katyja stood also and, placing the fingertips of one hand lightly against Yvaine's forehead when she halted before her, closed her eyes.

'Do not speak,' she instructed.

Silence fell; even the karls and slaves stopped their chatter to watch and listen. After several minutes, Yvaine began to relax. This was nothing more than mummery, she thought. There was no chanting of incantations or mixing of potions. Katyja merely appeared to be in some sort of trance.

Then with a small jolt she saw that the witch's eyes had opened. For a second she started blankly at Yvaine, then her vision cleared and she lowered her hand.

'You don't believe,' she said at once. 'But no matter. When the time comes, you'll remember my words and be strong. Listen well, golden child. I could not see all. Only a journey and two ships. One fleeing, one pursuing. And before that, danger. A threat that reaches back beyond your time. One thing more. Do not falter. Death surrounds you, but it does not touch you.'

'That's enough, Katyja!' Rorik shot to his feet and strode around the firepit to pull Yvaine into his arms. 'What in Thor's name do you mean by frightening my wife with your talk of danger and death?'

'I'm sorry, Rorik.' Katyja took a step back. 'I don't speak so by choice, but 'tis good that you're swift to protect her. You will always be so, I think.'

'There's no need to think about it,' he snapped. ''Tis my duty to protect my wife.'

'Not duty. You fight the true cause, but there's no need. You'll each give strength to the other.'

Rorik's eyes narrowed. 'You ramble, woman. Let us hope your ramblings are more propitious next time you visit. Tonight you've said enough.'

'But, Rorik, Katyja has yet to read the flames.' Gunhild, listening avidly, was clearly not pleased by this abrupt termination of the evening's entertainment.

Rorik turned an icy gaze on her. 'Another time, Gunhild. My father, your husband, is dying. I'm going to sit with him, and I'm not leaving Yvaine to any more predictions of doom and death.'

Gunhild coloured angrily. 'A Norsewoman wouldn't fear anything Katyja has to say,' she retorted, and, rising, she stalked into Egil's chamber.

Rorik turned back to Katyja, his expression shuttered. 'My thanks for what you did earlier for my father. You're welcome to rest by the fire for the night and take what provisions you need for your journey.'

'Thank you, Rorik. And I'm sorry if—'

She was cut off as a shrill cry echoed from the solar. Ingerd rushed into the hall, staggering and waving her arms. 'Dead,' she shrieked. 'The jarl is dead.'

Instantly, a long wailing arose from the women's bench.

'Oh, Rorik,' Yvaine turned in his arms and put her own around him.

He grasped her shoulders and set her aside. 'My father wouldn't want all this weeping and wailing over him,' he said. 'Send those slaves to bed, then get yourself hence. I'll see you in the morning.'

'But—'

But Rorik was already striding away. Yvaine gazed after him, feeling as if he'd slapped her. And yet, what more did she expect? Rorik didn't need her. Or rather, he wanted something from her that had no place elsewhere in his life. Even when Katyja's ominous prophecies had caused him to leap to her defence, he'd spoken only of duty.

Oh, wasn't this the very thing she'd feared? That despite Rorik's desire for her, she would live the rest of her life with the sting of rejection, with this cold feeling of being on the outside?

Trembling, feeling tears fill her eyes, she turned away, trying to regain some composure before doing as Rorik bade her. The touch of catskin against her hand brought her up short.

'Let him go, child. He doesn't yet accept what is.' Katyja smiled in understanding. 'I wish I could help you further, but only the Norns know our fates for certain. I'm permitted to see but a little.'

'Norns? Oh…the three spinners.'

'Aye. The spinners who sit by the Well of Fate. Past, Present and Future. They weave each person's thread into the tapestry of life, and when our time here is past, the thread is cut. 'Tis fore-ordained.

'And 'tis time we retired,' she added, patting Yvaine's hand again. 'Do as your husband bids you, little one. And try not to fret. I might not have seen all, but I saw how he watches you. If you would have more, you must show him the way.'

And how was she to do that? Yvaine asked herself the next morning as Anna braided her hair. Rorik hadn't even shared their bed last night, although at one point she'd thought she'd heard the door close. The sound hadn't been loud enough to rouse her fully. In her dreaming, half-dozing state she'd merely sensed a presence, but there'd been no other sound, no movement, and when she'd opened her eyes—she wasn't sure how long after—the tiny room had been empty, the pillow next to hers unused.

'Are you sure 'tis wise to go out, my lady?' Anna murmured, covering her hair with a fresh linen kerchief. 'Rorik has gone off to supervise the digging of some sort of burial mound, and I don't like the notion of you walking alone. There's a strange air about the place today.'

'I won't go far.' She peered into the metal plate Anna was holding up for her, wondering if she should thank her maid for informing her of her husband's plans. 'Has Katyja left?' she asked, nodding absent approval at her reflection.

'At dawn.' Anna laid the plate aside. 'Gunhild wasn't too happy about it. She seemed more upset about Katyja saying she came to see you than at losing her husband. I'd stay out of her way if I were you.'

'Don't concern yourself. I intend to. The last thing I need is to be told, yet again, that I'm not wanted here.'

'Er, no, my lady. I mean, there doesn't seem to be anything for you to do. Ingerd insisted on preparing Egil for burial and no one is arguing with her.'

''Tis the last thing she can do for him, I suppose. And at least her grief seems genuine.' She turned. 'I've been meaning to ask you, Anna, how do you go on with Ingerd? She seems…strange.'

'Oh, she's a harmless old crone. She's so ancient the other slaves treat her with some respect, which pleases her. Of course she thinks she knows everything. She's been hinting all morning that Gunhild's rule will continue, despite the jarl's death.'

Yvaine shrugged. ''Tis only natural her loyalty is to Gunhild. And it matters not, so long as she's not unkind to you.'

'No, she's not unkind. And the others have been friendly. 'Tis surprising really, because they take their orders from Gunhild. Perhaps they don't agree with Ingerd's predictions and think to curry favour. After all, you'll be mistress here now.'

'Mayhap,' agreed Yvaine, but she didn't pursue the subject. The gossip and petty quarrels that went on amongst the women of a household had never interested her. Nor did she have any intention of taking

Gunhild's place until Rorik had arranged for his stepmother to live elsewhere. She'd learned all too well, at Selsey, that a household could have only one mistress.

'I'm going to walk down to the fjord again,' she said, rising. 'Don't worry, Anna. I'll stay within sight of the house. I might even meet Rorik on his way back.'

But when she entered the hall a few minutes later, she saw that her walk would have to wait. Gunhild was nowhere in sight, and the slaves were milling about, apparently having nothing better to do than glance towards the solar—where she could see Ingerd moving about—and give vent to loud lamentations.

Training and instinct took over. In less than a minute Yvaine had the slaves busy with preparations for the noon dinner—Rorik would just have to make do with something cold, she decided, when he didn't turn up for the meal. Once the remains were cleared away, work began with a vengeance. A house karl was directed to replenish the oil in the lamps; the floor was swept clear of scraps discarded by the dogs; the two centre chairs rubbed until the wood gleamed. She even had the huge shield hanging over Egil's chair taken down and polished so the gold and jewels flashed and glittered in the lamp-light.

So fascinated was she with the shield, with its painted images of gods and heroes, that by the time she thought to take her walk, the sun was more than halfway between its apex and the peaks of the western mountain range.

No matter, she thought, escaping from the hall at last and starting down the path leading to the fjord. At this time of year the light lasted for hours, and she'd been inside all day. She needed fresh air, and solitude.

But solitude was not to be granted her. The first person she saw as she crossed the meadow was Gunhild. The woman was standing alone by the pier, watching her.

Telling herself she could hardly turn around and go off in the opposite direction, Yvaine summoned a sympathetic smile.

'I suppose I should thank you,' Gunhild said without preamble as she approached. 'Ingerd tells me you've kept the slaves from idle chatter all day.'

'It seemed the sensible thing to do,' Yvaine responded, wondering when Ingerd had spoken to her mistress.

'Oh, I wasn't criticising.' Gunhild's lips pursed in a tight smile. 'I'm grateful. I couldn't stay in there a moment longer this morning. All that weeping and wringing of hands.'

Sympathy flickered. So, too, did a touch of guilt. Had she misjudged Gunhild? Had the woman merely reacted with spite to the threat of displacement before rational thought had reasserted itself?

'Would you like to walk with me, Gunhild?' she asked on impulse. ''Tis pleasant out here, and peaceful.' She glanced about, suddenly realising just how peaceful it was. 'Where are all the men?'

'At the burial mound, with the rest of the family. I've just come from there.' Gunhild watched her closely, as though awaiting some response. When none was forthcoming, she turned and gestured in the direction Yvaine had been heading. 'The bathhouse lies this way. Have you seen it?'

'No.' Yvaine fell into step beside her, telling herself she would not feel excluded. She'd had better things to do than stand around all day watching men dig a hole in the ground. Even if the rest of the family had been there. 'You have a house especially for baths?'

'I'm surprised Rorik hasn't shown it to you.' Gunhild sent her another prim-lipped little smile. 'A hot bath can be soothing. Although you appear to be walking a little easier today.'

Yvaine kept her face impassive.

'No doubt the very brief demands he made on you last night helped in that respect. You must be thankful, since you were wed only for convenience.'

So Rorik had entered their bedchamber last night; had stood there, watching her sleep. Why hadn't he stayed?

'I see no convenience for Rorik,' she answered, determined not to let Gunhild see that her barbs, if barbs were intended, had struck home.

'That's because you're ignorant of our ways.' Gunhild indicated a fork in the path that veered uphill, away from the fjord. They started climbing. 'You were virtuous, I admit it. And to lie with a virgin gives a warrior strength and protection in battle.'

'Rorik didn't need to marry me to take me to his bed.'

'No,' agreed Gunhild slowly. 'He didn't.' She sent Yvaine a quick sidelong glance, then gestured to a small wooden building that stood to the side of the path. 'But here we are. As you see, we're not far from the fjord, so water can be easily fetched.'

Metal clinked as Gunhild drew up the chain hanging from her left-hand brooch and selected a key. She inserted it into the lock on the door and turned it.

'We keep the bathhouse locked to discourage the karls and slaves from using it as a trysting place,' she explained, pushing the door open. ''Tis a secluded spot.'

It was indeed. Yvaine glanced around. The light was much dimmer here, beneath the trees. The breeze whispered through the pines like the sighs of departing souls; leaves rustled in the undergrowth as some small creature fled from the sound of their voices. She remembered telling Anna that she would stay within sight of the house.

Still, it was less than a minute's walk from the main buildings if one took a direct route through the forest. A[illegible] wasn't alone.

[illegible]rugging off the strange feeling of unease that had come over her, she followed Gunhild over the threshold. And was instantly entranced.

The room was larger than she'd thought, and made snug with furs hanging from the walls and heaped on a bench set to one side. A firepit, laid with kindling, was placed at an angle to the bench, creating a cosy corner. Cauldrons, already filled with water, hung on tripods above it. But it was the tub, just above waist-height and occupying most of the remaining space, that held her bemused gaze. It looked big enough to accommodate the entire household.

'Saints above,' she exclaimed. 'You could swim in it.'

'Not quite.' Gunhild bent to strike a flint and hold the flame to the kindling. 'Would you like a bath?' she asked, straightening. 'You probably feel covered in dust after working all day. I'll send a slave with drying cloths, and to haul more water.'

Yvaine considered the offer. Gunhild was being positively helpful. It didn't quite ring true, but she could see no point in challenging the woman. Gunhild could well have thought twice about antagonising the new mistress of Einervik. And a hot bath sounded wonderful.

'Thank you, Gunhild. Would you send Anna, too, with clean clothes? I appreciate the thought.'

''Tis nought.' Gunhild gave her that tight-lipped little smile again. 'You'll have plenty of time before the men return, so don't hurry. A burial mound takes some digging, since it needs to be large enough to take a ship and Egil's horse and dogs. They'll be kil[illegible] graveside.'

Yvaine repressed a shudder. She knew from [illegible] Norse sagas that a wealthy man was buried with his weapons and other amenities, sometimes even slave girls, to provide comfort for the afterlife, but foreknowledge didn't lessen the impact of Gunhild's statement.

Was the woman hoping she'd shame herself by causing a scene at the funeral? she wondered, as Gunhild gave her a brisk nod and departed. Though she seemed more amenable, most of her remarks had had an edge to them.

Perhaps she was merely tactless, Yvaine thought, trying to be charitable. Then turned her head sharply as an odd little snick sounded. 'Gunhild?'

No answer.

Heart pounding, she rushed over to the door, seized the latch and tugged. It didn't move. She stared at it in disbelief then, realising what had happened, sprang for the small window beside the door.

But when she finally got the shutter open, fumbling in her haste, only the empty forest met her gaze.

'Oh, *stupid*!' She slumped against the wall, cursing herself for being so easily tricked. But at least her fear of being locked in, hidden from the world, had abated at the affirmation, seen beyond the window, that there was a world out there.

Nor was she helpless. The window was too small to climb through, but if Gunhild didn't send slaves as promised, she'd shout until someone heard her.

Indeed, Gunhild would know that, she thought, frowning. If she'd been locked in by intent, surely she wouldn't have been left free to call for help? Also, Rorik would start asking questions if she didn't turn up by nightfall.

Yvaine shook her head. She'd become so used to being on guard against malice, she'd panicked without cause. Gunhild had probably locked the door from habit. Or to ensure she had privacy in case she hopped into the bath before anyone other than Anna arrived.

Taking a steadying breath, she straightened and began wandering around the room, pausing when she discovered a trio of oil lamps on spikes in the corner opposite the firepit. That answered the question of how people could see to wash themselves in the middle of winter, when they'd hardly leave the door and window open.

She was about to cross to the fire, to search out a burning twig to light the lamps, when the key rattled again in the lock. She turned, a smile of greeting on her lips.

It winked out the instant Othar strolled into the room.

'What are you doing here?' she demanded at once, and could have kicked herself when her voice shook. She reached out and gripped the edge of the tub. There was no need to panic. Anna would be here at any moment.

Othar grinned and kicked the door shut behind him. The movement made him stagger slightly. 'Rorik ordered me to clean up before the funeral feast tomorrow.' He stuck his thumbs in his belt and rocked back on his heels. 'I didn't expect to have company, but since you're here…'

'But you must have known.' Yvaine frowned, not sure if Othar *had* known the bathhouse was occupied. Perhaps Gunhild wasn't the only one with a key. Perhaps Othar had come straight from the burial mound. He certainly needed a bath; she could smell the sour ale on him from where she stood.

'Then I'll leave you to bathe,' she said as calmly as she could. Forcing herself to relinquish her grip on the tub, she took a step forward.

Othar stayed where he was.

'Please let me pass, Othar. If Rorik finds you here—'

'Afraid he'll divorce you? Don't be. If you please me, I'll look after you.'

'I'll pretend I didn't hear that,' she said sternly. 'Now—'

He took a step forward.

Yvaine sent one quick glance towards the door, then retreated, her mind racing as she tried to think of a way out. If she could get Othar to follow her, perhaps she could make a dash for freedom once he was on the far side of the tub. He hadn't locked the door, and the ale in him might slow him down.

Or it could make him more vicious. Perhaps she'd be wiser to keep a solid object between them.

Wild visions of being chased around the tub until someone came to her rescue flashed through her mind. She took another step—and felt ice spill through her veins as her foot came up hard against another solid object. She was trapped.

She glanced down. Three wooden steps, obviously intended to facilitate climbing into the tub, barred her path. On the other side of the steps, a wide conduit led from the tub to a hole in the wall.

'Don't bother trying to jump the steps and the drain in those long skirts,' Othar advised. 'You might hurt yourself.'

'You'll be the one hurt if you don't get out of here,' Yvaine warned. 'Anna and a couple of slaves are on their way.'

His smile was enough to make her doubt that last statement. She immediately seized the more likely threat. 'Then what of Rorik? You're mad if you think—'

'Don't you say that!' he yelled. 'Don't you ever say that!'

He sprang forward, anticipation turning to rage so swiftly, Yvaine had no time to dodge before Othar seized her arm. At the same moment, a branch in the firepit burst into flames, lighting his face from below with a reddish glow that turned his expression demonic.

She screamed as he yanked her against him. 'I'll show you,' he snarled. 'I'll show you I'm a man and not the boy everyone thinks me.'

Her stomach roiled as the stench of sour ale struck her face, but his words restored reason. She was facing a human fiend, not a supernatural one. It was human force trying to turn her, to pin her against the tub. She screamed again, this time more in rage than fear. She got her hands up, wedged her fists against his chest, and was just drawing breath for another scream, when the door slammed open.

Rorik strode into the boathouse, seized Othar by the collar of his tunic and seemingly with nothing more than a flick of his wrist hurled his brother through the open doorway.

Yvaine watched in awe as Othar skidded on his side through a carpet of pine needles and crashed into a tree. She'd known Rorik was powerful, but the strength needed to send a man almost as tall as himself tumbling and threshing helplessly across the ground was terrifying. She gazed up at him, unable to control the fine shivering that seized her limbs.

'Did Othar touch you?' he demanded, every word edged with ice.

'Not…not the way you mean.'

'But he was going to.'

When she didn't answer, he turned and advanced on his brother.

Yvaine got one brief glimpse of the murderous fury on his face and dashed after him. 'No! Don't kill him. He's drunk, I think.'

'Drunk or sober, he knows better than to intrude on my wife in the bathhouse.'

'She asked me to meet her here,' Othar yelled, stumbling to his feet. 'She planned it. To escape from you.'

Yvaine gaped at him in horror. She'd all but forgotten the vague plans she'd made on the ship to enlist Othar's help. Now she felt memory stamp itself on her face in a rush of guilty colour. 'No! Gunhild locked me in.' She turned to Rorik, knowing she was babbling but terrified he wouldn't believe her. 'I don't know how Othar got the key…mayhap they're scattered all over the place, but…'

A sharp movement of his hand cut her off.

'I know enough of my wife to know you're lying, Othar,' he said still in that chillingly level tone. 'I'll have no man here I can't trust. Drunk or not, you've run wild long enough. After the funeral tomorrow, you will leave Einervik until you learn how to behave.'

'Leave?' Othar's eyes widened. 'You're banishing me? You can't do that.'

'I have done it. Now get out of my sight, before I forget you're my younger brother and give you the thrashing you deserve.'

'But—'

'Move!'

Othar staggered back, his mouth opening and closing. 'We'll see about this,' he got out before lurching away through the forest.

Yvaine didn't watch him go. Her entire attention was on Rorik. He turned, pinned her gaze with his, and started forward.

The implacable purpose in his eyes had the strength draining from her limbs in a heartbeat. 'Rorik…'

'Don't stop me.'

Her eyes went wide. Her heart bounded into her throat, its frantic beat racing faster with every step he took. He reached her, wrapped his big hands around her shoulders and drew her against him. She gasped as their bodies touched. He was rigid, hard all over. Sensation after sensation rioted through her. Before she could sort them out, his mouth came down on hers.

He kissed her as if he hungered, as if he craved. Every instinct she possessed longed to satisfy that hunger, appease his craving.

'I have to do this,' he said hoarsely between kisses. 'I can't stand to see another man's hands on you, when I—' He shuddered, held her tighter. 'I have to know you're mine. *Mine.* Yvaine.'

Her eyes widened in the second before he started kissing her again. Had that been desperation in his voice? How could she tell when her senses were reeling? When he was holding her locked against him so that she didn't know who was shaking, whose heart was racing; knew only that the world could have exploded around them and his hold wouldn't have slackened.

'Release me from my promise,' he said against her mouth. 'I need you…need you…'

She tried to answer, couldn't. He was kissing her too desperately. She couldn't even think. She made a small, frantic sound and he drew back; enough to give her air at least, to tremble at the desire blazing in his eyes. The full force of his will washed over her in a wave of fierce demand, yet she wasn't afraid. This was right. This was the moment.

'Rorik…'

'Do you trust me not to hurt you?' he asked, every word sounding as though it was torn from him.

When she nodded, he swept her close again, his face buried in her hair. 'Then let that be enough,' he groaned. 'Please let that be enough for now.'

'Aye,' she whispered. And lifted a hand to his cheek. ''Tis enough, Rorik.'

He held her a moment longer, shudders racking his powerful body. Then with an almost agonized sound of yearning, he picked her up and carried her into the bathhouse.

Firelight flickered, sending showers dancing across the walls, as he stood her beside the bench. He stepped away once, to wrench the key from the lock, slam the door and lock it. Then he was back, his hands going to the brooches holding her outer garment in place.

Yvaine trembled as she watched him. His eyes were narrowed, wholly focused on the task of releasing the clasps, of lifting the woollen garment from her and tossing it aside. Desire drew the lines of his face taut, but she sensed the fierce control he had over himself. When he loosened the neck of her shift, it was she who pushed the sleeves down, letting the soft linen slip to the floor, she who reached to unfasten the ties of her undershift. He would not merely take. She would give.

But shyness intruded. Her hands fumbled on the ties. She had never stood before a man, naked. And he was still fully clothed.

She looked up, uncertain, and understanding gentled his face. Holding her gaze, he stripped off his tunic and undershirt in one swift movement and reached for her.

Yvaine gasped as his hands encircled her waist, gasped again when he drew her against him. Her flimsy undershift was no barrier at all to the heat, the exciting friction of hair-roughened muscle against her softer flesh. The assault on her senses was almost too much. She whimpered and he held her tighter, bending his head to hers.

'I went to the house,' he said hoarsely, his mouth buried in her hair. 'You weren't there.'

'No.' She frowned, struggled free of the drugging pleasure of being in his arms. A strange, elusive awareness teased the back of her mind, that there was more here than mere desire.

But the thought slipped away. Reason was impossible when he held her like this, while his hands moved over her with barely restrained urgency, caressing, possessing. Need rose, the need to mate with him, to be one with him. Love welled, filling her heart until it eclipsed all else. She was his. It was as simple as that.

'I was here,' she answered softly. 'I knew you'd come.'

'Always.' He drew back, his heart pounding against her breast as he lifted her off her feet, holding her with one arm while he tossed the bench furs on to the floor. For an instant the room swung dizzily, then he laid her gently on the makeshift bed, quickly stripped off his remaining garments and came down beside her.

'Always,' he repeated, and slowly drew her undershift away.

Apprehension washed over her, just for a moment as he leant over her. He was big, incredibly powerful. The muscles beneath her hands were like tempered steel, but suddenly she realised he was shaking. His skin burned as though he was in the grip of fever. She was helpless against his much greater strength, but as his gaze followed the firelight flickering over her body, she saw that against his need of her, so too, was he. In their private world of passion, vulnerability was shared; they both held power here.

The knowledge enthralled her, but then he made a rough sound in his throat, covered her breast with his hand, and excitement shivered through her on a ripple of heat.

'I've ached to see you again like this,' he said very low. 'To touch you like this. To know you in every way there is.'

She turned her face into his shoulder. 'I ache, too,' she whispered. 'Somewhere inside. 'Tis the strangest feeling.'

The soft confession drew a groan from him. Holding her close, he stroked his hand down her body until his fingers tangled in the honey-gold curls between her legs. 'Here?' he asked, and, parting the soft folds, touched her with exquisite care.

She cried out, arching into his touch. Her head fell back, and with an almost savage sound of triumph he covered her mouth with his.

She expected a swift possession; tried to brace herself for it. Instead he kissed her with heart-shaking tenderness, until she was responding without thought. Caressed her until she was almost insensate with need. Only when she was moving helplessly beneath him, breathless little cries breaking from her throat, did he move to cover her body with his.

He framed her face between his hands, holding her still for his gaze as he began to enter her. Her breath caught at the blazing intensity in his eyes, at the sheer intimacy of the act. Firelight flickered, sending light and shadow chasing over him with every slow thrust of his body. There was pain; she'd expected it. Despite his promise, he was too big not to hurt her this first time. But, oh, the wonder of feeling him become part of her, the wild excitement of being held captive beneath him, the sheer delight of giving. Sweet, honeyed weakness invaded every limb, softening muscles that had tensed, easing the burning sensation as he pushed deeper, until he was seated to the hilt, until all she could feel was him, his hand clamping her lower body to his until she wondered that their very bones didn't meld.

She felt her inner flesh quiver around him and cried out as indescribable pleasure speared through her.

'Gods,' he groaned. 'Don't do that.'

He raised himself on one forearm, easing some of his weight from her. He saw her eyes widen as the shift pressed him impossibly deeper, and possessiveness flared, warring with needs that were just this side of violent. He was almost afraid to move, afraid he'd lose control. She made him feel all powerful, yet terrifyingly vulnerable. The conqueror triumphant; a supplicant at her feet.

'Are you all right?' he asked, and barely recognised the hoarse sound of his voice.

She nodded. At least, she thought she did. How could she tell when she was stretched on a rack of unbearable anticipation? He seemed to understand for he began to move, slowly at first, and then with a power that swept her beyond thought, beyond awareness of anything but the two of them, enveloped by firelight, moving as one.

Trembling became tension, coiling tighter and tighter. Her heart felt like a tiny battering ram, hammering against her ribs until she wondered why it simply didn't burst under the assault. Her body arched, wanting, needing. Oh, the need… She closed her eyes, clinging to him, unaware that the frantic sounds she was making threatened to drive him to madness. He slid his hand between their bodies, pressed his fingers to the point where they joined, and suddenly the tension exploded. Her body clenched and released, flooding her with sensations she could never have imagined. Indescribable pleasure; the sweetest madness.

She felt him go rigid, felt the harsh groan that tore from his throat, and with a helpless little sob, yielded control of her senses to him, surrendered utterly to the waves of ecstasy washing over her. Until there was nothing but peace, and the gentle heat of the fire, and Rorik holding her as if he'd never let her go.

Soft, trusting, she lay in his arms.

He watched her as she dozed. She had surrendered with such sweet abandon, had rendered herself so open and vulnerable at the moment of completion, he'd all but lost his mind, had been taken to the very edge of consciousness by the force of his release.

It should have been enough.

It wasn't.

He frowned into the shadows beyond the firelight, fighting the urge to hold Yvaine closer, to wake her, as though in sleep she might drift away from him. He wanted her again, would always want her, but it was more than desire that prowled just beyond his understanding. More even than the need to protect her. It was as if some part of him was missing. And she was that part.

She could bring him to his knees.

He shook his head sharply, and as though she sensed the sudden tension in him, her lashes fluttered open. She looked up at him. And smiled.

A velvet-covered fist slammed straight into his heart. Her smile held such sweet, shy, feminine knowledge that, had he been standing, he would, indeed, have fallen to his knees.

He bent his head and buried his face in her hair. He, who had never before hidden from anything or anyone in his life. 'Sweet sorceress,' he growled beneath his breath. 'What is it about you?'

He felt her fingers touch his shoulder, a caress too swiftly gone. 'Rorik?'

The uncertainty in her voice brought him back. She wasn't responsible for the turmoil within him. At least, not intentionally. After her first time with a man, she needed petting and reassurance, not a husband who was suddenly groping about in the dark cavern that had become his mind.

He lifted his head. 'Now you're my wife in every way.'

Well, that was certainly reassuring. A blunt statement of possession.

But she made a humming sound of agreement in her throat that brought his body to instant readiness. He leashed the need to simply spread her legs and take her. The faint tell-tale stain on her inner thigh told him it was too soon for that. Oh, he'd pleasure her again, he'd bind her to him with every physical chain he could think of, but his own needs could wait until she'd healed.

'I hurt you,' he murmured, touching his fingers to the stain. 'I'm sorry.'

An echo of pleasure shimmered through Yvaine at his touch. 'Only for a moment.'

He bent to kiss the curve of her shoulder. ''Twill be easier next time. *Elskling min.*'

The last was said so low she barely caught the words, was too distracted by the heat of his body as he leaned over her, the tender note in his voice, the nibbling little kisses that moved up her throat. Had he said 'my darling'? She couldn't be sure. It was all mixed up with her own feelings, with trying to fathom his. So much had happened; impressions tumbled on top of each other, overwhelming her.

But hope was strong.

'Fortunately,' he went on in that soft murmur, 'we have the means to ease the hurt right here to hand.'

She blinked, trying to keep up with him. 'We do?'

His mouth curved against her ear. 'The bath. I presume that's why you came here.'

'Well, aye, but...' She shivered as he tasted the tip of her ear, then memory rushed back. 'Rorik, you don't believe—?'

'No, never.' He lifted his head, suddenly intent, and framed her face between his hands. 'I would never doubt your honour, Yvaine. But...for your own safety, don't come here alone. At least, not until Othar has left Einervik.'

'I won't, but, Rorik, Gunhild was with me.'

'Gunhild?' His eyes narrowed, and she realised his rage at finding Othar in the bathhouse with her had deafened him to her earlier explanation.

'Aye. She promised to send Anna and some slaves, then locked me in. Mayhap Othar has another key, but…'

'He'd have no need for one,' he interrupted. 'The place is never locked. There's a key for privacy if needed, but it hangs on a hook beside the door.'

'Oh.' She frowned, not wishing to be the bearer of tales, but puzzled. 'Gunhild told me 'twas always kept locked to prevent the slaves from using it as, uh, a trysting place.'

That brought his smile back. 'Aye, she may have caught a couple here when they should have been about their work. I'll question her about it. However—' He glanced over at the wisps of steam rising from the cauldrons hanging over the fire, then looked back at her. His smile turned wicked. 'Since we're here, and since the water is now warm…'

Yvaine had to laugh, happiness bubbling up inside her at his quick change of mood even as she measured the cauldrons with a doubtful eye. 'If you mean for us to bathe, I think we'll need more than three loads to fill that tub.'

The gleam in his eyes was suddenly very male, and utterly sure. 'Trust me,' he murmured, bending to brush her lips with his. 'There'll be plenty for what I have in mind.'

Chapter Eleven

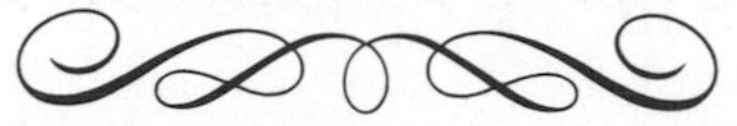

Gunhild claimed to have passed the key to Othar when she'd met him on her way back to the house, with instructions to give it to Anna, because a minor accident, requiring her presence, had occurred in the dairy. She had been all polite apologies for the trouble Othar had caused. Aye, he certainly needed to realise that boyish mischief, fuelled by too much ale, would not be tolerated.

It had all sounded eminently reasonable when the matter had been broached on their return to the house last night. And Yvaine hadn't believed a word of it.

She was still brooding over the tale the following morning as she watched the slaves set up trestles for the funeral feast. Unfortunately, she was fast coming to the conclusion that she had to let the matter rest. Without evidence that there was more to Othar's invasion of the bathhouse than a moment of misguided mischief, any expression of disbelief in Gunhild's story would make her look foolish, or worse, a troublemaker. Rorik might be patient with her doubts, but what could he do about suspicions that were so vague she couldn't even explain them to herself?

No. Better to stay silent and make sure she was never alone with Gunhild or Othar again. It wouldn't be difficult. They would be gone in a day or two, and besides, she had sweeter memories to savour: memories of the fierce restraint with which Rorik had taken her, of sensations beyond belief, his tenderness afterwards. And then the playfulness he'd shown her in the tub.

He'd been right, she thought, with a secret smile. There had been plenty of water for what he'd had in mind. She was still wondering at the pleasure that could be wrought upon her senses in a few inches of the stuff. Saints! A week ago she wouldn't have thought herself capable of frolicking, naked, in a tub with a man, let alone surrendering the secrets of her body to him with such wanton delight. There hadn't been an inch of her Rorik hadn't kissed or touched. And then, later, when they'd returned to the house and retired, he'd held her in his arms while they'd slept.

She gave a little skip of happiness, hugging herself as anticipation welled inside her. Then glanced around the hall to make sure no one had noticed. Really. She was supposed to be supervising the few slaves who had remained behind to prepare the funeral feast. At least, that was the reason Rorik had given, when, knowing parts of the ceremony would distress her, he'd stopped her attending Egil's burial.

His care for her made her feel warm inside. Even cherished, she thought, as she wandered over to the jarl's chair under the guise of straightening the trestle in front of it. Rorik might be driven only by desire at present, but the future was suddenly bright and full of promise. As glittering as the jewels decorating the great shield above her.

She looked up at it, remembering the excuse she'd given for accompanying Rorik to Norway without an argument, that of replacing her manuscripts. The purpose was still valid, she mused. When everything was settled, she would ask Rorik to procure some quills and vellum for her so she could start—

'You seem fascinated by Ragnarök, dear sister,' murmured a smooth voice behind her. 'Praying for the Doom of the Gods, no doubt.'

Yvaine turned quickly, startled both by Othar's approach and his mode of address—although, by Norse law, she supposed she was his sister. The notion didn't comfort her. Her mood of happy anticipation took a slight dip.

'You Norse believe it will come,' she answered warily, glancing past him to make sure the slaves were still in the room, 'since your gods are not immortal.'

'As you say.' He looked up at the shield and nodded. 'There on the left you see Odin being eaten by the wolf Fenrir, while below him Thor wrestles the serpent Midgarthsorm who will rise from the sea to do battle. He defeats the serpent, but dies from its venom. A useful lesson in that, perhaps, sister.'

'And on the right?' Yvaine asked evenly.

'Ah. There we see a happier outcome. The hero Sigurd slays the dragon Fafnir. After drinking its blood he understands the language of the birds, and they tell him where to find the dragon's gold.'

'Hmm. Most interesting. Well, if you'll excuse me, Othar, I must see how the preparations for the feast are progressing. If everyone has returned—'

'Oh, I left the burial ground early. No need to watch them throw dirt on the old man. He never liked me, anyway.'

The words were tossed out carelessly, like pebbles into a pond, but Othar's tone was bitter. Yvaine had a sudden vision of that bitterness rippling outward, consuming every other emotion.

'I'm sorry,' she said awkwardly. 'That must have made you…unhappy.'

'Aye, you understand, don't you?' He seized her arm, his eyes gleaming with a kind of feverish avidity that had both pity and revulsion roiling within her. But when she tried to free herself, temper flashed. 'I didn't want to hurt you yesterday,' he muttered. ''Twas your own fault.'

'Then loose my wrist,' she ordered, as though to a child on the verge of anger. His touch made her skin crawl, and yet she did understand his bitterness. On the other hand, that didn't mean she had to put up with a bruised arm. 'We have guests coming. I must return to my duties.'

For a moment she thought Othar might use his advantage of superior strength to detain her. His fingers tightened painfully, then he released her and stepped back.

'Rorik might think he's banished me,' he said, his face falling into its usual sullen lines. 'But he'll soon learn his mistake. You'll be mine. It will all be mine.'

He wheeled about and almost collided with Ingerd, who had come in unnoticed by either of them. The old crone waved a gnarled finger at him. 'Woe to the man who would steal his brother's wife,' she shrilled.

'Out of my way, you old bag of bones,' snarled Othar, shoving her aside.

Ingerd lurched to the edge of the platform, screeching in terror as she saw the fire below her. She grabbed for Othar, but he was already past her, storming towards the group of slaves who scattered like terrified mice at his approach. Ingerd's foot slipped over the edge of the platform. Arms flailing, she swayed towards the glowing stones on the hearth.

Yvaine sprang forward, seized a handful of Ingerd's clothing and tugged with all her strength. Her action sent them both crashing to the floor, but at a safe distance from the fire.

She sat up, waving the other women back to their work as they scurried forward to help. 'We're all right. At least—' she searched Ingerd for signs of smouldering clothes '—are you hurt, Ingerd?'

The old woman ceased her lamentations at finding herself in such an undignified position. 'My foot touched the fire,' she whimpered. 'It hurts.'

'Let me see.' She pushed Ingerd's skirts up an inch or two and eased her soft skin shoe off. 'There. 'Tis as I thought. The shoe protected you. See, your foot is only a little reddened, but stay off it for the rest of the day if you wish.'

She got to her feet and bent to help Ingerd on to the bench. 'I think you should rest here awhile in any event. You've had a bad fright.' She hesitated. 'I don't think Othar meant—'

'Hah!'

The exclamation came with such strength, Yvaine blinked in surprise. Ingerd immediately cast a quick glance about the hall, her voice lowering to its usual soft whine. 'You're kind, Rorik's wife. I'll warn you. Why should that young wastrel have it all his own way?'

She drew closer, wrapping bony fingers around Yvaine's arm. 'Did you see his eyes?' she hissed. 'Take care, girl. He spoke of madness, but I thought he was raving. The rest was true. I knew at the time there was something going on that morning, though we slaves had been sent out to the fields. Had to get the harvest in quickly, or some such excuse. But the madness… I never saw such a curse in Egil, nor in his father and grandfather before him.'

'You've been here that long, Ingerd?' Yvaine drew the old woman over to the bench, quelling an urge to prise the clutching fingers from her arm.

'Aye, that long. I'm old, girl, very old. And always a slave. 'Twas always "Ingerd, do this" or "Let Ingerd do it". But not for much longer.'

She glared at Yvaine with sudden malice and leaned closer. 'Why should you be free, English girl, because Rorik wanted you? He's not like his grandfather, though. Eirik the Just they called him, but what justice did I have once he'd taken his pleasure of me?'

The question was a little too apt for comfort. Yvaine banished the thought of her probable fate if Rorik hadn't married her. 'Men don't always understand what we women consider important,' she murmured. 'I'll speak to Rorik, Ingerd. I'm sure after all these years of service—'

'No! You don't understand.' Ingerd shook Yvaine's arm. 'Gunhild says I'm going to be free. I told her everything last night, you see. I thought about it all day and decided she was the one. But the boy…I didn't think about the boy…'

The old woman cast another nervous glance over her shoulder as voices sounded in the entrance passage, then leaned forward to hiss in Yvaine's ear. 'Listen well, Rorik's lady. I don't trust Othar, and Gunhild's his mother when all's said and done. If ought befalls me, seek out Thorkill. He was here that day. He knows the truth.'

'If ought… Truth?' She drew back. 'Ingerd, what are you talking about?'

But Ingerd looked around, cringing as she saw Gunhild approach. She released Yvaine's arm and rose, scuttling away from the bench like a small, startled crab.

Gunhild's eyes narrowed. 'I thought you were supposed to be watching for the men to return, Ingerd.'

'I thought they had, Gunhild.' Ingerd sidled towards the door. 'But I'll watch. Oh, aye…I'll watch…'

Cackling, she scurried out of the hall.

Gunhild raised her brows. 'Is it my fancy,' she asked Yvaine, 'or is Ingerd more than normally doltish today?'

'Ingerd had a bad fright, Gunhild. She almost fell into the fire.'

'Hmph. The old fool's getting past her usefulness. Now—' She turned to her slaves.

Yvaine decided to retire to her bedchamber until Rorik returned. Gunhild's callous remark, coming on top of Ingerd's raving, had unease creeping back. She'd thought Ingerd's warning had been meant for her, but did the old woman expect herself to become the victim of some nameless threat? If so, what could the unknown Thorkill do about it? Ingerd had said seek out Thorkill *if* something happened. In other words, afterwards. Where was the sense in that?

The funeral feast was almost over before Yvaine realised that Ingerd was not at her usual place on the women's bench. The discovery gave her such a jolt, she forgot her fascination with observing Rorik in a more formal setting.

That was one thing about being relegated to the women's bench in this all-male company. She'd been able to watch him to her heart's content, listening as one man after another roared out a tale of Egil's deeds—or misdeeds—that had the company laughing or yelling approval.

But now, as the slaves cleared the trestles away and the guests began to look about for cloaks and caps, she tried to recall seeing Ingerd during the meal and could not.

She slid a sideways glance at Gunhild, who seemed not to have noticed that her guests, although perfectly friendly to Yvaine, had paid her scant attention. Instead, she was smiling.

Yvaine shivered. It was strange how a smile could look so threatening. Especially when she could see no threat. Ingerd had been shaken by her fall and had probably retired to her loft in one of the storage *burs*. As soon as she was free of the hall, she'd check on the old woman and take her something to eat. It wouldn't be long. Already some of the guests were on their feet. The jarl sitting next to Rorik clapped him on the shoulder as he rose and spoke in a jovial tone that reached every corner of the hall.

'You'll have to take your place among us at the Allthing, Rorik, now that you've succeeded to Egil's chair. No more whiling away the summers raiding England.'

There was a short, embarrassed silence. Everyone very busily avoided looking at Yvaine.

Except Gunhild, who sent her a swift raking glance as if to say raiding England hadn't netted them much.

'You shouldn't be so hasty with your invitations, Hingvar,' she advised. 'Nor so quick in your assumptions. Rorik would do better to return to his raiding, than remain Jarl of Einervik.'

Several heads turned.

Rorik also looked at his stepmother. He seemed no more than mildly impatient at her intrusion into the conversation, but Othar, Yvaine noticed, was leaning forward, watching his mother with avid anticipation.

The food she'd just eaten dropped like a stone to the pit of her stomach. There was no reason for it, but she was suddenly braced, as though about to confront some unseen danger. When Rorik spoke into the hush that had fallen, she almost flinched.

'Why would I do that, Gunhild?'

Gunhild set her knife at a precise angle on her trencher and folded her hands. 'Because, Rorik, only a true-born son may inherit his father's chair.'

This time the silence fell like a pall. It was finally broken when Thorolf rose to his feet.

'What folly is this, Gunhild? You—'

Rorik silenced him with a gesture. He leaned forward, his eyes narrowed on his stepmother's face. 'Explain that statement, Gunhild. If you can.'

'Oh, I can, Rorik, but are you sure you wish your guests to hear such a tale of deceit as I shall tell?'

An elderly Norseman, his richly embroidered, fur-trimmed tunic proclaiming a jarl of some standing, also sat forward and spoke with authority. 'If there's any doubt in your mind, Gunhild, as to Rorik's right of inheritance, it must be stated before witnesses.'

'In fact, I insist on it.' Rorik rose and nodded to the man who had spoken. 'Ragnald, I'd like you and Hingvar to stay. I regret that I must ask the rest of you to leave,' he added, raising his voice to address the company at large. 'My thanks for honouring my father's memory and our house with your presence.'

Those guests still seated rose as one, hiding their curiosity behind polite faces. Gunhild ignored the speculative glances thrown her way and continued to sit, hands folded, a prim little smile on her lips. For all the world, Yvaine thought, like a cat that had got into the dairy.

She saw Anna pass her and realised the slaves, too, were being dismissed. On impulse, she caught the girl's hand. 'See if you can find Ingerd,' she whispered.

Anna nodded and followed the others, pulling the door shut behind her. Yvaine debated the wisdom of putting the length of the women's bench between herself and Gunhild against the risk of being noticed if she moved. She and Rorik might be closer physically, but, her earlier euphoria aside, she couldn't be sure that closeness would hold under these circumstances. And she had no intention of leaving. Whether he admitted it or not, he might need her.

He sat down again, exchanging a brief word with Thorolf, who had moved up the bench to sit next to him. Ragnald and Hingvar seated themselves opposite. Othar lounged at the other end of the room, a smile curling his lips.

'You may speak, Gunhild.' Rorik turned hard grey eyes on his stepmother. 'And I hope you have good reason for curtailing the hospitality of this house at such a time.'

'Oh, I think you'll find it very interesting, Rorik. I certainly did. It concerns your mother.'

Rorik frowned. 'What do you know of my mother? She died years before you came to Einervik.'

'True,' put in Ragnald sternly. 'Not only that, but when you married Egil there was no one here who even remembered Rorik's mother.'

'Except Ingerd,' Gunhild pointed out.

'If this is nothing more than women's gossip,' Hingvar grumbled, 'we don't wish to hear it.'

'Not gossip, my lord, but fact.' Gunhild rose and, facing the elderly jarls, clasped her hands in supplication. 'My lords, I appeal to you. A grave wrong has been done here, to me and to my son. 'Tis not Rorik who should inherit his father's chair this day, but Othar, who is legitimate. Rorik's mother was never married to Egil.'

'What?' exclaimed Thorolf.

Yvaine glanced quickly from him to the others. Rorik was watching his stepmother, his eyes narrowed. The two older jarls appeared thoughtful but not particularly perturbed. Othar still lounged at his ease, but his face gave him away. He was watching Rorik with a malicious gleam that sent ice sliding through her veins.

He knows, she thought. But how? Why didn't he say something yesterday when Rorik banished him?

'I see no need for all this drama,' Ragnald observed. 'A concubine's son is equal under the law and is entitled to a share of his father's estate.'

Hingvar nodded. 'Aye. What difference does it make if Rorik's mother was concubine or wife?'

'It makes this difference,' stated Gunhild, abandoning her pose of wronged widow. 'Othar should be Jarl of Einervik now. Not only that, but—'

'Hold! You go too fast, Gunhild.' Ragnald's bushy brows drew together. 'As far as I can see, you've only got the word of some old woman to verify a tale nigh on thirty years past. Did Egil say anything to you, Rorik, that might clarify your mother's position?'

'He never mentioned her,' Rorik said slowly. 'Until I brought my wife home. Then, 'twas only to say he'd cared for her.'

'Cared!' Gunhild glared at her. 'What did that unfeeling old man know of caring? He married me for the wealth I brought him, then tried to deny me a child.' Her lips curled back in a sneer. 'Now I know 'twas so his bastard son could inherit. And he used to speak of honour.'

'Egil believed in honour, Gunhild. Too much so to relate such a tale to a slave. If Ingerd knew my mother was a concubine, why didn't she say so earlier?'

'A good point,' Ragnald agreed. 'Egil wouldn't have spoken to a slave while his son remained ignorant. The woman is trying to cause mischief.'

'Egil was on his deathbed,' Gunhild insisted. 'For the brief time he spoke, Ingerd was alone with him. Then he fell senseless and remained so until he died. Ingerd was disturbed by what she'd learned and came straight to me, thinking, quite rightly, that I should be told.'

'And she didn't think I had that right?' Rorik asked sardonically.

'You have no rights,' she hissed, turning on him. 'Because your mother was not even a concubine. No! Egil couldn't maintain even that much propriety.' Her voice rose as she pointed an accusing finger at him. 'You're nothing but the son of a slave,' she shrilled. 'And worse! Your mother was not even Norse, but English. A captive such as your wife!'

Rorik shot to his feet. 'By the runes, Gunhild, you'd better have proof of this. You say Ingerd knows? Then let her be fetched.'

A timid knock sounded on the door as he spoke. For an instant no one moved. Then Thorolf rose, strode forward and yanked the door open.

Ingerd tottered into the room, supported by Anna.

The wave of relief that swept over Yvaine left her shaking. But what had she expected? Ingerd looked as if she'd been abruptly jerked from sleep, staring about as though unsure of her surroundings, but she was alive.

'Ah.' Gunhild crooked a finger. 'A happy chance, Ingerd. We were about to send for you.' She waved Anna off. 'We don't need you, girl. Return to your quarters.'

With a disdainful air that would have done credit to a Christian martyr, Anna ignored her. 'My lady?'

''Tis all right, Anna. You may wait in my bedchamber. Thank you for bringing Ingerd.'

She knew immediately that she shouldn't have spoken. Rorik's gaze flashed to her, his eyes so cold, so distant, her heart shuddered once, as if she was the one about to be interrogated.

'You, too, Yvaine. There's no need for you to witness this.'

'For once we are in agreement, Rorik.' Gunhild sent her a smug smile. 'But at least we know, now, why you married the wench. Like calls to like, does it not?'

Rorik ignored her and jerked his head from Yvaine to the door. 'Leave us.'

She stood. 'Rorik—'

'Leave us, damn it!'

'No,' she said very quietly. Keeping her gaze on his, she crossed the room to his side. 'You once said my place is with you. I'm your wife, and have a right to stay.'

Something fierce blazed in his eyes, only to be instantly extinguished by Ragnald's measured words.

'Your lady is right, Rorik. This concerns her. She may be English, but you married her by Norse law and if Gunhild's claim is true, Yvaine may wish to be free of the marriage.'

'No! I didn't mean—'

'Oh, I don't know, Ragnald.' Gunhild's harsh tones overrode her easily. 'They seem to be rather well-matched. Between them there is more English blood than Norse.'

A muscle flickered in Rorik's jaw. 'We're discussing my parentage, Gunhild, not my marriage.' He nodded at the woman now standing at Gunhild's side. 'Tell us what you know, Ingerd.'

The old slave turned shakily towards him. She appeared so frail, Yvaine wondered that the gentle draught from the window didn't knock her over. There was something *wrong* here, she thought. She could sense it, like a sound just out of hearing, a shadow just out of reach. But there was no time to search, to listen for that faint whisper. Ingerd was speaking, seeming to choose her words with care as a tale unfolded that closely mirrored Yvaine's own. Except in one crucial detail.

How ironic, she thought as she listened. Egil had claimed to care about Rorik's mother but he hadn't married her, had forced her to bear an illegitimate child. Rorik didn't love her, and yet—

'Do you think Egil was raving?' Ragnald demanded, drawing her attention back to him.

'No.' Ingerd shook her head. 'He knew me and asked if I remembered Alicia. Your mother, Rorik. He muttered about seeing the past repeated when you returned with your lady. But you were stronger, he said. You married Yvaine, whereas Alicia remained a thrall after he brought her from England, and he was shamed that he'd put family pride before her and you would suffer for it. So after—'

'Thank you, Ingerd. That's all we need to know.' Gunhild gestured smoothly, reclaiming everyone's attention. 'No doubt Egil did regret Rorik's position. A man on his deathbed will always think of things not done and mistakes made. However, my lords 'tis the future that concerns us now, and I will see my son in his rightful place.'

Hingvar sat back, looking worried. He and Ragnald consulted together in low tones. Rorik watched them. He hadn't moved, but Yvaine sensed the tension in him; that of a predator waiting to spring.

She caught Thorolf's eye. He was frowning, but he gave her a brief nod and motioned for her to sit on the long bench. After one glance at Rorik's stony profile, she complied.

Gunhild was bending solicitously over Ingerd. Yvaine frowned as she watched them. It was all wrong, she thought again. But how? *Why?*

'My lords.' Gunhild looked up from her quiet conversation with Ingerd. 'Of your kindness, allow me to dismiss my woman. She is old and frail and has endured much this day. If Rorik has any more questions they may be asked tomorrow.'

Rorik nodded before the other men could speak.

As she watched Ingerd shuffle from the hall, Yvaine had to stop herself running after the old woman. She wanted to question Ingerd *now*. The feeling that tomorrow might be too late was almost overwhelming, but she didn't want to leave Rorik. Surely a few hours would make little difference. Perhaps…

'Rorik.' Ragnald rose to his feet. 'Hingvar and I feel this matter is serious enough to be put before the court. I can't believe Egil would have left the succession so uncertain, and yet the slave, Ingerd, seems definite in what she says. It must be judged in the proper manner.'

'And in the meantime?' demanded Gunhild. ''Twill be nigh on a year before the law-speakers meet again at the Allthing. Is Othar to be kept waiting while this son of an English slave rules a Norse estate? Even Thorolf has a better claim.'

'Now look here, Gunhild—'

'Proper observance of the law must be made, Gunhild,' stated Ragnald, firmly interrupting Thorolf. 'Whatever Rorik's mother may have been, Egil acknowledged him as his son and he should share in the estate.'

'I have no intention of depriving Rorik of his share, my lords.'

Othar beamed as every head turned towards him. He waited, clearly savouring the moment, then stood up with lazy arrogance. 'No, Mother, let me speak,' he said as Gunhild opened her mouth. 'I'm as shocked as any of you to hear what my father has done, but Rorik isn't to blame. He'll always have a home here, and I hope he'll consider running the place for me.'

Rorik turned slowly. From where she sat, Yvaine couldn't see his expression, but the false smile slid from Othar's face. He took a step back.

Rorik shifted his gaze to Ragnald and Hingvar. 'There's no need to drag our private business through the courts,' he said quietly. 'And no need to waste any more of your time. Ingerd spoke the truth.'

'What!' Gunhild's voice rose to a shriek. 'You *knew*? And would have robbed my—'

'No.' His flat response cut off Gunhild in mid-screech. 'I knew nothing until a few minutes ago, but the things my father said to me on the day he died now make sense.' He drew in a long breath and Yvaine sensed the shudder that went through him. 'I believe Ingerd's story.'

'Well, if you're sure, Rorik,' Ragnald cast a doubtful glance at Othar and shook his head. 'I'm not certain this outcome is what Egil would have wanted.'

'Then he should have thought of that earlier,' Rorik snarled. He controlled himself almost immediately, but Yvaine saw his fists clench so tight the knuckles whitened.

Unable to bear the tension in him, she reached out and touched his hand. Without so much as a glance at her, he jerked away. 'My thanks for your time and forbearance, Ragnald. And yours, Hingvar. I'm sure you'll understand that we'd prefer to discuss anything further in private.'

'Of course, of course.' Hingvar, looking flustered, rose quickly and made for the door.

Ragnald followed, but paused on his way out, looking back. 'Don't decide anything hastily, Rorik. You're still your father's son. If you need advice or help, please come to me.'

The door closed on a heavy silence.

For several seconds, no one moved. Then Rorik stepped away from the jarl's chair and turned, and Yvaine saw his face for the first time.

Rage. Violent and barely controlled. But behind the fury in his eyes, she saw something that tore at her heart. She longed to go to him, to touch him—never mind that he'd rejected her comfort with a gesture that had stung like a slap—and knew this wasn't the time.

He looked at Othar and indicated his father's chair. 'Yours, I believe, brother.'

Othar came forward with alacrity. He flung himself into the chair and cast a satisfied glance around the hall. 'Well, I must say you're surprisingly calm about all this, Rorik. Are you sure you didn't know the truth? I mean, 'tis you who are at risk of banishment now, isn't it? I couldn't say so in front of Ragnald and Hingvar, of course, cautious old fools, but unless you're willing to continue raiding to contribute to the family coffers, you'll have to leave. We could live down your being a bastard, but your English blood is a bit much to take.'

'Aye, I can just see what the estate'll be worth with you in charge,' Thorolf retorted. 'You'll bleed it dry in less than a year. Something Egil knew well, I warrant. No wonder he stayed silent. As for banishing Rorik for something he can't help—'

'I'll banish whomever I please,' yelled Othar, jerking upright. 'And you'll be one of the first to go, Thorolf. You've always been against me, carrying tales to my father and getting me into trouble.'

'Thor! The suckling's run mad!'

'You and Rorik can both get out now,' Othar screamed. 'I've had enough of you.'

'No.' Yvaine rose, hardly aware of speaking. 'Egil didn't mean this to happen. There's something wrong.'

'What would you know, English slut?' Gunhild turned on her, her lips curling back in a sneer. 'Coming here from some tavern or gutter with your innocent looks and fawning ways. I should've—'

'Enough!' Rorik's command cut through his stepmother's tirade like an axe shredding silk. 'Yvaine might be married to a half-English bastard, but her blood is a damn sight better than yours, Lady of Einervik. She was cousin to King Alfred.'

'Indeed? Well, her royal blood won't be added to this family.' Hatred twisted Gunhild's face. 'Nor yours, bastard spawn of an English slave. You should have been killed long since in some raid.'

Rorik gave a short, mirthless laugh. 'So that's why you were so assiduous in wanting vengeance for Sitric. I sometimes wondered.'

'Don't mention that name to me,' shrieked Gunhild. 'He was another such as you. Arrogant, mocking, taking no account of what I brought to the family. Well—' with a vicious glance at Yvaine '—better to be married for money than for vengeance.'

'Vengeance?' Yvaine looked from Gunhild to Rorik. Pain, anger, every emotion she'd felt in the past hour suddenly coalesced into one thing. Fear. 'Rorik—'

'We'll talk later, Yvaine. Leave us now.'

'Why should she, Rorik? Have you lied to her as well? Poor girl. Doesn't she know 'twas her royal cousin who had Sitric put to death? Dear me, no, I can see she does not.'

Othar laughed, his good humour apparently restored by this turn of events. 'Don't fret, Mother. I'm sure we can find a suitable position for our little English slave. Preferably—'

He broke off with a startled yell as Rorik wheeled, grabbed Othar by the tunic and hauled him out of the chair.

Yvaine didn't wait to see more. Reeling from what she'd just heard, she dashed out of the hall and into her bedchamber. The sight of Anna, sitting on the clothes chest, brought her up short.

'I don't believe it,' Anna said at once.

Yvaine stared at her, fighting back tears. 'You heard?'

'The way they were all shouting in there? 'Twas difficult not to hear.' Anna rose and came forward to take her hand. 'My lady, don't take any notice of that spiteful Norse bitch. If Rorik's motive was vengeance he would've ruined you, not married you.'

'Perhaps he married me in a fit of conscience.' Yvaine swayed, and a small sound of pain parted her lips. 'Dear God. I don't know which is worse. Revenge or pity.'

'But, my lady, think. King Alfred has been dead these five years past. Why take revenge now?'

'Norse honour,' she whispered. 'Individuals don't matter. A wrong was done to Rorik's family by mine, and my cousin, Edward, still lives, so...' She stopped, then closed her eyes briefly as if to shut out the truth. 'Oh, Anna, 'tis all too likely Rorik's motive was vengeance. On the ship, he wanted to know about my family. I wondered at the time why he seemed so bitter whenever Alfred's name was mentioned. He must have realised as soon as he knew who—'

She broke off, staggering against the door as the truth struck home. The knowledge was like a knife-thrust to her heart; the pain stole her breath, would have doubled her over if Anna hadn't been there. Even then she had to snatch her hand free, clasp her arms across her body, to hold on, somehow, before she shattered. Shattered into a million shards, never to be whole again.

'Oh, God,' she whispered. 'He must have known the instant he saw the royal standard flying over Selsey.'

Anna frowned. 'There's something wrong with the reasoning, but I don't know what it is.' She studied her mistress's face. 'And you're in no fit state to think it through. Come and sit down, lady. God knows, you've been through enough today. But remember, so, too, has Rorik. What did you make of Ingerd's tale?'

'I don't know.' She knew Anna was trying to distract her, to give her time to gather herself. She wondered if she could do it. It was taking all her willpower to thrust pain into a dark corner of her mind where she wouldn't have to face it, wouldn't have to acknowledge it. Even then it prowled, a hungry predator, waiting for that one unguarded moment when it could reach out and rend her heart with vicious claws. She couldn't think and speak as well, while that fiercer battle waged within her, when the future she'd hoped for had been ripped from its still-fragile foundation.

'Do you think Ingerd spoke the truth?' Anna persisted.

'Rorik believed her.' Holy Mother, had he really kept her for revenge once he'd learned who she was? The fact that he'd married her made no difference. As far as Edward was concerned, she would be ruined, except—

Edward didn't know who had taken her.

A tiny seed of hope stirred. Like the first small bud of spring, tentative, vulnerable, afraid to burst through the still-cold ground, but compelled by a force that bade it grasp its chance at life, and hold on.

She sat up straighter, loosened the tight grip on herself.

Think.

Ingerd. Rorik's mother. The truth of his birth. He'd lost everything, she realised. If Ingerd had told the truth, he'd lost his home, his name, the very foundation on which his life had been based. And yet…

'There's something missing,' she murmured. 'I sensed it before, but thought 'twas because Ingerd had got the tale wrong somehow.'

Anna frowned. 'Something missing? What?'

'I'm not sure. But I know one thing, Anna. Egil didn't mean for this to happen. He was so proud of Rorik. I think...I think he even *cared* about him. At least, as much as these Norsemen seem to care about anyone. If he told Ingerd the truth, there must be more.'

'Then why didn't she say so? You'd think—'

'Because Gunhild stopped her,' Yvaine said slowly. And in her mind's eye, she saw, again, Gunhild bending over Ingerd, her attitude one of solicitous concern that had rung entirely false.

'Anna, I think we should find Ingerd and—'

She stopped, thought suspended, as a noise she'd been vaguely aware of for the past few seconds, suddenly increased in volume. Awareness flashed into Anna's eyes at the same moment.

Screaming. Women wailing and screaming.

Chapter Twelve

'Holy saints, what now?' Anna leapt for the door, Yvaine right behind her. They ran into the hall, only to find it deserted.

'Outside.' Yvaine was already darting through the doorway. She blinked as the late afternoon sun struck her eyes. The wailing had subsided, but there was a crowd down by the fjord, exclaiming and crying out. Nearer, Thorolf was moving swiftly across the meadow towards them.

'What is it?' Yvaine called, running to meet him. 'What's happened?'

'Ingerd,' he said curtly. 'She's been found in the fjord.'

'Dead?' The meadow grass seemed to rush towards her.

'Here, steady,' exclaimed Thorolf, catching her as she swayed. 'Come on. Back to the house. You, too, Anna.'

'No!' She looked over her shoulder. 'Where's Rorik? Please, Thorolf, tell me what happened. Anna and I were coming to look for Ingerd. To ask her some questions.'

'Well, she won't be answering any questions now.' Thorolf steered her into the hall, his face grim. 'Odin curse it. I had a few myself.'

'But how...?'

'I don't know.' He led her over to a bench and made her sit down. 'Get your mistress something to drink, Anna, She's as pale as wax.'

Anna hurried to obey. 'There's some ale left from the feast. Here, my lady.'

'I'm all right,' Yvaine protested, but she took a few sips before laying the drinking horn aside. If nothing else, the ale might wash away the cold knot in the pit of her stomach. 'Thorolf, where's Rorik?'

'He went up the mountain.' Thorolf thrust his fingers through his hair and took a few hurried paces about the hall. 'Thank the Gods I saw him head that way myself, otherwise we'd have Gunhild accusing him of pushing Ingerd into the fjord.'

'Blessed Jesu!' Anna crossed herself. 'Was she pushed?'

But Thorolf was watching relief flood Yvaine's eyes. 'You didn't think—?'

'No. At least, I know he wouldn't attack Ingerd. But, Thorolf, he was so angry, so...hurt. What did he do to Othar?'

'Nothing. What would be the point? When all's said and done, they're half-brothers. Rorik's been getting Othar out of trouble since the whelp reached manhood. Before, if truth be told. He merely threw him to the ground and left.'

He thought back, and grinned suddenly. 'Gunhild started ranting at him, but Rorik just walked out in the middle of it. Can't say I blame him. Nothing worse than a nagging woman.'

'This is no laughing matter,' Anna scolded.

'Well, I've got to admit there's been little to laugh at today, but if you'd seen Gunhild's face when Rorik just turned and stalked off without a word— But never mind that. We have to discover how Ingerd came to fall in the water and drown.'

'If she fell,' Yvaine said.

Thorolf frowned. 'You'd better keep that suspicion to yourself, Yvaine. At least until Rorik and I get some answers.'

'If he comes back.'

'If, if, if. Of course he'll be back. By the runes, woman, he's just found out his mother was a slave and English to boot. Let him have some time to sort it out. Thor! I'm shocked myself. I never would have thought that Egil of all people—'

'But that's just it, Thorolf.' Yvaine leaned forward, hands clasped in unconscious appeal. 'Egil spoke to me about honour. He was absolutely clear on the subject. He would never have left Rorik in such a position. Ingerd knew more, I'm sure of it. And she was afraid of that knowledge,' she added, remembering her encounter with the old slave. 'She didn't fall, she was pushed.'

'In broad daylight? With people all over the place?' Thorolf shook his head. 'Besides, Gunhild and Othar are down there now, lamenting with the rest, but until the clamour started, they were here in the hall.'

But Yvaine wasn't listening. 'Ingerd, herself, warned me,' she murmured. 'God forgive me, I thought she was raving, but 'twas fear. She didn't even go to

Gunhild with what she knew until the night after Egil died. She must have wondered all that day who to tell.'

Anna nodded. 'You're right, lady. I thought Ingerd was acting strangely that day. Poor old woman. I suppose loyalty to her mistress had become a habit. As for Gunhild and Othar, I've known they were conspiring all along. Especially after the bathhouse.'

Thorolf looked from one to the other. 'Bathhouse?'

He was ignored.

'Aye. I don't care how far-fetched it sounds. Gunhild or Othar killed Ingerd. Do you remember how she looked, Anna? She could hardly stand upright. I thought maybe you'd woken her too quickly, but what if…?'

'What if she was given some draught,' Anna suggested when she hesitated. 'Enough to dull her mind and render her unsuspecting.'

'That doesn't explain why Othar tried to attack me in the bathhouse.'

'They didn't know about Rorik's mother then. They had to get rid of Rorik another way, short of actual murder. I suppose even Gunhild quailed at the thought of the fuss that'd follow if Rorik died suspiciously, but if you'd been disgraced, if he'd divorced you in consequence and returned to his raiding—'

'Aye.' Yvaine shivered. ''Tis what Gunhild said in the hall. "You should have been killed long since in some raid."'

Thorolf grabbed Yvaine's drinking horn, took a long swallow, and replaced it with the air of a man now equipped to deal with two females who were way ahead of him. 'I shouldn't have stayed away so long.

Listen, you two. I'm going after Rorik. Until we get back, don't go anywhere and don't ask any questions.'

'Very well, Thorolf, but—' she put out a hand as Thorolf turned to leave '—Ingerd spoke of one Thorkill. Do you know him?'

'Thorkill?' He shrugged. 'There's no one here of that name, but 'tis a common enough one in Norway. What of him?'

'I'm not sure.' Yvaine shook her head. 'If only I'd listened more closely to Ingerd. Othar had been rough with her, and she must have wondered then if she was in danger because she knew too much. She said if ought befell her to seek out Thorkill. He knows the truth.'

Thorolf frowned. 'Rorik might know the man, but first I'll have to find him, and Odin's ravens know how far he's gone. Yvaine, you'd best wait in your bedchamber until we return. You stay with her, Anna, at least until the other slaves are back. I don't want you wandering around alone.'

Anna flushed, surprised out of her usual composure. 'Very well, Thorolf,' she said, quite meekly for her.

He grinned and patted her cheek. 'Sorry if I sounded as though Rorik's mother being English was shameful,' he apologised. He turned to Yvaine. 'I doubt Rorik would've thought twice about it once he got to know you, but there's no denying that the way Sitric died has haunted him for years. He admired his cousin a great deal. I didn't know Sitric well myself, but he always seemed larger than life when Rorik and I were boys. One of those big, roaring men capable of every heroic deed in the sagas.'

He shook his head, murmured, 'What a mess,' and strode from the hall.

'I suppose that was meant to be reassuring,' Yvaine muttered as she and Anna shut themselves in her bedchamber. 'But the fact is, I'm married to a man whose heroic cousin was killed in some apparently shameful manner by a cousin of mine. Alfred was heroic, too, let me tell you. He wouldn't order a man's death lightly.'

'I'm more concerned about Gunhild,' Anna said. 'It may be foolish, lady, but I can't help remembering that witch's warning. Especially the part about death surrounding you.'

Yvaine gave a little shiver, but rallied. 'What did Katyja really say, Anna? She saw a journey. Well, how else would we get here?'

'And the two ships?'

'Hmm. Mayhap Edward came after me, then turned back, not knowing which way to follow. As for the bit about death, anyone could tell that Egil was dying.'

She fully expected Anna to point out that Egil's wasn't the only death in recent hours, but the girl merely shook her head. 'I'll be glad when Rorik and Thorolf return,' was all she said.

Yvaine nodded. She, too, would feel safer when Rorik returned, and yet the thought of facing him again filled her with dread. If he turned that remote, utterly expressionless gaze on her again, she thought she would shrivel inside. And yet, like someone with an aching wound who knows a touch will cause pain but is unable to resist gently probing, she knew she had to find out the truth of why he'd taken her, why he'd married her.

Hope could not be so easily abandoned, she'd discovered. Not where she loved. Even if it meant exposing its fragile petals to the icy blast of Rorik's indifference.

Rorik stood in the shadow of a grove of pines, leaning against a solid trunk, his gaze on the western mountain range, glowing palely golden as the setting sun struck the distant peaks. A stream bubbled past his feet, tumbling cheerfully over its rocky bed, before plummeting down the mountainside to the fjord far below.

This had been the place where he'd dreamed boyhood dreams, of heroic battles and voyages to far-off lands. The place where he'd found surcease from the spite of a bitter and jealous woman. It was a place of wild beauty, a place he'd made his own, but it was still just a place. He could walk away from it and not look back. It hadn't become part of him in one brief night of sweet desire; it didn't hold his heart in the palm of one small hand.

He closed his eyes briefly and let his head fall back against the tree behind him. Then straightened, whirling about, instinct bringing him to battle-readiness before he heard the sound of footsteps over the rushing water.

'A bit risky, being up here alone,' Thorolf observed by way of greeting. 'I could have been anyone.'

Rorik relaxed out of the fighting stance he'd assumed. 'Only you and I know of this place.'

'Aye, but the climb seemed a lot easier when we were boys.'

When Rorik made no response to this, Thorolf decided shock tactics were called for. 'Ingerd's dead,' he announced.

Rorik raised a brow. 'Well, she's old, and after the day we've had—'

'It wasn't old age. She drowned in the fjord. Yvaine thinks it was deliberate.'

Pain slashed through him at the sound of her name. The same savage blow that had struck with brutal intensity in the hall when he'd realised, finally, what he stood to lose. The knowledge had been shattering, almost paralysing him, until he'd managed to cage it, to conceal the terrifying awareness of his own vulnerability behind a wall of cool indifference. He'd done it then, he thought, turning away. He could do it now.

'Why would she think that?'

'She believes there's more to the story Egil told Ingerd before he died.'

A short laugh tore from his throat, the sound so harsh a flock of birds exploded from the branches above them, shrieking in alarm.

And as though their sudden flight snapped the brittle tension binding him, he whirled and struck the tree with his clenched fist. 'Hel! What more does she need to hear? Betrayed by my own father. What better revenge for her?'

'I don't believe that any more than I believe you married her for revenge,' Thorolf said. 'But if you're not ready to listen to reason, I'll wait. Not too long, I hope. It gets damned cold up here at night.'

'No one's asking you to stay.' Rorik sent his friend a narrow-eyed glare as Thorolf made himself comfortable on a patch of grass. 'Can't you take a hint?'

'No. Besides, compared to the mayhem going on at Einervik, 'tis nice and peaceful up here. I may stay the night, after all.'

'Mayhem? What mayhem? And what the Hel were you thinking of, leaving Yvaine alone down there? I thought I asked you to keep an eye on things until I got back.'

He started down the path, moving so quickly that by the time Thorolf realised his friend's intent and leapt up, he had several yards to cover before he could speak again.

'Yvaine's safe for the moment. I told her to stay in her chamber. Besides, she wouldn't thank me for trying to take your place as her protector. 'Tis you she married, Rorik.'

'I didn't give her much choice.' *Not then, not later.* 'But I'm going to.'

'What does that mean?'

'I'm taking Yvaine back to England, to her cousin.'

Thorolf stared at him. 'To ransom her? Won't they think she's been…uh…?'

'No, not for ransom. As for the other…' Rorik halted his swift descent down the mountainside and fixed Thorolf with a grim look. 'I'll meet that when I come to it.'

'Hmm. You might have to postpone the trip. Know anyone named Thorkill?'

'What in the three worlds has Thorkill got to do with any of this?'

'He exists then? Who is he?'

'An old man who used to go a-viking with my—with Egil. I haven't seen him for years. He lives in a *shieling* in the mountains.'

Thorolf gaped at him in horror. 'All year round?'

Reluctant amusement flared briefly. 'Anyone would think you'd never spent a night in the open during winter, not to mention being half-drowned at sea. The man likes his privacy. A pity we aren't all so fortunate.'

Thorolf ignored this broad hint. 'Well, Ingerd told Yvaine that if anything happened to her, Thorkill knows the truth.'

'What truth?'

'How the Hel do I know? But I know one thing, Rorik. Egil was no fool. Runes! He didn't even want Othar born, so he wouldn't want him inheriting more than his younger son's portion. Find this Thorkill, hear what he has to say.'

Rorik gestured impatiently. 'Nothing he says will alter the fact that my mother was English and a slave.' He was silent a moment, then added, 'It explains one or two things, though.'

'Such as?'

'Why my father hardly blinked at my marriage to Yvaine, for one. Ill or not, he would've ranted and raved despite knowing he'd never change my mind. I thought 'twas because he wanted me home and thought she'd keep me here.'

'He did,' agreed Thorolf, pouncing on this point. 'What's more—'

'It also explains why I've never wanted to stay. Why I'm always drawn back…'

'To England?' Thorolf frowned. 'I thought 'twas because of Sitric.'

'No. And now there's another reason to go.'

'Well, I don't intend to stay here watching power go to Othar's head, and I'd have trouble keeping my eye on that pert little maid of Yvaine's from here, so count me in.'

For the first time that day, Rorik felt a genuine smile touch his mouth. 'Thanks, my friend.'

'No need for thanks, nor for thinking that the men won't follow you, Rorik. Who cares if you're half-English? 'Tis the Danes who are at war with Edward now, not us. As for your mother being a slave, who's to say Egil wouldn't have married her if she'd lived? Perhaps this Thorkill might know if he had such a plan in mind. I think you should see him, if only to find out what else Ingerd knew, and was prevented from telling.'

Rorik's eyes narrowed. 'You think she was murdered?'

'She could have slipped fetching water, I suppose, but Yvaine says something's not right. She and Anna seem to have it all worked out between them, but they lost me when they started babbling about the bathhouse.'

Rorik bit off a curse and started walking again, fast. 'Damn it, I'd forgotten that.'

'Forgotten what?'

'Othar threatened Yvaine in the bathhouse. I thought it no more than drunken impulse. 'Twas why I banished him. But Yvaine swore she'd been locked in after Gunhild showed her the place. In which case…'

'In which case they might have planned it to discredit her.' Thorolf gave a silent whistle. 'So that's what Anna meant. Perhaps you'd better take Yvaine with you when you visit Thorkill.'

'I don't intend to waste my time chasing proof of a tale I already believe. I've got a crew to collect and the ship to prepare.'

'I can do that while you and Yvaine hunt out Thorkill. The trip will do you both good.' Thorolf sent a quick glance at Rorik, then studied the sky with innocent assessment. 'Weather's fine. It'll give you a chance to convince Yvaine you didn't marry her for revenge.'

For a moment he thought he might have gone too far with that remark. Rorik sent him a look that could have pierced mail at a hundred paces.

'There's a faster way down this mountain, my friend, if you'd prefer to take it.'

'Uh, no thanks, Rorik.' Thorolf smiled winningly. 'I'd rather be alive at the end of the trip.'

'Hmm.'

The rest of the trek was accomplished in silence.

A like silence greeted them when they reached the house. No surprise there, it was late; the sun which never quite sank below the horizon during the fleeting northern summer, now lay shrouded in the grey mists of night.

Murmuring something about food, Thorolf entered the hall, but Rorik strode directly to his bedchamber. He didn't feel like encountering any of his family, and food was the last thing on his mind.

He hesitated at the door, realising he didn't know quite what to expect. After what Yvaine had learned in the hall, and his harsh dismissal of her, he could be faced with anything from tears to stony silence. Not that it mattered. He'd made his decision.

Grasping the latch, he lifted it and pushed the door open.

She was sitting bolt upright on the side of the bed, her hands clenched in her lap. Despite the late hour, she was fully dressed, even her hair was still covered. She watched him with the wary eyes of a wild creature, waiting to see what he would do.

He pushed the door shut behind him and forced the words out, before he couldn't say them at all. 'I'm taking you back to England.'

Her eyelids flickered, her only reaction.

'Well?' he demanded, flayed by her silence 'I'd think you'd be pleased. You were trying to reach your cousin the day I—'

'Pleased? To return shamed so your revenge will be complete?'

Her voice was low, but he heard the tremor in it, saw the pallor on her cheeks. He couldn't do it. Not even for the time he'd sworn to keep his distance from her could he let her think he'd used her like that. Oh, aye, he'd told himself revenge had tangled with the other reasons he'd taken her, because that was easier than looking too closely at something he hadn't understood. But he was long past lying to himself. And he could never lie to her.

'Yvaine, I'd never use a woman for revenge. Please believe that.'

She continued to watch him, her eyes dark, fathomless. 'You asked about my family on the ship. You recognised the royal standard flying over Selsey.'

'Aye, but that had nothing to do with revenge. You didn't cause Sitric's death. Besides, once you'd recovered and I knew—'

He stopped dead and turned away, leaving her prey to a myriad tormenting questions. What did you know? she asked silently. That you wanted me? Do you want me still?

'Then why take me to England?' she whispered.

He moved abruptly, as though about to pace before remembering he couldn't stride freely in the tiny room. She saw his jaw lock tight. 'I'm not about to repeat my father's mistakes.'

She flinched as if he'd struck her, every word piercing her heart. 'Of course. You'd rather your children be more Norse than English. I understand completely.'

'I doubt it,' Rorik snarled, wheeling to face her. Then he went still, a strange expression in his eyes. 'You could be with child. You'll tell me if 'tis so, won't you, Yvaine?'

It was more command than request, but Yvaine nodded, knowing she'd never use that circumstance to hold him.

But there'd been something in his voice, in the sudden stillness of his body. Something…hopeful?

No, she thought as he glanced away again and started unbuckling his belt. Hope was too strong a word. He'd sounded more cautious, as if too wary to hope. Did that mean he wanted a child? Their child? But in that case, why return her to Edward?

Then all at once she thought she knew, and defeat almost doubled her over. Darkness seemed to drop between her and the rest of the world, leaving only one harsh sliver of light, and within that glaring flame burned a single word.

Ransom.

Aye, she thought, closing her eyes as unbearable pressure built inside her. Hadn't she'd thought of this before, on Rorik's ship? How much more likely was that explanation now? He'd been exiled from his home; he'd need money to start again. It was perfectly logical. No one would think anything of his decision; ransom was a business.

Oh, God, she couldn't think about it now. Couldn't ask him if it was so. An affirmation would crush her completely. And yet if she didn't speak, if she didn't break the grip of the talons buried in heart, *she* would break, screaming, crying, beating at him with her fists. Or worse, begging him to keep her.

'Did Thorolf tell you about Ingerd?' she got out on a ragged sigh. 'About Thorkill?'

'Aye.' He looked around, frowning. 'And about your suspicions, but unless Gunhild or Othar have developed a talent for being in two places at once, 'tis more than likely that Ingerd slipped fetching water.'

She shook her head, clutching this new argument to her like a shield. 'Ingerd never fetched water. She was too old to carry heavy pails across the meadow.'

'Then she went for a walk and missed her step.'

She frowned at him. 'Ingerd was in no condition to go walking. Why are you ignoring this? Go and see Thorkill and—'

'Damn it! To what point?' he yelled suddenly.

'Because your father was an honourable man,' she yelled back, and the heat of anger was momentarily fiercer than the pain. 'He wouldn't have told Ingerd such a tale if that was all there was to it.'

'Oh, you knew him so well, did you? After a day's acquaintance?'

'I certainly knew enough of him to want to know more. If you won't see Thorkill, I'll find someone who knows where he lives, and go there myself.'

'Don't be ridiculous,' he said, but more quietly.

'Is it not more ridiculous to ignore what happened to Ingerd? I can't, Rorik. I...' She faltered; her voice breaking. It wasn't only Ingerd's death that tore at her so. Her emotions were balanced on a knife-edge, terror that Rorik no longer wanted her warring with pain and love and rage that he couldn't see it, couldn't see what she was fighting for.

'Yvaine—' He took a step towards her, hesitated, then sat down on the edge of the bed, leaving a couple of feet between them. As if she was a pile of flints that could explode in his face at any moment, she thought furiously.

'What does it matter if Ingerd didn't relate the whole story? What she did say was the truth.'

'Surely it matters that she was killed.'

'You really believe that?'

'Aye. I have to find out, Rorik. I feel so...guilty. If I'd taken more notice of her warnings, she might still be alive.'

'You mustn't think that,' he said at once, and gave a bitter laugh. 'You weren't to know the mess my father was to leave behind.'

The echo of pain in his voice momentarily steadied her. He'd lost everything, she reminded herself, her heart aching for him. She reached out, unthinking, and touched his hand. 'Rorik, your father wouldn't have betrayed you. I know it.'

He shot off the bed as though launched from a catapult. 'That remains to be seen,' he growled, reaching for the door. 'But 'tis clear I'm not going to get any peace until we do see it. If you're determined to question Thorkill, you'd better get undressed and get under the covers. 'Tis a long trip. You'll need your sleep.'

'Well, my thanks for your gracious indulgence,' she cried. 'Holy Saints! 'Tis for you I'm doing—'

But she couldn't go on, couldn't speak the lie. It was for Rorik she was doing this, aye, but it was for herself as well, and if she failed she didn't know how she would bear it.

'Yvaine…' He halted, surprise in his eyes, and she realised tears were spilling over her lashes. He put out a hand, touched her cheek…

'Leave me alone,' she cried fiercely, pushing at his hand before scrambling across the bed out of reach. She swiped her hand across her cheek, brushing away the tears. 'I don't want *kindness*. After we've seen Thorkill you can take me back to England and be rid of me. I'll be glad to go. Glad, I tell you! And I hope—'

'All right!' he roared 'You don't have to make yourself clearer. Gods! Anyone would think I'd been about to rape you.'

He flung the door open, then turned back to grab his belt. 'You didn't object to my touch last night,' he bit out. 'But that was before you found out I was the son of a slave.'

'You fool!' Yvaine bounced to her feet, all but sizzling at this injustice. 'If you were the *King*'s son you'd still be a thick-headed barbarian who wouldn't know what was right in front of your eyes if it bit you.'

'I hadn't got around to biting,' he purred with a smile that could have cut glass. 'But don't worry. From now on you can consider yourself free of me. I won't bother you again.'

The door slammed behind him with enough force to shake the entire house.

They left at dawn in one of the small *faerings*—and in a silence broken only by the passage of oars through water. Even that ceased abruptly when the sun was high above them and Rorik stopped rowing so they could eat a simple meal.

Unbearably conscious of the hurtful words they'd flung at each other last night, Yvaine glanced about them. They were now deep into the mountain range. The fjord had gradually narrowed until sheer cliffs rose on either side, spearing towards the heavens. Beyond each bend another snow-capped pinnacle had loomed above them until she felt surrounded, overwhelmed by the stark, terrible beauty of the mountains.

Despite the warmth of the sun, she shivered as she gazed up at the towering peaks. How insignificant were their human desires and foibles, she mused, compared to these creations of time beyond the memory of man.

A distant rumbling made her start, and she glanced at Rorik in nervous enquiry.

'Avalanche,' he said briefly, and handed her a chunk of bread and some goat's cheese.

It was the first word spoken between them since the previous night. He'd eventually returned to their bed-chamber. She had heard his low-voiced conversation with Thorolf in the entrance hall, then he'd slipped quietly into the room to wait out the hours before morning.

Yvaine had lain awake also, too afraid to close her eyes in case she slept past dawn and he left without her. The fact that he'd agreed to go at all had puzzled her once she'd calmed down. She'd spent the remainder of the night torn between hope that Rorik might change his mind about taking her to England, and the heart-wrenching suspicion that he was only delaying the journey to ease her guilt over Ingerd.

The frozen silence in which they'd spent the morning had threatened to bury hope beneath an avalanche of despair as crushing as anything the mountains could produce.

And yet the long hours had given her time to think, to question. If Rorik wouldn't use a woman for revenge, would he also not use a woman for financial gain? Other men would, aye, without thought, conscience, or even a flicker of awareness of the lady's feelings in the matter, but Rorik was not like other men.

Oh, was she foolish to think so? Despite all that had passed between them, she still didn't know him, was achingly aware that part of him remained closed to her. Was she foolish to wonder if his determination to return her to England sprang merely from his innate sense of honour—which might mean that he cared for her? He hadn't touched her in any way; seemed scarcely able to look at her. What sort of woman held on to hope in the face of the stony wall he'd erected between them?

One who loved, she thought, closing her eyes briefly. One who still cherished hope, because the alternative was simply too painful to contemplate. No matter what it cost her, she would do anything to keep him with her a while longer. To restore the terrifyingly fragile link between them.

'Is it dangerous, the avalanche?' she ventured.

Rorik shook his head. 'Too far away.' He leaned forward to take up the oars again, his eyes holding hers, guarded, yet searching.

Unwilling to let him see too deeply, Yvaine glanced away. 'I think this must be the land the *skald* told me about,' she said, indicating the mountains. 'The land of the Frost Giants.'

'The Frost Giants live in one of the three worlds of myth.'

She looked back at him as the boat began to move forward again. 'Three worlds?'

'Aye.' He sent her that wary, probing look again. 'We Vikings have a legend about a world tree, Yggdrasil's Ash. It holds up the sky, and beneath its branches lies Asgarth, home of the Gods. Beneath that again are the roots, each covering the three worlds of myth. Midgarth, the world of men; the world of the Frost Giants, who are the mortal enemies of the Gods; and Hel, the world of the dead.'

'We Christians believe in Hell, also.'

'You mean your priests threaten people with everlasting punishment so they remain under the rule of the Church. Our Hel is merely a place for the dead.'

'I've never thought of it quite like that,' Yvaine murmured. She remembered the fat, greedy priest at Selsey, thundering out promises of eternal damnation if anyone disobeyed Ceawlin no matter what cruelties he inflicted upon them. 'Some priests take advantage of the ignorant and simple, I suppose, but there are others who are good. It seems very far away now.'

He frowned. 'Then you're not afraid for your immortal soul, Yvaine? You've been unable to hear the Mass or confess. In England you'd be considered my mistress, not my wife. Do you think your God will forgive you a sin you couldn't help?'

'I wasn't that helpless,' she murmured, but the harsh note in his voice intrigued her. She opened her mouth to ask how he knew so much about Christianity.

'Well, don't worry,' he muttered before she could speak. 'No one in England need know of our marriage unless you tell of it.' He gave such a violent pull on the oars the little *faering* almost flew out of the water. 'Odin knows what your priests would do with you. Probably lock you away for the rest of your life. Hel!'

'Yours or mine?' she asked whimsically, and dragged a reluctant laugh out of him.

And suddenly it was all right again. The grim look disappeared from Rorik's eyes, and when he started to tell her of other legends, the constraint between them eased. By the time he moored the boat to a jutting rock, where a barely discernible path meandered up the mountainside, Yvaine discovered that the tiny bud of hope was again blooming, fragile but persistent, in her heart.

'Stay close,' he said taking her hand as they started upwards, and even that small contact warmed her.

The climb, too, lifted her spirits. She was stiff from sitting in the boat for so long and the stony path, though precipitous, was easy enough to follow. Every so often Rorik would lift her over the roughest patches. Yvaine started counting the number of seconds that passed before he released her, then wondered if she was fooling herself that they seemed to be increasing.

So absorbed was she in these intriguing calculations that she didn't notice Rorik had stopped walking until she bumped into him. He steadied her, but kept his gaze on the path behind them.

'What is it?' she asked, immediately forgetting sums and glancing back. After Rorik's tales of myths and monsters, she wouldn't have been surprised to see a Frost Giant or two, but the empty silence of the mountains surrounded them, as if they were the only people alive in the world.

'I thought I heard something,' he said. 'Another boat.'

'Thorkill?'

'No. His boat was already there, tied under an overhang.' He listened a moment. ''Twas probably nought. Sound carries in the mountains.'

But before they walked on, his gaze swept the rugged terrain as though examining every leaf and twig, and Yvaine felt a chill brush the back of her neck. As far as she knew, only Thorolf and Anna were aware of Thorkill's existence, but what if someone had heard her and Rorik arguing last night? They hadn't exactly been talking in whispers.

Worse, what if Gunhild had overheard enough of Ingerd's warning to make her suspicious? She'd been close enough by the time Ingerd had noticed her and fallen silent. Without hearing all, conscious of her own secrets, might not Gunhild have set a watch on them?

'Rorik—'

'Aye,' he said as if his thoughts had been racing along similar lines. 'We're being followed. Quick! Up here.'

He virtually propelled her up the next section of rocky slope by the sheer force of his body. Heart pounding, Yvaine scrambled over a jutting ledge and found herself on a plateau overlooking the fjord. She had a dizzying view of the drop below them before Rorik pulled her across to the far side and shoved her behind him.

He'd barely done so when a man leapt on to the rocky shelf from the path they'd climbed. He was armed with spear and axe, and in his eyes she saw a cold, emotionless purpose that stopped her heart. Without a word, he drew the axe from its loop on his belt, hefted it, then levelled the spear and spread his legs in a stance that looked terrifyingly efficient.

Rorik's hand had gone to his sword-hilt as soon as the man appeared, but now he let it fall to his side as he, too, widened his stance. 'Move back out of reach and get down,' he said, not taking his eyes from his opponent.

Too terrified even to tremble, Yvaine forced herself to move, thinking he needed room to manoeuvre—although with his sword still in its scabbard, how was he going to deflect a thrown spear? Dear God, what if the man threw both weapons at once? The distance between them was so short, she doubted Rorik would have time to dodge in either direction.

No, she thought, grasping at reason, their attacker wouldn't do that. He'd save the axe for close combat in case Rorik was merely wounded. Oh, Mother of God—

The prayer winked out of her mind as a death's-head grin spread over the man's face. Taking a short backswing, he launched the spear straight at Rorik's heart.

Yvaine didn't even have time to scream. In a blur of movement so fast she would have missed it if she'd blinked, Rorik dodged to the side, caught the weapon as it flashed past, swung his arm in a backward arc and returned the weapon with a force that buried it deep in its owner's chest.

The man dropped the axe in his hand, his eyes widening in stunned disbelief as he stared down at the spear piercing his chest. His lips parted; he lifted a hand towards the weapon. His fingers never reached their goal. He staggered and dropped to the ground, choking.

Yvaine got shakily to her feet, hardly daring to believe it was over. So dazed was she by the rapid shift from danger to safety that when a voice spoke behind them she didn't even flinch.

'In all my life I have seen but one man perform that feat. Your father taught you well, son of Egil Strongarm.'

Rorik turned. 'Thorkill,' he acknowledged. His gaze went to the sword in the older man's hand. 'Were you intending to use that?'

'If yonder assassin had succeeded in killing you, aye.' Thorkill jerked his head sideways. 'The vermin still lives. You might discover his reason for an attack that was clearly intended to come from behind.'

'I don't need to ask.' But after a quick glance at Yvaine, Rorik walked over to look down into rapidly glazing eyes. 'Gunhild sent you, didn't she?'

The man stared up at him. 'I was…to silence Thorkill. Or kill you…and the girl…if you got there first.' His teeth bared in a hideous travesty of his earlier grin. 'The old woman was easy…' A rattle replaced the rest, and there was silence.

Rorik stood for a moment, his mouth set hard, then with a gesture that spoke louder than any words, he shoved the body to the edge of the plateau with his foot. One kick and it dropped like a stone to disappear beneath the dark waters of the fjord.

Thorkill nodded in satisfaction. 'A fitting end for a hired killer.'

Yvaine finally unlocked her frozen muscles enough to turn. As she did so, Rorik came to her side and put his arm around her. 'Are you all right, sweeting?'

She nodded; the only response she could manage, and he drew her closer.

'This lady is my wife, Yvaine,' he said to Thorkill. 'We come with news of Egil's death, and with questions.'

Thorkill glanced at the abandoned axe. 'Questions with a high price, it would seem. But come. You're both welcome to my home. It lies beyond the next bend.'

They started up the path, Yvaine grateful for the supporting arm Rorik kept about her waist. She felt numb, as though she was surrounded by a veil of silence. Rorik glanced down at her a couple of times as he and Thorkill talked across her, and gradually, warmed by his concern and the heat of his body, the feeling lessened and she could hear again.

'I'm saddened to learn of Egil's death, Rorik. And that trouble has come upon you because of it. Egil hoped you wouldn't need the stone.'

'Stone?'

'Ah. You don't know it all.'

'I know enough,' Rorik said grimly. ''Tis Yvaine who would come. But since we're here, I might as well know what else Gunhild was at such pains to prevent me hearing.'

'First we'll eat,' said Thorkill, and indicated a turf and stone hut ahead of them.

The *shieling* nestled snugly against the mountainside, sheltered by a craggy overhang. Rorik had to duck his head as they entered, but the interior was roomy; a smaller version of the hall at Einervik.

As Yvaine sank on to one of the fur-covered benches in front of the firepit, Thorkill gestured to an ale jug on a nearby shelf. 'Pour your lady a drink, Rorik. She looks like she needs one.' He took up a ladle to stir the fragrant contents of a cauldron hanging over the fire. 'Tell me, how does your *Sea Dragon* sail these days? Egil sent word that you were trying a longer steering-oar.'

Yvaine leaned back against the wall, listening with only half an ear to Rorik's reply. Her senses might have returned to something like normal, but she was glad to let the conversation flow over her, to study their host while he and Rorik swapped seafaring stories. Thorkill reminded her of Egil, she thought idly, except that he still enjoyed robust health. His skin was weathered and lined, his hands gnarled, but his stature was straight and his white hair and beard were still thick. His clear blue eyes twinkled often, and she marvelled that a man so friendly and hospitable had once looted and killed at will.

But that was long past. Lulled by the warmth of the fire and the tasty stew they were served, she sat quietly, almost dozing, until Thorkill rose and went to a chest against the far wall. Opening it, he lifted out an object wrapped in oilskin and returned with it to his seat.

'This is what you seek, Rorik.'

Alert again, Yvaine drew closer as Rorik took the object and parted the skin wrappings.

'Why, 'tis only an old stone,' she exclaimed, surprised and little disappointed.

'A rune stone, love,' Rorik corrected, turning the stone over in his hands. It was small, only about a foot long and rounded at one end. Both sides were covered with strange symbols that Yvaine knew represented some sort of written word—unusual among the Norse. With vellum so rare and valuable, their stories were more often passed down by word of mouth. Only the laws, and the occasional grave marker, were carved in stone.

'Can you read it?' she asked.

Rorik glanced from her to Thorkill, turned the stone over again and began to read. '"Read these runes. Egil, son of Eirik, son of Rorik, son of Einer, lay with a slave, Alicia, who bore him a son. Afterwards she died. The son Rorik lived and was duly adopted by law to be equal with any other children of his father. And being the only son and older than those who may come after, he must take his father's house, allotting shares to his brothers should any be born. The law-speaker Gudrik carved these runes."'

There was a long silence when Rorik finished reading. He laid the stone on the bench and stared thoughtfully into the fire.

'This is what Egil told Ingerd,' Yvaine said at last, working it out. 'What Gunhild stopped her from telling us yesterday. That man…'

'Aye.' Rorik briefly covered her hand with his. 'He killed Ingerd.'

'A defenceless old woman,' she said angrily. 'I'm glad you kicked him over the cliff.'

Thorkill laughed. 'Spoken like a true Norsewoman. But your wife is English, Rorik, like your mother!'

'Does that matter?' Yvaine turned to him. 'Surely the rune stone proves that Rorik is his father's heir, whatever his mother's blood. Oh, Rorik, don't you see? There's no need for you to leave Einervik now.'

He gave her a quick glance, but was distracted by Thorkill.

'You were leaving, Rorik?'

'Othar banished me. Not that I took any notice of that. I was planning to leave anyway.'

'That whelp!' Thorkhill snorted. 'I might have known he'd cause trouble, or rather, that his mother would. Not that Egil ever expected it. He hadn't even met Gunhild when that stone was carved, but he wanted everything done to protect you, Rorik. After all, the son of a concubine is one thing. He has rights. The son of a slave becomes a slave also, regardless of who sires him. Egil wanted you recognised as his legal heir. He even held the full adoption ceremony. I was one of the witnesses.'

'I knew nothing of this,' Rorik said.

'Well, you wouldn't recall it, of course. It must be twenty-five years ago. I think you were about three. Egil slaughtered an ox and made a boot from the hide of the beast's right leg. Then we all set our right foot in it, one after the other, including you.'

'It must have caused some stir, surely,' Yvaine said. 'A ceremony so elaborate.'

'Egil kept it quiet. As far as everyone knew, when Egil took Rorik to Einervik, he was the son of a woman he'd met on his travels, married, and left her with her people because he wasn't ready to settle. He took Alicia away after she quickened. To some distant farm where you were looked after, Rorik, until you were old enough to take part in the adoption ceremony.'

'Wouldn't it have been easier to have simply married my mother?' Rorik asked drily. 'Especially if Egil cared about her as he claimed.'

Thorkill pursed his lips. 'That I can't say. She was English and a slave, and he was always proud, always aware of his position. But then you were born. His son. I think it took him by surprise, the feeling he had for you. He certainly settled down then, never went on another raid.'

'A little too late for my mother.'

'Aye, but you have to remember that when all this happened we were at war with the English. Runes! We've always been land-poor in Norway and there was England, divided into warring kingdoms, just waiting to be taken.

'And, by Odin's beard, we did it!' he added, waving his drinking-horn in a toast to those long-ago days. 'The very year you were born, Rorik, there was a Norwegian ruling the north from Jorvik. York, t'was once called. Only Alfred of Wessex held against us. A great warrior. A great king. And you needn't remind me of Sitric.'

'I wasn't going to,' Rorik murmured. 'Would I be so uncivil to my host?'

'I think 'tis the thought of my old bones that restrains you.' Thorkill chuckled. 'And they grow weary.' He rose, stretching. 'I sleep outside during the summer months,' he announced, his eyes twinkling with mischief. ''Tis good for the blood. So you'll be quite private here.'

Before either of his guests could reply, he scooped up a fur from the bench, gave them a grin, and departed.

'He thinks frozen blood is good?' muttered Yvaine, suddenly wide-awake at this abrupt end to the evening. She hadn't expected to be alone with Rorik; wasn't sure what to do. The opportunity to renew the physical bond between them was here, but in the face of his reaction to her touch last night...

'Would you rather have the hut to yourself?' he asked quietly, getting to his feet.

'No,' she whispered, and, gathering all her resolution, looked up. 'I want to be with you.'

She wondered if he would understand her deeper meaning; could read nothing in his eyes. He nodded and crossed to the door.

'I'll be back,' he said shortly. 'I've one or two questions still to ask of Thorkill.'

Well, at least he hadn't refused to sleep in the same room with her, Yvaine encouraged herself as he shut the door.

She rose, tossed some furs on to the floor for a bed, and started to unfasten her brooches. She wasn't sure what she would do. Frolicking in a tub when she was already naked and lying in Rorik's arms was one thing; her heart threatened to lodge in her throat at the thought of tempting him by sitting naked by the fire—although, unbound, her hair would cover her to her hips. Only one thing kept her resolve alive. An endearment she wasn't even sure he'd been aware of uttering. *A rune stone, love.*

That sweet single word was enough. Enough to hope he might change his mind about taking her to England. Enough to dare to reach out, to find out if he still wanted her. She would think only of that.

Rorik closed the door quietly behind him, looked up and went utterly still. Even his heart stopped. He had no need of it, nor for the breath that caught in his throat. *She* was life to him. She was everything.

She sat by the fire, combing her hair, her bare legs curled to the side. The honey-gold mass fell over her shoulders like a silken cloak, parting slightly with the movement of her arm to show tantalising glimpses of the curve of her hip or the graceful sweep of her back.

She glanced up at the closing of the door, her lovely eyes wide, enigmatic, but behind the shadows he thought he saw a shy, fugitive longing.

It was almost like the first time he'd seen her, he thought. Except that this time she wasn't hurt. And this time he wasn't going to reach out and take.

But what if she wanted to give? If only he could read the mysteries in her eyes. Her pose was temptation incarnate, but he couldn't be sure it wasn't his own need that had him seeing an invitation where there was none. Yet she'd removed every stitch of clothing.

He realised, without surprise, that a fine tremor vibrated through his limbs. How could he walk out of here and not try to bind her to him with every tie he could think of? Not try to imprint himself on her, mind, body, soul, so she could never forget him?

He came forward slowly, as though any sudden movement might startle her. He went down on one knee, reached out a hand to cradle her face. Just like that first time, he thought again. But though her eyes held a hint of uncertainty, there was no fear, and this time, when he parted her hair to reveal the soft curves of her body, he knew he would be lost forever. Knew and cared not.

She shivered a little as he looked at her, the movement sending firelight flickering over her skin, warming her, creating a rosy flush. No, not just the fire's heat, he thought, as he watched her nipples tighten. The way he was watching her was doing that. Her body knew him, wanted him.

Gods, she was beautiful. He could have gone on looking at her, just looking, for hours, even while the yearning in his soul, the throbbing in his loins, made him ache beyond bearing.

''Tis not just…kindness?'

The whisper reached him, drawing his gaze upward. 'Kindness?' he echoed. Suddenly the hesitation in her eyes was unbearable. His hands went to her waist. He stood, pulling her up with him and into his arms. His mouth was on hers before the answer reached his lips.

'Does this feel like kindness?' he demanded between kisses. 'Does *this*—' he let her feel his teeth against her throat '—or *this*—' he arched her over his arm, clamped his mouth over her nipple.

Yvaine cried out, ceasing to think, ceasing to hear or see. She could only feel. Feel the violent pounding of his heart, the hard strength of his arms, the almost brutal demand of his mouth. She clung to him, wanting to get closer, to ease the throbbing between her legs that was growing hotter and wilder with every strong movement of his lips at her breast.

With an almost agonised groan, he released her and started stripping off his clothes, heedless of ripped seams and dangling laces. Yvaine swayed, she couldn't stand, her legs felt like water. She trembled uncontrollably at the fierce intent in his eyes, would have dropped to the floor had he not hurled the last of his clothing away and bent to her. With a powerful movement that wrenched a wild cry of excitement from her, he lifted her against him and lowered them both to the fur bedding.

'If this is kindness,' he growled against her mouth, ''tis for myself.'

'It doesn't matter,' she gasped, clinging to him. 'Rorik. It doesn't matter.'

But he drew back, his hands gripping her face, forcing her to look at him. His thighs held hers wide apart; she could feel the hot, powerful length of him pressed against her, but he held still, the strain of control making him shudder with every breath. 'It does matter. Yvaine, I wasn't going to take you again until you could choose.'

She heard the words, understood them, but dimly. It didn't matter. He could have said nought and she would still be his. 'I have chosen,' she murmured, and arched beneath him in frantic feminine demand.

He almost heard the explosion as his control cracked. She was quivering beneath him, soft, open, wanting. Forgetting everything but the blind need to possess her, to be inside her, part of her, he joined their bodies with a powerful thrust that had her screaming under the sudden lash of ecstasy.

He closed his mouth over hers, knowing with one last vestige of sanity that she'd be embarrassed later if she thought Thorkill had heard. Then the sweet hot pulsing of her body around him was too much. A harsh groan tore from his throat. Holding her as if the world itself had vanished around them, he unleashed the full force of his need, until she cried out again and again, lost in total surrender; until the hot spurting of his seed inside her joined them for all time, creating new life.

If he was very, very lucky, Rorik amended, when his heartbeat returned to something like normal and he could think.

Yvaine lay beneath him, so still, so utterly limp, she seemed scarcely to breathe. He lifted his head sharply, remembering the unrestrained power with which he'd taken her. She was still new to love-making, and so delicate, so soft. Wondering at the slenderness of a body that could cling to him with such passion, he raised himself on one arm, splaying his fingers across her belly, pressing gently.

She could be with child. He was torn between the violently primitive need to make it so, and the yearning to have her come to him freely.

Her lashes fluttered open. She looked up at him, and smiled. Just as she had that first time. And again, he had to break the connection, to let his head fall forward until his brow rested on hers. That smile of shy feminine knowledge was going to strike straight at his heart every time he saw it.

Not only at his heart, he realised wryly, as renewed tension invaded his muscles.

He lifted his head, watched her eyes widen as she felt him quicken inside her. Her inner muscles quivered delicately around him, making him groan with the exquisite pleasure of it. The need for completion hammered at him, but not this time…not this time…

'Did you think once would be enough?' he murmured against her lips. He began to move again, a gentle, rocking motion designed to draw this out until they were both sated, both senseless with pleasure. She gasped and trembled beneath him. 'A hundred times,' he whispered. 'A thousand. 'Twill never be enough.'

No, never, she thought as a tide of voluptuous weakness washed over her, ecstasy building, flowing, gently tumbling her over a crest before building again.

She'd wanted to talk to him. To ease her uncertainty about what he intended to do now that he knew the truth of his birth. But it didn't matter; there was time enough for that. She couldn't think of anything but the heat of his body, the coiled power of the muscles beneath her hands, the sweetness of his kisses after the whirlwind that had gone before.

England, his family, everything could wait.

Chapter Thirteen

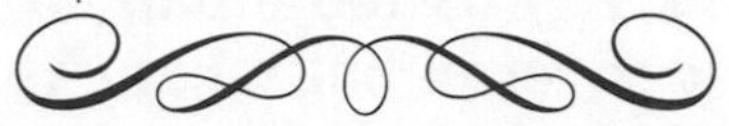

But Gunhild and Othar hadn't waited.

'Gone? What do you mean they've gone?' Rorik stared narrow-eyed at Thorolf over the remains of their supper. He and Yvaine had reached Einervik that afternoon. In the presence of the free karls and slaves of the estate, he'd produced the rune stone and related Thorkill's account of the adoption ceremony.

There had been much talk and wonderment over the supper table, but now, taking advantage of the long summer evening, the slaves had drifted away to their own affairs, and Yvaine had retired to their bedchamber. It was time to deal with his stepmother and brother.

'Othar said he was taking Gunhild to stay with a friend, and he wanted us gone by the time he got back,' Thorolf reported.

Rorik frowned. 'That doesn't make sense. By morning, everyone up and down the fjord will know of the rune stone. Why assume we're still leaving?'

'Well, I'm preparing for a voyage regardless.' Thorolf shrugged. 'Perhaps they're hoping you're still taking Yvaine to England, and that their version of Egil's story will be forgotten by the time you get back.'

'Hmm. Staying with a friend? The woman doesn't have any friends.'

'Then perhaps he's taken her to Kaupang. Who knows? The point is, Rorik, they have reason to lie low until we've gone. I think Ingerd might have been dead before she went into the water. There was a tear in the back of her shift. It was too small to be caused by a dagger so I can't be sure, but when Anna and I hunted around we found some blood in a clearing above the fjord. If the killer lured Ingerd there and stabbed her, say with a cloak pin, then rolled her body into the water, from a distance 'twould look as though she'd slipped and tumbled down the slope. Of course, nobody can remember seeing anything. Bunch of fools.'

'The murderer seems to have had a fondness for sharp weapons,' Rorik murmured. 'Although he tried something a little larger on us.'

'What!' Thorolf sat bolt upright. 'Are you saying…?'

'Aye.' Rorik tipped his drinking-horn at his friend. 'Gunhild does indeed have reason to lie low. Her intent was to silence Thorkill before he could speak, or to kill us all if Yvaine and I got there first.'

'Gods! Did they think *I*'d stay silent if you all ended up dead?'

'Probably not, but with the three of us gone and the rune stone destroyed, you'd have no proof that Gunhild had a motive for murder, let alone had one committed. I'd confirmed Othar as Jarl, openly before witnesses. In fact—' he leaned back in his chair, gazing into the fire '—as a plan it wasn't badly thought out. If you went looking for evidence that Othar had usurped my position, then silenced those of us who knew about the stone, I warrant all you'd find would be the remains of a tragic fire in Thorkill's *shieling*. As for Ingerd, could you swear the blood you found and the tear in her clothing wasn't caused by her striking something sharp when she fell?'

'No, but... Hel, Rorik, what in the three worlds made them think you'd be easy to kill? 'Tis like Othar to act first, then panic at the thought that you might survive, but I would've thought Gunhild had more sense.'

'I'd rather know why she isn't here to brazen it out. We either wouldn't have returned, thereby making her safe, or we'd return with a tale that merely removed Othar from his chair. All she had to do was claim that Ingerd didn't tell her the whole story.'

'And your would-be murderer?'

'Deny all knowledge; suggest we were set upon by an outlaw. Although in this case, one who talked before he died. That possibility might be keeping her in hiding until we've sailed.'

'I should think it would. By the Runes, Rorik, you could have them outlawed and banished from Norway for this.'

'Very likely. But I've got no time and less inclination to chase after my ambitious relatives. Let them creep back when they hear we've gone. How soon can we get a crew together?'

Thorolf frowned at this apparent end to the discussion, but answered readily enough. 'Another day. I didn't send out a war arrow, but I made it clear that men were needed in a hurry.'

'You did tell them we're not going a-viking.'

'Of course. And, uh, speaking of such things, I want to buy Anna's freedom.'

Rorik's brows went up. 'You have been busy.'

A sheepish expression crossed Thorolf's face. 'I knew she was going to be trouble,' he said with comically false gloom. 'Right from the start. Do you think Yvaine will mind losing her maid?'

'Of course not. Anna will still be her friend. But I don't want payment, Thorolf. When we get to England, they'll both be free.' He gave a short laugh. 'Or have you forgotten that things are different there?'

Thorolf stretched his legs out and contemplated the toes of his boots. ''Twas good enough for you, once. You were even—'

'Enough!' Rorik stood up and strode over to the fire. He threw the dregs of his ale into the flames with a quick, jerky movement, causing sparks to fly. When they subsided he turned back to Thorolf.

'Sorry,' he said abruptly. 'Of course you know what returning to England will mean. I wish you luck with your Anna.'

'Thanks. But, Rorik, what are you going to do about Gunhild and Othar? 'Tis all very well to say let them creep back. You can't be thinking of leaving them in charge here. Apart from their crimes, you should have heard the orders Othar was giving yesterday, contradicting himself, and—well, never mind. Sometimes I think he's not sane.'

'There's a real possibility that you're right,' Rorik said quietly.

Thorolf blinked at him. 'Hel, I was only jesting.'

'Aye, but you're remembering, aren't you?' Rorik nodded as memory and comprehension chased each other across Thorolf's face. 'Remembering those uncontrollable rages Othar used to fall into as a child if he was thwarted in the smallest way. How he always accuses people of being against him. According to Thorkill, when my father married Gunhild there were rumours of an ancestor or two who'd been locked away. 'Twas why Egil tried to prevent Gunhild from bearing a child.'

'Thor's hammer! Does Yvaine know?'

'Of course not. I spoke to Thorkill alone so as not to frighten her. I couldn't understand why, if I was legally adopted, my father still worried about Gunhild conceiving. After all, a man wants many sons.'

'Not with the curse of madness.' Thorolf shook his head. 'What will you do?'

Rorik returned to his chair and sat down. 'Tomorrow I'll see Ragnald about selling the estate.'

'Selling!' Thorolf sat upright, startled all over again. 'That's a bit final, isn't it?'

'You know I've never been content here. I'll leave Othar enough to support himself and his mother, but—'

'What!'

'I can't leave them with nothing,' he said impatiently. 'Besides, I warrant 'tis Gunhild who's behind everything. Othar might have thought to suppress some of the tale, but I can't see him coolly waiting until after the funeral so Ingerd could give just enough evidence to convince everyone I was the son of a slave, then arranging to have her killed. Left to his own devices, he would have confronted me the minute he heard the truth.'

Remembering Othar's avid anticipation when his mother had announced the partial truth of Rorik's birth, Thorolf had to agree, but he looked far from satisfied.

'I hate to think of Gunhild being left with anything,' he grumbled. 'Damn it, she's getting away with murder.'

'Ingerd's killer is dead and disposed of without comforts for the Otherworld. As for Gunhild, she'll lose wealth, power, and position. In all but country, 'twill mean banishment in truth.'

'But what about you? You'll still need a base.'

Rorik merely shrugged.

Thorolf's eyes narrowed. 'Ragnald might be interested in buying Einervik,' he said slowly, watching his friend. 'Three of his sons are married with families, and he mentioned at the funeral that Ari was thinking of moving to Iceland to ease the problem of overcrowding.'

'That would certainly simplify matters.' Rorik rose and stretched. 'Well, I'm for my bed. I'll see Ragnald in the morning and settle on a fair price. You'll need your share, too, Thorolf. My father would have wished it.'

'Thanks, but 'tis not necessary. Unlike you, I picked up the odd piece of gold and silver whenever we raided England.' He continued to watch Rorik as he added, 'Not that I'm going to do that this time. I'm merely coming along to make sure you don't put your head in a noose.'

Rorik cocked a quizzical brow as he turned away. 'Why would I do that?' he asked lightly.

'Why indeed?' muttered Thorolf, but he said it into his drinking horn as he watched his friend walk out of the hall. He had a niggling feeling that he might already know the answer. An answer that solved the puzzle of why Rorik was selling Einervik with no plans to settle elsewhere. An answer that made reparation to the English king for Yvaine's abduction while allowing Rorik to avenge Sitric's death. An answer he couldn't oppose without impugning his friend's honour.

Rorik intended to offer himself in single combat against Edward. And unless he was willing to kill Yvaine's cousin, he didn't expect to survive the encounter.

Something was very wrong.

Yvaine stood in the sunlit doorway overlooking the fjord and cast her mind back over the past few hours. Everything was packed and, even as she watched, being stowed on board *Sea Dragon*.

That was the problem. *Everything* was packed. Or in readiness to be loaded at the last minute. The great shield had been taken down; the fur of Rorik's ice-bear rolled and tied with rope. Even Egil's elaborately carved bed had been dismantled and taken on board. It was a wonder *she* still had a bed to sleep in that night.

And that wasn't all. Beyond the household walls, a steward was totting up what was owed to the karls, several slaves were being freed, children given small trinkets. It was perfectly obvious, even if she hadn't learned what had passed between Rorik and Thorolf from Anna, that Rorik didn't intend to return to Einervik.

She shifted uneasily, cursing herself for falling asleep last night the moment her head touched the pillow. Understandable after two virtually sleepless nights, but in light of the fact that she'd neither heard Rorik enter their chamber, nor leave it at what must have been an ungodly hour this morning, more than a little disastrous. Now she was groping about in the dark, knowing what he intended, but not knowing why.

She frowned in the direction of the pier, noting the empty space beside *Sea Dragon*. Othar must have taken Egil's longship to go into hiding with his mother. They must have gone some distance, she decided, if he needed a ship instead of one of the smaller *faerings*.

But that wasn't her concern. Seeing Thorolf, standing in the stern in solemn consultation with a crewman, she started down towards the water. Then halted. Even if Thorolf knew more than he'd told Anna, she doubted he'd enlighten her. In truth, she didn't want company, which was why she'd escaped from the house after helping Anna pack up their belongings. She needed to clear her mind, to think how she would tackle Rorik when he returned.

She turned to look up at the mountain behind her. A thick pine forest covered the slope to a considerable height, but sunlight streamed through the trees, creating glades of light and shade. Perhaps she could sit there, within sight of the hall, and sort out the questions in her head while she watched for Rorik's return.

The sound of a door slamming inside the house decided her. Yvaine began to climb, trying to make sense of the nameless dread that brushed, a ghostly whisper, across the back of her mind.

Something had changed. From the moment they'd left Thorkill's *shieling*, there'd been a calm, implacable purpose about Rorik that unnerved her. She felt as if the passion they'd shared had been but a moment snatched out of time, the memory of a dream. He wasn't cold towards her, or even distant, but since she'd woken yesterday, he'd been treating her with the grave, gentle courtesy he might have used towards a guest who had been tipped over the edge of the world and almost devoured by the dragons who awaited her there.

Was that why he was taking her to England? she wondered suddenly. To recover? What did he think would happen to her there, where dragons of another sort lay waiting, ready to strip her of all chance at happiness? He must know she would be whisked away from him the instant Edward clapped eyes on her.

A fine shivering started deep inside her. Surely there was no longer any reason to return to England. A message to Edward, in her own hand, explaining what had happened—with certain facts omitted—and assuring her cousin that she was honourably wed and content, would allay immediate reprisal from that quarter. Their time in Thorkill's hut had convinced her Rorik still desired her. He no longer had reason to leave Einervik. Why was he cutting all ties with Norway? Why did he need so much money that he had to sell his home?

Unless…

Dear God, was he thinking of offering Edward some sort of…*compensation*? As if the two nights they'd shared, the happiest, the most wondrous of her life, had rendered her less worthy.

She stopped walking, wrapping her arms around herself and blinking away a tear. That would be *worse* than being used for ransom. Surely Rorik couldn't have shared those nights with her, taken her with such fierceness, such heart-shattering tenderness, and still give her back—with payment for damage done? She couldn't think it of him. And yet…he was taking her to England.

The sharp snap of a broken twig jerked her out of her thoughts. She blinked, looking around, a startled exclamation parting her lips as she realised that, deep in thought, she'd climbed higher than she'd intended.

She turned to peer through the trees, searching for a glimpse of the fjord. A flash of water reassured her, but the sunny glade she'd seen from the house was now far below her and to the left, and here, deep in the pines, the light was muted.

It was very quiet. Even the breeze had dropped. Uneasiness of another sort stole over her. She glanced over her shoulder, straining to hear any sound that would convince her the snapped twig had been caused by the passing of some small creature. The shadowy forest seemed to listen with her. Silent. Waiting.

Nothing stirred.

She shook her head and started downhill, scolding herself every step of the way. She hadn't even managed to climb in a straight line, for heaven's sake. But no matter. With the fjord to guide her she could go straight down to the meadow and walk back along the shore.

In the open.

'Silly,' she muttered, her heartbeat slowing as the edge of the forest came into view a few minutes later. With Gunhild and Othar gone there was no danger. Funny, though, how it was easier to believe that when she stepped into the sunlight.

She glanced around, realising she was further from the house than she'd anticipated. The hall was out of sight, around a slight bend. In front of her, midway between fjord and forest, a great pile of earth blocked her view of the shore. She'd stumbled on to Egil's burial mound.

There was no gravestone, she saw as she approached, but no doubt Rorik would leave instructions to have one erected. She wondered idly if she might have come to like the old man, given time. She thought so. He'd made mistakes, aye, but he'd paid for them with years of loss and regret.

She stared at the bare earth that, by next summer, would be covered with sweet-smelling meadow grass and wildflowers. Which of his father's mistakes, she wondered uneasily, was Rorik determined not to repeat?

A cloud passed over the sun as if in answer. She shivered, looking skyward.

Strange. There were no clouds. Then what…

Pain exploded in her head before she could finish the question. She gasped, staggered, lifted a hand. When her fingers touched nothing she tried to turn, to cry out, but the mound of earth was rushing towards her, darkness closing. Another shadow moved. She had one brief glimpse of a grinning face, floating, amorphous…then everything went black.

She knew what had happened the instant she woke, and terror bludgeoned her like a war club. Her heart stopped; her vision hazed, the scene before her wavering in cloudy patterns as memory clashed with cruel reality.

A ship, like *Sea Dragon* but not. A crew of Vikings, but a scarce half-dozen of them. A leader who was tall and fair, but whose eyes were a cold blue, and whose face wore an expression of such vicious triumph she stayed prone on the deck, eyes squeezed shut again, too terrified to move in case Othar discovered she was conscious.

The sun beat down on her aching head. She ignored it; an aching head was nothing compared to the panic churning inside her.

How long had she been lying here? She had no idea, but it helped to concentrate on the question. Not much, but enough to steady her disordered senses, to resist the urge to fling herself into the sea. Rorik would come after her. She knew that beyond any doubt. All she had to do was survive until he found her.

Where was Othar taking her? By the motion of the ship they were already at sea, but—

'She's been lying senseless a long time. How hard did you hit her?'

Othar's voice directly above her had her fingers pressing into the deck. Her breath seized.

'Not that hard,' growled a second voice. 'The wench should have stirred long since. Who is she, anyway?'

'You're right,' muttered Othar, ignoring the question. 'She sleeps overlong for a simple tap on the head.'

He kicked her in the ribs.

Shock wrenched a cry from her. Knowing that feigning sleep was now impossible, she let herself roll with the blow and sat up. The movement made her head swim dizzily, but she'd put a few inches between herself and Othar.

Waving away his crewman, Othar sat down on an upturned pail and smiled at her. 'Good,' he said, as if she'd woken quite naturally. 'You're awake. I was getting bored with no one to talk to.'

Yvaine could only stare at him. Her head seemed to be stuffed with feathers. She couldn't think, couldn't reconcile this pleasant, smiling Othar with the vicious, self-indulgent youth who'd had her knocked senseless and kidnapped. 'Your men,' she finally got out.

'I can't tell *them* anything,' he scoffed. 'They wouldn't understand. I suppose you don't either, but when I've explained everything, you'll be grateful.'

'Grateful...'

'For saving your life. My mother would've had you killed.'

'She tried...that man...'

'Aye. She sent Hjorr after you. I told her the scheme wouldn't work. I've seen Rorik fight, so I knew Hjorr wouldn't stand a chance. She should've listened to me.'

'You didn't go away,' she murmured, struggling to work it out.

'No. At least, only to an island a few miles down the fjord. Far enough away so Rorik wouldn't know I was waiting. I knew you'd come back with the stone. I told my mother so, but she hated Rorik so much she wouldn't listen to me.'

Othar leaned forward. 'I think she's gone a little mad,' he confided. 'I couldn't tell if she was talking about Rorik or Sitric. She hated you, too. It changed her. She was quite clever until then, but now I'm in charge.'

Everything in her recoiled at his closeness, at the smiling face, the gleaming, feverish eyes. She forced herself to stay still, to keep her voice steady. 'Where is your mother, Othar?'

'On the island. She would have tried again, you see. I couldn't let her kill you. Besides,' he added with a touch of spite, 'she didn't think I could plan, but she was wrong.'

'You left Gunhild on an island?'

'Something like that,' he answered vaguely, waving a hand.

Yvaine swallowed against the sudden tightness in her throat. A hideous thought had struck her, a suspicion more chilling than all the rest, but she wouldn't let herself think about it.

Othar tapped her arm, smiling again. 'I've been very clever,' he boasted. 'I'll show Rorik that I can have everything, too. I've got a ship and some men, and now you.'

'Where are we going?' she managed. Aye, keep him in this complacent, satisfied mood. It was eerie in its unfamiliarity, but, blessed Mother, better that than violence.

'Ireland. You'll like it. My mother didn't. 'Twas another plan she wouldn't consider. I always thought she was on my side, but she turned against me like everyone else. You won't, will you? You understood about my father.'

Yvaine shook her head even as her mind raced. Ireland! Would Rorik remember that Othar had mentioned Ireland on board *Sea Dragon*? Would he discover which way they'd gone, or would he cross the North Sea directly to England? Dear God, he could go anywhere.

'How long will it take?' she whispered.

'Oh, a few days. We have to stay close to land. You see how clever I am? I don't know as much about sailing as Rorik, so we'll go up the west coast of Norway and straight across to the Orkneys. Then we'll follow the islands and the English coast. Don't you think that's a good idea?'

'Aye, very good.'

Othar looked pleased. 'I knew you'd think so. 'Twas my plan to take you, also. I thought we'd have to draw you into the forest with a message of some sort so we could take you overland to the ship, but you made it easier by turning up at the burial mound. No one would've thought anything of it, if they'd seen me there.'

Yvaine cleared her throat. 'A message. Is that how… Ingerd…?'

'Hasn't Rorik discovered that yet? He's not so smart, after all. Aye, my mother told Ingerd to meet Hjorr in a clearing above the fjord. She thought 'twas where she'd get her reward.' Othar laughed. 'She got her reward all right, and so will anyone who goes against me.' He threw back his head as he spoke, wild exultation in his eyes, but an instant later he hunched forward again, glancing quickly from side to side. 'You'll have to keep a lookout for Rorik,' he whispered. 'No one knows where we've gone, but Rorik's good. He used to take me hunting, so I know he's good. You'll tell me if you see anything, won't you? I'm going to be very busy with my ship.'

Yvaine nodded, surprised she could make even that response. When Othar rose and left her, she was incapable of movement for several seconds. It was plain that she, the crew and the ship were in the hands of a madman. A madman who didn't have a tithe of Rorik's strength, endurance or experience.

The knowledge beat at her, over and over, until, finally, the pitching of the ship broke through the hammer blows of fear. She edged back until she could sit against the side. She had to stay calm. It was no use panicking about Othar's madness or lack of seamanship. While the sea remained calm there was little danger, and the crew, at least, appeared to know what they were doing.

She studied the men cautiously, making sure she didn't meet anyone's eyes. Unkempt hair and beards made them look uncannily alike. None were familiar. She remembered Gunnar and Ketil, and was suddenly thankful that one had left Rorik's ship at Kaupang and the other was at the bottom of the sea.

On the other hand, she thought as she intercepted a sly, sidelong glance, these could be worse.

Shuddering, she raised herself and peered over the side. Far behind them a dark grey line marked the horizon. It could have been cloud, or the fast disappearing shores of Norway. There was no other land in sight. They had begun the crossing westward.

Yvaine sank back to the deck and gingerly probed the tender spot at the back of her head. Her hair was still braided, but her headkerchief was missing. She had no recollection of losing it. Given how far they'd come, and the position of the sun, she must have been unconscious most of the day.

The thought of being handled by Othar and his men while she lay senseless had her stomach heaving, but she forced the images away, reached instead for a waterbag that lay nearby. The cool trickle of liquid sliding down her throat made her feel immeasurably better.

She would survive this, she vowed, fisting her hands around the bag. While they were at sea, with the ship undermanned and Othar intent on getting away from

Rorik, she might be reasonably safe. The real danger would come when they landed. But no matter what, she would survive.

And that had been an empty vow, or no, she thought two days later as she rubbed eyes burning from the strain of watching the equally empty sea.

Oh, she survived. Had she been hungry, thirsty, abused, she would still have held on to life. But she had water. Othar tossed her some food whenever he ate. Someone had even handed her a bucket when she'd eyed the communal slop-pail with a mixture of embarrassment and despair.

When the demands of nature had to be met, she arranged her long skirts to retain some degree of modesty, even though the chuckles, the leers, the whispered jests, flayed her spirit. So she survived.

But, by the saints, she was tired. The strain of being constantly on guard was sapping her strength, stripping her nerves raw. Too afraid to sleep, she dozed for minutes only, jerking awake at any sound or movement that came too close.

She'd made a place for herself between a sea-chest and a cross-rib near Othar's station at the stern, thinking that if he was bent on emulating Rorik, he wouldn't be inclined to share her. At least not immediately.

She'd been right, but there was a chilling flaw in her strategy. Othar chatted to her incessantly, pointing out how clever he'd been as though seeking her approval. And she was forced to respond, to keep him in his smug, self-satisfied mood, to avoid tipping him over the edge into the violence that simmered just beneath the surface.

For it was there. It shrilled in his voice whenever the men were too slow to carry out an order; it twisted his face whenever the wind drifted and he had to change course. It was there when he fixed her with the hungry stare she'd seen in the bathhouse, and she dreaded the moment when they'd be alone, knowing her apparent acquiescence, now, would make rejection that much more dangerous.

Yet what else could she do? Tell the men Othar had kidnapped his brother's wife? Force a confrontation at sea where escape was impossible? She couldn't be sure they would take her part, especially when one of them knew she'd been taken near Einervik and had helped Othar in the taking. Even if she threatened them with Rorik's vengeance she might not be safe. To men of little thought and brutish instincts, the threat of vengeance had few teeth when there was no sign of the avenger. They could rape her, throw her overboard and disperse to lie low the minute they landed. She was balanced on a knife-edge. Like the line she walked with Othar, danger threatened no matter what course she chose.

And she might be forced to choose soon, she thought, hugging herself against a chill as evening closed in on the second day. The western isles and the north of England were now within easy reach and, for the better part of an hour, the men had been demanding to go ashore to take on more provisions. Both areas were settled by Norsemen and thus safe ports, but Othar was making no move to change course.

She didn't know whether to add her voice to the men's in the hope that Othar might listen to her. Landing would slow them down, give Rorik a chance to catch them. But if they beached the ship for the night, she would be staring danger in the face before ever they reached Ireland.

Heaven save her, she didn't know what to do, what to pray for. Was no longer sure her prayers would be heard. Battered by fear and exhaustion, she felt utterly alone. Had God forsaken her because she loved a heathen? she wondered vaguely, staring at the distant horizon. The priests would say so. They would denounce her love for Rorik as a sin.

Then I am indeed a sinner, she thought, clenching her fists on top of the side in a burst of defiance. For I love him and always will. If that makes me a heathen, too, then so be it.

And in that moment when anger and fierce resolve burned away some of her tiredness, an image of Katyja flashed through her mind. The words she'd dismissed and long forgotten echoed as clearly as though the witch stood beside her.

You will remember my words and be strong. Two ships...one fleeing, one pursuing. Death surrounds you, but it does not touch you.

'Two ships,' she whispered. 'Oh, Rorik.'

She sank to her knees, folding her arms on the topmost plank as she strained to see in the dimming light. The horizon misted before her eyes, creating wavering patterns, so that, for an instant, she thought she'd seen something. A flash, as though the setting sun had struck something bright.

She squeezed her eyes shut, looked again.

Nothing. And yet, she could have sworn—

'And I say we *are* going to Ireland.'

She sprang up, turning and slamming against the side as Othar shouted the words behind her. He was still at the steering oar, but the other men had left their posts to confront him in a group, the man who had knocked her senseless a pace ahead of the rest.

'We're not here to throw our lives away,' he growled. 'You never mentioned Ireland.'

'Well, I'm telling you now. *I*'m the leader of this ship, Kalf, and—'

'Leaders can be replaced,' Kalf interrupted. 'Especially one who lies. You promised us loot in England if we didn't interfere with your business.' He jerked a thumb at Yvaine. ''Tis time to deliver.'

At a rumble of agreement from the others, some of Othar's bluster wavered. 'You'll get your loot,' he said sulkily. 'No one's asking you to stay in Ireland. You can leave us and go. You can even take the ship,' he added, as though coming up with a brilliant idea.

''Twould be difficult to go anywhere without it,' Kalf snapped. He bit out a curse and gestured with rough impatience. 'You fool! The Celts drove us Norsemen from Ireland a few months past. Aided by the Danes, Odin curse them. Haven't you seen the beacons along the coast? We've been spotted. If we land, our lives won't be worth a thrall's ransom.'

'But we have to go to Ireland,' Othar yelled. 'Rorik won't look for us there.'

'Rorik?' Kalf's eyes narrowed. 'Why would Rorik be looking for you, Othar? You said he'd been banished.'

Yvaine's lips parted. She took a step forward, glanced over her shoulder.

Nothing.

When she looked back, Othar was speaking again, his face sullen.

'It doesn't matter. You were the one who wanted provisions, Kalf. Here's your chance.'

'Not in Ireland. You change course for England, or we'll do it for you. By morning we'll be off the northernmost part of the Danelaw. Get the Danes to take you to Ireland if you're set on losing your life.'

Othar's lips thinned, but it must have been plain, even to his deranged mind, that he was outnumbered.

'All right,' he muttered. 'We'll take on more food in England. Raid a town or two.'

Looking thoughtful, the men nodded, dispersing to their places in a silence that spoke louder than words. Kalf sent her a long look, before he, too, turned away.

Yvaine sank back against the side, her heart pounding. One more night. One more night before she would have to face Othar, or try to escape.

Could she do it? They would be landing very close to the border, which dissected England roughly from south-east to north-west. Once on land, could she risk asking Kalf to help her? He alone of the crew seemed wary of Rorik. Would that wariness incline him to stand alone against his leader—in Norse law a crime punishable by death—or would he throw in his lot with the others?

She didn't know, but there was one thing she was sure of. The question was going to keep her awake for another night.

'They've changed course for England.'

Out of sight, below the horizon, the lookout on a

ship with a gilded wind-vane yelled the information down to his leader's second-in-command.

Thorolf nodded and strode aft to pass the news to Rorik.

'Do you think they saw us?' he asked, when there was no response.

Rorik tore his gaze from the seamless line dividing sea and sky. 'If our informant was right,' he said curtly, 'Othar has a half-dozen men. He can't afford to have someone on the mast as lookout.' His hand clenched around the steering oar with so much force he wondered the wood didn't crack. 'I hope.'

'Aye. His crew must have barely enough time to sleep. Even Othar will have to pull his weight.'

'Aye. He won't have time to—' His teeth snapped shut on the rest.

'She'll be all right, Rorik. Tonight we'll get close enough to chase him into land, or board him at dawn, before he has much warning. You'll get her back.'

A muscle flickered in Rorik's jaw. Aye, he'd get Yvaine back, he vowed, and stopped his thoughts right there.

Because if he let himself consider the alternative he'd lose his mind. Even the thought of Yvaine in the hands of brutal warriors for one more night caused his gut to tie itself in knots. Every instinct he possessed was screaming at him to give chase *now*, to close the distance between the two ships and snatch her to safety before daylight was lost.

And he knew he had to wait, to give Othar as little warning as possible. His brother was too unpredictable. If he turned on Yvaine before they were close enough to save her, Rorik knew he would go mad. And if he lost the rigid control he was hanging on to by a thread, he'd be no help to anyone.

He would get her back.

He wouldn't let himself believe anything else.

Chapter Fourteen

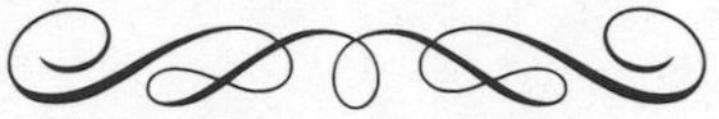

Shouts ripped through the curtain of sleep that had fallen over her like a pall.

Yvaine sat bolt upright, blinking in the grey light. Dawn had crept up on her while she'd succumbed to exhaustion. Before she saw the danger accompanying it, a hand fisted around her braid and hauled her to her feet.

'Bitch!' Othar screamed. 'You were supposed to keep watch. You were supposed to warn me.' His free hand flashed upward, catching the side of her face without any warning. Her involuntary cry was cut off when his arm swung back the other way. This time his fist was clenched; this time he let her fall.

She dropped to the deck and lay motionless, her mind hazing. Then, spurred by the vague thought that she wouldn't cower at his feet, she forced her head up.

Othar was storming about the ship in a mindless frenzy. She flinched as he kicked a pail out of his path. He snatched an oar from one of the men and swung it at the mast. The crack of shattering wood had her flattening herself to the deck as splinters flew.

'We don't need oars,' he yelled. 'We have to get away. Hoist the sail!'

She blinked at the sail. It bellied out in the wind as it had for the past few days.

Before she could wonder why Othar couldn't see it, he rushed past her. 'No, we'll land. That's it. We'll land and run. You hear me, Kalf? Why aren't the oars out?'

'Holy Mother of God,' she whispered. 'He's run mad.' She wasn't sure if she crossed herself; her mind was drifting like fog. Moving as if she was crawling through the stuff, she pulled herself up against the side. One side of her face felt numb; her legs barely supported her. She hung on, trying to see through the mist in front of her eyes.

Something wavered in the distance. Land. They'd sailed into a wide bay; hills surrounded them on three sides. And ahead…

She narrowed her eyes. Were those tents on the hill above the beach? She couldn't see, couldn't be sure. But even if a bustling city loomed ahead of them, why would Othar descend into raving incoherence?

She turned her head in time to see him throw a sea-chest over the side. There was an immediate explosion of rage from its owner.

'Fool!' Othar swung a fist at the man even as he looked around for something else to jettison. 'We have to go faster! He's put up a red shield. He wants to fight.'

Fight? Who?

Still clinging to the side, Yvaine peered toward the stem.

Sea Dragon. Oh, God, it was real. There was the red and white sail, billowing in the wind. The fierce dragon's head on the prow dipped towards the water, cleaving the waves as though devouring them. A red shield hung from her prow, a challenge to battle. She looked warlike, menacing and unstoppable. And she was gaining on them fast.

'Rorik!'

Her scream was snatched away by the wind, but her movement as she staggered sternward alerted Othar. He sprang to intercept her, dragging her back against him and wrapping an arm around her throat.

'I'm not finished with you,' he shrieked. 'Not finished.'

'Leave her alone, Othar.' It was Kalf, looking as if he'd finally realised there was more to her presence than the simple kidnapping of an unwilling wench. 'You're behaving like a fool. If that is Rorik behind us, he doesn't intend to fight a battle at sea, his sail is still up.'

'Of course it's *Sea Dragon*, you dolt. Do you think I don't know my brother's ship?' Othar's arm tightened, almost cutting off her breath.

'All right, 'tis Rorik. Then you'd better have a good reason before I go against him.'

'I'm Rorik's wife,' gasped Yvaine, barely able to get the words out. 'Othar—'

'Be silent.' Othar's voice was suddenly ice-cold. As cold as the dagger he drew and pressed to her throat.

I've felt this before, she thought through the roaring in her ears. That night on the beach…

But the memory vanished as Othar's grip shifted. He began to crowd her against the side, one hand fisting in the neck of her shift as he forced her upper body over the rail. 'Don't move, Kalf, or I'll slit her throat.'

Kalf obeyed. The others stood like statues.

No help there, Yvaine decided, fighting dizziness as the sea rushed past her eyes. But helpless or no, she would not die. She would not die with Rorik so close.

'Othar, if you kill me, Rorik will hunt you to the edge of the world. He'll—'

'I'm not going to kill you,' he snarled. 'I'm going to slow Rorik down. And I hope you drown before he gets to you.'

She felt a hard shove, Othar's hands on her hips. Then there was nothing around her but air.

'He's less than a quarter-mile ahead, Rorik. You were right. The battle challenge made him run for shore. He's trapped.'

Rorik held the ship steady into the waves, grateful for the grim concentration needed to overtake Othar. The distance between the two vessels was shrinking rapidly. He could see people moving about on Othar's ship now, but the sun was bursting over the hills ahead of them, shining right in his eyes. He couldn't tell which one was Yvaine.

'He won't have time to hurt her if he's worrying about me catching him,' he muttered, and tried to believe it.

'She's alive,' yelled Thorolf, shading his eyes with his hand. 'There, amidships, with Othar. What in the name of… He's throwing her overboard!'

Rorik shoved the steering oar violently to one side as the shout left Thorolf's lips. The big vessel listed dangerously, almost taking the mast overboard, then steadied and leapt forward, a hound freed from the leash.

At the same time Yvaine disappeared beneath a rolling wave.

Rorik grabbed Thorolf, spinning him around with an iron-fisted grip on his shoulder as his friend sprang for the side. 'Take the *styri*,' he ordered, unbuckling his belt. He flung his sword to the deck and stripped off his tunic and undershirt.

'No, wait.' Thorolf cast an anxious glance at Rorik's set face. 'The ship will get there faster. Yvaine can swim, remember? She kept on telling you so. She'll be all right. Wait until I have to bring the ship into the wind.'

Rorik didn't answer. He was poised on the side, every muscle tense, as he scanned the surface of the water. 'Why doesn't she come up?' he said through his teeth.

'She can swim,' Thorolf repeated, hoping to the Gods Yvaine was still alive to give truth to the statement.

'She's fully clothed. And with those damned brooches—*there!*' He went over the side in a low, powerful dive that took him well clear of the ship.

Cursing helplessly, Thorolf yanked on the steering oar as he saw why Rorik hadn't waited. An off-shore current was sweeping Yvaine right into the path of the speeding, oncoming ship. He'd have to slow down or alter course to avoid running over her; both alternatives would waste precious time.

But Rorik was a powerful swimmer. Thorolf prayed his friend would reach Yvaine before she tired.

The shock of cold water closing over her head jolted Yvaine back to full awareness. That was something to be grateful for, she thought grimly as she kicked towards the surface. Nothing happened; her legs were tangled in her skirts. She reached down to pull them free of the heavy wool and sank deeper. Panic clawed at her throat. She fought it back, struggling to rid herself of her heavy brooches. Her chest was burning, she couldn't see…

Ah. The second brooch opened, her top garment floated free. Her head broke the surface seconds later and she gulped in air, letting the waves take her as she turned this way and that, searching frantically for Rorik's ship. Before she could locate it she was swept down into a deep trough.

She couldn't even see the land from here, she realised, panic raking fresh claws across her throat. Waves were all around her, surrounding her, huge swells carrying her across the bay, not directly into shore. She might stay afloat if she got rid of her outer shift, but swimming against such a heavy sea was impossible. Already the effort of keeping her head above water was sapping her strength. Her light skin shoes felt like logs tied to her ankles; her shift tangled about her legs, hampering her movements and threatening to drag her under again. She struggled with the wet ties at her throat, almost sobbing when the sodden knots defeated her.

Suddenly *Sea Dragon* loomed ahead. She opened her mouth to cry out, swallowed salt water instead as a wave slapped her in the face. The ship was lost to sight as she slid down the other side of the rolling swell.

Then, out of nowhere, a strong arm gripped her from behind.

''Tis all right, my darling girl. My brave love. I've got you.'

'Rorik…' She choked on another mouthful of water, tried to turn her head.

'Hush. Be still. We're almost there.'

And they were. The ship was beside them, a solid haven of safety. Hands reached over the side to pull her from the clinging embrace of the sea. A moment later Rorik hauled himself on board, water streaming from his powerful body.

He took her from Thorolf, pulled her into his arms and held her as if defying the very Gods themselves to wrench her from his embrace.

'I didn't think I'd be in time,' he said hoarsely. 'You didn't come up and I thought—' He broke off, shuddered.

'I'm all right,' she whispered. And burying her face in his shoulder, she burst into tears.

The storm didn't last long; a few seconds only to let all the tightly stoppered fear burst forth, to give in to relief at seeing him again, at being safe in his arms. Rorik held her, saying nothing until she gulped, sniffed and fell silent.

Then he tipped her face up to his, his eyes going the colour of ice as they narrowed on her jaw. 'Did Othar try to knock you senseless before he threw you into the sea?'

'No.' She covered his hand with hers when he lifted it to cradle her cheek. The numbness was wearing off, a painful throbbing was taking its place. 'This was earlier. He ran mad…lost all reason. Oh, Rorik, you don't know. I think Othar has killed Gunhild.'

'Aye.' He drew her closer, as though he would shield her from the knowledge. 'We found her on one of the islands in the fjord. Strangled.'

'Strangled!' She gazed up at him in horror. 'God have mercy.'

'Don't waste your pity,' said Thorolf behind her. 'The woman cold-bloodedly used Ingerd, then had her killed, and had no compunction about sending her hired assassin after you and Rorik.'

'I know, but to plot like that for Othar only to have him turn against her—' She shivered, then realised she'd been shivering all along.

'Hel!' Seeing it at the same time, Rorik turned his head. 'Get the sail down,' he yelled to his men. 'We're going in under oars. Any of you look this way for the next few minutes, you'll be going in without your heads.'

He bent, picked her up and carried her to the stem. 'Here, sweetheart, get out of those wet clothes. You can wear my tunic.'

'There's a mantle here somewhere,' Thorolf offered as Rorik set her down near the steering oar. He turned away to rummage behind a pile of axes. 'You were wearing it when we left.'

'Aye.' Drawing his dagger, Rorik sliced through the ties at the neck of her two remaining garments and stripped them down her body. He tossed his shirt and tunic over her head and yanked them into place.

Yvaine hugged the warm garments to her as Rorik rolled the sleeves up past her hands. She had to smile wryly at the picture she made, but Rorik's expression remained carved from stone. He took his mantle from

Thorolf, wrapped it around her waist and fastened it with the pin to make a rough skirt.

'You'll have to hold it up to walk,' he said. 'But 'tis better than nought.'

'Aye. Rorik, what—?'

'You haven't slept,' he interrupted, and stroked his thumb across her cheekbone.

She studied him, seeing the shadows beneath his eyes, the way the skin was drawn tight across his cheekbones, the rigid line of his jaw. 'Nor have you.'

'No. There were enough nightmares chasing me without leaving that door wide open. The same nightmare that chased you, I expect.' He lowered his hand, gently touched her aching jaw. 'Was this all?' he asked very low.

'Aye. I'm all right, Rorik. Just…' Her lower lip quivered. She blinked hard against another onrush of tears. Tears of relief this time as she realised she'd probably escaped being alone with Othar by mere minutes. 'Just tired.'

'Aye. You'll be able to rest soon, sweetheart.' His voice was impossibly tender as he urged her to sit down on the deck. No sea-chests this time, she thought vaguely. There was nothing on board but men and weapons.

'Othar won't come near you again,' he vowed as he stood and began to untie the lashing on the steering-oar. He called out an order to his men and the ship began to move forward again.

The abrupt change from bobbing about on the waves to purpose and power had Yvaine's tears drying in a second. 'Where are we going?' As if she didn't know.

'After Othar.'

'But…to take him back to Norway?'

'No.'

The single word had her scrambling to her feet, her heart in her throat. 'Rorik, no. You mean to kill him, don't you?'

He didn't even glance at her. 'Othar brought about his own death the minute he took you.'

'But the hand he dies by will be yours. Please. Don't do it.'

That brought his head around. 'You care what happens to Othar?'

'No.' Her lashes quivered at the glittering intensity in his eyes, but she held his gaze. 'I care what it will do to you. He's your brother. And he's not…sane. Besides, he didn't intend to kill me. He threw me overboard to give himself time to get away from you.'

'If he did,' Thorolf put in, 'he's not going far.' He'd been standing nearby, ostensibly studying the shore, but able to hear every word. Now he glanced over his shoulder. 'We might have more to deal with than Othar, Rorik.'

Rorik continued to watch her for several unnerving seconds, then narrowed his eyes at the beach. 'Looks like Othar has run into soldiers of some sort.'

'Aye. Just what we need. To land in the middle of a battle that's none of our business.'

Yvaine peered towards the beach; it seemed to be swarming with men. She had to suppress a craven desire to suggest that they simply turn around and sail away. She'd had enough of violence and fear and uncertainty.

'Have someone take that red shield down,' Rorik ordered. 'Put up a white one.'

'What does that mean?' she asked.

'A white shield means we want to talk, to treat. If they're Danish they'll know that.'

'And if they're English?'

'We hope they'll know that.'

'Dear God. Rorik, Othar isn't worth—' She stopped as a fluttering movement far above them caught her eye. Those *were* tents on top of the hill, she realised, lifting a hand to shade her eyes from the sun. Several of them. And flying from the largest…

She stared in disbelief for several seconds before excited recognition dawned. 'The standard of Wessex,' she cried, turning and gripping Rorik's arm. 'Rorik, look. 'Tis the standard of Wessex. 'Tis Edward.'

The ship slid gently into the sandy shallows as the words left her lips.

'What do you think?' asked Thorolf, low-voiced, when they were immediately surrounded by soldiers.

'I think Edward is going to ask questions first.' Rorik took Yvaine's hand and led her towards the side. 'Tell the men to stay on board. If anyone reaches for a weapon, he'll answer to me.'

'As if we have a choice.' Thorolf eyed the small army surrounding them and tried a smile. No one smiled back.

Yvaine looked from the phalanx of unmoving warriors to Rorik's face and felt excitement metamorphose into dread. He had that implacable air of resolve about him again, as though nothing and no one was going to swerve him from his course. 'Rorik, I'll speak to Edward first. He'll—'

'No.' He released her hand, vaulted down to the sand, then turned and lifted her over the side.

As he did so, a soldier came striding along the beach towards them, sword in hand. He was tall, brown-haired, and dressed in a businesslike leather tunic and woollen chausses. A leather helm covered his head, but left his bearded face bare. Alert blue eyes swept over the ship, lingered on the white shield, then came to rest on Yvaine.

After another quick glance at Rorik's face, she grabbed up her makeshift skirts, darted past him, and raced down the beach to throw herself into her cousin's arms. 'Edward! Don't kill anyone. *Please*.'

'Yvaine?' Edward removed the arms she'd flung around his neck to prevent any murderous impulse and held her back a few inches. 'By the Rood, it *is* you. We thought you lost. Your priest at Selsey sent word that you'd been taken by Norsemen, and— But the why and the how can wait,' he amended, his keen eyes studying her face. 'The bastard who tried to kill you won't bother anyone again. Whoever these fellows may be, I owe them my thanks for your life.'

'Indeed you do,' she affirmed, nodding rapidly. Then stopped. 'You saw what happened?'

'Enough to have men waiting when those savages landed. Their leader came charging up the beach, offering me the Lady Yvaine of Einervik or some such nonsense. He was raving; a madman, but when he said your name I knew he was the one who'd taken you. I despatched him.'

'Oh.' She drew back, her gaze falling on Edward's bloodied sword. 'You killed Othar.' Explanations whirled in her brain. Before she could pick out the least dangerous one, she felt Edward's hands tense around her arms. She looked up. His gaze was fixed on a point beyond her. Surprise flickered, then his face went very still.

'Greetings, Edward.'

Yvaine felt her own face go blank. A strange humming filled her ears. She had to force herself to move, to step out of the king's hold and turn so she could see Rorik.

His gaze held her cousin's, but beneath the cool glitter in his eyes a spark of amusement showed.

'Rorik,' Edward said, equally coolly. 'You've caused me quite a deal of trouble over the past few years. Cost me nigh on a company of soldiers. I suppose I'll have to forget that now.'

'You know why.'

'Aye.' Edward cocked a sardonic brow. 'Is it over, or is my life about to be forfeit for Sitric?'

''Tis over,' Rorik said curtly. Then added, 'You were never at risk.'

'My relief knows no bounds.'

Yvaine shook her head. She was getting dizzy again from watching one hard face then the other, but one thing was perfectly clear.

'You know each other.'

Both men turned to look at her.

As if they'd just remembered she was there, she thought, anger spearing through the discomfort of her wet hair and still-damp flesh.

But Edward's eyes widened as he got his first good look at her. 'Blood of the saints! This is no place for you, Yvaine. Look at you. 'Tis a wonder you're still on your feet, and—'

'Oh?' Yvaine plunked her hands on her hips. 'Why would you think so, cousin? I've only been kidnapped, thrown into the sea, rescued by a man who doesn't listen to a word I say, and now I discover that the two of you know each other well enough to share some stupid notion of male humour that escapes those of us with more than half a wit. Why would I be anything less than perfectly well?'

Rorik's lips twitched. 'She's perfectly well.'

'So I see,' Edward retorted. 'Obviously the child I sent to Selsey has grown a full complement of female fangs.'

'Indeed she has,' Yvaine agreed, holding his gaze with grim meaning. 'And because you sent that child to Selsey, Edward, you owe me now.'

'Enough, little cat.' Rorik took a step forward, closed his hand around her arm. 'Your cousin isn't used to your methods of negotiation. He and I will sort this out.'

'But—' Aware that the king's brows were climbing towards his helm, Yvaine searched frantically for an explanation that wouldn't put a noose around Rorik's neck.

'You'll have to let me catch up first,' Edward said tartly before she could speak. 'I presume by your tone, cousin, you had some complaint about your husband.'

'You must have known she would,' Rorik said far too softly.

His words alone, never mind the menace in his voice, were enough to have the king glaring. 'Am I a soothsayer? 'Twas arranged through intermediaries as these things are. By the saints, my father had just died. I was up to my ears in council meetings and...' He trailed off as he registered the icy glitter in Rorik's eyes. 'And I didn't know the man,' he finished, frowning.

Rorik's voice went even softer, even more dangerous. 'Then let me enlighten you.'

But Edward's eyes were narrowing as realisation dawned. 'What is this?' he demanded. 'You had time to exchange life sagas while you fished Yvaine out of the sea? Perhaps I was over-hasty in despatching the scum who tried to kill her.'

Rorik shrugged. 'If you hadn't done it, I would have.'

'Oh, no, Rorik...'

He glanced down at her, but not in answer. His fingers tightened briefly about her arm, then he pushed her gently in Edward's direction and released her; a move that threatened to break her heart.

'Yvaine shouldn't be here,' he said. 'Are there women in your camp who can care for her while we talk?'

Edward's gaze shifted. 'Of course! What am I thinking of? Wulf—' He clicked his fingers to summon one of his men. 'Take the Lady Yvaine up to the camp. That wench whose bed you've been warming is about the same size. Make sure she looks after my cousin well.'

'But—'

'Go up to the camp, Yvaine.' Rorik's quiet command cut her off. 'Nothing's going to happen that you need witness.'

What about the things she wasn't going to witness?

'Aye.' Edward agreed. 'This is no place for you. We'll be along in a moment. After I despatch the rest of those pirates.'

She'd forgotten all about Othar's men. With a shocked exclamation she glanced past Edward. Several yards away Othar's crew had been lined up and forced to their knees, their hands bound behind their backs. They were still alive, staring sullenly before them, but—

She didn't see anything else. Rorik seized her arm and whipped her around to face him before she fully realised the bundle of clothes at the end of the line had been Othar. 'I see you heed your cousin as little as you heed me,' he said through his teeth. 'I didn't fish you out of the sea to have you catch a fever. Go! Or I'll carry you up to the camp myself.'

At least that would get him out of Edward's reach. But exhausted, all too aware such a reprieve would be temporary, she capitulated. 'All right, I'll go, but only if you swear not to kill anyone.'

'I have no intention of killing anyone.'

For some reason that made her feel more afraid than ever. She turned her head. 'Edward?'

The king's gaze was shifting back and forth between her and Rorik. 'Is this the debt you mentioned, Yvaine? I am to kill no one involved in your disappearance?' He glanced again at Rorik, speculation in his eyes. 'Very well. I grant your boon.'

''Twas Othar who intended to harm me,' she said, as though in explanation. 'The others didn't know who…who I was…'

She stumbled over that, let it go. Edward could make of it what he would. He was no fool; he knew there was more to the story, but at least she didn't have to worry about her husband and her cousin killing each other.

That left one other thing. The insidious fear that, now she was safe and back in England, Rorik might sail away without seeing her or speaking to her again.

She looked up at him, striving for a courteous tone that no one would question, while her eyes sent a very different message. 'I would like to thank you properly, my lord, for your care of me, for saving my life.' She might as well bludgeon Edward over the head with that as often as possible. 'Perhaps later…'

His mouth twitched; amusement sprang into his eyes. She suddenly realised how absurd she must look, chin held at a dignified lady of the manor angle while her hair dripped down her back and she clutched his mantle to her to avoid tripping over it.

But as her lashes quivered, as anxiety and doubt clouded her eyes, his expression gentled and the cold hand fisted around her heart eased its grip. He took her free hand, lifted it to his lips and pressed a kiss into her palm.

'Don't worry,' he said in a voice meant only for her ears. 'I'll find you. Wherever you are.'

Several hours later she was beginning to doubt that statement. Rorik hadn't found her and she had been summoned before the king.

She obeyed the summons with a mixture of hope and trepidation. Hope when she remembered the way Rorik had held her when he'd plucked her out of the sea. Trepidation because she didn't know what he'd told

Edward and feared it had been the stark, unadorned truth.

Was that why she hadn't seen him all day? she wondered. Because, unable to kill Rorik, Edward had sent him away, and he'd agreed to go out of a sense of honour? True, she'd spent most of the day sleeping, but now the sun was laying a shimmering golden path across the sea, and 'I'll find you wherever you are' was taking on an ominous new meaning. As if some time was going to elapse before he started looking.

She glanced down at herself as she followed Wulf through the camp, unhappily aware that, though she was grateful for the borrowed clothes, a mantle of Lincoln green and a primrose woollen gown were not the most seductive of garments.

On the other hand, a modest appearance was probably more appropriate for her coming interview with the king. Especially given the way she'd behaved on the beach.

She bit her lip, barely suppressing a wince. What had possessed her to speak to her liege lord and sovereign like that? She remembered Edward as a young prince when she'd first come to court. He'd been kind enough, in the distant, careless way of a much older cousin, but he'd been ruler for five years now; had ruthlessly held his crown against another cousin whom many felt had had a stronger claim, and she doubted he'd tolerate such licence again. If he'd been told the truth of her kidnapping, she wasn't even sure which Edward she'd be facing. The kind, older cousin or the king whose ruthless ambition was to rule all England.

She was about to find out. Wulf paused outside a large tent, pulled aside the leather flap across the entrance and motioned her inside. Heart thumping, she stepped over the threshold.

'Ah, cousin.' Edward rose from his chair behind a plain work table and came forward.

'Edward, where is Rorik? What did he tell you? Where are the ships and all his men?'

The minute the words were out, she closed her eyes in despair. 'I…I mean…Sire!' She sank into a deep curtsy.

'Oh, don't spoil it,' he said with more than a touch of sarcasm. 'I've been dealing all afternoon with people who should be grateful they're keeping their heads, but apparently don't share that view.'

She looked up. 'Who?'

'Hmm. Still the direct, straight-to-the-point girl who informed me she'd accept my choice of husband for her as her way of fighting for my crown, but I'd better not forget it.'

He motioned for her to rise and walked around the table to sit again. 'Well, Yvaine, if it's any consolation, Rorik told me what Ceawlin did to you. I suppose I should have sent someone to make sure you were well treated, but why in the name of God didn't you write asking for help?'

'I did,' she retorted, frustrated that he'd ignored her question. 'Ceawlin read the first letter and tore it up. When he made it plain that a messenger would be spared only if he approved my missives, I gave the next one to the priest. He returned it to Ceawlin and I was locked in the solar and starved for two days. The slaves were too afraid to help me, the churls likewise. Besides,' she added, relenting a little as Edward grimaced, ''twas only that one time that he actually beat me.'

'Aye, so Rorik said.' He waved her impatiently to a chair. 'Clearly, he knew what he was about when he carried you off for ransom.'

'Ransom,' she repeated, seating herself in obedience to his gesture. Despite her best efforts, she couldn't keep the tartness out of her voice. 'I see. How much was I worth?'

Edward waved that off. 'The subject was dropped once the reason was given. Rorik merely said that he found his father dying, discovered his mother was English, and decided he'd taken enough revenge for his cousin's death. He swore he was about to bring you home when his brother ran off with you. And, I tell you, Yvaine, I will never understand the Norse.' He thumped his fist on the table, making her jump.

She blinked at him, still grappling with this drastically abbreviated version of events in Norway.

'The man decides to take revenge on his own people, killing off my soldiers year after year because Sitric's stupidity got himself and his men hanged, and yet when I kill his brother, Rorik tells me he would've hanged Othar like the rabid dog he was, rather than give him an honourable death by the sword. Incomprehensible!'

'His own people?' She shook her head. 'Rorik didn't know about his mother at the time of Sitric's death.'

'No, but you mistake my meaning. For a long time I'd thought of Rorik as one of us. Saints, there's only five years between us, we were friends, God damn it. He'd even been Christened.'

'What!'

'You didn't know that?' Edward's brows rose. He was still a moment, then he leaned back in his chair, watching her. 'Well, how should you? Unconscious, taken for ransom. Why would Rorik discuss such matters with you?'

'Why indeed?' Yvaine said grimly. But she couldn't afford the luxury of taking offence now. 'The Norse have a rigid code of vengeance,' she began.

'Good God, girl, you don't need to tell me that!' This time the chair arm received a thump. ''Tis not so different from our Saxon wergild. A man's blood-price should his life be taken. Saves on soldiers,' he added with heavy meaning.

Yvaine winced. Better get off that subject. 'How did Rorik come to be Christened?' she ventured.

The king eyed her narrowly. 'The subject interests you?'

'I know 'tis not an unusual occurrence.' Oh, aye, she could play the game of giving an answer without answering as well as anyone. Edward seemed to accept it, though, for his scowl eased slightly.

'I suppose it began when my father signed that treaty with Guthrum years ago, creating the Danelaw. Guthrum became a Christian, and when Rorik signed on with him a few years later he was properly Christened as well. Guthrum only lived a month or so after that, however, and on his death some of his followers decided the treaty no longer applied to them. The Danes rebelled, and the Norse started raiding the continent.'

'What did Rorik do?'

'When Sitric went off to Normandy with the rest, Rorik came over to us. He was still young, only twenty, and had been used as a messenger between Guthrum and our court several times. My father took an interest in him. Indeed, 'tis a wonder you never met the man, but you were only a babe, and we were away more often than not.'

She shifted restlessly; it wasn't her childhood she needed to hear about. 'And?'

Edward shrugged. 'Rorik divided his time between England and Norway. He'd just returned from a visit home when we heard there'd been a battle at sea against the Danes.' His frown returned. 'My father was building a navy so we could protect the coast, but this particular day was disastrous. The five vessels we had ran aground on a sandbar and the men were slaughtered like rats in a trap. Our soldiers had to watch from the shore, helpless. Their only redress came when the Danish ships were damaged as well, and the crews were forced to land.'

'What happened?' Yvaine asked, as Edward paused.

'Father had the Danes brought to Winchester and hanged for treason. Somehow Sitric and his men were in the middle of it.'

'So they were hanged, too.'

'Aye. Rorik spoke for them but to no avail. He left, swearing vengeance.'

'But he never threatened you or Alfred.'

'Is that supposed to make me look more kindly on his actions now?' Edward demanded, thumping the chair arm again.

'He did bring me back, and…and I should thank him for saving my life. Twice, if you count taking me from Ceawlin.' She thought that was a nice touch. 'If he's still here…'

'Oh, he's here somewhere.' Edward jerked an impatient thumb to indicate the camp. 'You didn't see the ships because Rorik's *Sea Dragon* has been pulled up to the foot of the cliff and Thorolf has taken the other, and the crew, back to Norway. Since you insisted on sparing the lives of the vermin who served Rorik's brother, they went with him, in chains. It was that or be left here without food and weapons when we break camp.'

'Oh.' She wondered if she was supposed to feel guilty for depriving Edward of a mass hanging. 'I don't even know where we are.'

'Near Chester,' he said curtly. 'I'm thinking of restoring the town as a military base.'

'Oh. Well.' She managed a shrug. 'I suppose Rorik will have to wait for Thorolf to return then.'

'I suppose he will.'

She winced at the short agreement. Obviously, leading up to the question she really wanted to ask was not the best way to placate the king's temper. 'Edward, will you please tell me what you've done with him?'

'Done with him? You took care of that when you insisted I didn't kill anyone. A rather rash request when you think what else I could do, but, putting that aside, I'd think you'd be more concerned for your own future.'

'What do you mean?'

'You're a wealthy widow, cousin. Or had you forgotten? You'll need a husband to hold your lands. I intend to look into the matter.'

She gaped at him, her voice rising in horror. 'You'd send me back to Selsey?'

'Why not? Ceawlin's gone.'

'But—'

'A strong man, of course, to weed out any remnants of rebellion there. One who has no lands of his own to divide his loyalties. Not to mention one who can handle this tendency you've developed to make demands.'

'But—'

She couldn't go on. Her throat was too tight. Dear God, how had it come to this? What was she to do? It was no use telling Edward she was already married to Rorik. He'd consign such a union to oblivion; dismiss it out of hand. *She*'d dismissed it, she remembered. *A few heathen words over a cup of ale doesn't make me your wife*, she'd said, and Edward would agree wholeheartedly. And then marry her off with indecent haste in case there were any little consequences.

She couldn't let it happen. She couldn't—

''Twill give you something to think about on your way back to Winchester tomorrow,' Edward concluded.

'What?' She struggled to take it in. 'Winchester? You're sending me away? *Tomorrow?*'

'Aye. In fact—' He clapped his hands and Wulf stepped through the entrance. 'You'd best be off. 'Tis a long journey and you'll need to rest. I think we've said all we need to at present. I'll send a message when arrangements are made.'

It was dismissal. She couldn't believe it. How could he arrange her future like that, and sit calmly waiting for her to leave?

Dazed, sick to her stomach, Yvaine rose. Wulf was holding back the curtain. She barely had enough wit to drop a curtsy to the king before she followed the young man from the tent. Her legs were shaking; her mind hazed…

No! She wouldn't panic. There was a solution somewhere. She just had to find it.

Chapter Fifteen

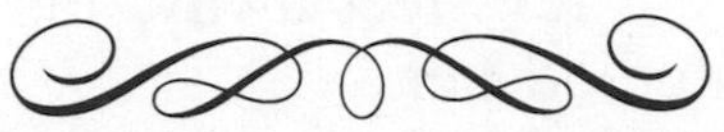

The sun had vanished completely by the time Yvaine found Rorik's tent. And though the soft, pearly light of the summer evening would last for an hour or two yet, a few fires had been lit about the camp. The scent of wood smoke drifted on the breeze, mingling with the mouthwatering aromas wafting from the cooks' fires. Several men were strolling in that direction, thinking of their supper; others gathered around the largest fire where a noisy dice game was in progress. No one was paying her any attention.

Hefting the bundle of clothes that was her excuse should anyone question her, she scratched at the leather curtain hanging across the front of the tent.

'Enter.'

A shiver went through her at the sound of Rorik's voice. Her heartbeat picking up, Yvaine obeyed.

He was standing behind a table, his hands braced on either side of a scattered pile of parchments as he leaned forward to study them. A pallet bed occupied the space to one side of the tent; a chest and two chairs the other. Though daylight prevailed outside, here the light was muted; the candles in the branched holder on the table had not yet been lit.

He glanced up as she entered, then straightened and strode swiftly around the table towards her. 'Yvaine. When I enquired of Wulf's girl, she said you were like to sleep until morning.'

'I woke up.' She'd had some vague plan of throwing herself into his arms the moment she saw him, but he stopped abruptly a few feet away, his brows drawing together as he studied her.

A cold fist uncurled in her stomach. She didn't know what he was searching for, but she had the horrible feeling he wasn't finding it. 'I've been with Edward,' she hazarded. 'Or I would've come sooner.'

'You shouldn't be here at all,' he said. His eyes narrowed further. 'Are you all right?'

'Aye. Although I know this bruise looks…'

He moved abruptly; stilled. Then, as she hesitated, he came forward and touched his fingers fleetingly to her jaw. 'You look as fragile as mist. But…that wasn't what I meant. You shouldn't be here, alone with me, at this hour.'

Given all that had passed between them she had to smile, even as her heart sank a little. ''Tis not so late. I thought you might need the clothes you lent me.'

'Aye. Thank you.' But he made no move to take them; just stood there, watching her, so close she could feel the warmth of his body.

'I'm glad Thorolf has gone back to Norway so quickly,' she said into the silence. 'Anna must be out of her wits with worry by now.'

'Aye.' He glanced towards the entrance. 'I think…'

Oh, no. He wasn't getting rid of her that easily. Before he could take her arm, she slipped away from him, placed his clothes on a chair, then crossed the small space to sit down on the bed. She hoped Rorik couldn't see how precarious was her calm pose of being at home in his quarters. *Calm*. That was a jest. How could she be calm when her entire future depended on this last desperate throw of the dice, when her heart was still beating too quickly, her mind a prey to fear and doubt?

When he stood there by the entrance, that remote stillness cloaking him again, as though waiting to take her back to her tent.

'Rorik, will you tell me…about Sitric?' She closed her eyes, cursing herself for her cowardice, then opened them on the realisation that it might be better this way. If they could talk, dispel the distant air that had fallen over him…

'What do you want to know?'

She shook her head, pulled her thoughts together. 'Why did you spend years avenging him when he brought about his own death?'

He hesitated, as if contemplating the option of picking her up and removing her bodily from the tent, but he must have sensed her determination to stay, to have answers at least, for he turned on his heel and walked across to the empty chair.

''Twas Sitric's men who were avenged,' he said curtly, sitting down. 'Not him.'

She nodded. 'I don't think you could have killed Alfred or Edward, Rorik.'

'Maybe not.' He paused, shrugged. 'At the time I was furious enough to kill anyone, but 'twas anger at Sitric as much as at Alfred. I felt betrayed by them both. By Sitric for turning his back on Guthrum's peace, and by Alfred for condemning Sitric to the death of a common felon. To a Norseman, hanging is the most shameful of deaths. My father nearly went mad when he heard. It shattered his health.'

'So you appeased his family honour with a vow of vengeance,' she murmured. 'Only to think he'd betrayed you in turn.'

'I wasn't exactly loath,' he said dryly. 'Sitric's men didn't deserve to die that way, since they'd only been following orders. For all they knew, outright war had been declared.'

She had to smile. 'Your male reasoning defeats me, but I suppose only a warrior can see different degrees of death. They all look rather final to me.'

'I suppose they do,' he said soberly. 'When you've come as close to it as you did this morning.'

'But you were there. You saved me.'

'After putting you at risk in the first place.'

She frowned. 'How so?'

He gestured impatiently, indicating her bruised face, her borrowed clothes. 'None of this would have happened if I hadn't left you at Einervik that morning.'

'As well say none of it would have happened if I hadn't walked into the forest,' she retorted. 'Or if I hadn't pestered you to seek out Thorkill.'

A faint smile crossed his face at that.

Encouraged—dear God, it didn't take much; she would have stayed if only to savour these few precious moments with him—she pressed on. 'How did you know where Othar had taken me?'

The smile vanished. 'An old karl who had sailed with my father recognised the ship some miles down the fjord. He thought it odd that 'twas moored at an island where there was no farm or village and suspected it might have been stolen. He arrived at Einervik soon after I got back from visiting Ragnald. And just as we discovered you were missing.'

She squelched a twinge of guilt. 'I suppose I shouldn't have walked so far, but, truly, I thought there was no danger.'

'A mistake I made, myself,' he said grimly. 'And for which I'll never forgive myself.'

'Oh, no, Rorik. It wasn't your fault. Were you supposed to know Othar's mind?'

'Perhaps not.' His tone said he should have. 'Anyway, we spent some time searching for you. Several of the men had seen you start towards the forest, but then you apparently vanished like smoke. I decided to investigate the old man's story. When we got to the island the birds were disturbed. Screaming and flying about. For a few minutes…I thought—'

Her heart leapt. Surely it was more than desire for her that had his face tightening like that, his body bracing as if for a blow. She almost rose to go to him, but he sat forward suddenly, resting his forearms on his thighs and gazing down at his linked fingers.

''Twas Gunhild, as you guessed. I went back, collected the crew and set sail, only stopping at the coastal villages until we found the one where Othar had picked up more men. It didn't take long to discover his route. Word spreads when men speak too freely in an alehouse. Although there was no talk of a struggle when you were taken on board.'

'I'd been struck over the head,' she explained. 'Othar had been waiting, watching for an opportunity to get my attention or summon me by some ruse. He followed me, knocked me unconscious and had me carried overland to his ship.'

Rorik's fingers locked tight.

'I swear, Rorik, Othar didn't hurt me again until this morning.'

'Being so undermanned probably hampered his usual style,' he muttered. 'But whatever it was, I thank the Gods for it.' He rose abruptly and strode over to the entrance, lifting the curtain aside and looking out at the camp. The light was dimmer now; from the side she couldn't see his expression.

But then he turned his head and her breath caught. Though he still held the curtain aside, he was focused on her with an intensity that, weeks ago, would have stopped her heart. It did now, but for a different reason.

'Yvaine, why did you run to Edward like that? On the beach.'

She stared at him. That was the last question she'd expected. 'I was afraid of what he might do if you told him that you were the one who carried me off.'

'I did tell him that. I just gave him a reason for it he could understand.'

She nodded. 'Ransom. Revenge.'

'Better that than confounding him with the knowledge that I wouldn't have trusted anyone else to look after you. Couldn't have borne not knowing what had happened to you.'

Her eyes widened, but before she could do more than form a silent 'Oh' of wonder, he glanced away, jerking his head toward the camp. 'Come. It grows dark. I'll take you back to your tent.'

He thought he could leave her to mull over *that* for the rest of the night? Not while she had wits in her head. And not while he was standing there gripping the curtain as if about to wrench it from its moorings.

'Well,' she said mildly, 'it seems perfectly obvious that nothing I said or did on the beach was necessary? Since you and Edward are such good friends.'

'Oh, it was necessary. But this isn't the time or the place to discuss it. I'll have no gossip about you. Bad enough that I carried you off, but at least Anna was with you then.'

He would have no…

Bad enough…

Now he was concerned for her reputation?

She clamped her hands around the edge of the pallet and resisted the urge to scream. Impatience with male reasoning would get her nowhere and screaming would only bring soldiers on the run. Soldiers wouldn't help. If her plan was to work, it was time to bring out the warships.

'Oh, I wouldn't worry about that,' she said, waving a hand with airy unconcern. She hoped he wouldn't notice the tremor in her voice. 'When I left Edward, he was busy planning my next marriage.'

The weatherbeaten leather in his hand buckled with a crunch. Rorik wheeled to face her, his eyes slitted. 'I wondered if you were going to mention it,' he said through his teeth. 'Oh, aye, you may well look surprised. Did you think Edward wouldn't inform me of his plans for you? Dangle her before some thegn who's still questioning his loyalties, he said. Get her safely married and breeding, he said. You don't seem particularly upset by the prospect.'

'Well, I was at first, but—'

'What?'

'I said I—'

She broke off with a jerk as he dropped the curtain and strode over to the table. He snatched up the candle-sconce and turned to glare at her.

'Stay there,' he ground out, stabbing a finger at the bed. 'Stay right there. Don't move!'

'What about my rep—?' she began, but he was already out of the tent.

She wondered if the tremulous smile curving her lips constituted movement. She was still debating the point when Rorik returned with the candles lit. The short trip didn't appear to have improved his mood. He dumped the sconce down on the table with so much force, the flames flickered wildly and nearly went out. She wiped the smile off her face.

'You were upset at first, but now you're not?' he snarled. 'Edward's planning another political marriage for you and you're not saying a word in protest?'

'No. You see—'

The rest vanished on a gasp when he took the two strides necessary to haul her off the bed and into his arms. 'Three times I've thought I'd lost you,' he said, no discernible change in his expression. 'That's three times too many. I'm not standing still for a fourth.'

'Three?' she managed. She could feel the smile coming back. There was still an obstacle in their path, a kingly obstacle, but her heart was soaring with happiness. Rorik was crushing her against him, glaring at her, but he was shaking as if with a fever.

'When I found out I was the son of a slave; when Othar took you; when you ran to Edward on the beach as though you couldn't wait to get away from me.'

'Oh, no, Rorik.' She flung her arms around his neck, clung. 'It wasn't like that.'

'Gods.' The shaking increased. He bent suddenly and buried his face in her hair. 'I thought you wanted to be free of me. I thought...just now...you spoke of Edward's plans as if going to another man meant nothing to you.'

'Only because I was so unsure. I needed to know how you felt about me, and I didn't know how to ask without making you feel bound by honour. Or worse, if you'd felt only pity. Not upset? This past hour I've been desperate.'

The shaking stopped. He lifted his head and she caught her breath at the smile that transformed his face. In that fleeting, precious moment, she saw the boy he'd been, before the years of vengeance had carved the stern lines on his face.

'Desperate?'

'Beyond despair.' Wonderingly, she touched a hand to his face. The smile was fading, but he wasn't distant now. Raw emotion darkened his eyes, love, longing, a burning desire that yet was achingly tender. 'You went away,' she explained. 'After that night in Thorkill's hut, and again this morning. Somewhere deep inside yourself where I couldn't follow.'

'Did you want to?' he asked very low.

She nodded, and, raising herself on tiptoe, touched her lips to his. 'I would follow you over the edge of the world itself, Rorik. I love you.'

'I didn't know how much I needed to hear those words,' he said huskily. 'Didn't know that I loved you from the moment I saw you lying in that hall, so hurt, so courageous. It wasn't until the truth of my birth came out. Losing everything didn't matter then. You were all I wanted.'

Tears welled in her eyes and he shifted his hold, cradling her face between his hands. 'What? What is it?'

'I needed the words, too,' she said, smiling through the misty veil.

'Then take them,' he murmured. 'For you are everything to me. All that is good and true and gentle in my life.' He bent and kissed her. '*Elsknan*. Beloved. Keeper of my heart.'

Her lips parted as he folded her close again, his kiss gentle, cherishing, and yet so deeply possessive she lost all sense of self, of separateness. He was hers; she was his. For eternity. It was there in the beating of his heart against her breast. In the whispered words that made no sense, and yet held all the meaning in the world. It was there in the sweet delirium of desire, simmering beneath the surface of a tenderness she had only dreamed of.

And when he lifted his head, it was there in the look they exchanged, of love, immeasurable and everlasting.

'I'll never let you go,' he said. ''Twould tear me apart to see you married to another.'

'It won't happen,' she assured him. 'You see—'

'By every god in Asgarth, it won't happen,' he vowed before she could explain. 'I'll tell Edward you're with child by me and make sure every prospective bridegroom hears the same story if I have to.'

'What?' She clutched at him, alarm crashing through her euphoria. 'The only reason you're not already meeting Edward on the battlefield tomorrow is because you saved my life.'

'He promised he wouldn't kill anyone involved in your kidnapping.'

'Then he'll have someone else challenge you. He'll do *something*. We'll have to get away, but—' Dismay widened her eyes. 'But how? You have no crew, and by the time Thorolf gets back—'

'Hush, little love.' He reinforced the tender command by kissing her. 'I was planning to kidnap you again even before I knew your response to Edward's plans. To hold you until I won your heart, or we knew there was a child.'

'Holy Saints! You were going to force the king's hand?'

'If you loved me. Or even if you didn't,' he added, a wicked smile dawning through the implacable purpose in his eyes. 'I knew you didn't hate me. I was going to build on that.'

'I think I should protest that,' she said, frowning. 'But since I do love you, it seems foolish to worry about it.' She shook her head; she had worse fears. 'But what shall we do? Where—?'

A scratch at the curtain interrupted her. Yvaine froze, her fingers digging into Rorik's shoulders.

He loosened her grip, set her gently aside and strode over to the entrance. When he drew the curtain back, Wulf was standing in the aperture. She wondered uneasily how long he'd been there—and what he'd overheard.

'My lord. The king sends this message.' The young man grinned at Yvaine, seeming not the least surprised to see her there, and handed over a rolled parchment. 'It doesn't require an answer,' he said, and strolled away with a wave of his hand.

Rorik stared after him for a moment, then let the curtain drop and unfurled the parchment.

'What does it say?' Yvaine whispered, bracing herself for the worst.

To her utter astonishment, a grin very like Wulf's lit his face. He finished reading, threw back his head and laughed until he was breathless. All she could do was watch and wonder if the news was so disastrous he'd lost his mind.

'It seems,' he said when he recovered and realised she was staring at him in dismayed enquiry, 'that Edward has decided I can best repay him for depleting his army by supervising the improvement of his navy. My vow of allegiance would be required, of course, and to ensure it he's suggested that I marry a certain widow.'

She gasped. 'Marry? A certain… Ohhhh!' Her fists clenched.

'If I wish to accept his terms, I'm to present myself, with said widow, at his quarters in an hour's time when his priest will be available to marry us. An hour's time,' he repeated thoughtfully.

But Yvaine was still spluttering. 'I'll never forgive him for this. All that time he was tormenting us. Playing with us, when… But *why*?'

'To punish me,' Rorik said drily. 'A blind fool would have seen my reaction to his plans for you. Knowing threats wouldn't keep me in line, he decided to employ a subtler bait. And got a little vengeance of his own into the bargain.'

'Well, *I* didn't kill off a whole lot of soldiers. What about my feelings?'

'He used them, you little innocent. The cunning bastard is probably laughing himself into fits right now, having watched you run straight to me.'

'I didn't run straight to you,' she said with dignity. 'I picked up your clothes first.' Then, narrowing her eyes. 'But I'll still never forgive him. I was sick with dread until I remembered the one escape left to me.'

He looked up, still amused, from another perusal of Edward's message. 'What was that?'

'I was trying to tell you before. All I had to do was publicly announce that my conscience dictate I enter the cloister and that would have been the end of any marriage plans. Edward couldn't gainsay me without defying Holy Mother Church, and that he would never do. It wouldn't have mattered then, you see.' A little smile touched her mouth, that held all the sadness she'd been braced to bear. 'If you didn't love me, nothing would have mattered.'

'Oh, sweetheart.' His smile gentled into a look of love, so all-encompassing, so heartfelt, she felt tears prick her eyes again. He tossed the missive aside and reached out to take her in his arms. 'There'll never be a day when I won't love you,' he murmured against her mouth. 'Never a day when I won't need you.'

'And I you,' she whispered back. 'Make love to me, Rorik. I want to be close to you again. I need to feel safe.'

'Safe? Like this?' His low laugh sent a cascade of delicious shivers down her spine. 'There's a misguided notion if ever I heard one, but—' he started backing her towards the pallet '—far be it from me to deny a lady's wish.'

Already quivering in anticipation, Yvaine waited for him to lift her on to the bed. Instead, he lifted her against him, turned and sat down on the edge of the pallet, settling her on his lap, facing him. Instinctively she shifted her legs, straddling him, her eyes widening in surprise. 'Like this?'

'This isn't our feather bed at Einervik,' he murmured. 'You're too small and delicate to lie between me and an army pallet. And we have scant privacy here. This way we can keep our clothes on and still be close.'

'Oh.' She glanced towards the entrance. 'You think someone will intrude?'

'If they do, they'll soon leave,' he said, grinning. Then he took her face between his hands. 'But if you want to wait until we're married…'

She shook her head. She didn't think she could wait. And judging by the hard evidence separated from her by just two layers of clothing, she doubted Rorik could either. And yet, he was holding back, waiting for her answer, because she'd felt that slightest hesitation.

Something opened, flowered, deep inside her. Love welled, springing free with nothing held back; a flowing tide that she knew would toss her hither and yon over the years, but would always return her to this place of safety, to his arms. He was ruthless, she knew. He would always have that hard edge of danger. But he loved her. That made them equal.

'Until we're married?' she repeated softly. She gave him an innocent smile from beneath her lashes and wriggled against him. 'Oh, you mean as Christians?'

'Little witch,' he growled on a sharp intake of air. He lifted her slightly to push her skirts out of the way. 'You knew.'

'I learned of it from Edward.' She gasped as his hand found her, stroked. 'When were you going to tell me…ohhh?'

'I didn't mean to keep it from you,' he whispered. 'I'd buried it deep.' He moved his hand again, one long finger pressing inward, circling. 'As deep as I'm going to bury myself in you.'

She cried out, wanting more, and with a muttered imprecation, he withdrew his hand to wrench open his chausses, before urging her close again.

The first demanding touch of his body had her shaking with mingled need and doubt as she realised suddenly how vulnerable she was in this position. He gently opened her, pushed upward, stroking her as he thrust so that she trembled in his hold even as her thighs tightened in an instinctive attempt to stop the invasion, to slow it at least, to let herself adjust.

''Tis all right,' he whispered. 'You know I won't hurt you.'

'Rorik…no…I can't…'

'Aye, you can,' he murmured. 'That's it. Give yourself to me. My own sweetheart.'

His words flowed over her, easing her tension. Somewhere beneath the flood-tide of passion waiting to sweep her away, she knew he was asking for more than her body. Knew he wanted her acceptance of all that he was; her acknowledgement of the ruthlessness that was an integral part of his nature, her trust that he would never use it to hurt her. He wanted her completely open to him. Vulnerable. His.

Desire replaced doubt as sensations, more thrilling than any he'd shown her before, washed over her. She felt the liquid pulses of her response around him; those wickedly clever fingers never left her. Knowing that what he was doing was hidden excited her unbearably. The fact that she couldn't control it, couldn't close her legs or retreat against his restraining arm, had her trembling in helpless surrender.

Only trust, she realised dimly. Only utter trust could make it like this. And love.

Then with a groan that came from deep within him, he crushed her against him, forcing her forward and reaching so deep, he had to stop her scream of ecstasy with his mouth. She clung to him, sobbing with the intensity of the pleasure flooding her senses, holding him close as she felt his own release shudder through him, making him, in that sweet, incomparable moment, as vulnerable as she. Hers. Until, with passion spent, they simply held each other, still joined, her head tucked into his shoulder as their heartbeats slowed and their breathing levelled.

Eventually, when an errant breeze found a gap beneath the tent, making her shiver slightly, he lifted her, gently disengaged their bodies and stood to return their clothing to a state of respectability.

'I think I could sleep for a sen'night,' she said dreamily, standing up on shaky legs as he straightened her skirts.

'Tonight you'll sleep in my arms.' He gave her a wicked grin as he steadied her, but sobered almost immediately to frame her face between his hands. 'Will you forgive me, sweetheart? For not telling you I was a Christian?'

'Aye.' She smiled up at him; there'd never been any doubt. 'For you've told me the most important thing.'

'Always,' he said. 'I will love you through this life and beyond. That is my troth. The vow I give you before we meet any priest.'

'And I give you all that I am, Rorik of Einervik. My vow of love, for all eternity. No matter what words are spoken to bind us.'

He smiled, took her hand and led her towards the entrance. 'Then come, sweet wife. We have an appointment to keep.'

Outside, all was calm and still. Guards patrolled the camp, but at a distance. Dogs slept. Horses dozed. In an indigo sky scattered with diamonds, the moon sailed across the heavens on its endless journey. The warm clasp of Rorik's hand around hers was sure and strong.

And when they reached the king's tent, the golden glow reflecting from the candles within seemed to reach out and enfold them, as, hand in hand, they stepped over the threshold to claim their future.

* * * * *

HISTORICAL ROMANCE™

LARGE PRINT

THE MATCHMAKER'S MARRIAGE

Meg Alexander

Despite constant admonitions to be discreet, Amy Wentworth had never learned to hold her tongue! Bright, honest and forthright, she couldn't bear any form of unkindness, and it was her good nature that made her take Miss Charlotte Skelmersdale under her wing.

But, though it had *seemed* a good idea to make a match for Charlotte with her good friend Sir James Richmond, somehow Amy found she couldn't do it. She'd realised James was everything Amy herself wanted in a husband—and now she just needed to convince him!

ONE NIGHT IN PARADISE

Juliet Landon

Queen Elizabeth I's court at Richmond was rife with intrigues and liaisons. Beautiful Adorna Pickering had grown practised in the art of flirtation, although the moment an admirer became too ardent she promptly sought the protection of her father, the Master of Revels.

One man alone held the power to overcome her skittish ways—decisive, commanding Sir Nicholas Rayne. But, knowing his reputation for keeping countless mistresses, Adorna was not prepared to become another easy conquest—as much as she might dream of shadowy, seductive gardens and a night spent in his arms…

Reign of Elizabeth I
…courtly love, intrigues, passions…

MILLS & BOON®

HIST1003 LP

HISTORICAL ROMANCE™

LARGE PRINT

WAYWARD WIDOW

Nicola Cornick

Lady Juliana Myfleet scandalises the ton with her risqué behaviour—and gets more outrageous by the day… Her reputation is nearly in tatters. One thing only will save her from ruin—marriage—but Juliana has vowed *never* to marry again!

Martin Davencourt knows there's more to Juliana than gossip and scandal. What has happened to the innocent to whom he once proposed? His rising political career is delicately poised, so he'd be reckless to consider any close association with her. Still, he's enchanted—and willing to risk all…

MY LADY'S DARE

Gayle Wilson

The Earl of Dare was an enigma, even to those who professed to know him well. For while his morals seemed suspect and his leisure pursuits as reckless as any of his well-heeled peers', something dark and dangerous lurked beneath the façade of good looks, wit and charm.

But he was still a highly eligible catch, until the night Dare wagered a small fortune for a French gambler's English mistress, and won. Now, with the stunning widow installed at his town house, society matchmakers doubted that he'd ever recover his name. Most especially when the infamous Mrs Carstairs appeared all set to become his bride…

MILLS & BOON®

HIST1103 LP

HISTORICAL ROMANCE™

LARGE PRINT

BELOVED VIRAGO

Anne Ashley

Spirited Katherine O'Malley, sent to France to flush out a traitor, is prepared for discomfort, fear, even danger in her country's service. She *isn't* prepared to work with handsome rake Major Daniel Ross – posing as his wife! Katherine knows all about his womanising ways and she's determined to resist his charms – no matter how strongly they affect her.

But when Napoleon's escape from Elba forces the pretend couple to flee across hostile France, Katherine has to trust Daniel absolutely. Even if that means letting him get intimately close…

RAKE'S REWARD

Joanna Maitland

As companion to the Dowager Lady Luce, Marina Beaumont is under strict instruction to restrain the older woman's gambling habit. So when the Dowager loses a fortune to the renowned rake Kit Stratton, Marina's position is in serious jeopardy.

She secretly visits Kit to ask him to forfeit the money he's owed – and he surprisingly agrees. But only if Marina gives him the reward he desires…

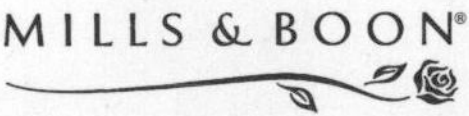

Live the emotion

HIST1203 LP